# BLUNT

## THOMAS EASLEY

where words connect

*The most difficult thing,
when confronted with madness,
is not to go mad yourself ...to look past
what offends to something higher...*

# BLUNT

1. Not sharp, unsharpened dull dulled worn down.
2. Straightforward, frank, plain-spoken, candid, direct bluff, to the point, forthright, unequivocal, point-blank unceremonious, undiplomatic, indelicate, brusque, abrupt.
3. A hollowed-out cigar filled with marijuana.

# BLUNT

ISBN: 978-1-946274-88-5 (Paperback)
ISBN: 978-1-946274-89-2 (eBook)
Library of Congress Control Number: 2022915902

Cover Design: Okomota
Interior Design: Amit Dey

Twitter: wordeeeupdates
Facebook: facebook.com/wordeee/
E-mail: contact@wordeee.com

Published by Wordeee Beacon, NY
Website: www.wordeee.com

Printed in the USA

# ONE

I walk into the bar first. Sally just behind me. We stop together. Scan for an empty table. A street view by the far window is unoccupied. I nod. We walk to the table, sit down, relax, I rearrange the table setting, open the menu.

"Are you hungry?"

"No, not really. I'm thirsty. Thirsty and tired."

Sally's albino lashes flatter her green eyes. She looks at you, always, never over or around you. And she never burps, never vacates, pops the cap. Rare. That's what she is. But who decides what makes something rare? Do they wear uniforms, the deciders? Would we recognize them?

I glance down at the menu. The placemat, the Formica tabletop. All the scratches, beverage stains, the incomplete stories every surface tries to tell.

"I'm ordering a plate of wings, spicy. Very hot," I say. "You can have some. If you want." I always say that, if you want, line. Makes the period at the end of a sentence last longer.

"Why very hot?"

"No reason. Not really." I sneeze. Pull a napkin from the black metal holder. Wipe my nose. Cats. Sally loves cats. Sometimes she looks like a cat, smiles like a cat.

"I'm still mad at you," she says.

I push back in my chair. Finger the menu corner bending it back and forth.

"The fag in the dress shop? That! You're still mad about that?"

"Benjamin! You can't say fag. Not anymore. Homosexuals are a protected class."

My chair is hardwood, very uncomfortable. I turn, look out the window. A new world. A go with the flow world. Maybe. Maybe not. If the herd is going in the wrong direction... should we follow it?

"It's just talk, Sal. Words mean whatever people want them to mean, what people need them to mean. The point is how to live with each other, not change each other. Christ! I'm basic survival primitive, male primitive. I don't give a shit about "preferences." In their beds, closets, wherever, fags can have at it all they want. Who cares? I don't. I love women, adore women, adore you. That's all."

"But you must, Ben. You must care. Caring changes the world, can change it." Sally is adamant, her eyes burning crosses in my logic. Young people searching for a cause to give them value. They all do it. I did.

"Why?" I say, "I have little interest in guys, no interest at all in guys that have no interest in girls, and less than no interest in politics. Listen, Sal," I bend my fork backward for no reason and the spoon. "A fag can call me white trash, homophobic, breeder. Breeder's a favorite. Redneck, whatever derogatory name he wants. Doesn't matter, not to me. No offense taken. I don't give a fuck, it's all fine, and nobody's going to lose a job, a vote, trash their reputation by calling me a breeder, a redneck. But if I say 'fag,' every PC mafia weathervane in the country knots up and pisses on free speech. 'Protected class.' What the fuck does that mean, anyway? Prostitutes, fat people, tattooed people, poor people, farmers, women, war vets, the President, they're not protected. I can say what I want about them. Call the president Hitler incarnate if I want. No Jack Boots drop down from the sky to chastise me. And black folks, look at the crap they live with. Who's protecting them. And how come child molestation, abuse, and trafficking isn't a higher priority on the liberal agenda than sex changes and gender acrobatics? All the Epstein prevention blockades, where are they? Fuck! Guys like me, we should be a protected class. Guys who fought to keep their hometown safe. Normal guys. Honest, hardworking company men, who's protecting us?"

It begins to rain. Hard. A good rain. Could have used it months back.

2

"What other people think of me, I don't give a fuck. You're getting testy. Don't. I'm old, pissed off and disillusioned. Look at us, our home. Paradise. Burned to shit. Eight-six people dead. Who cares? Our lives have been transformed from fishing, day hikes and happy hours to ashes and blood. We live in a homeless town, Sal, a lost paradise, a faltering democracy, and there's something wrong with me calling some smartass, tippy-toe fuck in a dress shop a fag? Christ!"

"Calm down Ben."

"How Sal? I went to war; did terrible things to people I didn't know for the right to speak freely. Now, look at the White House, at Trump; Putin's test dummy manipulating the levers of power, digging for cash to pay his bills, polish his ego. We have problems much bigger than offensive words. Much bigger." I sneeze, lean back, picture Sally lifting her shirt for the first time. A cotton T-shirt with a deep V neck. No bra. Amazing how seeing tits soothes the mind, even a quick glance.

"You're a boomer, Ben." Sally sits up; lecture erect. "Your generation was the first to gain political influence as teenagers. Your protests, drugs, vain idealism—all the changes you don't like now, got us here. What's happening in the world, boomers made it happen."

The bar smells of cigarette smoke, old smoke trapped in the wood panels, countertops, furniture, curtains, the strained faces at the bar hunched over drinks—loyal regulars. Paradise before the fire. Regulars remember. They remember everything.

"You're right, Sally! All those degenerates, tie-dyed, throw-trash-in-the-woods, panhandling Haight-Ashbury hippies. They brought on the Trashager Age, not me. The Sixties were great, a braless wonderland. I got that. But I was no hippy. 'If you can't be with the one you love, love the one you're with.' 'Make love, not war.' Yeah, the sex was great, easy to come by, but how did all that lead to the political correctness we're suffering through today? And who decides what is and is not correct? No one elected, no one we've agreed upon. Political Correctness is a moral deceit, a headless punitive autocracy, a free speech muzzle. Change mailman to mail carrier? Why? Mailman, garbage man, chairman, fireman, businessman, taxman, they work just fine. And who gave the OK to change, men, to people, in the Constitution's "All men are created equal" line? Fuck." I pause, draw a long slow breath. Try to relax, can't do it, continue talking.

"Who would have thought saying 'Merry Christmas' could get you in trouble? Waving a photo of the Dalai Lama in China; that can get you in trouble. I can see that. I don't agree, but I can see it. Here, it's safer to say, 'Fuck you' than 'Merry Christmas.'"

Sally. Sometimes I keep talking, give myself greater reason to lose my way in her look, her revealing beauty. She does that to me; she takes me places without moving.

"An equal and fair world, Sal. We're not in one. Never have been, never will be. I know what man is, how petty, ego-driven, and selfish he is. I don't hate fags, homos, dykes, no reason to. They've always been there. But I didn't kill people in 'Nam so I could come home to reprimands for using a three-lettered word PC judgementalists don't like. Why don't my "feelings" matter? What about what *I* don't like? I'll say what I want when I want."

"Not when it affects me, Ben. Offends me."

"That! See what I mean...." I bent the knife.

Sally interrupts. "Lower your voice, Ben."

"Right there. That. You see that? That's what I'm saying. Political correctness. Used to be that people feared offending God, some dictator or king. Now they fear offending homosexuals, fags, fairies, homos, girly men, whatever. That's what I'm saying."

"Ben, you're turning red."

A couple of college kids enter the bar. They're already drunk. Isn't even noon. Maybe they are students, maybe not. Maybe they're dropouts, corner cutters, slackers. They take seats at the bar.

Sally is tall, about five to six inches taller than me. Amazonian. Never a problem sitting with her back to the door. She grew up tough but not intimidated. Had a bastard of a mother...loaned her out to the highest bidder. The weak controlling the weaker. Sally turns slightly, runs her gaze over the men at the counter. I wait for her to speak, think about silence, the distance between words when we don't know what to say. She turns back to me.

"It's hard being you, Ben. I know that," she says, reaching over, pressing my cheek with her palm. "Remembering what it was like before political correctness, before 911 and AIDS, must be hard, growing older in a world—a golden age, that no longer belongs to you, to anyone like you. You comfort yourself by devaluing life, by thinking everyone will lose in the end. Change offends you, that's all. But I love you. I'm going to marry you, and we're going to have kids, lots of kids."

Kids....

"Are you ready to eat?" I ask. "Do you want a beer? I'm buying."

"You're buying!"

"Right. A beer. Do you want one?"

"No. Vodka and coffee."

"What?"

"I want vodka and coffee."

"Why?"

A body goddess, Sally. A woman at peace with her sexuality, open for worship...she turns seedy into rapture. Rejection into sensuality. Every guy in the room, I can feel their eyes staring, even when they aren't looking. Sally's mystic white skin, her red lips, they hover in your mind, eager to make a man of you, a man you have no idea you can become. Guys look at her reflexively, women too. They all want her, a part of her, something to keep safe inside themselves, to enjoy when no one else is looking.

"Just kidding, Ben, coffee is fine. Too early for vodka. And Ben," she leans across the table, her perfect breasts stressing the loose buttons on her blouse. "Your black friends, you wouldn't call them nigger, would you?"

"Right. I see. OK, Sal, I'll stop saying fag. I'll try...for you."

When the waitress came, I ordered two beers.

# TWO

"So, this is where we are."

I look around the bar, out the window. Still raining. An old tube TV hanging from faded parachute straps in a high corner is showing *Friends* reruns. There are only two women in the bar, Sally, and an attractive black lady, sitting with several men in business suits.

"I'm tired of living in two trailers, Sal. Tired of charred air and empty people. Vacant dreams dulling my mind. Let's move. Go someplace far away, someplace warm, and friendly. Make something of ourselves. Something unexpected."

"How, Ben?" Sally puts her hand on mine, rubs my thick knuckles. "Whatever you are going to become, you already became it. A long time ago. There's no 'making you' into anything. Me, though? I could do fashion. Maybe porn. Become an actress."

Sharing herself. Sally does that. No hesitation, no fear of carnal reality.

"Porn. You could, Sal. You could definitely do porn. Become an actress, a fearless player unlike any other, and I know where. Florida! Key West! Remember? 'All the happy hours you can drink, music for-free Key West.' We can move there. It's almost Cuba. Lots of wild chickens and cocks. They're everywhere. They walk the streets. Alligators and naked people. Key Wester's love nude. Beaches are filled with skin, all kinds of skin. Streets are filled with skin. And lots of tourists. We could buy a camera, sell photos of Key West with you in them. Get ourselves a store window, spend our nights at the bars soliciting clients, making friends, living again. Lots of bars in Key West."

A gust of rain smacks the window, interrupts me, feels good to stop talking. The sound of my voice. I don't like it. Never think about why.

"OK, Ben, why not. It's a good idea."

"Really! You agree?"

"Yes, really."

Sally agrees.

Suddenly I feel rich, selfish. With her, with Sally on my arm, everyone in Key West will want to know me, to get close to her, to touch her. Kids think she's an angel. She's money. The kind that makes every man proud. "Great!" I say, and I take another swallow of beer. Prefer wine, good wine, but can't afford it, so I drink beer and smoke pot. Have a great pipe, a comfort pipe. It cradles weed like a fine wine glass cradles wine. Potheads. I might be one. How does one measure that?

"In my teens, Sal, I hitchhiked everywhere. It was almost as good as owning a car."

"Hitchhike!" She's indignant, abrupt, beautiful. "Is that what you're thinking? To Florida! You want us to hitchhike across the country. No fucking way! I'm not giving hand jobs to truck drivers. Not one. Your memories Ben, they're out of date, and the world is too far ahead of them for you to catch up. People don't think like that, they don't think like you, because they don't remember what you remember. They don't care that you remember anything. Nobody hitchhikes, not today. Besides, who would stop for an old man and a gangly albino?"

"Guys would stop for you Sally. You're not gangly, not at all. Nuns would stop for you. Damn, a hurricane would stop. I could hide nearby, wait for a ride to pull over, then pop out like I'd been taking a leak. Once a guy stops, gets a closer look at you, even now realizing you are not alone, he'd think of giving us a ride because he'd get to sit next to you. We'd be on our way."

Sally gave me a look. A deep, admonishing look, silent around the orbital parts of her eyes but blasting away at the center.

"OK, Sal," I say. "A bad idea, very bad. How about a bus?"

"Ben. We're driving."

"Driving?"

"Your Jeep."

"My Jeep!"

"Yes, your Jeep."

"It's three thousand miles, Sal. At least that. A long way for an old Jeep."

"Doesn't matter. It's time to leave."

"You're right. I know. Paradise is burnt to shit. It's left us already. 2018 Camp Creek Fire. Deadliest in California history. Fuck. Fires are blind, lethal blind...ashes to ashes. No more foreplay stops on Camp Creek Road. No more picnics, gooey peanut butter and jelly sandwiches and 69ers in the tall grass. Foothill's serenity, gone."

"They're memories, Ben. Our memories. We'll pack them up and take them with us."

Do we ever save memories intentionally? I fix my mind on the idea, study the curve of Sally's lips, her dimpled cheeks.

"Our years here have been good. We've been lucky, mostly." Sally says.

"My Grandpa, he died in a fire. Did I tell you?"

"You did, Ben, several times."

"Right. Grandpa and Grandma. They're both buried here. Too many old people in Paradise, always have been. Retirees from Sacramento. I'll miss our neighbors, especially the Websters."

Sally smiles. "The fat ones at the court entrance with all the bird cages?"

An image of Sally in a tight black skirt slips in, gives me an idea. "I know. Let's go through Vegas. Play the casinos, pick up some extra money before they throw us out."

Sally winks with both eyes, drops her jaw and blows me a kiss. I feel the wetness of it on my lips, the taste.

"No one can count cards like you, Sal. Count anything like you count."

Tricks she'd picked up from the sleazes her mother hung around, worked with. They traveled, those guys. They knew people. You had to know people to cheat them. That's what they told her, what Sally learned from them—how they expected to win, expected the mark to lose; a Turkish thing to do. She learned a lot early in life, and she's smart. Sally can pick blackjack winners in three-deck stacks. Tahoe casinos know her, but not Vegas. Our best nights would bring in over a thousand before the fisheyes overhead figured out, she is counting.

"Vegas. Sure, Ben. 'Sin is good.' My mother said that every time she peed."

"Every time she peed? That's odd."

"Yeah, it was."

The rain stops. Sunlight, softened by mist, lights Sally's face. She's almost see-through, something you can't imagine being real.

"Then it's decided. We're leaving Paradise. We're moving."

"Yes. Decided."

The waitress returns. Lays down two more cork coasters and two empty glasses, scratches a couple of dark hairs on her chin, stares out the window, turns and walks back to the kitchen.

I tilt my glass, drink the last of my beer.

"A couple of hundred people lived in Paradise when I was born," I say. "A few less, a few more. Mountain people. Adults, mostly. I remember them as a memory without shape or detail, a blur of something trying to become something. Paradise was a tree place. An animal place. No Oroville Dam, boats, weekenders. I liked growing up here."

"I know, Ben. But what does it have to do with us leaving this bar, this town, this life?"

"Nothing, I guess. I'm just thinking, waiting for words to clarify something I'm trying to remember. As a kid, for extra money, I sold hides and meat, mostly venison—some bear and beaver. I chiseled animals out of wood, very rough, used old tree trunks. Hey, that's it, in Key West. Right! That's what I was thinking. In Key West, I could chisel palm trees, carve alligators, big snakes, put them in our shop window, stand them outside to attract customers."

Sally sits up. "And I could pose like you said. Show a little flesh, pretend to adjust our window display, play with the camera. My favorite number is 826. 826 breaks down to 7 numerologically, a lucky number. Maybe we can find a shop with that number. It's a good idea, Ben. Maybe a *Vogue* editor will see me. Invite me to join *Vogue*. *Exotic*. Or *Playboy*. *Playboy* would be good."

"Sure, Sally, why not? You don't look thirty-three, maybe twenty-eight, a well-preserved twenty-eight that could be mistaken for twenty-four. Sure, it could work. Why not? We're good people. Nice things can happen to good people."

"Not the good people of Paradise."

"Yeah. Fuck. Camp Fire did them in. PG 'n E did them in. Faulty electric line. Fucking electric companies. Monetary cannibals, that's what they are. All big companies. They consume everything in their path. Trusted lifestyles disappear in the wake of rising profits, and no one cares. Lifestyle extinction. It's all very normal now. Family farms, hometown doctors, mom-and-pop grocery stores. Gone. Small people becoming smaller. Climate refugees, donors to lost causes. Extinction.

"We should start packing."

# THREE

**M**y trailer, a dull brown. Modular. Sits next to Sally's. She has a small picket fence. Not quite the American dream. We thought about connecting our trailers with a plank between our porches. And we thought about walking the plank at night, naked. Walking like Neanderthals emerging from our caves heaving with animal lust, ready for sex, propagation of the species, and the riotous thrill of clubbing, with mammoth bones, saber tooth tigers, giant sloths, and mice…big mice. We did put a plank there, but the court manager, Bill Green, told us he would charge us extra for a larger size lot. Big pockets digging into smaller ones. Humans behaving badly.

It didn't take long to pack. Our trailers are small, our belongings few. The fire missed us, but we were so far behind in rent that we left the trailers to Bill, told him to sell them and keep whatever was left. Fuck. How did I get here…did we get here? No point in thinking about it. Not today.

We climb into the Jeep. Jill the Jeep. My '98 Grand Cherokee, an off-road, soot-black baby. Her body, interior, rims, seats—all black. I turn the key. The V-8 ignites with hunger, hefty hunger, a big dog ready for road food, rolling wheels, wind across its hood. New beginnings. We feel like I imagine we would feel in a world where people treat us right, don't steal from us, lie to us, betray us.

A last look. Our eyes run a full 360° scan. Not much left, nothing golden to remember. Not in what we see, not without effort. Seeing through loss to what remains that's good, salvaging the positive. Sally can do that. I can't, not yet, maybe never.

"OK?"

"Yes. OK."

I have the wheel, Sally, shotgun. A big age difference between us. Big height difference. Doesn't feel like it, and it doesn't matter. We're a perfect fit. Her needing unconditional love, me needing her acceptance. Sometimes I tell jokes, lame jokes with happy endings. Was always good at fixing things, violently protective when required, and fit, exceptionally fit—mountain genes, a blend of rocks, bushes, and ice-cold water. Love ice cold water. Still, Sally could have anyone. I thought so. Maybe she did, on the side, and never told me. I wouldn't care if she did. She is young for me, but I never think of her as *too* young, just more energetic. Backing away from the trailers, I feel no regrets.

I began working at age seven, maybe seven and a half. Having a family but no family life, had rarely been fun. The thought of being "happy" wasn't something I grew up with. Happiness comes from feeling safe, and I never felt safe. But I love Sally, and as much as love can make a man happy, I am happy.

Very little traffic on 191.

We're on our way.

# FOUR

Lake Tahoe. Our first stop. Second actually. The first was a couple of miles before the 20/I-80 junction

"Pull over! Pull over!"

Splaying, holding her hand over her mouth and rolling down the window, Sally still looks great. A vision of all that's right in the world.

I did, I pulled over just past the turnout where a wooden water flue crosses under the road. An old flue. Before Sally, on hot days, I would stop, walk along the flue, toss my clothes, then jump into the water once I was out of sight. Sally and I did the same many times, made sport of it. We'd strip down, frolic, make love in the rushing water. Erotic water pulling us together, pushing us apart, pulling and pushing, pulling, and pushing…primal messaging, Morse Code for aliens. "Focus, Ben." I need to do that.

Car sick, again. Sally throws open the door, hurls out, and let's go. How she held it as long as she did, who knows.

"Christ, Sally! Are you OK?"

With her back to me, she gives me an "I'm OK" wave, walks to the flue, rinses her mouth several times, bends over slowly and begins to sway a bit, to wiggle, to tease an old man. She boosts her skirt, hooks a thumb around her panty band and begins sliding it down her legs, slowly, stops.

"I've got to pee," she says, and she squats behind the Jeep, just out of view from the road.

At first, I hear a dim trickling sound, then louder, then a rushing splashing brawl. Humans pissing. The sound of humans pissing. I don't like it.

Sally finishes, smiles, dismisses my obvious angst. Washes in the flue. "All better," she says, and she gets back in the jeep.

"I hate the sound of pee." I say, talking over the steering wheel, trying to remember an odious past without feeling it. "I was in a cult once."

"A cult!?"

"Yeah, one of those manipulative family substitutes promising a resplendent self-image; an exclusive relationship with God though a divine leader. I was nineteen, maybe twenty. The leader was bent. Had to have young men around him all the time, and boys. All helping him do "God's work.""

"It's always God, isn't it, Ben. The God men use to control other men."

"Yeah. The God men use to control other men was used to control me. I was brought on to chauffeur the leader, R.B. When, and wherever he wanted to go, I drove him, and there were never any girl attendants."

"No girls?"

"Right. No girls, Sal, just guys. Straight guys like me, each one of us, our conscience weakened by the belief that we were working for a higher good, made us easy to manipulate. Christ's disciples reborn. That's who we thought we were, how we saw ourselves. The "chosen" ones. We ate together at the same table, sat next to each other in the car, shared small rooms and small bathrooms. Everyone could hear everyone else, smell everyone. Being around guys all the time, guys smelling like guys, behaving like guys, apish body hair crawling out collars and cuffs, dirty socks, rank flatulence, fat sweat, toothpaste spit in the sink, stupid jokes, macho indifference—all of it disgusted me. But male smells and pissing sounds were the worst. I hate pissing sounds."

Sally looks at me, stares. "You want me to pee without making a sound?"

Soundless piss—I think about it, try to imagine what it would take to invent soundless piss.

"Maybe, but no, not that. You're not a guy."

"And...."

"I don't know. Guys, we're like slugs with muscles. Girls, they're butterflies...something like that."

Sally cups her breasts. "Forget all that Ben. You owe me. It's my turn."

Her first, me second, me first, her second, and both of us at once whenever possible. Sex. No matter what people say, whatever religion they follow, whatever beliefs they have, life is sex. Everything we do, we do for sex. Orgasm heaven, everyone wants to be there. Sally loves sex. I love sex. Grail orgasms. With every decisive coupling we think we've found it – the meaning of life.

Sex is big. That's all. Fact number one in the creation handbook. There's no hiding it, no hiding from it. Religion is all about sex, that's it. Reproduction control rules religion, all religions. The power of nature, of God, is in reproduction. Control sex, control reproduction and you control life, define life. Sex control…it's hidden behind all the candles, all the hush-hush prayers, the sanctuary rooms, the corner confessionals. "Come Ye forth," say the candles, the prayers, all the bowing, "fear being ruled by pleasure instead of guilt and pain." That's what they say. And they say Christ wants that! That God wants it.

I doubt it.

Happiness on earth. If everybody could make love when they want to, how they want to, there would be no war. Hippies. That part. They got that part right.

Sally takes the driver's seat, lifts a leg over the stick, gives me full access. Her turn. I take my time. A warm day, Paradise behind us. A lucky man. I am…more than lucky.

For a few hours, life is good.

# FIVE

---

"Sal, can I tell you something?"

She's drifting, her eyes reflecting the warm light of early evening coloring her features in sunset hues. An ethereal witness; maiden of the misty universe. I imagine she can fly, breathe underwater, dance on the head of a pin. She puts her hand on my shoulder, plays with the keys hanging from the ignition.

"Sure," she says. "Whatever you want."

"The cult thing…the pissing."

She sticks her finger in my mouth, corners my tongue, makes it hard to talk.

"That again? It's not important, Ben."

"I know," I said, "but still, it's a thought, Sal, that's all. One more thought."

Another Sally look…how many are there?

I continue. "Horses, dogs, goats, and cats taking a leak, and donkeys, and elephants. I can manage that. Guys pissing. Like I said, that's something else. The latrine piss, the wall piss, the splashing on pavement piss, the pissing on trees piss — cult memories return every time. It's tiring. A memory delete tab. I need one. Maybe I'm older than I think, or something's broken in me, but I don't hear music, Sal. It's not music. Sounds can be reconfigured to make melodies, lots of sounds, but not pissing sounds."

"You need help, Ben."

"I know."

"Really. No one will think you insane, demented or deranged. I wouldn't use those words. Extreme. You're that, but what controls you? Anger? Bully memories? Fear of failure? Who knows? You can say anything, sometimes the wrong thing, and people get hurt. You're too blunt, Ben, break the rules too often. Followers don't like that."

"They're not my rules."

Sally adjusts her legs—her long white legs—rolls her window down, runs her fingers through my hair, curls my ears (not sure how).

"Sometimes, you shouldn't talk, Ben. That's all. People misunderstand you. Control, that's what you need. If you are not in control of your mind, someone, or something else will be. I'm telling you."

"But what does that have to do with pissing sounds?"

"Whatever you want."

*She's right. Sally's always right. Mostly always. She's a woman. Women know stuff.* I understand wanting to get on top of them, who doesn't? But holding them down, that's wrong. Lots of guys (especially the architects of religious text) fear having no authority over their attraction to women. To lessen their fear, they subjugate women. Nothing manly in that.

We reach the top of Donner Summit, a little over seven thousand feet. The sky is clear, more glass-like than porous, very still. What she said, Sally...my bluntness, my uncertain control...I imagine those few moments before a tsunami hits. Everything is calm. Calm and comforting. Then, with one stroke, everything changes. Maybe I am old. Is sixty-four old? I have energy, as much as I did in my thirties, look fifteen to twenty years younger, eat well, exercise, but more is needed. A change in myself I can't make. Or can I?

"Ben?"

"Yes."

"I know you say so. Lots of people say so, but do you really think I'm pretty? My face. I feel like my thinking distorts it. Makes me look old. I think too much, talk too little, and often badly...but am I still pretty?"

"From the moment I saw you, Sal, I couldn't imagine seeing any woman's face more frequently than yours. You're not just beautiful, you're magnificent. Everything about you is divine. Children call you angel woman. You know that? Pretty? Yes, you're pretty, and you're the most complete woman I've ever met."

She smiles. Winks. "What are we going to name our first baby?"

# SIX

We arrive at Sun-Day Lodge on Tahoe's West shore an hour before twilight. Stop in front of the entrance. Old pinewood columns led the way to beams bleached almost bone white and a wide stairway. A young man, smart-looking, wearing a Sun-Day Lodge shirt, white with green letters, greets us at the bottom of the stairs.

"Do you need help?" he asks.

That question. In my mind, that question is always answered with my grandfather's voice, and his face smiling down at me.

"My wife thinks so," I say, just like grandpa.

The attendant doesn't blink. "Are you checking in, Sir?"

You know how, when you go back and read something—a grade school paper, a letter, an old email—and you think of the person you were when you wrote it as being someone you don't know, because you can't remember who you were at the time, and you can't quite grasp not knowing what the difference between who you were then and who you are now means, so you abandon the thought? I do that. Did that. When the attendant asked, "Are you checking in, Sir?" I heard myself asking the same question. It was something I said dozens of times a day working summer jobs at the casinos. I couldn't recognize the person I was then in the person I am now.

Confused, I stood there staring at the attendant. "Yes," I said, "we're checking in."

"Oh," Sally gets out of the Jeep. "Don't mind him. He's old."

# SEVEN

---

**S**ally chooses a room with bay windows facing the lake. One large, two small. I sat down on the bigger ledge cushion, put a foot up, lit a joint. Sun-Day Lodge, it smells old but not broken or neglected. Sally begins to undress.

"I'm taking a shower," she says.

"OK."

"You can join me."

"OK."

I want to. Imagine Sally doing things to me, in the wet, in the heat. She knows me, knows what keeps me sane, but I can't get up—the view, it has me. Looking out the window, across the lake, silhouette ridges turning to shadow, bits of daylight chalked into the fading sky, they brought back memories.

> My family, what there was of it, spent summers at Tahoe, not the whole summer but most of it, most of the time. A lot of dirt roads, few people. Desolation Wilderness, no people at all. Loved Desolation. Sometimes I would stay on at a friend's house, go out, fish, hunt, climb the ridges, disappear into the woods for days. I'd get as far away from adults as I could. In the forest, there's always something...something that knows me, trusts me. I loved the forest, and the forest loved me. I thought so. Then I realized if I fell, if I broke a leg, hit my head, got trapped in a ravine. If a cat attacked, caught me off guard and killed me, the forest wouldn't care. It was not made to care. Life was not made to care. Still, I loved the forest. Love is not being loved back; it's just loving.

"Ben, where are you?"

The bathroom door is open. An invitation. The shower glass fogged just enough to draw faces; I can see her figure through it. Her hand size breasts, the glow of her contradictory skin, her hair darkened by warm water conforming to each move of her body. I did want her, every second of the day, but I couldn't move, memories were spent, my mind, I couldn't take my mind off the lake, off the secret's surfaces conceal. The lake surface…beneath it…all the bodies I skied over, their liquid eyes gazing up from a forgotten past. I know they're there, calling for remembrance. The first biped to fall into the lake. Indians and miners who never learned to swim. Water-skiers, divers who ran out of air, flipped over kayakers, drunks walking on water (without Jesus), witnesses, gangsters, and snitches (mouths duct-taped, hands tied behind their backs, chains around the legs, no last words), all the rodent-size dogs that yap too much, how many of them are down there calling? Vietnam calling, demanding I remember. Dying men. Dying friends. Dying enemies, down there. Calling, calling, calling. They are there. I hear them, and they hear me listening.

"Ben! I'm waiting."

Reality. Back to it, to Sally's magnificent body, pending erections, ejaculations, cold beer afterward. Before and afterward.

"Baby names, Ben," she calls out. "I'm thinking baby names."

Sally turns off the shower, steps out. A beautiful woman, the promise of a fulfilled life, a story that must be told. I turn toward her, stretch out my legs, drop them abruptly, smile. She drifts over, sloshing, skin steaming, pulls up my shirt, removes it. Unbuckles and unzips my pants, slides them off.

"Me first," she says.

We rolled it on the floor. Did the happy dirty with alternate glances at the beamed ceiling—the white pine with dozens of cracks and knots, cobwebs in the corners. The carpet looks clean but close up smells of old dust, cigarette smoke, years of absorbing dirt and cleaning solutions.

"Baby names." Sally rolls onto her side. Reaches for me. Stops. "Maybe we can wait on names."

"Sure. I can do that."

"Let's eat."

"Yeah."

# EIGHT

Not for my eyes only, Sally puts on a see-through blouse, no bra, white trousers, sandals. A warm night. The Tahoe smell–a combined fragrance of pine trees, lake evaporation and altitude—it captivates me. The world's smells. I've become intimately related to many of them, (sometimes regrettably). No other place has what Tahoe has. People who know Tahoe, know the Tahoe smell like a dog knows his favorite tree, food bowl, the cat next door...the dog next door.

We take a table on the deck with a view of the night sky and lights far away.

The waitress, her name is Suzy, skips over to our table. Acts eager to meet us. Maybe she is eager.

I order steak, rare, bacon and cottage cheese on the side, large curd, a bottle of wine. Wine with steak, have to have it, a cheap bottle. Sally orders arugula avocado salad on top of brown rice. We share the wine.

"You're an animal, Ben."

"I eat animals."

"You do, yes, you eat too many animals, too much steak, too thick, too raw."

"That's what the wines for. What the steak clogs up, wine unclogs."

"Nonsense, Ben. How are we to marry, make it to the Keys, start a family, keep trying to make babies, often, if your heart stops?"

"It's not going to stop, Sal. No worries. I'm a mountain man. I ate rocks and bushes as a kid. Made me strong and fibrous, long-lived."

"Hard on the teeth, I imagine."

"Yeah, it was. Definitely."

Suzy returns. She's cute without trying to be. Younger than Sally. Flirtatious, but not with me. I catch her eye as she serves the avocado salad. Sally's blouse is open, inviting inspection. Suzy inspects, likes what she sees.

She likes me too, but not as much.

A quiet dinner. We talk, but nothing serious. Old movies, childhood infatuations. Mine, one of them, was chewing on the bone. And still, I like chewing, gnawing the bone. Certain parts of the bone. Some ancient temperament still active in my blood. An animal thing, maybe. Can humans, certain humans, can they have animal blood—dog blood, cat, bear? Skunk blood would be interesting. I get lost in my steak, the bone, and wine, Sally in her greens and rice. Not many patrons, not that I can see. The moon rises—a full moon. Yellow-brown and bright. We watch it make a ghost of the night, the trees. Feel chilly, always cooler in the evening. Tahoe. It snowed in August once. Desolation. A week-long fishing trip, Rubicon Reservoir. Rained the last three days, then snowed, dropped a load of Sierra Cement on me, cold slush. A miserable hike out.

"More wine?"

"Sure."

We finish the bottle. Order another.

"So, driver man," Sally sets down her fork, stops chewing, looks at me. "Tomorrow, where to?" Suzy comes up, pours more water.

"Emerald Bay," I say. "First thing after breakfast. Then Myers, Hope Valley after Myers, then a bar I know in Markleeville. Can't remember the real name. Locals call it the Bra Bar. Lots of bras hanging from the ceiling. Girls boozing it, making dares, making bets, then one lets go. In front of everyone, she yanks off her bra, leaves her tits out to catch air as she tosses her bra toward the ceiling. Tries to hook it on something, misses, tosses until it catches. Guys love that bar, and girls. You'll love it, Sal."

Tits. Female breasts. Beautiful breasts are one of nature's most flawless compositions. Like beautiful faces, beautiful breasts radiate perfection, but most of the time, they're hidden behind bra bars: tit hijabs. That's what bras are, tit hijabs. Bikini tops, and bright yellow pasties, they're a good step forward. Along with beauty contests, we should have beautiful tits contests. Imagine that? An international most beautiful tits competition.

Nothing in nature is more balanced than beauty? Beauty appreciation. We need more of it, much more.

"After Markleeville, we'll head down 395 along the Sierra, past Mono Lake, then on to Vegas. Or Death Valley. Maybe both."

Suzy finishes pouring, adjusts the condiment tray. I study her, undress her, can't help it. Her hoots, they're pressing hard against her light blue waitress shirt, a short T-shirt with Sun-Day Lodge written on it. It stops just above her navel. A little blue apron tied in a bow, hangs below the shirt covering the black skirt underneath. I wonder if she's knickered up. A guy thought. Typical. Suzy asks if there's anything else we need, suggests a dessert—very special, but only available through room service.

"We'd love that, Suzy, "Sally says. "Can you take the order?"

"I can." And she does. I sign for the meal, leave a good tip. We go back to our room.

People of a like kind recognize each other. Always have. Like homing pigeons, they pick up the cues. Maybe it's the world they inhabit, the world we inhabit. The places we end up…maybe places decide for us. Maybe places are like people…the thinking, making decisions, making plans, throwing out lines to catch us, kind of people.

"Ben, we're going to have fun. I know what this dessert is."

"She likes you, Sal."

"Yes, she does."

"And me?"

"And you, Ben…yes," she says, and she smiles, a casual lift in the cheeks. A smile with eyes, ears, and dilated lips.

I go into the bathroom to brush my teeth. Hear the knock, check the mirror. It's Suzy. Dessert. She's changed into a light green dress, tight, very short, a deep V-neck, split sleeves open at the sides, nothing on underneath. My chest tightens, my royal tightens, begins to surge. Suzy closes the door, walks toward the bed unzipping her dress. It falls to the floor making sounds heard only in the mind and one's expectations. I drop my toothbrush in the sink. It bounces around, splattering the mirror. I pull off my shirt, unbuckle my belt, drop my pants, turn toward Suzy. Sally steps in between us, naked. Holds me, stares albino-like at

23

Suzy. The lights are on, the curtains open. Eyes on the dock. People having drinks on their boats. Fish, if they're looking, they can see us. The distant peaks, the stars, they can see us.

Erotic primetime theater. Classic Bolero unwinding the clock. We go sauna all in, body to body rapture hunters scalding the air, searing the night. Water in the bedside pitcher begins to boil, blankets melt, nylon curtains shrivel up, the bed catches fire. Semen is cooked and out the gate. Christ rising from the dead. Vesuvius, Mount St. Helens, Krakatoa. I hit full stride. A sperm geyser knocking on heaven's door, kicking the wind. Feels like it will never stop. It does.

Sixty-four and still in the game. I smile.

The girls lean over me, touch each other. Tasty touches. I want back in. No ticket.

Sally takes pity, pulls me over. A good time to die, a good death. I want both.

# NINE

Another sweltering day. We skip Emerald Bay, too thick with tourists. Tourists who drive big Winnebago's. They block the road, drive five miles an hour around turns, clog local arteries. RV flatlanders, cartoon people. Globs with faces, webbed feet, and octopus' hands, that's what they are. With a tank I would crush them, push them off the road, blow them off the road. Anger rolling down the windows, turning up the heat, again. Control it? Should I?

There's a brief rise on Tahoe's southwest side highway, between Cascade Lake and Emerald Bay, a small stretch, twenty to thirty feet, where you can see Greater Tahoe ahead of you, Cascade Lake on the right and Emerald Bay on the left. It's one of the most magnificent highway moments in the world. Breathtaking. Impossibly beautiful on a perfect day. We drive those twenty to thirty feet at two miles an hour, one mile an hour, maybe. Take in the view, try to make it last. A big-ass RV pulling a Mercedes sports car comes up behind us. The driver honks. Twice, three times. The third time he sits on his horn, looms over us.

I stop at the highest point of the rise, get out, walk up to the RV driver. Years of festering resentment toward the world, especially slow-moving RVs with absurd and contradictory names like Ghost Rider, Prowler, Outlaw, Renegade, take hold. I hate how RV drivers block the road ignoring long lines of cars behind them, cut turns too wide, pause to take in the view rather than pull over. How many times have I endured that?

"A thousand times," I shout. "A thousand times I've been stuck behind a big-ass RV driver like you, and the one time I decide to go slow, for just a few minutes, to enjoy the view with my girl, you honk at me. You honk like it's your road. Well, fuck you! This is *my* road, asshole," I shout and then, even louder, I say. "You see me on it, standing here? You see me? This is my road!"

His hands on the wheel, he stares, horn blaring.

What can I do? What do I want to do? I can stand in his way, say nasty things. I was doing that. Or I can walk over to his door, open it, pull him out and stuff him into the trunk of his Mercedes.

He keeps on his horn, keeps staring. I turn around, pull down my pants, moon him, moon the woman sitting next to him. The woman begins hitting him. He let off the horn, doesn't move. I don't move. We stare. Eye rage, it can get ugly, very ugly.

I smile. "All the people backed up behind you," I say. I don't shout, no need to. "The next time one of them gets in front of you, like I am now, right here, now, you might not be so lucky. I don't need to know who you are to dislike you. Neither does anyone else." I flip off the woman, give the man both fingers, get back in the Jeep, feel better. Much better.

"Ben," Sally reaches over, turns my face toward her as I sit down, buckles my seat belt. "That was fun. I'm all excited. So manly. So brave, a real turn on."

"It was?"

"Yes. And now you owe me," she says as she grabs my Johnny Royal, ignites the urge for sensual reprieve—the thirst that follows a pleasurable fit of anger.

I shift gears, step on the gas, leave the past to fend for itself.

# TEN

Markleeville. The Bra Bar.

Windows are open, the place busy but not crowded. Rock and roll plays over three corner speakers. Feels welcoming, very friendly. A guy and a girl, they look like a couple, are shooting pool, the familiar click of pool balls accenting the music. Pool is my game, but I never talk about it, not with anyone but Sally. It's my wild card, always good for a few bucks and several rounds of beer.

We sit at the bar, order two Buds, sandwiches, ask for water with ice. Ice water. I love ice water, always love ice water, have a good reason to love it, many good reasons. Carefree erotic memories. Ice cold water. Walruses and polar bears, with better management, could patent ice cold water, make enough money to buy off global warming.

Two men at the end of the bar are drinking hard stuff. They have a bottle. We can hear them. They sound a little like me and my brother when we talked. The conversations we had, something I should remember. Wasn't sure if I did. We fought more than we talked.

"You see, Jonas, I understand that, I do." The guy with a baseball cap on took a drink. A backwards baseball cap. "Tits. I'm saying. Listen up," he says, "The professor's talking here. Tits are lifesaving. Who did not suck tits as a baby? No one. Right. We like tits, need tits. Boys, girls, mammals, we're born tit-suckers, all of us. But guys, the scepter and jewels we're born with, they don't belong to us. They belong to girls. I'm telling you. The professor knows. That's it."

I get his meaning. Think I do. Am sure they know the girls there, the owner.

The cap guy takes another drink. Empties his glass, refills it. Local guys. They look local. "That women have any interest in us is a mystery," says the cap guy, emphasizing his words with bloated expressions, his sausage veins popping out. An odd look. "How they do? I don't know, but I'm glad they do."

"Me, too," says the other guy. He's bald, thin mustache, sharp eyes. "You've seen my wife."

"I've seen her, sure. Many times."

"She's more than her looks, and she looks great. She's smart. Whip smart, money smart."

"You're right, Sam Long. You prick. And you always add that, y'know? The 'she's smart' bit. You always say that after saying she's beautiful, like it means more than her looks. Her looks are what attracts you, not her smarts. Who fucks smarts?"

They're drunk. Those men.

"Up yours, Jonas."

Sam Long slaps his hands together, takes a long swig, cranks up his voice, his sudden belligerence.

"I have four sons. You have three girls. My wife's a boy maker. That's better. Yours is a girl maker. My boys are going to kick the socks up stream, Cuz. Knock up your girls! Then we'll see who's the who here?"

"Your boys, Sam. I love you, man. You're my favorite relative, but I'm sayin,' just sayin,' those boys of yours, they're going homo on you. An end to your family line."

The bigger guy, he must have been six-four, stands up and steps toward the pool table. The couple back up.

"We're too close to them, Ben," Sally whispers. "Maybe we should move away from the bar. It's taking forever to get served and they're not even busy."

"You're hungry. I know. Food's coming, we've only been here for ten minutes, less. No worries, Sal."

"Ten minutes, or less, that's too long. And why did we come here anyway?"

Sally, I stare at her reflexively. She' like a web…her beauty, it catches you and instantly you pray she'll never let go.

"The hot springs, Sal. I told you about it, remember? In my teens, the band days. We came here at night. After performing at the American Legion Hall, there would be girls. They waited for us. Groupies. They were too young, most of the time, but not always. The older ones, we'd bring them here."

"And that's why we came here?"

"Right. And this bar. The bras, like I said." I get up, hand Sally her beer, pull out a chair at one of the nearby tables, a safer spot for her to sit, point to all the bras hanging from the ceiling. Mast flags giving directions, clothes on a line drying in the sun, cleaning rags, plastic bags caught in trees. At a glance, the bras could have been any of those things.

"Fuck you!" Says the cap guy as he steps to the side, slid some to avoid the other man's fist as it shot past his left ear.

I stand up, can't stop myself. Vets with PTSD. Too many dead, not enough dead. I shout, "What the fuck guys! Christ! Are you going to do that now? For Christ fucking sake. You're scaring my girlfriend."

The bartender looks on, uneasily. Starts shuffling around behind the counter. Looking for something. A gun, maybe a bat. Bats are good.

"And who the fuck are you?" The smaller bald guy belched his words. Did his best to appear menacing.

"I'm the happy man," I say. "I'm here to make you happy." The eight or ten people in the bar turn to watch. "That's all, a peace maker. That's who I am."

Both men are bigger than me. I walk over to them. "Look gentlemen, you don't know me, sure. Who the fuck am I, right? And why have I interrupted your quarrel? I like a good fight. The raw meat in it. I didn't interrupt to stop you from breaking teeth, spilling blood. Bleeding is good. Lewis and Clark, all those early frontier guys, they used leeches, knives to bleed people. Bleeding was good then. Still is. Bleed all you want. I don't care but stop scaring my Sally. That's all I'm saying. She's albino. She scares easy." I close my mouth, harden my eyes, consider the idea of torture, of using excessive pain to learn the truth, to subdue a challenger.

The cap guy says, "Maybe I should go a full round with her, give her reason to fear. Right here, right now, put you in second place, old man.

And why the fuck would a gorgeous woman like that want to be with some dead branch, like you?"

I wince, drop my eyes, check my stance, my leverage. "I wonder that as well," I say, nodding, and I'm thinking, *Ben, what are you doing, this is a bad idea. Too late....*

The big guy puts a hand on my shoulder, tries to push me aside. I look up at him, grin meekly, then put my boot toe into the smaller guy's balls, hard. As he doubles over, the big one looks at him, exposes his jaw line. I put an elbow into that jaw, his jaw, feels good. He stumbles backward, falls onto the pool table, fucks up the young couple's game, kicks a little trying to right himself. Sits up. The bartender pulls out a bat.

Sally pushes her chair aside, steadies her glass of water, and begins unbuttoning her blouse. "Guys, guys! Everybody! I know what you want."

All eyes turn, focus on Sally. She's good. You can't miss her, don't want to miss her. A new bra for the bar, all eyes are on her, the room still, shuttered in silence. With each button, the silence deepens. People stop breathing, couldn't hear them breathing. They're eager. Button by button, Sally leads all eyes to her soothing milk mounds, nipples pink with desire, a thousand babies crying to suck them. Her blouse flies open, she removes it, tosses it up. It caught on the ceiling fan. The fan threw it across the room. Another woman, not so attractive but decent, grabs it. She opens her shirt. Takes off her bra. A damn big one, bright red. Ties it to Sally's blouse and throws the two pieces over the beam above her. It catches. Everyone in the bar cheers and claps, and claps and claps. Feels like they clap forever, like the moment stays in the same place but keeps stretching, reaching further ahead, and back to help us find our way.

We run out laughing. Sally bare-breasted, bouncing, irresistibly bouncing. It's still warm, the end of day pulling twilight curtains across the sky. We get in the Jeep. Jill the Jeep. Drive to the hot springs. Sneak in and spend the next three hours pretending we're the first life forms on earth sorting out reproduction like modern day dolphins, seahorses, sardines, bristlemouth...anything with fins.

# ELEVEN

**"S**hit! We forgot to pay our bill."

"We did, Ben. We did, we forgot. Should we go back!"

"Too late." My immediate response.

Being told what to do, made to do, told what to say. No one likes being told. Told to come or go, how to think, what to think. I keep driving, began debating the pros and cons of not paying the bill. It's illegal, must be, but how illegal? Enough for me to feel I'd done something wrong, something so wrong that I should turn around, drive back, prostrate myself before the bar owner? Does it matter? The cap guy. Really? Put me in second place. He thought he knew me. Sally saved him. Moron. I should've paid the bill.

Self-explaining, accommodating truths that cannot be denied, justified learning, I do that, often. It's like medicine for the incomplete soul. You explain yourself to yourself as if you're not who you are, so you can see who you are—if you are. I have good reason for thinking the way I do, acting the way I do. I think so, every man does. Feel no need to justify myself, to inject visuals of how I resolve what's caused me grief into Sally's mind.

Bad men, predator dictators, the many faces of selfish want. Fuck it. I served my country…those bastards included.

"What's wrong, Ben?"

"Nothing, Sal."

"Ben…."

"Yeah, nothing. Memory embers trying to reignite. They come up sometimes, walk around my head, uproot the past. Not a lot of light in them. That's all, give me a few minutes. I'm dissolving them with the view, with you."

Sally, she smiles, refills my empty eyes.

"Highway 395 is just ahead."

A right turn, our first big right. Grand vistas. US 395 has grand vistas. Nature, throughout our lives she carves indelible images in the mind, gifts us glorious sunsets, massive waterfalls, canyons, oceans. We're cruising, feeling alive, optimistic. Sally hands me an apple. Takes one for herself. The morning is bright, sunny, a little cool, a relief.

We skirt Bridgeport, one of those American towns that never grows up, gets a bit bigger every year but never grows up. We keep south. Mono Lake on our left, a brine-rich blue. On our right the clawing teeth of the Sierra Nevada, shooting up at odd angles and distances. The sky is food to them. The clouds are food. The Sierra eats the clouds. The Rockies eats them. The Alps. Himalayas, the Andes— sky hunters, cloud eaters, all of them.

Mountains. I couldn't get enough of them when I was in them and always missed them when I was gone. Room to breathe. The forest gives me room to breathe. Cities are suffocating, straitjackets of conformity city dwellers bow to. Wasn't good at bowing. Too willful. Couldn't imagine riding an elevator to get home. People above me. Under me. Next to me; all the time. Everyday. An end to the fenceless frontier we took from the Indians. Everything is owned now or will be soon. Humans, we're greedy fucks. We want more. Always. Throughout my life, for the most part, I've lived outside cities. When I worked, I worked as an inventor/problem-solver, hitman in my dreams. Had no title. I made things, fixed things, forgot things. Memory's becoming unreliable little by little. I accomplish less each year and work harder to do so. Get paid too little to do so. I make extra money shooting pool, selling home grown weed and casino-hopping. Now, when I hop, I hop with Sally.

Hopping with Sally, it's a thing, it's more than a thing, it's more than fun. It's what fun is, but on top of fun it's hypnotic, something like having a part in a movie you're watching, and you can't wait until your little scene comes up. That's it. That's what I want to do with the rest of my life. Hop with Sally.

She tilts her seat back, rolls down the window, begins massaging herself; verifies the utility of relaxation. Changing air patterns in the Jeep filter through her loose blouse, enhance the view. A tits man, that's what I am, and Sally is a give-you-all-the-tits-you-want woman. We're a perfect match. The day a perfect day. We leave 395 around noon, continue south on 136 and turn east on 190, head for Death Valley. It's hot and getting hotter. Late June.

"Ben. Christ! Why so hot?"

"The windows are down, Sal. The way we like it. Air feely flowing is more alive, even when it's hot air, right."

"Fuck! It's hot, Ben! Fucking hot!"

Sally doesn't swear much. Not like I do. I swear as often as possible.

There are too many things that piss me off. Too many rules, too many things wrong with too many people in too many places too much of the time. A world without swear words, I couldn't live in it. Swear words are the worst you can do without becoming physical. A way to fight the big dicks, to stick it to them, like cutting corners, smoking in banks while making a big deposit, drinking in public, running stop signs, red lights, eating the occasional food item without paying for it. Rules. Who makes them? Old guys...balding fucks with shriveled hearts, false teeth, glass eyes, ingrown toe-nails...dictators, CEOs, politicians, priests.

"Fuck," Sally says again. "Look at me, every inch of my body is visible. I'm soaked."

Naked with clothes on, naked with clothes off. Doesn't matter, I celebrate every Sally moment, every enticing part of her body, her skin, breasts, legs, her radiant face, her walk-through eyes.

"Desert, Sal, desert plays a role. Summer plays a role. Global warming, the sun heating up. It's hot, that's all. I'm hot, you're hot."

"I know, Mr. Ben, that's what I said. I'm hot." She puts her feet on the dash. Begins slicing her hand through the air rushing past. I love watching her relax, a vicarious comfort of some kind.

We stop at Furnace Creek for lunch. There are buildings. Homes. Trees. People live there. They have a golf course with a pond. The world's lowest elevation golf course. 214 feet below sea level. The course is green, the greens are green–214 feet, below the sea, and green. We park outside the19$^{th}$ hole. A lodge or something. It looks deserted. The whole town looks deserted. A hundred and nine degrees. I walk around the Jeep inspecting the tires. Feels like they're sticking to the road. Maybe they are. They're shiny, they look wet. It's a good idea to skip Badwater. The novelty of standing on the lowest patch of ground in the US, on this day, is a novelty too dear.

"They must have food in there."

"Yeah. We saw houses. Cars."

"Do you see any lights?"

Sally puts her face to the glass door. "No."

"I don't remember it being like this."

"You've been here before?"

"A long time ago, yes. Let's go."

Something troubles me. Sally knows. She always knows. Doesn't matter what it is. Shadows, there is more in them than the absence of light. I fill our water tank with an outside hose. We get back in the Jeep. No cars on 190. No people. The sky has an odd, rose-white hue to it, a strange glow. Aliens, where the fuck are they? Have they outgrown God? Is this the day, the place? Terminators, no Arnold.

A half-dozen bikers appear on the road ahead of us. Death Valley. Hell's Angels. Seems like a good fit. They pass us, in slow motion. Eye us, each one. We eye them, each one. Big guys. Angels. They probably have guns. The last guy passing us doesn't look. His eyes fix straight ahead. As he passes, he flips us the bird.

Asshole! Before I can stop myself, my finger is out the window. "Fuck you!"

I never wanted to fight. Not in 'Nam not anywhere. I tried, and try, to avoid fighting. But I always feel like a good fight solves problems. Blowing shit up solves problems, can end starvation, injustice, all the crap living bestows upon the weakest in life. A dumb thought, but I always think it. An inner toy I play with to keep myself sane.

Are they going to turn around? I keep watching, checking my mirrors. The road is long and straight. I can see them fading. The line of their bikes merging into a dot. Then nothing. Nothing for a long time. A bend in the road erases my worries. They're gone.

"You shouldn't do that Ben."

"I know. Didn't mean to."

"Yes, you did. You can't stop yourself, even if it hurts me."

"I can Sally. I'll try harder. I know better. I do."

She's right. How can I love her as I do and behave so carelessly? The bra Bar was a lucky escape. I've always been lucky with Sally. Sally changed the direction of my life. Childhood never leaves you. Mine was ugly. Bitter. I grew up angry. Stayed angry. Sally changed that, is changing it, a lot of it.

"I've got this Sal. I'll do better. Promise."

Guys are always promising shit. In the past I didn't give a fuck. What were the consequences anyway? It was just me and I cared less for myself than anyone trying to harm me. This time, this promise—I have to keep it.

Can I?

# TWELVE

We make Vegas before sunset.

Stop at the weed dispensary across from the Trump hotel, pick up a half ounce. Trump. His real name. It might not be Trump. It might be Grump, or Bump, maybe Runt…how is one to know? So many lies and pretensions to choose from. The weed. A weed store. Lots of oils, Indica drops, some new combination. I don't care. For a golden age boomer, a sixties kid, buying pot legally is magic. Standing in line. Looking at all the glass display cases. All the names you can give a simple little weed, a weed that wore sandals when it was a man walking the desert, teaching people to do unto others as you would have them do unto you. I love it. No cops. No handcuffs. This could be progress for a country otherwise going to hell.

Body searched, imagine that. For no reason, at a young age, 14. I was stopped in the LA airport, taken to a room where a machine with lots of whirling parts, probed my private anatomy for any hint of illicit drugs. Lots of airport cops all around, many waiting in line. Wasn't sure what for. Lots of rooms, mostly empty with ugly wallpaper, plastic folding chairs, and vending machines.

A tall, blond Viking looking guy, staring down, his hulking torso blocking the light. "Mister Mamott, Come with me."

"Why. I'm just a kid," I say. "What do you want with me?"

"It's not you, it's your girlfriend."

"My girlfriend! Sir, I don't have a girlfriend."

"You do now."

Some girl, pleasant to look at. She was three, maybe four years older than me. She saw me in line, told the cops that grabbed her that I was with her. That I gave her the pot she had in her pocket. Fuck.

"I don't know her," I said. "She's lying."

"She's a Christian."

"So...."

"Are you a Christian?"

"No. But I was made to go to church."

"Fine," he says, "now you're going to jail."

"Why? Because I was made to go to church?"

"Marijuana's illegal."

"It's not mine."

"I've heard that before, Mamott. You should have learned to pray while you were in church."

"Pray!"

"That girl," he points, "she prays every day. She said so, and Christians don't lie."

"I never pray. Why would God listen to me, listen to anybody?"

"God listens to Christians," he says, and he handcuffs me. A kid. Locks me in a small cell for three days. Three days in a cage with a fat smelly man. All night and all day he would lose it, that man. And he cried, loudly. All night. All day. He cried.

That's what happens. When a kid is made to go to church but doesn't want to...that's what happens.

At the drugstore (they sell everything in Vegas drug stores.) We picked up a few sandwiches, some cottage cheese, milk, nuts, two six packs of Bud and a bottle of Seven Deadly Zins. Fits right in with the world we're living in. It's cheap but not too cheap. We have a veterans' discount for the Trump hotel. My brother sends me these deals just to stay in touch. It works. I call to check on him. He's the oldest now. The next in line.

The lounge is grand. Lots of busy people hurrying about. Important people, every one of them, you can tell. When people think they're important, you can tell. We check in. Go to our room. Twelfth floor. Get undressed, open the Zin, roll a joint and step into the six-person, three-nozzle shower, complete with a marble bench, polished handrails, free shampoos, all with Trump's name on them. Trump's name is everywhere. On the towels, water bottles, coasters, soaps, even on the paper doilies at the bottom of trash cans. An ego rampage, that's what it is. Trash, maybe his name is Trash. Donald Trash. Unbelievable. The man in the Whitehouse, he's like a dog that can't stop licking his own balls. And he licks publicly, wants everyone to see.

Christ!

A great shower. We make love on the shower floor, pulses of warm water splashing, flowing all around us. Liquid memories. The Trump hotel. A big, shiny, gaudy, dick hotel. Skyscrapers? Maybe they should call them Dickscrapers.

"Ben."

That sound, how she says my name. I love it.

"Have you ever thought about humans, like you would think about cattle, goats, or pigs? Thought of them, us, as meat?"

"Meat? I don't know. Bears think of us like that, gators do, wolves, lions, sharks, they think of us as meat. Cannibals think the same. I don't, though. I haven't thought...."

"Why not? Think about it now. Imagine how many mouths human meat would feed, who or what it would feed if we were being farmed for our meat. And what would we do if God, the big guy with all the heavy artillery is behind it, if, in this case God, whomever or whatever that is, is the farmer?"

"Sally, really...."

We're stoned. Our brains loaded with strange text. Human pages in an open book waving at strangers. Empty teapots whistling on a hot stove. Can't think. Not immediately. Maybe it's the weed. It's good weed. I'm sure it's the weed.

"You think God is a farmer?"

"No. A rancher."

"OK."

We use room service for dinner. Watch a movie called "300", drink all our beer, empty the Zin, smoke some pot with a tin foil pipe, call the front desk, ask for two girls to 'massage' us—Vegas style. The girls come, promptly, like they were next door waiting. They're Haitian. Strong, beautiful, illegal, probably. Naked but for oil bottles hanging from their waist belts. They sponge us down in the shower, dry us off, oil us, set up their tables in front of the windows, put on meditation music, light scented candles, lay us down, face up.

Working girls. We love working girls. Want better lives for them at the same time we take pleasure in the services they provide. Standing between us, they work our chests, stomachs, thighs, inner thighs. Slowly, deliberately—feels like a sacred event, a prayer, the worshiping of private sensation. Warm oil, a warm room, soothing hands, professional hands. We slip into their good graces, gave up our bodies to them. They're good. Feels like my member is in my toes when they work my toes, in my neck when they work my neck, my shoulders when they work my shoulders, everywhere they touch.

Time loses its way. We can be anywhere, any place. Steady strokes, a dance routine, they take us away, let us drift… magic carpets, lost worlds, ritual silence. Orgasm hit without warning. It's there suddenly, in every pore of our bodies, no time to think. They keep massaging, easing the dissipating heat into our pores, into our memories. And pressing, they keep pressing with tender hands, caring fingers smoothing the sheets, our perfectly made bed. Wonderful…it is, pleasure refreshing the senses, wonderful. More than wonderful, it's something complete in an incomplete world, a blessing.

They step back, wait for further instruction.

Sally lays her arm across my chest. A happy ending. All stories should have a happy ending. I think so.

We sit up. Smile at the girls.

"How did you do that?"

"Voodoo," they say. "Will there be anything else?"

# THIRTEEN

**M**orning came early. It always does, but it feels earlier today, like the sun is cheating. I get up, wander into the bathroom, close the curtains, load our tin foil pipe, take a hit, go back to bed. Sally snuggles in. We sleep until noon.

"Are we hopping today, Sal?" She opens her eyes, turns to me.

"Sure. That's why we're here."

"Yeah, that's why."

I get up, walk over to the window. Look out. Train tracks. Cars. Buildings. The weed dispensary. Distant mountains. An OK view.

"Ben, how much money do you have? Do we have?"

I open my wallet. "Credit cards, no debt on them, checks, a couple of thousand in hundreds. Not much, but we're good."

A safety deposit box, Paradise. I have fifty thousand stashed away. Emergency money. Sally knows the money's there, where it is, where the key is stashed. We never talk money. Not seriously. We need it like everyone needs it, but we don't think it, plan it. Not much. Not often. Often enough to beat the casinos. That often. Beating the house. It's a good feeling. Little animals acting ferociously toward big animals they know won't hurt them. We're little animals; disposable citizens. Ferocious feels good. The money is extra.

"Money," Sally says, and she sits up, straightens up, combs her hair with her fingers. For a second her fingers look like combs. "You're right. It's time to hop."

We dress. I help with Sally's buttons, mostly fumble with them. Want to wait on hopping. No rush. No rush at all. That's what I'm thinking.

"Ben, are you done? How long can it take to button five buttons?"
Smiling, I button her last button, think to unbutton it.
"Done!"
"OK. Let's hop!"

# FOURTEEN

Casinos. Slot bells. Lots of slots. Lots of bells. Synthetic noise. People drifting, meandering, walking around with drinks, cigarettes, dressed to lose. Girls on the arms of guys. Girls alone, guys alone. Couples. Groups. Old men bussed in from nursing homes, short sleeve shirts, pot bellies, withered arms pulling steel levers, drinking, dreaming of impossible riches. Empty gazes. A wedding party dancing to the music. Dealers standing. Dealers dealing. Wheels turning, dice rolling, cards scraping the felt, more drinks. The occasional child, stunned and dismayed, held tightly in hand by a parent, pedophile, kidnapper looking for an exit. Intercom voices. Money making money, being money. Cameras watching, recording every suspicious move, clandestine glance, spilled drink, cleavage view, disheveled wig, nose job.

Casinos look like girl scouts but they're dirty sex.

Animals can look like casinos. Can't think of what kind.

It's noon. Our first hop. We walk around. Adjust to casino climate. Spend a few bucks watching the white tiger show at the Mirage. Tigers.... Massive animals. Beautiful. The tricks are good, the cats magnificent. Easier to imagine being hunted by one than hunting one. Not sure why. Too beautiful to hunt, maybe. A hungry man would think differently.

The Strip is packed. Tourists, hundreds of them. Thousands. Vegas. De Wallen of the West. The desert version. No French accent. Every casino window, entrance, neon sign shouts, "Cum one. Cum all. Vegas is a red-light-means-go town. Go all the way all day. And Nevada is a red-light state.

We pause on one of the crossover bridges. Watch the traffic. Guys with cardboard signs asking for money, smoking joints, drinking from bottles wrapped in brown paper bags. Addicts, drunks, mad men, it doesn't matter. I give them money. A couple of bucks. The 'there but for the grace of God,' thing playing in my head. Lots of kids with tattoos, dyed hair, torn jeans, pierced head to toe. College kids. They look like college kids. Lots of kids look like college kids.

"Hey," I call to one of them, "are you a college kid?"

"Fuck you, mister."

He walks off. Must be college.

Sally stops a couple of Swedes, two girls, both are taller than her, asks for a cigarette. They don't smoke. Sally doesn't smoke. Beautiful girls. I start to think, what ifs, fun ifs. Stop myself. A hot day. Every day is hot, nature turning on us. Sally takes my hand, walks us to the nearest casino, the Venetian. An amazing lobby. We pass the slots. Lots of ass fat hanging over slot stools. People who'll die soon from eating too much genetically altered food. Theater signs lit and blinking, spectators watching roulette, baccarat, craps. Sally's stride is casual, uncommitted, her lose clothing animating wants we fear will shame us. Beautiful. An angel in a house of sin. Camera eyes watch her, operator fingers pushing the zoom in button. Magic. It's the only way to think about her.

She skips the first blackjack table, the first half dozen, looking a little lost, acting nonchalantly attracted to a particular game, then she walks back to a table she'd just passed. Before taking a seat, she knows the odds—the house percentage taken off every game. She knows how many face cards remains in any deck size and when the face cards will come up. She knows when to split, double down, surrender. Numbers talk to her, tell her things, other players tell her things, she watches them, how they play, how they choose to take risks. Finding her advantage, it's so natural for her, graceful, that even if someone knew she was going to win, they didn't care. Might be an albino thing, maybe. Maybe alien.

"Here," she says. A blackjack table in the middle of the main casino floor, inset ceiling overhead, Tiepolo reproductions pretending to have historical value, glass chandeliers. She reaches for a stool, the middle one, sits down, buys chips, makes herself comfortable. A twenty-five-dollar minimum table. There are two other players. I take the stool next to her. Turn my back to the table, begin looking for a cocktail waitress. They're young, the waitresses, and attractive, all of them.

Sally places her bet. The dealer's a woman. Small bird tattoos under each ear, bald. (Lots of bald out there.) She likes Sally. Sally studies her. Studies the other players, analyzes how they're playing, how they see the game, how long they look at their cards, how they arrange their chips, how frequently they ask for drinks, or don't ask. How they smoke, if they smoke. How they adjust their posture. How much they bet. How happy they are, she notices. She notices if they're alone, have someone with them, someone nearby. She notices everything. And she counts.

A good table. Sally pulls three winning hands. Earns us a couple of hundred dollars. We get up. Walk away, go to another room, another table. No waitresses, odd, I look around. Give up. Go to the bar, purchase a couple of beers. By the time I get back, Sally has returned two 50-dollar chips to the house. Deliberately.

I sit down next to her. Give her a beer. She keeps her eyes on the dealer. Androgynous. Boy or girl. It/them/they. Pronoun acrobatics. I can't tell, not immediately. Gender equivalence? No longer a boy girl world. Wasn't simple anymore. I like simple. Have to adjust, see no reason to. I told Sally I would try. I did, but being forced to have an interest in something I can't relate to and have no interest in, how am I to do that?

"What's your name?" The dealer's polite. His/her job.

"Sally."

"You're not from here."

Sally looks around. Watches a family of five. Kids with balloons, stuffed toys. They're huddled together on the escalator. A game of some kind. One of the balloons, a red one, gets loose. Then a blue one. They rise to the ceiling, block one of the cameras.

"No one's from here," Sally says.

"Right." The dealer smiles, slides Sally her cards, deals the other players, pulls his/her own cards.

Sally doesn't look down. She keeps her eyes on Androgynous.

"I'll take a card. A six would be nice."

The dealer gives her a five. Twenty.

The other two players bust. Get picked off by face cards. The dealer hit for eighteen. Sally wins.

The dealer: "Do you like music?" Androgynous has a guy package. I can tell now, and he fancies Sally unwrapping a few boxes. Understandable.

"Hey, buddy." It's the cowboy near the end of the table, finger tattoos, a wrinkled look on his face. He taps on the table, says, "Just deal, OK? No one's paying you to talk." The guy is losing. Androgynous acknowledges his displeasure, glances at Sally.

"I do like music," Sally says. "Don't like noise."

The other two players, are big, (Why are guys always big?) Cowboy hats, boots, sweat-stained shirts, face scars, wedding rings. Drooling over Sally makes them weak. She takes control, pulls information from their eyes, somehow. Wins two more hands, gets chatty with Androgynous, makes it harder for them to concentrate, to win. Maybe she doesn't like them. They keep at it, keep trying, lose three more hands, win one. Sally folds twice.

"Lady, you're beautiful." The taller of the two announces, like he's informing the world of something only he knows.

"You are, I'll drink to that," he adds. "But you talk too much."

The man closest to her stands up. "Right. Jim. Let's try roulette." They leave.

A handsome, somewhat handsome, couple take seats at the table next to us. We note their arrival. Don't look. A raw moment, something about them, something like us about them, but not us. Are they hustlers? Grifters. Cons. The casino's covert eyes on the floor? Are we being watched? I think so. I would watch us.

Sally wins four more hands. We are up $750.

"Are you hungry?"

I am, and I'm thinking. There are people who have never paid rent. People who have never had a hot shower, an alcoholic drink, sex, never eaten bacon. Can't imagine going through life without eating bacon?

"Yeah. I'm hungry."

"Chinese? Mexican? Italian? Ben, you decide."

"Friday's bacon burger."

"OK."

# FIFTEEN

The Strip, walking. Heat of the day fading. Tired of walking, tired of Ubers, taxis, people. Tired of disliking myself, always tired of that. Doing better with Sally. We found a Friday's. Why no Saturday's, Sunday's, or Monday's? Mondays could work. "Take a bite out of your week. Eat Monday's." Everything on the menu but rattlesnake. I order my burger, two patties, extra bacon, beer. Beer and bacon. Sally goes animal. She does that sometimes. Friday's signature steak, well done. She orders it, gives me half, eats all the seasonal vegetables, gives me more than half her mashed potatoes—watching her figure. Burger, bacon, beer, mashed potatoes. More beer, more bacon. Real gut food. We pay the bill, leave, go back to walking. I feel bloated, like my belly is a dog on a leash running ahead of me looking for more food, sniffing the ground, trash cans, people's pockets. Consider a quick curbside heave, decide against it.

Sally nudges my shoulder, laughs softly. "Remember," she says, "that old line. 'It's a man's world.'"

"Sure. I remember."

"Well. It's not."

"Not what?"

At the end of each sentence Sally closes her eyes, adds to the wonder of what goes on behind her eyes. A ladies' lady. She doesn't need approval but waits for it all the same. A need without definition, like so many needs are. I study the pores of her skin as she speaks. They're small, compact, unnaturally smooth, more like a suit than skin. People continue to walk around us.

"It's not a man's world, Ben. It's a sperm's world. Competitive and fast. Guys," she says, "only mimic sperms. But it's not the guys, it's the sperm that rules. Men are like sperm. Being first. Winning the race. It's a sperm thing. Men never stop being sperm. But not you, Ben. You always put me first. That's why I love you."

What everything she said means, exactly, I don't know. But what do I say? When she says that, tells me she loves me, why she loves me. Can I say anything equivalent? "What I think," my hands fall to Sally's waist. I pull her close. "I think having your own toilet, a toilet only you can use. Your very own. That's what life is all about."

"Ben." Another Sally look, exorcising my shameless immaturity, eyes swallowing me whole.

A woman bumps into us. An off-duty cocktail waitress. Crooked teeth, orange hair, a full rack taxing their constraints. She steps on my foot. I don't care, her tits have me. They're the kind a sixteen-year-old would be proud to show off in the girl's locker room. I stare.

"Sorry, mister."

Sally takes my hand. Pushes it under her blouse. Holds it to her breasts. Right there. On the street. Lots of hungry eyes watching. Camera eyes. Telescope eyes looking down. Telescopes on the moon, on Mars, looking down.

"These are all the tits you need, Ben. And don't change the subject. Having your own toilet has nothing to do with sperm. Do you agree with me or not?"

"Yes," I say, "It's a sperm's world. Yes indeed. Sperm has it."

There was a time when I thought I could make it big. I lived on the East Coast for the first part of the 90s. Took a small, one bedroom cottage in Pleasantville, New York. Worked for IMC. Their Armonk location. A stoic structure, intimidating, the runway model's look—unflinching chiseled eyes, cold certainty in every step. The "I'm-perfectly-turned-out-get-paid-a-shit-load-of-money-so-don't-fuck-with-me" look. Was better in the summer than winter. New York winters are gray things, heartless months of barren cold. IMC work was tedious. I had an idea. An ambient light retrieval system. That's what I called it. A brilliant idea, I thought so. A best seller for sure. As soon as the idea came to mind, I imagined everyone loving me. The wealth, the travel, famous beauties knocking on my door—movie stars, models, athletes, princesses, other men's mistresses. All of them wanting a piece of me. The fame. The fortune. The pride of power.... not really me, that... it doesn't matter. They want me, I want them, that's all. The idea was simple. Make a lampshade, wallpaper, and paint capable of absorbing and conducting electricity. Collect the lamp's own light bulb light and any other ambient light collected by the walls to feed the lamp's bulb. Perpetual motion lighting. Something like that. Low maintenance lighting, individualized for every home. It would save billions, last for years. I worked on it through three winters. Our prototype was giving us a couple of hours of light a day. It all stopped, suddenly, no explanation, no money, no Hollywood girls knocking on my door, no knocking at all.

It was a good idea, until I had it.

# SIXTEEN

The Bellagio lounge bar. Old time cabaret, piano and voice. We take a table with a good view of the stage, make a point of spending no money at the Trump. Even plan to lift all the shampoos, shower caps, soaps, water, and a few towels for wiping dirt off my Jeep. Sally sits across from me, sipping her third gin and tonic. Her face pinched between her palms. Elbows on the table. The cabaret lady has a thick voice. Wears a '40s-style dress and hairdo. Her best years spent long ago. The piano guy looks about my age, if I looked older than I do. His white patent leather shoes, black bowtie, and cropped hair bob to his routine. I imagine the two of them on stage in a live show. She throws down the mic, kicks the piano stool, knocks the man down as a dance pole comes up through the floor. He gets up, tosses his shoes with a flare, his bowtie, leans her back against the pole, she legs the pole like a pro, her veins bulging, lips flaring, knees bending, creaking some… It's weird, even disgusting. Fuck. Somebody in my head without an invitation. Lots of back doors to the brain. I pick up my glass–gin, no tonic. Relight my joint, toast Sally. She toasts back.

"IMC betrayed me, Sal."

"I know, you've told me the story twenty times."

I empty my glass, keep a cube to suck on.

"Only twenty?"

"Only twenty, maybe less."

"They stole my one great idea."

"Don't worry, Ben. New ideas will come. A better idea. You'll have one. I'm sure of it."

Sally puts her face in my face. Rubs her nose against mine. Sucks on my bottom lip, grabs my ass. She's good. She knows me. Women how often they pull us back from the edge.

"Ready for another hop?"

"OK. Yeah."

"Great."

I pinch out the joint.

# SEVENTEEN

The sidewalks are crowded, almost impossible to move. Claustrophobia, sidewalk claustrophobia, congestion claustrophobia. They can make one suicidal, make a guy rip open his shirt, scream, "Bloody Hell!" and chase down old, surgically enhanced fat ladies with paper shopping bags, steal all their food, choke their little dogs, have a shootout with police? Suicidal. Completely. Very hard to walk. I pull Sally toward the street. No room. We cut off, go into Caesars Palace. Cartoon architecture. The usual noise, people, smells. Always people smells. Every casino smells of people. Not drug stores, business lobbies, they don't smell of people. They smell of something, but not people.

Sally cuts through the ambient froth to find the right table, the right players, the best odds of winning, of passing through unnoticed. We stroll for three, maybe four minutes, pick up drinks. Gin and tonic, Sally's favorite. Different casinos, look different but sound the same. Sally finds her table. Three players, two women (about the same age), one darker than the other, short hair, both attractive, curious. And an old man, a '60s guy, '50s, maybe, '40s, maybe '40s. Gray ponytail tied back, uneven teeth, denim shirt. The dealer is South Indian, African, my guess, as black as Sally is white, cheerful eyes, alert, sincere.

"I have to get a dress."

"What?"

About to sit down, Sally has a sudden urge. Something. She leaves me at the table. Just, leaves. Curious, but not worried, I hold her place. Play a couple of decoy hands. Begin looking for a cocktail waitress. Maybe Caesars hires more of them. Can never have too many cocktail waitresses.

I play a couple more hands. Fingers feel thick, like they're at the end of something, but not my hands. Odd. I pick up eighty bucks. Need another joint, a pipeful, a cigarette, cigar. The older I get, the more I smoke. Alcohol, when I drink, I drink more, something strong, stronger, need to feel the hit, make it last. Always another man inside of me trying to take over. Fuck. Do I need a new me? Does anyone? Age denial and so much more. Substances, the poppies of life vitalizing and renewing perception…and worse, breaking the control chains social programming has on defining who we are. I wave for a waitress. A tiny Filipino girl, maybe four foot tall, her smile half made, eyes sharp, she sees me, walks over. I look down. Wonder if Sally, when she looks down at me from her towering height, thinks of me as I think of the waitress. She is way down there, the waitress, way down there. I order three bourbons straight up. A change.

That's when they came back, and right up to me. The hustlers from the Venetian, spooks, headhunters, whatever. The girl is wearing a tight-fitting leather skirt, black, an open blouse over a white T-shirt, cuffs curled up. No bra—I always look for bra signs, the absence of bra signs. A guy habit, shit that doesn't matter. There's always shit that doesn't matter. She stands close. Nudges me. I like it. I look at the guy, he must be six-two, blotchy skin but OK otherwise. Impassive eyes, bodyguard eyes.

"Sally sent us." The girl takes my chin, eyes me. "Your Sally. She has a surprise for you."

I relax. "How's that?"

"Walking by the dress shop. I saw her changing. She left the door open, so I went in, and we talked. Now I've come to get you. We've come to get you. I'm Becky, he's Joe. And you're Ben, we know. Come. Bring your drink."

No time to tell the waitress. I leave a five on the table.

Sally isn't an Amazon, not that. She isn't a Gal Godot Wonder Woman, or a young, sexually liberated Mother Teresa. She's remarkable alchemy, a vision of beauty extracted from another world. Life clings to her, wants something from her, something more than life has to give. How everyone else is made human, I get that. What makes Sally human? I have no idea. She is magic. That's all.

Becky takes my hand. Joe follows behind us.

"Where are you taking me?"

"You can trust your Sally, Ben, no worries. Come," she says.

We leave Caesars. Walk out. An Uber is waiting for us. The driver is a girl, mid-twenties, John Lennon glasses, a black ladybug tattooed on her visible earlobe. She drives oddly, keeps changing directions, changing roads. I used to know Vegas…I used to know a lot of things. Too warm in the Uber. After ten, twenty minutes, we stop at a small building in the Arts District. Unassuming, big windows, white curtains, polished cement entry, a bright red tongue-shaped welcome mat on the front step, a flashing neon sign over the double doors.

*Up-Slide-Down…Up-Slide-Down*

Sally comes out. Smiling, her hair tied back. What looks like a loose hospital gown drifting from her body, waving at hidden admirers, secret admires; all those people unknown to history who stood where I'm standing now. She opens the car door.

"I love you, Ben."

Damn. Every time she says that. A man like me. No real value. How did it happen?

Life.

Sally.

Life works in mysterious ways. Doesn't ask God for directions.

# EIGHTEEN

The lobby is small. An antique desk on a silk carpet faces the door.
The walls are painted panels with exposed wood grain. A willowy
Monet knock-off hangs behind the desk. Water lilies. The frame is faux-
carved. There are two curtained doorways on each side of the desk.
Several sofas. The girl behind the desk is topless. Maybe bottomless. An
unmistakable absence of urgency. Soft eyes, pulpy cheeks, a moonlike
face. Lots of beautiful women in Vegas, and secrets. And secret places.
And people who knew the places. Sally knew.

"We're next! My gift to you, Ben. What they call the 'couples
drop,' we're going to try that."

We sit down. An overhead fan with enlarged blades strokes the air.
The blades are carved wood. Makes the room more inviting, mysterious.

"A gift?"

"Yes, Ben, my dear Ben. A treat for my protector."

Compliments that make me feel good confuse me…I smile, that's it.

Becky and Joe walk through the left curtain. Another couple, sitting
across from us, both in their early twenties. They look hesitant, unassuming, young. I imagine they've just gotten married, that this place,
whatever it is, was a surprise for them. A gift from one of them to the
other, maybe not. Surprises make people nervous. Becky and Joe, what
they want is unclear. Something.

The girl behind the desk stands up. She's wearing a pair of pink
bunny slippers. That's all.

"Please, come with me," she says.

There are six rooms. Ours is called Tropical Sanctuary. It has a heated floor, a red, shell-and-sand look, puffs of warm mist fill the room, shift with our movements, an abstract dance routine. Wall screens with drifting scenic vistas magnify our perception of depth. Fractured rays of sunlight filter through the jungle canopy, animals seeking shade or food hurry along the floor, muddy rivers washing away the sins of the earth. I can hear distant waves. Gull sounds.

Two inversion tables, well made, lay flat in front of us. Expensive. Waterproof. I have questions. Doesn't matter. Two girls come in, naked but for head hair, their skin moist, shiny, almost drinkable. One is from the desk, the other from the waiting room—the girl from the couple. I thought they were married. The girls offer us a hookah, a glass of wine. We take both, surrender our defenses.

"May I?"

The desk girl. Her body is inches away, her features enlarged. She looks up at me. A full look, healthy, generations of genetic good fortune flowing in her veins. Beautiful. Her name is Ellie. She unbuckles me, pulls the zip. My trousers drop to the floor. No underwear. Almost never wear underwear. Underwear suffocates. Fear of being trapped, restricted, unable to move, I have that fear. Can't remember not having it. A man of many fears. I am. All men are, but most don't know it.

Ellie smiles. Fear retreats. A master in her world. She's well trained, no hesitation, no apologies.

From the lobby, the young guy, the not-married-married guy, he comes in. Hair oiled down, red lipstick, shaved clean like a plucked bird, a hairless, chicken, ready for the pot. Odd. An odd look. Hairless lipstick men, tattooed girls. The guy is there for Sally, there to massage her, to clamp our ankles and invert us.

I'm first to go upside down. Then Sally. In front of each other. Upside down, blood rushing to our heads. We try to kiss. The girls begin pouring warm oil over our feet. Soothing warm oil. Desert fragrances mixing in the mist. Flute sounds. Water sounds. Warm oil finding its way. Warm hands. They're not Haitian. But they could be. Vegas style voodoo shifting gears, readying a romp with the beast of pleasure.

Sally moans softly. They work our legs, press oil between our toes, erase hours of walking from our feet with smooth, deep pressing hands. They work us. Sing to us with oil sounds. Tactile rubbing.

Our two tables pull apart. The guy stands in front of Sally. Ellie stands in front of me. I study her feet, a dancer's feet, perfectly shaped.

Something about her reminds me of Bethann Webb. Bethann was the first to let me in. Pope Beach. A warm summer night. A full moon. We were young, knew nothing of love, had no need of love, just a sense of things only youth can feel.

The Vegas upside-down massage, explicit, bewitching, exalting. The saints of pleasure competing with God. Waves of erotic attention swell our bodies. Tectonic plates shift. Light at the beginning of the world, we feel it. Sally is ready, she's reaching deep. I know her. I feel her. I'm ready, all resistance leaves me, attachment to identity suffering leaves me. Sally catches me in her eyes. Through the legs of our attendants, we can see each other. Sally's teeth are straight, perfectly straight, no gaps between them, invisible when she wears white lipstick. A glorious contrast to her green eyes, moisture rich, flaring with expectation.

The pace, hands mauling us with erotic affection, the rhythm of it all is on us. The belief that good in the world can bear fruit cheers us. Full waves of soothing warmth guide our way. Our fingers touch. Tips to palms. We push to feel more of ourselves, to will our senses into a voracious appetite for life, to blow out, discharge desire...lava escaping its molten bed...bats leaving the cave. Ejaculation lightning strikes, orgasm weightlessness takes us. A drifting sensation. No direction. Spent. We're spent. I'm spent. Every pain, stress, disfigured moral judgement, every self-flagellating remorse, dark memory, the insult of sins I cannot forgive, abuses I cannot forget, betrayals and wrongs only hate can answer, they leave me. Suffering—and all its hollow tributes to revenge—they run from the heat, they run.

Erotic burn...passing the torch, the one thing God got right.

I relax. Fully. The rush: sensual glory, it passes too quickly. The present moment, no harness on it. Here and gone at the same time. Enlightenment, is that what it is, being here and gone at the same time? Sally knows, she's albino, alien, a fish with mammalian lungs.

"Life," she says, "lives in the present. Ego lives in our head through past remembrance and future imagining. To be enlightened is to live. Ego is the absence of life," she says, and she holds out her arm, her lithe and very white arm. "Putting one's arm out is easy. Keeping it out is hard. Being in the present is easy. Staying in the present is hard. Life is not given, life is earned, or not lived at all."

Sally, she's my present.

Our tables return to the flat position, blood rushes back to our heads. The thickness and warmth of the mist increases, makes the room feel juicy. Warm, damp towels are laid across us. The moment slipping by, details and feelings easing their way into memory. A leisurely retreat from heaven's door.

"Well?"

Sally looks directly at me, amplifies my thoughts before I think them.

"I'm thinking," I say. And I am. What can I say?

The albino, all a man can desire. *For* her I would do anything. Bad things, good things, whatever. A red light on every corner. Vegas. The inverted massage.

What happens in Vegas, stays in Vegas.

Fuck that. I'm going to tell everyone.

Fucking everyone.

How does Sally know this place?

# NINETEEN

---

**B**ecky and Joe are waiting in the lobby. New clothes. High on something illegal, likely illegal. We never make it back to the hotel. Don't bother to check out. No Trump soaps, shampoos, shower caps. No towels for cleaning my Jeep. Trump. Fuck. How people allow themselves to think more of him than they do of themselves, of their own families and friends. I don't understand. Trump's an easy read…he lies to keep himself out of prison. That's it. A junkyard conscience. Fuck him. We borrow a local phone, send Trump, via the Trump, a Facebook message, visible to all. "Sorry, Cheeto. We've left the state unexpectedly. Please secure our heirloom bags at reception, they're worth a fortune."

A dumb idea. A little animal idea. Doesn't matter. They're shit bags. Nothing notable in them. No plan to pick them up, to pay the bill. A gesture of disdain for Trump's betrayal, for his treasonous adoration of Putin, his shaming America, selling America, poisoning it, poisoning us, robbing it, robbing us, trashing the constitution. And fuck Republicans, fuck Democrats…the Cock and Pussy parties popularizing specious want over collective need, manipulating us by different means, preventing us from looking past what offends to something higher. I'm becoming a political atheist, a loathing both sides centrist, a 'Nam hangover junkie. Trump. That fuck. He skipped Nam with the indifference of skipping a B movie, a boring social event, the funeral of a much-loved employee.

Ellie calls an Uber. Joe takes shotgun. Sally and Becky sit together. I get the boney drivers head to look at, a big fucking head, stuck right in front of me. No view. Feels like we're leaving town. A new moon night.

Very dark. We're going to a private tattoo party-art show, whatever the fuck that is. Why? I don't know. Joe's idea. I hate tattoos. Too late for me. I'm done. I just want to take Sally to bed, lay next to her, love her. I could open the door. Shout "Geronimo" and jump. I could speak up, say, "folks, I'm too tired, thank you, good night, take me home."

Trapped. Restrictions, I hate restrictions. Always something after me, something circling overhead, digging beneath my feet. Ecstasy. A good time to try it. Could be. Something strong, bewildering. I don't ask. Too tired to think. Joe keeps changing the music channel. We're still driving. Seems like a long time. Lots of new homes, big homes. An entrance road. A long road. Damn long. Could have been paved better. An uncomfortable seat. Sally and Becky talk the entire ride. Girl talk.

# TWENTY

**"S**top! Turn around!" Joe shouts suddenly. Confusing the driver. Confusing all of us. "I need some cash," he says "The party. I need cash for the party."

"I have cash," I say.

"Not your cash. My cash. I need it."

"Fine." The driver shrugs, comes to a stop. No cars. No problem turning around.

It's dark. Night sounds. Night smells. I roll down my window. A lucky escape. We drive toward town. The lights. The big noise. Very little traffic. It's late, almost midnight. Midnight! Inversion massage. Up-Slide-Down memories. Pleasant memories. Prostitutes, money without chains, pleasure without chains, judgment liberation. Can't feel sensations I remember, but I like to remember them anyway. Going back to town is fine. I drop my head back. Roll up the window. Relax. Everybody lives. Everybody dies. Material processors processing material...Man's essential duty. Who cares? Really.

"There!" Joe points, reaches for the wheel, grabs at it. The driver pushes his hand away.

"My ride, asshole!"

"Please." Joe demurs, makes his voice whiney, pathetic. "There," he says, "That gas station. Stop there. Please."

The driver relents, pulls up to the pumps. "Fine. I can use some gas," he says.

Sally sits up. Becky sits up. Joe throws open his door. Steps out. Becky joins him. Takes his arm as they walk in.

"Ben. I'm thirsty, and hungry. Aren't you?"

"Yeah, I am."

We get out. The driver, heavier than I thought, pulls the handle, sets the lever, begins pumping gas, picks up the squeegee, cleans his windows. Looks like he is going to light a cigarette! We go in.

A typical gas station mini mart, but bigger. If New York is the city that never sleeps, Vegas is the city that never went to bed in the first place.

"Sal, you want a beer?"

"I am thinking something stronger. Remy maybe. Maybe whiskey."

Joe begins arguing with the manager. We walk to the back of the store. The bathrooms are next to the tequila, the rum. I start thinking tequila.

"Ben. I have a joint. A mixed joint." Sally pulls me into the ladies' bathroom. "This Joe is weird," she says, "and Becky, but not so much."

"Yeah. Something's off. I know."

"What are we going to do?"

"What do you mean?"

"I don't trust them. Is there a back door? Can we slip out a back door? A bathroom window?"

"Maybe, but they're quite small. You can fit."

Sally lights the joint. Bipeds, we've been smoking weed for as long as we've had lungs to breathe, longer, even before we had lungs. Was probably the weed that kickstarted imagination, or mushrooms, or peyote? We find the back door, slip out just as a handgun goes off. Short, loud, sounded like a .35. The alarm blares, mixes in with confused shouting. We stay put, we're fenced in. Sirens in the distance, how far? Then, a helicopter, flashing lights. The cops are quick. We get down on our hands and knees, begin crawling along the side wall, get to the front in time to see Joe getting cuffed. Becky is screaming, waving her hands, crying. They cuff her too. And they cuff the driver. He is black. Always cuffing black guys.

Becky sees Sally. Turns her head to look. The cops look. The manager looks. We get up, raise our hands, and walk toward the store entrance, cop lights burning our eyes.

"We've done nothing wrong," I say. "These people, we just met them."

"Sure, you did."

They cuff us. Take us. No lady cops. Just guys. They take all of us. Joe shot the manager's dog. Un-fucking believable.

They put us in separate cells. I have a small eight by ten, with a metal cot. The mattress smells. Lost hours, lost lives, they find their way here. A toilet with no seat. Small sink. Outside the cell, a bare light bulb, about a thousand watts. Bare. Bright. Unblinking. Cells. You never forget a cell. They're all the same. In the end, they're all the same.

It's late. The guards have left. Rooms and halls are silent. Doors closed. Where's Sally? My job is to protect her. Paradise. The street I grew up on. The people I knew. They're gone. I'm gone. I can feel it. Everything goes, eventually. But not Sally.

Where is she?

I listen. Listen and listen. Four, five hours, six. Not sure how long.

"OK, Mr. Mamott. You can go, sir. Here's your things. There's the exit." A young guard. Tall. Some people are too tall, even when they're not taller than you. He's wearing a nose ring, a Swiss cow thing. I've seen them, Swiss cows. In the Alps, village roads. Cows with rings in their noses, walking along, just walking along. Vegas. Anything goes in Vegas. I begin walking toward the exit. An older man, another cop, stops me. Smiles.

"My Sally?" I ask.

"She's coming." He says, smiles again. "And the other girl, the two of them. They'll be here. And the guy, Joe Preston…you know him?"

"I met him yesterday. Maybe the day before. Like I said, I don't know him. Joe and Becky, we just met them. At the casino."

"I believe you, sir. Anyone who's done for this country the service you have deserves respect. How many lives did you save? I read about you. You're a hero, Mr. Mamott, sir. An honor to know you. To shake your hand." He does.

War credentials. Medals of honor. Men who kill people. Men who don't. A big difference between them. My get out of jail free card. Didn't know I had one.

"Any other trouble in Vegas, you call me. Here's my card. Call me." He hands me his card. Sheriff Graham Jones, Sr. Has a handgun embossed on it, in gold foil.

A sniper, in jungles mostly. Crosshair relationships, in the sights of my gun. Every face was personal. Always personal. My grade school principal. Every face was his face. No longer remember what he looked like. I did two tours. Worked for the DEA after 'Nam. A couple of precision cartel kills. Lost hope. Moved to New York. Joined IMC. Every day, every lamp shade reminds me of what IMC took from me, of how little value work has if it's not your own. A bum is better off. I gave up. Why not? Power always rises. If you have no power, you get pushed to the bottom. I headed back to Paradise. Crawled. Stopped at Tahoe for the winter. Skied Heavenly every day. Met Sally outside her salon. Jane Ireland's Wig Wum Wow Snip Shop, very casual, a quick hello in passing, but there was something between us, some kind of primal lust caught between shadows; something we knew about each other but didn't know why.

I was in the news awhile back. Maybe she read about me. Lots of people did. My knife sniper story. I was lucky. He was not, the other sniper. A small man. But they were all small. He was protecting missile batteries. We were losing planes. Skyhawks, A-4Es like McCain's. I was told to find him, kill him. I did. My gun, a Win 70. I trusted it, but my knife saved me. That's the story people read. "Sniper Knife-Thrower Beats the Bullet." I found the guy's nest. Stumbled into it. Too close. He heard me. Began to rotate his rifle. My knife, in hand from cutting vegetation, took control. It felt like that. As I had done so many times before, I threw. Caught him in the neck just as he fired...low. His bullet punctured my right thigh, went through, missed the bone. I tied off while he bled out. Then I shot him again, twice. Took his rifle. Traded it for a couple of beers, a pound of hash. Wasn't a day for heroes.

Footsteps on the concrete floor. Sally's voice, her laugher. A satis-fied laugh. I feel better.

Sally. She's magic. That's all.

We take a room on the edge of Vegas. Small. Ugly. Dirty. Cheap. Clean sheets and towels. TV with over a hundred channels. Dirt park-ing lot. My Jeep doesn't mind. We pick up a couple newspapers. Watch the news. What happened to Joe? Animals are property, even wild ones. Everything costs. What do they do to you in Nevada when you shoot a manager's dog?

Joe and Becky. We didn't know them. Didn't like or dislike them.

"Maybe we should hop, Ben. First thing tomorrow. Money. We need more of it."

"I know. A lot more if we want a shop, camera equipment, actors, a home, a family. Maybe we should rob a bank. Bonnie and Clyde, our way to Key West. That would be cool, damn cool."

"Sure. Except for the getting shot part."

"Right. That didn't end well. OK, let's hop. Maybe I'll come up with a new idea. A famous idea."

Hopping with Sally. Dancing in the wind.

I can do that.

# TWENTY ONE

"**F**uck!"

Sally swearing. I like it.

All the things we can't say about people, things we don't like about them, things we can't say about anything. Political incorrectness. Programmed to be what we are…are we?

I'm staring at the ceiling, thinking. "What?"

"This room, Ben…it stinks."

"It does. Yes."

Sally rolls over on the bed, her body camouflaged in white. White on white, captivating, alluring. An Artic rabbit playing in the snow. Her wide green eyes. It feels like nothing fills them before she opens them to look at you. Like you are being seen for the first time.

"Damn, woman. You're unbelievable, unbelievable. What it took for the universe to create you. I can't imagine."

"Alien DNA, "she says. "And I'm smart."

"Oh, yes. Damn smart."

"Do you think we should look for Joe and Becky?"

"Not today, Sal. We should hop. That's all."

"Right."

Sally pulls me to her. We make love. Fall back to sleep. Wake up to the hard vibration of motorcycle engines. Lots of them.

Mid-morning. Already warm. 98 degrees, dry. The bikes keep coming. Loud voices. Thick, broken laughter. Melodic Western songs blaring, shouting. We aren't ready to get up.

"See, Ben. This is what happens when we go cheap."

"I need a drink. A couple of hits…fuck."

"We could."

"What?"

"Toss a jolly, a morning jolly."

"With all this noise!"

"Sure. Skin doesn't hear. Your skin, for sure."

Sally…what can I do? She throws off the pillows, the bedspread, the sheet. Stands up on the bed bouncing over me. A leg on each side, bouncing. Bouncing and bouncing. Get me out of bed bouncing.

"Sally! Christ!"

She laughs, runs to the shower, and closes the door. A pathetic room. Old plastic curtains. The bathroom door is broken, doesn't close. It swings open. Sally peeing in the shower. I watch. She makes certain of it. A cure for piss phobia? Maybe. Everything has a cure.

"Sally! You're…"

"I know," she says, splashing water over the shower door. "Are you coming?"

"Yeah, I am. Outside. I want to take a look. Give me a sec. Sounds like a gang invasion."

I step to the window. Look through the curtain without touching it. Harleys, Nortons, Triumphs, one Honda. They fill the parking lot. Dust everywhere.

"Lots of guys my age, Sal." I speak loudly. "Long hair on some of them. A lot of them. Some with no hair. Leather. Hammock chains. Beards. Dirty beards, tattoos. They look like 'Nam guys. Retired cops, military maybe. War dogs without a bone to gnaw on. Oh…Fuck! It's the guys we passed in Death Valley. They're walking toward my Jeep. Shit!"

"What? Ben! I can't hear you!"

"Nothing, Sal. Just coughing."

Shit…shit, shit, shit.

"OK, Ben, but hurry. Really. This place probably heats its water on the stove. Won't last long."

They stop next to my Jeep. Don't appear to notice. Two guys standing in front of it, big guys, they block the plate. Lots of laughter, repeated greetings, back slapping, fist pumps, hugging. Everyone in a good mood. Several step away, walk toward the hotel office. They're checking in.

"I'm coming, Sal!"

Running shower water lessens the engine noise, the shouting. I back away from the window. Sally's singing, wind chimes with a human voice. I step into the shower.

"There you are. My handsome big Ben."

# TWENTY TWO

Decisions need to be made.

How long do we wish to stay in Vegas? Where do we want to go next? What roads should we take, what towns and attractions should we see? How much money do we need, exactly?

Florida. Sunny golden Florida. A long way away.

The bikers continue to mill around outside, only one or two bikes idling. They drink, smoke, put out cigarette butts with their boots, lean up against cars, sit on bikes. Bright out, very bright. I keep the curtains closed; the door bolted.

Sally is sitting on the edge of the bed rolling a joint, legs crossed, towel wrapped around her head.

"Sal, what help have you had with your life, your life before us? Connections, you know, family connections, help from friends, that kind of help?"

"Very little," she says, her voice flat, unattached. "My dad left when I was two. Mom was busy. Too famous in her own mind to see anything in me but a side show for her friends."

"I thought you loved your mom?"

"I did, before she began selling me."

"Selling you!"

"I worked, Ben. Gave myself purpose. That's what I did. I stitched socks, shirts, torn clothes. Sold sneak peeks to boys, up peeks, down peeks, a touch was more. And I sat babies, cleaned homes. I was little, maybe nine, ten years old. Fearing she would get caught, jailed for child abuse, mom sent me away to live with my father. I was fourteen. I didn't know him, or his wife. They hated me. Used me. Adults do that. He came into my room whenever she was out for the night. Never went all the way. He was too smart for that. But he made me do all kinds of things, things children shouldn't do, shouldn't know about. His wife was ugly, graphic ugly. She had a beak nose, looked exactly like a beak, and enlarged eyes that always looked frightened, a double chin, skinny arms and legs, straggly gray hair. I was pretty and young. She was neither."

"I'm sorry Sal. So sorry."

"Me too."

Dropping her head into her palms, she heaves softly, rolls her gaze across the dull carpet stains, frayed curtains, splintered lamp shades, aging dust. Bad idea to bring it up. Bad timing. Is reminding someone of hurtful memories ever good timing? Probably not.

"The silent ones?" she says. "The silent girls. The silent boys. Innocents feeding the world. I'm sorry for them more than for myself. Much more. So many don't make it. Boys molested by men, raped by men, they never talk, not until they're older, then they talk, maybe. Girls. It's bad for them, too. It was bad for me. I did a lot to adjust... to embrace what I couldn't change, to manage my trauma, give it a purpose of my choosing. Same sex rape, that's different. How is a boy to recover his masculinity? He bangs every girl he can to prove he's a man. Bangs, and bangs, and bangs. But even that, however great the relief of conquest, it can never make him clean again."

Air stops moving, goes cold. The raw unforgiving discomfort of fact. The silent boys. I recognize them. I'm one of them, and my brother. Should I tell her, my Sally, admit to myself that I was molested as a kid, a 7, 8-year-old kid? Our big-gutted, flat nose grade school principal. His weekend cabin. What he did to us. How he used us. The stink of sweating fat, male slime oozing from the dark, robbing us of childhood. Would she use it against me? Think less of me, more of me? Think it's nothing of importance. Talking. It's a risk... Sally transformed her abuse. Nothing. I say nothing.

"Christ, Sally." Suddenly I feel clever, certain, more like someone I can imagine myself to be than who I am. "Death—man's inevitable fall. It's not our problem, Sal. Fear of insignificance, that's our problem. We'll do anything to give ourselves value. To believe exception denotes significance. Molesting you. Your father loved that. All of them, the molesters, rapists, pedophiles. They all think they're exceptional because they break the rules and get away with it. That's what they think, what everyone thinks. We all think what we do, what we are, is exceptional. A black dot in the night sky is more exceptional. We delude ourselves. Self-medicate a 'purposeful' life."

Silence.

"Damn, Ben. Listen to us. So depressing. Jesus! Enough whining." Sally pulls the towel off her head, blows me a kiss. "That's why we're starting a new life. Why don't you pop out and get us something to eat? Probably too late but try the breakfast room. Breakfasts included with the room. And bring me some orange juice…please."

Two broken lives mending themselves into one. Is it like that for everybody? Are all of us broken halves of a whole trying to reconnect? If we are, why? Why write it that way, why produce the reality? To whose advantage? God's. Does God need an advantage?

I get dressed. Clothes are beginning to smell. Must be time to leave Vegas. The relentless, instantly dissolving moment. Nothing to hold on to. I walk out the door. It's painted a purple gray. Doesn't match the other doors. None of them match. The entire building is oddly colored. Novelty art up at bat, swinging for a home run, the novelty lottery. An attempt to transform a shit hotel into a shit work of art. Ugly as fuck installation hotel art. That's what it looks like. I make my way to the breakfast bar. The food is gone, most of it. All the tins are there. They're open. An old coffee warmer with near empty pots of coffee is still on. A few drying pieces of fruit, dirty wastebaskets with no plastic bags. I find some bread and jam. No butter. Drop the bread into a toaster. Get some orange juice from the juice machine, looks orange, not sure about the juice part, napkins, what's left of the eggs, and take a seat. An old picnic table. Uncomfortable. Neglected spills, table tattoos, scratches, cigarette burns. A stack of magazines in a torn box. *Scientific American* on top, for Chrissake! Cool! I pick it up, start leafing through. Find an article on magnetics. I love magnetics. Love science; evidence-based reality; proof before belief. In the future, the distant future, a more mature evidence-based human species will emerge to define what people believe, and what they don't believe. For today, I wonder…my life, our lives how different can they be from what they are? But that's always true. The life we're living, it can be different, can always be different, but it's not.

> I had an idea. Must have been in my forties. A *Magnet Motion Device*. That's what I called it. Something I visualized. A ring of magnets, set at different heights and powers that could pull, from magnet to magnet, a larger magnet attached to the end of an arm supported by a shaft driving up from the circle's center. The big magnet, after giving it a push, would be handed off from magnet to magnet, around and around the circle, generating energy. Clean, silent energy.

The toaster pops. Three of the Death Valley Angels walk in.

The biggest of the three, he's black, heavy, a man made for brawling, maybe 250 pounds, six-foot-five, terminator arms, red headband across his forehead, gray mustache, short, braided hair, copper middle finger earrings saying "Fuck you" with every move of his head. He takes a seat on the bench across from me. Struggles to get his legs under the table. The other two, also big but with less weight and height, fewer chains, reversed baseball hats. The brims cut off. They stand behind me, just beyond peripheral vision.

He doesn't talk, the seated guy staring at me, moving his mouth slowly like he's getting ready to chew. Nowhere to run. I stare back, not a desperate stare, more curious than cautious. Try to see the men behind me in his eyes. One of them takes hold of my neck and begins choking me. Slow at first. Not much pressure. The seated guy keeps staring. I keep staring, dig into his eyes. Big hands, the man choking me. My neck feels thin, turkey thin, goose thin. The choking gets worse, more real. I ignore it. Keep staring, don't blink. The guy across from me keeps staring. Doesn't blink. Waiting. Very difficult to breathe. Sally. Not a good time to die. I relax. Make it easier for the guy choking me. Nothing to lose. Nothing to prove. The strangler lets go. Backs up. The big guy leans toward me, smiles.

"So, what are you reading?"

"Science," I say. "Magnetics. I love magnetics."

# TWENTY THREE

War dogs with a bone. The Angels. I could be one. Maybe I was, without the bike. A Jeep Angel. They like me. Like Sally more. We stay a couple days. Make friends. Go to several Angel parties. Grand events. Uncoupled. Rowdy. Civil, somehow. Ace, Al, Deck Top, Herald, Sniper, James. Bad looking good guys. We get to know them, their stories. Everyone has stories. Stories they live on, stories they hide behind. We eat stories. Feed them to who we think we are, who we want to become.

"You were in 'Nam?" he asks. Ace, the guy who sat across from me at the breakfast table, gray mustache, braided hair, their main guy. I like him.

"Yeah," I say. "A sniper. Can we turn down the music? Hard to hear."

The bar, a raunchy, Western saloon knock off, with old style swinging doors. The doors are open, windows are open. A dry day, comfortably dry. It filters in, reminds me of the life Sally and I are not living.

Ace waves at the bartender. A big girl with purple hair, studs through her lips, her nose, tattoos from her fingers to her neck. Tattoos on girls reminds me of barcodes. She's a barcode girl. Lots of barcode girls. They can never be nude again, those girls. Never nude again tattoos, they hide what's lost. Ace points at his ear, palm down. She gets it.

"Kills?" he asks.

"Not many, but meaningful. I volunteered. Got tired of shooting deer."

"You volunteered, fuck! You're a beast, Ben, savage."

"Maybe. More of a revenge shooter. Something like that. Now I make things, invent things, fix things, smoke weed, drink, hang with Sal, hope the next day will be better than the last. We're driving to the Keys."

Ace likes a good chat, goes out of his way to incite conversation; cause to gnaw the bone.

"These guys," he says, looking around the bar, "they're grunts. Old shit-head grunts, still in the field, still angry. They all lost friends or family in 'Nam. Shit, they voted for Trump, that dick, right." He catches my look. "Me? Nah," he says, "I can't vote, you know. Might've though, I thought Trump was cool, entertaining. These guys did vote. They all regret it. Trump. He's a lying fuck. Personal advantage is all he thinks about. He hates people he can't use. And foreign leaders, Putin. When Trump talks to Putin you don't know whose side he's on, who we killed for? Who our guys are killing for today? Trump, he ran for office to pay his bills, to stay out of jail. He's shamed the nation. A traitor, straight up, no question, no doubt. We used to hang traitors. When we were men, that's what we did."

Everything about Ace is big. He sweats big, blows his nose big, coughs big. "Fuck us, Ben. The money game...Power. We have none."

"I know. Small people. No seats at the table for small people. Do you kill people for money?" I ask. "I've heard that Angels do that. That you're ruthless extortionists."

"Shit, Ben, we're retired cops, most of us. But there are times."

That day, on the road. They had guns, must have. "When you pulled into the hotel, saw my Jeep. What did you think?"

A big grin, then he begins laughing. "Your woman!" he says. "We all wanted another look at your woman. More than a look. After passing you, we couldn't stop thinking about her. An albino woman. Never seen one before. None of us. Beautiful. What the fuck is she doing with you? We wanted to know. Every guy in our gang thought he was a better match. That's why we stopped, Benjie. For her."

"Are you going to kill me? Try and take her from me?"

Ace drops his brow, a half curious stare.

"That won't happen," I said. "You know that."

"Yeah. We know."

When to worry? When not to worry? Is he joking? Can't tell. All those things we worried about that never happened. Would they have happened if we hadn't worried?

"Ever blacked out from drinking, Ben?"

"No...."

"Don't," he says, "Hey! You wanna try my bike?"

A damn big guy, Ace.

"Sure," I say. "Absolutely. That would be stunning."

"And while you're out...Sally?"

"Sally goes with me."

"Right," he smiles. "Sally goes with you."

# TWENTY FOUR

Temporary freedom is not freedom, but it feels good. For the next few hours, God is ours to create. No helmets. No seat belts. No street cages. No stop lights, stop signs, speed limit signs, double yellow lines. No censored storytelling, no sententious politically correct judgementalists impugning free speech, redesigning moral standards. Ace's Hog. A flaming Hog. Old, beat up, rusted in spots, chrome in need of polishing. Lots of road dirt, discolored grease, chipped paint. Still grand.

Outside Vegas, we take 147 toward Lake Mead. Immerse ourselves in the dry desert heat. The older I get, the more I long for hot days. Feel more like a lizard than a mammal, especially in the morning. Still plenty of stoke in my Jolly John. A good thing. No Viagra. Not yet. 147 connects to North Shore Road. A paved road. We turn right on 8 Mile, park some twenty feet from the water's edge.

> Waterskied Mead many times. Flew Hughes to Vegas, hitchhiked to Mead. I was a good skier. Always found a couple of girls to pull me, traded for instructions. I was young then. Lots of secret coves, hidden inlets, intimate islands. A big lake with private parts.

"Are you coming, Ben? Come on! Come on!"

Sally strips, runs naked to the shore and dives in. My mermaid. My tits bouncing, legs for fins, hair flowing like the sea, mermaid. Humans. Look at us. We're more afraid of exposing children to tits than we are a murder scene, horror movie, sodomy. Kids never see mermaid tits. They should. Tits should be out there with milk, breakfast cereal, donuts, and coffee. Tits for all occasions, and wine. Tits and wine. Eye candy for the masses. Christ, what happened to us? What made two simple mounds of fat and flesh so intimidating?

"Ben!"

"I'm coming, Sal! coming." I strip. Make my way to an outcrop. Dive in, swim to Sally. Just the two of us. Blue sky. No wind. No noise. Earth's early days. Cyanobacteria gatherings, sexy stromatolite orgies. Not likely. Budding flesh eaters, maybe.

Lake Mead. We do it, we go full on in the Mead, the secrets of sin playing games with our bodies. We let go, drop the reins. Age. Time. The importance of purpose melts away. Water all around. Warm pliant water. I feel younger with every thrust, with every kiss, with every hydraulic moment.

"Ben," softly. Her voice is soft, white like her skin.

"Ben. I stopped taking the pill."

"What?"

The pill...no longer there. Billions of little sperm heads, at this moment, racing for their reward. They have a target now. Guys, we don't think about babies. We have to. Do we? Babies. Really? That's not guy stuff.

"How long? When did you stop?"

Poor people beat the law by becoming cops. Rich people buy it. My thoughts scatter, run from my mind...singed horses fleeing a burning barn, and pigs, and bugs, and sensible bipeds, the ones with a human brain, that have use for a human brain. Can't think. Damn! Sally's off the pill.

# TWENTY FIVE

"Let's stay here, Ben. Spend the night. All the dull browns, the gnarly bush, the feelings of the place for itself, how it feels every day. I like it. Can we?"

Nights in the woods. I spent many nights in the woods, alone. Weeks away from people, showers, the need to feel human; to behave as expected. Humans make humans feel more possessive, defensive of possessions, defensive of attachments. Animals are safer, fewer rules, no rules. Animals are, or are not hungry, that's it. If you know that about them, you know enough. Humans are belief addicted. Difficult to calculate addiction, to talk honestly. Truth prosecutes, and it's foreign. It scares people. I've tried being honest, many times. Lost friends, many times. Maybe I didn't have friends. Maybe nobody does, though everyone thinks they do. Maybe Sally is my first friend, maybe, and she isn't even human. At night, when I sometimes watch her sleep, her body lifts off the bed between breaths as if the air in her lungs held her down, gave gravity something to hold onto. Alien, definitely, I think so. And if she is. If she really is alien. What that would mean...fuck.

"If you want, Sal. Sure. I guess. Don't see signs saying we can't."

There's a certain comfort in sparsity, a dry explosive comfort that satisfies the need for independence. Travelers understand sparsity, they travel light, few possessions...living life more than holding on to it, that's what they do. They're more death ready than homeowners.

In the distance, a couple of water skiers try a cross, crash. A good try. The boat circles back to pick them up, stops, they see us.

"You should put on a shirt, Sal." I grab a towel.

There are three guys and two girls on the boat. The skiers throw in their skis, sit down, take off their life jackets. They're far away but we can see them clearly. They're looking in our direction. Sally gets up, walks to the bike. Her shirt covers most of her. My towel did the job for me.

"Are they using binoculars?"

"Looks like."

"Are they looking at us?"

"They are. Our bare skin got their attention. We're covered now. They'll go away."

Another boat slows down, pulls up next to them. And beyond them, three more boats turn abruptly, head toward them. Not the widest part of the lake. Something's happening and it isn't us. Smoke, lots of gray-black smoke. The water skier's boat. People begin jumping into the water, leaping. A lot of splashing, screaming. The smoke blackens even more.

"Sally. I think we should leave."

"No, no. Let's watch."

We do. We watch. Fire erupts. The boat explodes, sinks in seconds. Mob movies, love mob movies. Are they making a movie? I immediately visualize wise guys tying weights to bodies and how that makes the body sink fast, very fast. The boat sank like that. Like a mob boat. Must have been. Maybe the boat snitched on some other boat, told the other boat's owner who it was that put a hit on his cousin's canoe. The boat that put out the hit is getting even. It all makes sense. Of course.

Roadside crashes, house fires, flooded streets. Entertainment suffering. Do animals like watching other animals suffer? Bugs? When an ant sees another ant suffer, what happens? Who knows? Humans. We're pathetic, I think so. Sally's right. I comfort myself by devaluing life, by thinking everyone will lose in the end. Life behind the curtains. Never sure of exactly whose life.

"Maybe we should head back to the hotel."

Florida. The Keys. Miles between us. Too many miles.

# TWENTY SIX

"**B**en! Slow down."

I am...I'm driving too fast, not sure why. Maybe I'm being covertly selfish, want to kill myself but don't know it. Once, not that long ago, while Sally was away for a few days and I was driving back to Paradise, I came up behind five cars following a dump truck stopping at every driveway to pick up garbage. The lead car refused to cross the double yellow to pass the truck when it had an opportunity. I waited; cars began building up behind me. Four cars, five cars, a bus. "Fuck it," I thought, and I throttled down, dropped into first and floored it, crossed the double yellow, passed all five cars and the truck on a blind curve, a hairpin curve, got in front of the truck with about ten feet to spare before hitting an oncoming SUV. I just made it. A death wish, love of risk, simple stupidity, an overreaction to highway claustrophobia...who knows, who cares? Sally. Sally cares.

"Sorry, Sal."

"It's OK, hubs. We're in no hurry. There's a roadside fountain up ahead on the left, let's stop."

We pull in, two other bikes there, no one around. The place is dusty, dust on the fountains. There are three of them, only one works. Not a popular stop.

"Ben, try this one."

I bend to take a drink, push harder on the lever, a tarantula climbs out from the drain, scares the shit out of me, tries crawling up the sink, keeps falling back.

"Fuck, Sally, look at this." The tarantula struggles can't get a grip on the fountain bowl. Keeps rolling backward.

"Kill it, Ben!! Christ, kill it!"

"Sure…with what? Not my knife. It's an enamel fountain. I can whack it with the handle. A rock might be better." I drop my eyes, search the ground, Sally runs to the bike, digs around Ace's satchel, searches for something, anything she can use, finds a gun, a .22 loaded with hollow points. "Back up, Ben…back up!"

"What? What are you doing?"

"Move, Ben!" She hurries by me, begins shooting at the spider, shatters the fountain's spout, water blows out like a lawn sprinkler. She keeps shooting, the spider runs, slides on the water (spider fountain surfing; a future entry for the bug Olympics), squeezes through the bullet holes overflowing the small sink and runs along the wall toward the other bikes.

"Wait, Sally! Stop!"

"He's not dead, Ben."

"Here, give me the gun. I'll do it."

She ignores me, runs forward pointing the gun at the spider, pulling the trigger. A cat appears at the end of the wall, runs toward the spider, grabs it and leaps over the wall. Sally empties the 22, shouts obscenities at the cat as it runs off with its meal.

"Damn," she throws down her arms, the empty handgun. "I wanted to kill it."

"The cat?"

"No, the spider! I love cats."

# TWENTY SEVEN

She does. Sally loves cats. "Cats make a home in your mind like no other," she says. "I learned that as a child."

Never sure what that means. Doesn't matter. She loves cats.

Cats and raisins.

We return Ace's bike, tanked up. Pack the Jeep. Not much to pack. Pay our bill. More miles, we're ready for more miles, eager to shorten the distance between Paradise and Heaven. Ace, and the other Death Valley guys come to see us off. To get one last look at Sally. A tit shot, maybe.

"Hey, stay on Ben, Sally. Why not. One more night? One more." Ace, he knows people, knows how to define weaknesses to his advantage. His eyes. Sitting there, hovering. Many reasons for doing something. I can see that, but not the reasons. He gives me a hug, sort of, just enough to justify giving Sally a hug.

"We're going to miss you folks. That's certain."

"Yeah. Us too," I say. "You guys have been great. Really."

Ace leans forward, whispers, "Listen, Benjie, there's a Thailand-themed strip show, a must see. 'Bean Balloons.' The name is Deck Top's idea. The show is one of ours, we own it. Nothing like it. Naked girls, model-level beauties popping balloons with beans shot from a straw stuck up their money maker. It's great stuff. Stay, Ben. You can bet on which balloons you think the girls will miss. Every miss gives you something free, whatever. One more night. What's your hurry?"

Thailand. The ugly man's paradise. Thailand was good to me. Bad for drug dealers, even suspected ones. Good for sex. Sandwich massages, three girls at once. They took you like whispers spreading secrets in the mind, their merciful female hands, the lightness of their fingers touching, they coax the gale, the fertile male roar crafted by their mastery of the senses. Eastern voodoo. Thailand, love Thailand.

"No hurry," I say. "It's time to go, that's all. We're trying to make Key West in time for Sally's birthday, August 1st. Earlier would be better. And Ace, you're going to need to reload that .22."

"Already did."

Sally puts her arm around me. Gives Ace a clean shot.

"I understand," he says. "You'll make the 1st, guaranteed."

The others agree. We shake hands, a round of hands. Get in the Jeep. Exit the hotel's disintegrating lot onto black asphalt. New asphalt. Smells new. Head East. A great relief.

Bikers. They're good guys but too extreme, unpredictable. Can't discipline extremes. Extreme people or extreme weather. Puerto Rico, Paradise, Northern Marianas, New Orleans. Weather with no mercy took them, beat them, ate them. Extremes arriving too frequently normalize the abnormal, make exception common place. I feel nauseous. Thinking can do that. Leaving hotels can do that. Within minutes we hit I-515. Minimal traffic, cut over to 93 toward Boulder City. No plan to stop at Hoover dam. Sun is setting. Beautiful. Children's story colors. Golden reds illuminating the clouds, the dry, scratching earth.

Sunsets. If I lived to eighty, eighty times 365 would give me, not counting leap years, 29,200 sunsets in my lifetime. Of those I'd lived so far, how many have I actually seen? And the one hovering in my rear-view mirror, which one is it? The thousandth? Did it matter? The universe is full of sunsets, millions every moment. A grand performance with no eyes to see it. A view of all sunsets in the universe. I try to imagine it.

Cruising. Everything slows down, the highway rolls. Sally drops her hand in my lap. Leans back in her seat, rolls up her window, up then down. She leaves it down, puts on sunglasses. Car lights bother her more than sunlight. Lots of cars passing us. Vegas is closing in on Lake Mead, the surrounding mountains, the desert. Population increase. More people. More rules. Less freedom.

I begin to drift. "A noiseless patient spider." Whitman. Drafts of air looking for direction come and go through open windows. The ride is smooth, the breeze comforting. Twilight hues pinch the horizon. East coast hunters shooting deer from tree stands. Tracking game with cameras. Unbelievable.

In Kashmir. At a hospital. Not sure why I was there. Men are lying in the hallway. There are several. One looks near death, very near. I point this out to the doctor I am with. He tells me not to worry. "If the man dies," he says, "he will be reincarnated."

A dyslexic mind struggling to right itself. I can't do it.
"Sally, you stopped taking the pill?"
"I did."
"You want kids?"
"I do."
"Should we get married?"
"We should."
"When?"
"Anytime."
"Where?"
"Anywhere."
"OK," I say. "We need to talk. I mean. There are places on the road. I think so. Every town has a church. Maybe we can find a near empty town. A small town. One of those cute western churches, painted white, thin steeple tower, bell hanging. Ringing at noon. Stained glass windows, if we're lucky. What do you think?"
"I like it," she says. "Let's stop. Make a baby."

"Maybe we have already."

"Maybe, but let's make sure. Find a place to pull over."

The last bit of semidarkness. A thin, blue-gray line of light fighting to keep the earth and sky separate. It fails. Stars come out. The moon comes up. Almost full. A place to stop. A side road. A turnout. We find one, stop, take the back seat, strip. Sex with clothes on is not sex. It's something, but not sex. We synchronize to the flicker of passing car lights. Pretend we're in a movie. A famous love story. *Gone with the Wind. Casablanca. When Harry Met Sally. Bonnie and Clyde*...without all the dead bodies. Not big on dead bodies. I've seen too many. Never been to a funeral. People disappear when they die. That's all. Tomorrow we'll look for a town. Just the right town. A church. Just the right church.

# TWENTY EIGHT

**R**oad sounds. Night driving. Time slips by, escapes notice. Orphan moments torn from the future, the past. The smell of sleep. Animals in their burrows. Clear sky, stars. Lots of stars. A topless earth. Few cars passing by. No one ahead of us, no one behind us. The hum of tire wear. A sweet darkness wrapped in forgiving warmth. A perfect night. I nudge Sally.

"Mm?"

"Superstition, Sal. Have you thought about it?"

"Not much." Sally presses the hair on the back of my neck. Massages my shoulders. Strong hands. Surprisingly strong.

"This is interesting." I begin playing with the high beams. Shut them off. Turn them on. Off, on. "If I told you, it's bad luck to pick up a penny, the next time you see a penny lying on the ground, you'll hesitate to pick it up, even if you think my saying it's bad luck is stupid. You can't stop the initial hesitation."

"OK."

"What does that mean?"

"You tell me, old man," she says. "Tell me what it means."

Teasing me. The cat in her. Her blouse, it's unbuttoned. I want to look. I do look. Guys, we always look. A black Sally. Somewhere in the world there must be a black Sally. Black breasts. Onyx nipples. Silken skin. Warm lips. Sharp wit. Another ideal woman.

"I don't know. Something. It means something. That we're programmed to believe lies. That we can be too easily convinced of something being true, even when it's not. That the prosecutorial nature of truth is too much for us. I don't know. My Dad. He died the day after his honorable discharge. Fell off a ladder. He used to rage. Hated Hitler. Called him a "jumper." Thought him a bent twitchy fuck, little boy bent. Still the Nazis followed him. Today's Trump supporters, same problem; "Father forgive them for they know not what they do." Why? Better for them to man up, admit that Trump lies to his benefit, not theirs. Trump. Fuck. Little boy bent. Is he? Very possible, more than possible."

"O…K…And that has what to do with superstition?"

"I don't know, Sal. Nothing, probably. I'm just talking. Trying to stay alert."

We drive on. Miles. Long slow miles. Easy miles filled with distracting mind odysseys, with forgetting, with remembering, with watching for animals crossing the road, elephants crossing, kangaroos, giraffes, Big Foot, alien ships landing on the divider, inviting us to tour the universe in 20 seconds.

We stop for gas in Kingsman, an uninteresting town, mostly recent construction that looks old, out of date. Some nice roads. Can't see much. After Kingman, lots of nothing. Scrub. Spent earth. Rock. Life feeding itself, somehow. We take I-40 to Flagstaff. Trees become more frequent. Shrub more frequent than trees, and the clutching grass camouflaged between the two, between cooler air, and the night.

"Sedona. Should we drop down? About thirty miles. Not far."

"Maybe." Sally smiles, turns toward me. A ghost. At night she's a ghost.

"Sedona. Ooh… Mysterious energy fields, ancient cave gateways to who-knows-what worlds beyond ours."

"Maybe," she says, and she smiles again, but longer. "Though we live it, life is a secret, something hidden in us that surrounds us."

I stop thinking, listen to her words echoing, wonder if I'm thinking in the first place, if I know how to think.

"Enlightened Indian elders, Sal. Some people believe they created Sedona's energy fields, the gateways. No credit, though. Even if it were true, they'd get no credit. Native American enlightened beings were here long before Christ. Before Buddha, Muhammad. Before all of them. Pre-Christian enlightenment of tribal elders worldwide made Christ's enlightenment possible. Credit that went to God should have gone to the Indians and shrooms."

"We can stop in Sedona. Sure."

Too tired. We pull into a Motel 6. More or less cheap, depending on management. This one should have paid us to check in and double that to spend the night. We take a room. Nasty. Go to bed. Hold each other. Close. Very close. Don't move. Don't dream. Don't…

An Indian chief. An elder. A wise man, enlightened. Sitting on a large flat stone overlooking a distant valley, rising hills, a thin blue ribbon of water. Animals grazing, birds flickering overhead. Can't see his face. A single feather in his hair, tilts to the side. He's old, very old. Where he is…where he's been…where he's going. He knows.

# TWENTY NINE

Rain. A gray rain, dark and heavy. By the time we check out, the streets are flooded. Water rushing, finding its roots, its arms, and legs. A heartless rain. Not a good day for the crusted red glory of Sedona. Meteor Crater. We'll stop there instead.

"Doesn't seem to bother your Jeep, Ben. All this water."

"Jeeps love water, Sal. They're taught to swim before their tires go on. I've seen it. They have big ponds at the manufactures, small lakes really. Jeeps are thrown in, told to kick. They do, they kick and frolic, dry off, then they head out to showroom floors. Jeeps are dogs, sort of."

"I see...."

Weed. I take another hit. Too potent? Not potent enough?

Sally pokes me, rolls down her window, soaks her face, her hair. Water runs down her blouse magnifying the fine contours of her breasts. Emasculate men. Poor fucks, they miss that. One of the greatest shows on earth, they miss it. Every moment without a tit shot is only half a moment. Have to concentrate on the road. Heavy rain. Lots of red lights ahead. Cars braking. Trucks braking. Traffic. A white Mustang passes us on the right. I'm driving five over the speed limit in the left lane. No one immediately ahead of us. The Mustang cuts in. Too soon. Speeds up to compensate. Hits something in the road, spins to the right across the slow lane. For a couple of seconds, he straightens out, then flips off the road, slides along the embankment, makes mud of the saturated earth. Tears up bushes. Comes to a stop.

Christ!

We pull over. I have an old pilot's hat, along with a cracked leather flight jacket for when it gets cold or wet. They're behind the back seat along with the toolbox, emergency flares, all manner of emergency stuff you have to have but almost never use. I fish out the hat, the jacket. Others pull over. A half dozen of us. A guy in a suit, some lady and her son, a teenager, me, Sally, a truck driver chewing tobacco.

The teenager arrives first. He steps back, fast. The Mustang's wheels are still spinning, throwing off water. I'm next. The man's dead. I know the look, feel the heat of absence; the path we're all on. I get down on my hands, my knees, sink into the mud. The last thought in the man's eyes, hovering, unattached, a vacant final proof of life. It's there, waiting to be recognized. Accident Theater. No rehearsals. He's gone. Rocks split open the car roof. A strip of metal, sharp, jagged. It cut through his skull, protrudes from his left ear, shiny at the tip. Bits of brain, flesh, hair...they cling to it. Blood flows over his face, a calm flow, almost soothing. Nothing can be done. I stand up. The others, they're standing, staring, saturated silhouettes, vague resemblance to human form. Nothing to say. Sirens in the distance. A gray rain. Dark, heavy. Death, The final frontier. Should have gone to Sedona.

The police take us to their station, all of us, we take seats, watch rain slam the windows, lots of rain, noodle-like rivulets streak the glass. Air feels second hand. Standing fans crank away on bad bearings. Several cops with their sleeves rolled up. One lady cop. Statements are taken. We drink coffee, a mud and burnt wood taste. Eat stale donuts and cookies, sit on plastic chairs, make scuff lines in the dust on the floor.

No word from the man's kin by the time we leave, and where the fuck are we anyway? Flagstaff, somewhere off Rte. 66? Winona. That's where. A dry riverbed town–but not today. Potash, helium, basalt, a lot of mining. It isn't Florida. A little after four. Thunder in the distance. Hours before sunset, already dark. A midnight mood. Thick clouds. Rain.

"I'm hungry."

"Me too."

"An ugly fucking day." Mud on my boots. Dull, blood brown mud. My pants. My shirt, my hands, I need to change. Too tired.

"There," Sally's white finger, her painted nail, it cuts the space between my eye and the road ahead. "There," she says. "A diner."

"Lights are on. An arrow pointing the way, blinking every few seconds, different colored bulbs. A diner/bar. Sixties architecture.

I drop Sally at the door. Park in the corner of the lot. Hate people dinging my doors. Get out. Water covers my boots. Noah. About time for another Noah. Two by Two. Not a good day, far from it. A fuck-all day. That's what it is. A fuck-all world. Jobs going to shit. Families going to shit. Moral justice shredded by the courts. A strip of metal. Sharp, jagged, piercing the skull. He was someone's husband, father, co-worker, boss, estranged sibling, mobster, fugitive—no one at all. A body now. A corpse. Fewer demands. Was money the only real difference between people? I walk to the diner. A Dutch door entrance. Dried Christmas wreath nailed to the frame, a string of lights, burned out, a discolored welcome mat. Nice inside. Warm. Friendly. A jovial lady takes our orders. Pigtails, a pink and white checked apron, thick soled shoes like the ones nurses wear. One cook. A black guy, big boned, full beard, bright red shirt with bright green triangles. Blacks can do that. Bright colors. "Stairway to Heaven" playing in the background. A dozen tables, a few booths. Sally's in a booth. I slip in next to her.

"A good choice."

"The table's clean."

"Right." I pick up the menu. "I feel small today."

"You are, Ben. Every day. Even when I go barefoot. You always feel small when you think about it. Don't think. Have a beer or two. You'll feel better."

"Not that kind of small. It's more like not being here. We are here, I know. But what difference does it make? Homeless self-worth. That guy's head. His eyes. What was...all that he knew himself to be...gone. Death is like that. It's always like that. Gone, that's all. Here, then gone."

"Benjamin," Sally puts her finger to my lips. "Think sun. Cresting waves. The blue expanse of open seas. Palm trees. Me with no clothes on, wading into the surf. Life. We're alive, Ben. Alive."

The waitress came to take our order.

"Welcome folks. I'm Peggy. Peggy Lynn Cranston. What can I get you?"

Peggy, she could lose a few pounds, more than a few. Altered food. Monsanto concentrate. Bad diet. Fat people eating, dripping, squishing. Food porn. Millions of Americans love food porn. They go all in, make living eating—an empty mouth impossible to satisfy. Her face is young, though. She's young. Bubbly. Good skin. On another body, a slimmer body, she would be a good catch, more than good.

I like her. Sally likes her.

Liking her feels good.

I order a hamburger. Hard to ruin a hamburger. And a beer. Sally orders a bowl of Raisin Bran, warm milk, lots of sugar. She loves raisins. Keeps a box of dried raisins in her pocket, her purse, the glovebox, anywhere. I begin playing with my napkin. Pick up my knife and fork. Poke the knife between the fork tines.

"It's OK, Ben. It's OK." Sally squeezes into me, slips her hand down my pants. Finds what she's looking for, rings my hollies. She knows how to calm me. A good size booth. Red patent-leather. Wood table. Real wood. Rusted napkin holder. Dried catsup on the catsup bottle, the mustard bottle. Side drippings. Saltshaker. Pepper shaker. Sugar bowl with a spoon. Crayons for kids. Placemats with games. I turn mine over. Prefer plain white. Fumble for the weed in my pocket. Take a vape hit. Two hits. Prime Indica. Wheels spinning. Death, its appetency momentarily gratified, we stop thinking about it. Try to stop. Arizona marijuana laws. What are they?

"We need to get to Florida."

"Yes. We do."

"Maybe we should sell your Jeep. Take a train."

Train?

"What?" Sally smiles, but not with her lips.

A dark day. A dark time. Rome fell. The Medici fell. The British fell. The USSR fell. The USA...Donald Wilkes Booth Trump. His evangelic oligarchical, Nazi right, versus the homo's PC pacifist, gender mania, open borders left. Primal foolishness. Nobody listening to the other side, nobody talking. The grand lady falling. Being made to fall by our own hand. Our enemies winning. A well-orchestrated Russian revenge consuming our victory's, our heroes.

"Sell my Jeep? A train?"

"Sure, why not. Trains are romantic. And no stress."

"Twenty years, Sally. I've had this Jeep for twenty years. An old man's living room chair. His all-is-well-in-the world chair. That's my Jeep. She looks new. Runs great. Who will take care of her if I sell her?"

The truck driver from the accident walks in, takes a seat at the counter. Chewing his tobacco, beard dripping. Big cheeks inhaling. He orders coffee.

Peggy arrives with our food. Jokes about the cook. Gives us extra napkins. Smiles. A genuine smile.

The truck driver hears us talking. Turns around. Looks at us. We look. Wheels spinning. Spinning and spinning. Eternal recurrence. Sightless eyes wandering through our minds. He turns back. We finish our meal. Thank Peggy.

Leave.

# THIRTY

The rain stops. Heat replaces it, searing heat.

We drive thirty minutes, maybe an hour, on I-40. Take the Meteor Crater exit. Mostly flat, few small hills, lumps of higher ground, ridges. Leave the pavement, go off-road. Scrub brush, always lots of scrub. Constant gray-brown scrub. Bleached grass. Rocks. Dust, dirt red. I make several loops, then swing back to the road, cross it. Hide behind a small hill. Fresh tracks make me uncomfortable. One a.m. 73 degrees. Finally dry. I lay down the seats. Make our bed. Sally removes her clothes. Takes the flashlight, a roll of toilet paper, the camp shovel. Walks into the pale hollow of the full moon.

"Watch out for snakes!"

"Always."

An albino in the high desert. I watch until she squats. The moment. It's still, very still. All moments are still.

I remove my shirt, my pants, my socks, lie back, leave the hatch open, my legs dangling over the back bumper, close my eyes. 'All men are created equal.' What bullshit. Would be great if we were. Pretending we are, denies the truth. The inevitability of evidence. Fuck. Why think about it? Paradise before the burn. Neighbors walking their dogs. Automatic lives. Waving with one hand, pooper-scooper in the other.

No wind. Every sound echoes against the night. Footsteps, almost noiseless. Sally, for how tall she is, gravity gives her little attention, at times ignores her completely. Something to think about.

Off road in Arizona. Everyone who knows us, has no idea where we are.

The Mustang. The wheels. The guy.

They have no idea. How could they?

# THIRTY ONE

My Jeep, a charcoaled blur on the landscape. A chunk of coal. No trains. No plan to sell her. Dust devils, three or four, wobble in the distance. Warm breeze. Blue sky. Contrails at 35 thousand feet. Economy passengers sleeping uncomfortably in economy seats, reading magazines, watching movies, college studs shopping the stewardesses. Our windows are down, the hatch open. Bird sounds ricochet off inert air. No idea which birds. The sun, just above the horizon; an orb muted by a dull sky, struggles to ascend the morning's gray/brown haze Voices. Far away. I roll over, fill my eyes with Sally, with her white hair running secret errands across the pillows, her shoulders, her breasts. I stare. Her skin doesn't age. Never see her cut her nails, her hair. She looks at me, beyond me. Her green eyes radiant, sensual, fragrant. Can eyes be fragrant?

We dress.

Sally complains, "Clothes. What do people fear more than nudity?"

"I don't know. Death? Injury? Pain? Not violence. We love violence."

I adjust my seat. The mirrors.

"Benjamin!"

"What!"

"Somebody's coming."

"Fuck."

A park ranger. Are we in the park? I'm not sure. He pulls up. Stops about thirty feet in front of us. White pickup truck. Lights on top. Dirty wheels. Dents. I get out. Sally gets out. The ranger gets out.

"You folks lost?" An average size man. My size. A cigarette hanging from his mouth. Eyes shaded by the brim of his hat. Round glasses with a thick frame. A tight beard.

"Yeah. A little. More like disorientated."

He relaxes his gun hand. Adjusts his glasses, his hat. "People follow off-road tracks and make more tracks. I follow them." He walks up to Sally. "You're a beauty, aren't you? Damn." Sally steps closer to me. Puts her arm around my waist.

"I can ticket you for trespassing. Hand you over to the local shields. Make you pay a hefty fine. Don't look like you have money."

"We don't," I say, "but I have this." I hand him Graham's card. Gold foil. Embossed handgun. He says to call him if I had any problems."

We're far from Vegas, but not too far.

He takes the card. Walks back to his truck flipping it between his fingers. Can't see his face or the inside of the truck. Too much reflection off the windshield. Standing. We keep standing. Waiting. Better not to move. Cops. Rangers are cops. Cops are dangerous. We wait. Ten minutes. More than ten. The morning warmth is no longer pleasant. He gets out of his truck. Walks over to my Jeep. Looks inside. Walks around it, continues flipping Graham's card between his fingers, comes back, stands directly in front of us, hands me the card.

"He says you're a war hero."

"I did my part."

"We like heroes." He looks at Sally, slowly, up, and down. "You are a beauty, lady. I'll have a look at your tits."

"What? Fuck You!" Sally lit up, steps behind me.

"No," said the ranger, "fuck you. And fuck your old war hero boyfriend. I'll see your tits, or you go to jail. Both of you."

"We've done nothing wrong."

"You don't have to." He spits. "This soil—the dried grass, the crater, everything you see here. It's my jurisdiction. All of it. What's right, what's wrong, I decide. Tits or jail." He spits again. "Your choice."

Did he know someone just died? The mustang. Would he care?

Sally steps from behind me. Begins unbuttoning her blouse, removes it—a white flag of surrender, drops it to the ground. The ranger steps forward. Licks his lips, eyes wide, moisture collecting on his stubbled cheeks, his nose, above his brows.

He raises his left hand. Right hand on his weapon. Opens his palm over Sally's breast. "A perfect fit," he says. "Perfect. Show me more." He stretches his neck then looks down. "Your prize basket," he says. "The prize this old man loves. Let me see it."

A slight shift in the air. My albino in the sun, her back to me, hair drifting. Humiliation, she feels it, turns. Takes me into her eyes. Holds me. Returns to the ranger. He moves several steps closer, unsnaps his holster.

"Gotta keep myself entertained," he says. "It's damn boring out here. Show me more."

"Ranger. Officer. Have you done this before?"

He pauses. My question distracts him.

"What?"

"Is this the first time you've used your legal authority to break the law?"

"No. No, man. Many times, it's a thing here. Was easier when I was a beat cop in Albuquerque. In general, I like them younger, but look at you. You're so white, slim, perfectly formed. Nooking you is going to be my best fuck yet. Enough talk. Down, down on the ground. And you. You back up. Way back."

Fear overwhelms Sally, the life in her body. I see it. Her man. Her protector, I see it race through her as she begins to unclip the fasteners of her denim skirt.

The nest. A sniper's perspective. Stillness, slow moving seconds. Waiting for the exact moment. I step back, pull my blade when he looks down to unzip his fly. Liquid anticipation in his eyes, the grotesque abuse of power glaring wide. His pants fall, gun belt hanging off his bare hip, he rips off his underwear.

"You'll like it. I can tell. I know women. Know what they want. What you want. On your knees."

Before Sal can move, I throw. One flip. Catch him in the ball sack, his back thigh, cut the lower side of his rod off. He screams, clutches at the knife, the blood, his hanging parts. Sally backs away. A spider running from fire. He goes for his gun. Tries. Still fast for my age. I'm on him. A heel between the eyes. I break his nose. He hits the ground, a solid hit.

"You fucker, shit head. I'll kill you!"

"Not today." I kick him in the groin, the stomach. Grab my blade. He tries to sit up. I kick him again. Military programming. I want to crush him. Another kick to the head. His eyes roll back. Broken teeth. Blood widening the sides of his mouth. I take his gun. Empty it. Break it apart. Wipe my prints. Scatter all the pieces. He sits up panting, whimpering, crying.

"This knife," I prod his nose with the blade tip. "It's a swear word with a more physical nature, you hear it?" I hold it up, turn it so he can watch his drying blood dull the blade's shine. "I could blind you," I say, and I slide the blade tip across his eyelids, cut them. Thin lines of blood ripen and drip over his lashes. "I can castrate you, cut your fucking dick clean off. Make you watch. Kill you." An angry man. People who hurt me and got away with it. The shots I missed. Buddies who died. Children I couldn't save. The ranger. Today they were his debt to pay. I slapped the flat of my blade against his cheek, lifted his chin with the point. More blood. No pity. Wars never end. "I can leave you here. Clear our tracks. Bury you alive, hands tied, legs tied, mouth gagged. No revenant revival. Park your truck off the main road at some shithole bar, a shit hotel."

"People know me. They'll find you."

"They? No. No, they won't. I choose when I'm found, and who will find me."

Marlboros in his pocket. I take one. Light it. Hover the hot ash in front of his eyes. "I'm going to let you live, what's left of you. No more masturbating in the ladies' bathroom. No more little girls intimidated by the badge." I take out my phone. Hit the play button.

"*We've done nothing wrong.*" "*You don't have to. This shit soil—the dried grass, the crater, everything you see here. It's my jurisdiction. All of it. What's right, what's wrong, I decide. Tits or jail...Your choice.*"

I click forward, "And here, listen to these lines. They're Hollywood, pure Hollywood."

*"Is this the first time you've used your legal authority to break the law?"*

*"No. No, man. Many times, it's a thing here. Was easier when I was a beat cop in Albuquerque. In general, I like them younger, but look at you. You're so white, slim, perfectly formed. Nooking you is going to be my best fuck yet. Enough talk. Down, down on the ground...And you...You back up. Way back."*

Control. It feels good. Dictators, do they feel good? I key in some addresses, make a show of emailing the recording to several of them.

"Your phone. Give it to me." He does. I take it, go to the truck. No dash cam. No record. No trail.

"We're leaving now." I squat, stare; something frozen in me, an identity, a decision, a man I barely know. I want to hit the ranger again. Again, and again. Rip him apart. Beat out of him all the anger I feel toward evil selfish men—all the memories loving Sally can't forgive. "You're going to get your shit together Mr. Ranger," I say. "See a doctor, make do with what's left of your manhood and crawl into a hole somewhere. You're in my world now. Bullets without a country, a master, a conscience. Laws can't protect you. You come after me, after us, hire someone to come after us? Anyone. I come after you."

I take his jaw in my hand, wade into his eyes. "Were you ever a good man?"

He glares, tries to glare.

"I doubt it. And how would you know the difference anyway? Forget us. Make a new life for yourself. "You understand, yes?" I tear into his cheeks, squeeze.

He nods. Face swollen. Eyes swollen. Lips dropping to one side.

"You're losing blood. Not much. Make up a story. You slipped on a bar of soap, fell down a hill, fell off a ladder, jacked off with a razor in your hand. I don't care. Don't make me come back. Don't follow us."

I grip his face, the fat in it, my fingernails wolfish, hungry for blood. "Are we clear?"

"Yes. Clear." He whimpers, mouths the words.

Can barely hear him.

Not listening.

Predation. It's a male disease, mostly male. Nothing to be proud of. I'm not listening.

99

# THIRTY TWO

Sally picks up her clothes, gets dressed behind the Jeep. Takes her seat. Looks out the window. Says nothing. Almost twenty minutes to the main road.

We hit I-40 and turn east.

Now she knows. She knows that her Ben is other than he appears to be. A real threat to anyone who would harm her. The stories are true. Nothing to say. We pass Winslow, cross the Little Colorado. An arid blend, scraping, clawing. A hard life for snails and slugs. A little past Holbrook, Sally unbuckles her seatbelt. Lies down, puts her head in my lap, her right arm over my legs, closes her eyes.

We skip the Petrified Forest; trees with hardened memories, cross into New Mexico, begin the tedious climb to Mentmore, Gallup, Renoboth. Homogenized America, manila paper colored clusters of small towns, spaces between them with nothing of their own to hold onto, barren reality. No white steeple churches. We cross the Continental Divide. Stop to read the sign, take a roadside break. 7,245 feet. That's what the sign says. We continue on. Pass Grants. Stay on I-40, mostly, take old 66 when we can, to Laguna, that's the plan. To stop in Laguna. Swim the river. Maybe.

"Tell me something, Ben. Anything."

"OK, sure."

*Anything* is a big word. Something funny. I try to think of something funny, make it up. Can't do it. Too many ranger images, bad guy images.

"In New York," I say, "I know a guy, knew a guy. Melih Abdul, a guilty name. I can say that now. I trusted him. Loved him like a brother.

He's Turkish. Average looking. A lying fuck. He married an English girl. Blond, disarming...he used her. Came to America with his hand out. Had a good tech idea. Solicited money from American investors. Built a company, made millions, over a billion. Did the utmost to fleece his founding investors. He's still fleecing them. Turks. They learn that at an early age. Many of them."

"Fuck, Ben...Power liars. One of those. You know one?"

Sally, how she says the word fuck. I love it. From her lips, with her voice, fuck becomes an eatable word, a high scoring wine.

"I do, yeah, God's pet sinners. I know one. Several, unfortunately. Money leaches. 'Power liars,' like you say. I try to think like an alien about them, imagine the point of view a higher disinterested intelligence would have. It makes everything else seem small, immaterial. So, I say to myself, 'Why think about it?' Corruption rules, that' all. Then I think about it, anyway. Grinding thoughts creep back in, enrage conscience. All the high-end cons, the untouchables for whom crime pays. I think about them, about how well they know people, know that most people can't determine value on their own, that they have to be told what to value, to be lied to. All the bankers, CEO's, cult leaders, religious leaders, political leaders. Trump. Putin. Modi. Xi. Orban. Duterte. Kim. Tokayev. Erdogan: dictators—the lies they tell shape our decisions, decide for us. Big Pharma drug lords decide for us. Orientation entrapment programs decide for us. Hospitals decide, fashion decides, insurance companies decide, pyramid schemes decide. Money games, money deciding everything, telling us what to do, how to think, what is correct behavior, what is not. Money, money, money. Money is the God of small minds." I stop, scratch my ear, an itchy ear, been itching for years. A dry itch. Might be ear wax. Too much ear wax. A gust of warm air fills the Jeep, tosses our unmade bed, a couple of plastic bags, empty raisin boxes.

"Sal, I've forgotten. Why was I saying all that?"

"I asked you to tell me something. Anything."

"Right."

"And the ranger?" She leans over, gives me a kiss. "What do you think about him?"

"He's lost his sense of humor. Definitely."

"Maybe he never had one?"

"Yeah. Maybe he never had one."

We drive in silence, a vacant slow-moving silence. Dry winds in the mind rearranging memory. Moments waiting to become moments. Remembering a smell but not what it smells like.

"Here's another thought, another something. A tale of great wit and bravery." I speak without turning my head.

"A Knight's Tale. Wonderful, Ben. I'm listening." She is. And reading a magazine, checking messages on her phone, looking out the window, unwrapping a candy bar.

"I looked into a bear's eyes once," I say.

"A bear? The *animal* bear?"

"That's right, a bear."

"OK, a bear."

"Crater Lake. It was at Crater Lake, Oregon. I was eighteen years old, maybe nineteen. I think eighteen. Nothing unusual about the day, the place. I was sitting at a picnic table. Eating a sandwich, planning a hike, a swim to the island, around it. There were lots of tables. Metal fire pits. Few people. No one near me. Suddenly I felt uneasy, like a weight with needles was poking the back of my neck. There was something behind me. I dropped my sandwich, turned to look. A bear. A black bear. Male. Fully grown, hundreds of pounds, ten, twelve feet away. My knife. Too small. Legs pinned under the table. "'Fuck!' That was all I could think. Useless to think it, but I did.

"Black bears were not unfamiliar to me, Sal. I grew up with them—chased them clapping my hands, shouting, banging sticks, pots, anything made of metal.

"Our eyes connect. The bears were hungry, hungry eyes searching, his nose sniffing, nothing personal in them, no moral expectations, just an assessment of what is, and what is not, food. That's all he looks for; all I can see of what he looks for. No favorites in nature. Food is food. My sandwich is food. Berries are food. A corpse is food. A dog, child, a man is food. Just food. Was I afraid? Couldn't tell. I turned suddenly, felt invincible, threw out my hands, waved my arms violently and shouted, yelled, really, 'Fuck you bear!' Very brave, right? And witty."

"Yes, Ben, very brave. And very witty." She toes me, continues flipping pages in her magazine.

"He did nothing," I say. "The bear. He did nothing. He just looked at me. Didn't rear up, didn't move, didn't blink, growl, lick his lips, nothing. He just stood there, indifferent, dismissive. I imagined him thinking. 'What the fuck, man? Swearing at a bear, how dumb is that?' After about five seconds—seemed like thirty—he blinked casually, even deliberately, turned, and walked away. Just, walked away."

Sally claps, drops her phone, eats the last of her candy bar.

"That was fun, Ben. Did you make it up, just now?"

"No, not at all. It happened. Really. It did. Just like I said."

"The bear...just like you said?"

"Well, he stuck out his tongue. I didn't tell you that."

"He did?"

"Yeah, he did, just before he turned to walked away. He stuck it out. A big tongue. Bears have really big tongues."

# THIRTY THREE

The first Laguna exit. I take it. A dirt road. Wrong exit. Turn around. Pick up a side road, more gravel than dirt. A guy walking in our direction. Mexican. Looks Mexican. Clean. Short. Short black hair, mustache, beige trousers crimped by a black belt at the waist. Plaid shirt. Open cuffs. America running on Mexican muscle. It does. Low wages. No thank yous.

I come to a stop. "Excuse me. Sir. Mister. We hear there's a river nearby. We'd like to swim. Is there a place? A park? The best road to take?"

The man looks at me. At us. Keeps walking. I follow, slightly behind him.

"You live here?"

He stops pivots toward me, his eyes bright with certainty. "I live here. Yes. I work here. I was born here. I will die here."

"OK," I consider my options. "Then you do know how to get to the river. Can you tell us? We won't litter, make noise, nothing like that. Just swim."

"You have a pen? Paper?"

"I do. We do." I look to Sally. She finds a Post-it pad. A pen. Two pens. Cheap, black plastic pens.

"What's your name, sir?"

He takes the pad and pen. Begins drawing.

"Anything else we should see?" I feel like talking. Maybe because he doesn't want to. "Know a good place to eat," I say, "drink. Get a cold beer?"

He keeps drawing.

Sally leans over. Excites me. A sudden urge. "Sir. We're really thirsty. The name of a bar. Do you know one?"

The man pauses, rotates the pad in his hand. A look of personal satisfaction. A perfectly kicked field goal. He hands me the pad. His map is good. Easy to follow. We're close to an accessible part of the river, what there is of it.

"And the church," he says. "You should see the church. Everyone sees the church."

"Church!" Sally and I speak at the same time.

"The San Jose de la Laguna Mission Church," he says, and he crosses himself. "Our mother church. She is here. On your way to the river. On your way back. Either one. You should see her. She will bless you," he says, and he skids slightly, descending the slight gradient in front of us. A cluster of homes, clay brick, concrete, flat roofs, hard packed roads, stick fences and a distant plateau dissolve him. It's well past noon. Very hot.

We skip the river. Go straight to the church, the San Jose de la Laguna Mission Church. A fortress. Two warning bells. No steeple. Old. Very old. Walled in. Plastered mortar and stone. Whitewashed mud-plaster inside. Well maintained. Dirt floor. Cool to bare feet. Sally's bare feet. A beamed wood ceiling. Wall art. Primitive. Dull yellows, blacks, greens, reds. Altar screen. Polished wooden pews. Candles.

A sign with big letters. "Wonderful world. Beautiful people. Redeemed in Love."

Church talk. Always church talk. Proof in words that facts lie. Nasty facts, beautiful lies. We covet beautiful lies, and good liars. They're more accommodating than the truth.

Sally takes my arm. Walks me to the altar. The empty pulpit. We sit down. The pew is hard, almost indecent. A front row view.

"I went to church as a child," she says, drops her gaze to the floor, to some depth in the floor eyes cannot see. "My mom sang in church."

"The same mother who loaned you out to pedophiles for cash?"

"The very same, yes. Church fed her illusions, her vanity, excused her wickedness, made her wickedness possible. She kept changing churches to keep singing. A good voice. I would sit. Listen to mom, listen to the priest, the whispering congregation, the muffled laughs of other children, wait for the bell. What choice did I have? I was there because of mom, for mom. On his podium, when the priest spoke, I listened intently, counted every word, heard him lie, saw in his eyes when he claimed to know God, that he made the claim to obligate believers, to make sure they paid their weekly tithe."

Sinners. Does God sin? Was creating man a sin?

A big sigh. I know that sigh.

"God! Dear God!" Sally grabs my hips, pulls me to her. "Now, God. I'm saying right here, right now. If you're there, God, here, if you exist, prove to me that you live in this house! Give me a sign, inconvertible proof. Please!"

Nothing.

No one in the room but us. An old truck in the parking lot. My Jeep. No sign of a monk, a priest, a nun. No word from God.

"See?" She pauses, looks around the room. Small windows. Vacant rows. "The righteous…To believe makes no one righteous. To verify does."

Sally turns abruptly, glowing, a magnetic glow. "Tell me Ben, if light is the measure of time, and we can stop light, but not time, what does that mean? What does it mean to man? That we will learn to control time?"

I scoff. Straighten my back. "Fuck if I know," I say. "And where did that come from? Damn. You're beyond exception, Sal. What does it mean? I have no idea. None whatever, none."

"Can belief in God create God? It's the same question, Ben."

"I don't know. A bit above my bandwidth. Very alien. I like it, like that you think like that. Means I don't have to. I would, though. I would think like that if it came naturally. Want to roll, now, sanctify this sacred dirt floor, give the sperm gang a good toss, here, now. Prove churches embrace sinners?"

"Sure," she says, and she takes my hand, presses it to her chest, her tommy. "But…." she pauses. "Let's get married first."

"Right." Have to wait. Don't want to. Guys, we never want to wait.

No pointy steeple but the church is white. It's old. All we need is a two-timing priest and two rings.

"I'll look for a priest," Sally says. "You find us rings."

"Right," I say again, turn and walk out the door.

Rings. Where?

I walk to the Jeep. Small dust puffs popping up with each step.

# THIRTY FOUR

Midday. Feels more like taking a nap time than getting married time. No cars. My Jeep. The truck. That's all. Fuck. Where am I going to find rings? I roll up my sleeves. Always wear long sleeve shirts. Almost always. Walk toward the river, see some buildings that look promising. They aren't. Little movement in the air. Hot. Dry. A few dogs. Strays, maybe. Can't tell. Nothing. Very still. A ghost town. Another one. I walk back to the Jeep.

"Run!" Someone shouting.

"Run!"

From what?

My blade. I go for it reflexively, rest my hand on the handle.

"Run!"

It's a boy—sixteen, seventeen maybe. Straight hair sticking up, cactus hair. His shirt and pants are torn. He's bleeding. Runs past me, fifty, sixty feet away. Two men are chasing him, two big men. With handguns. Christ! What the fuck is wrong with people, with life, with just living life? Impossible to get ahead with so many people sliding backward. Professional standards breaking down. Social standards breaking down. Strapped and stressed, civility gone, democracy wavering.

The men are sweating. Loose fitting clothes. Tattoos. Chains. The boy vanishes. Outruns them. They turn, see me. I open the passenger door, sit down. They lower their guns. Hide them under their shirts. One guy, the taller of the two, is wearing a red bandana around his neck. Could have been an Indian. The other guy is white. Red hair, thick eyebrows, mousy chin. He walks like he has hemorrhoids, a tumor...maybe.

They look, watch me. I look, watch them. *Think. Florida. Were we going to make it or not?* They begin walking toward me. A slow walk. Cautious. I wait. They stop ten feet away. The shorter of the two comes over, leans against my Jeep. Kicks the front wheel. Scatters dust from the wheel. Dust from his boots. Nice boots. I have boots, rarely wear them. His are better made.

"That kid owes us money."

"I don't care," I say, my voice flat, callous.

"A lot of money."

"I don't care."

"You don't care?"

The guy looks disappointed, glances down.

"No."

"Then what do you care about? And who are you?"

"What I care about? Who I am? Is none of your fucking business."

"You know who we are?"

"I don't care who you are."

They act surprised. My mood is grim and growing grimmer. I need to find rings. Marry Sally. Get to Florida. "You're two guys," I say. "That's all. Just two more dickheads making the world less fun to live in."

"Yeah, we are." They laugh. "You're right."

Smug looks. Hesitation. IQ circuit breakers flip on. My knife is ready. My eyes focused, unblinking. Reading faces. Listening. Calculating. Calm. Pressure. Pressure defines a man. I exhale, wait. Just the right moment...it will be there.

"Alright then. Enjoy the church."

They turn and walk away. Waddle away. Fat fucks. I open the glove box. Find two rubber bands. One blue. One green. Rings. I lock the Jeep. Walk back to the church. Go in. Sally is there. With a priest. They're talking.

Sally looks at me. Walks toward me. I wait at the door, scan the room. Listen, check for irregular shapes, forms, noises. Threat. No threat. Eyes in the church, ears outside it.

An unimpressive priest, a less impressive man. Butch haircut. No collar. No robe. A white shirt, sports jacket, trousers, black polished shoes, frayed laces.

> Talking to God through a burning bush. A fantastic tale. Too fantastic. Drugs. Moses on drugs—was he? Yes, he was, definitely. And Abraham, and David, the whole lot of them? And Jesus Christ...Yeshua...bastard birth...was he a good man? Who decides? We're a long way from the finish line. No second coming, just us and the mess we do or do not make struggling to convince ourselves of human worth.

Sally, halfway to me. I hold up my hand.
"I have rings."

# THIRTY FIVE

**N**oon. The sun directly overhead, pushing down. Cooler in the church. Beams of light cut through the open windows. Look solid–like something you could walk on, slice into parts, build with. Sally pulls me to her, whispers, "The priest, he's not a priest."

"What?"

"He's a court clerk."

"Clerk? He looks like a clerk."

"He is, he's a clerk." She whispers the words.

"Clerks can marry people?"

"They can. He can."

"He showed you, his credentials?"

"He did, yes. He's the priest's brother."

"Are they twins?"

"Maybe. Why?"

"Twins are interchangeable. Maybe he's the priest and his brother's the clerk."

"Ben, it doesn't matter," she says, and she goes to the door, acts like she just walked in. Kneels, crosses herself, ties her hair in a bun, attaches a red ribbon. She's wearing my only white shirt, long enough to be a dress. Clean but un-ironed. Curled collar tips. A short white skirt. Bare feet. She begins walking up the aisle. Slow motion. Legs shimmering, eyes alight with joy. A vision. Angelic. The clerk, the brother, he sucks it in, opens his bible, begins humming "Here comes the bride!"

"Too loud, sir, and too soon!" Sally hurries to him, covers his mouth. "Wait please! We want to marry as no one has married before us. A consummation marriage. No words. No bible talk. No pretense. No clothes. You stand there. Doors open. Windows open. You stand. Watch us, preside over us on behalf of God as we fornicate right here on your holy dirt floor."

"Ma'am? Excuse me?"

"Sir, Mr. Clerk," she says, and she takes his hand, presses it, captures his attention, takes him places unknown to him, to anyone. "As we begin," she continues, "you know, to have sex…churches, all the altar boys; the dark corners where God and Satan act as one, excuse carnal abuse, you know."

"Ma'am….?

"Libidinous sex, sir, when we begin to extract life's purpose, that's when you start humming 'Here comes the bride.' And you keep humming. Humming and humming. You hum louder as we go. Loudest when I begin to come, when we begin to come."

"Ma'am…"

Wisps of air rustle the trees, the bushes. Quiet inside. Quiet outside. Lizards scurrying across empty roads, over crumbling brick walls. I hear them. Snakes. Birds, I feel them. High above us, outside the windows, the air. The living air. I feel it. My senses are on, locked on, ever present.

The clerk begins to hum.

I lay down on the floor in front of Sally, look up, do all I can to absorb the moment, expand it, immortalize it. Slowly, Sally's nimble fingers move down her wedding dress (my white shirt) from button to button, a cloud unmasking high peaks…the shirt gives way, splits open abruptly. The clerk gasps, stops humming. Sally reprimands him. Removes the shirt entirely, the red ribbon, drops them to the floor, tucks her toe into my belly, pushes against my zipper. Steps back, unzips her skirt, drops it. The clerk chokes, loses his way, begins again.

"Hmmm, hmmm, hmm-hmm…"

Floor feels cool against my back. And Sally, a weightless waterfall, warm to the touch as she drops to my chest, kisses me sweetly. Damn. I feel good.

The clerk begins to stutter. Continues humming.

"Faster!" Sally calls to him as she shifts her angle, removes my shirt, begins singing, not really a song, something ancient, seems ancient.

"God! I do. I do." All I can think of is "Yes, I do. Yes!"

The clerk keeps up. No rush. An even hum, playing his part.

I laid my arms out, dust absorbing into my skin, my damp flesh

"Hmmm, hmmm, hmm-hmm. Hmmm, hmmm, hmm-hmm…"

Sally. The baby maker, my wife to be. We pace ourselves in time with the humming. An increasing hum. Faster and faster. Pots on the stove. Deserts weaned from the sun. Primal heat. Our reproductive calling…I can feel the heads shouting, the race of the rising crowd. On the mission floor, a sight for eyes to see, no dark corners. The clerk, almost frantic, hums louder, faster, screams, loses his voice, begins to screech. "Here comes…"

He drops his Bible, struggles to breathe, grabs the edge of the altar, draws a deep breath, looks at his shoe, there are drops of sweat on it, looks at us.

"I now pronounce you man, and wife!"

Done. The clerk wipes his chin, his lips, hands me a handwritten wedding certificate. Signed and dated, complete with the Laguna Mission monogram, and a cat for a witness. A cat. She was there the whole time, watching.

"Christ!" Was Christ a cat?

Sally collapses on me. Limp, warm, soothing, complete. We inhale together. Exhale together. Baby-making. Purpose fulfilled. I roll my head to the right.

Eyes…. The cat staring. Rust brown. Black paws, gray ears. Our witness. Face to face. I stare. She stares.

Cats can't smile.

Sally glances at the clerk, disheveled, confused, shock intoxication. "He looks dead," she says.

"Really?" I turn, study him. No movement. "Maybe he fell asleep."

"We should go."

"Right. Time to go."

We dress, straighten our clothes. Roll up our certificate. Walk outside.

Very dry, hot, warm breezes press against us, marriage memories hurry to get in line, take seats in our minds as we climb into the Jeep.

We head back to Old Route 66, not much left of it. Pass a dog walking with a limp. Crows following the dog. I look back. Lots of small birds pecking for seeds along the wall. Vacant dust. Somebody calls the dog. He wags his tail.

Married.

I like it.

Hope the clerk isn't dead. What would we do if he were?

# THIRTY SIX

A man. A woman. Married. A man becoming a man, in the full sense of the term, as the Talmud says. Very cool.

Mine is the green rubber band, hers the blue. Marriage isn't ownership but it feels like it.

"We'll get real rings in Florida, maybe New Orleans."

"I know." Sally smiles. Presses her finger to my lips, relaxes, reaches behind us, opens the back windows. Human odors. Sally has none. She never sweats. Rarely blinks. Never pops the cap, never.

"I like my rubber band," she says. "Everyone should wear rubber band wedding rings. Marriage is flexible. The rings are a good reminder."

My Sally, she's always thinking.

Open windows. A beautiful clear sky. The pressure to elevate personal value forcing us to think less of other people; the instinctive urge to take rather than give, it left us, utterly. For the moment, another moment, life is good. The moment passes. It always does.

We pick up I-40 at Mestia, head for Albuquerque. Plan to drive through. Lots of sunlight. Hours before dark. Everywhere in America, the same signs, the same buildings. Roads that look the same. Malls that look the same. The same junkyards. The same car lots, restaurants, banks, school buses, red lights, green lights, stops signs, road signs, truck stops, drug stores, gas stations, baseball fields, golf courses, racetracks, railroad crossings, movie theaters, pawn shops, stadiums, airports, bus stations, palm readers, tattoo parlors, hospitals, graveyards.

One country, one people. We are, whether we like it or not. Face it or not. *Are prepared, or not.*

We drive. Barren hills, ravines, bushes. Jagged shapes, crumbling earth. The isolation of decay. I feel it. A familiar feeling. Friendship decay, it happens. Never a worry about losing enemies.

"Hubs! I can call you Hubs now." Sally blows me a kiss, pinches my cheek, tosses a raisin in her mouth.

"Yes, you can. Of course. Are you hungry?"

"I feel pregnant."

"Already! You know what that feels like?"

"Of course, I know."

"OK."

"And I'm hungry."

"I know, I can feel your hunger."

"You can?"

"Not really, but I want to."

Sally's always hungry on many levels, and always giving. Whatever she takes into her mind, her body, her heart, she gives back manyfold in greater value. She makes kids smile, wonder, ask questions. Gives vitality to old people (me included), hope to those in despair. I watch her. Wherever we are, people just walk up like they know her, have seen her, met her before, and they ask her to give them hope, with just a touch, if she would only touch them. An angel who grants wishes. And she does, every time, whoever they are, she touches them, and they feel better. The most remarkable woman I've ever met, she's utterly unique. And she loves me. Maybe it is just charity, loving me. I don't care. Why a person loves…do we ever know, really?

"Sure," I say. "The next restaurant. My appetite is minimal, nonexistent, but I can eat, watch you eat, order a beer."

Left lane. The fast lane. 75 miles an hour. We're doing 83. Few cars. Lots of trucks. Beautiful American trucks. Chrome mudflaps. Exquisite detailing. Shiny. Clean. Brake lights, ahead, dozens of them, traffic slowing down. Too many trucks in the slow lane to pull ahead. Slower still. More brake lights. Under the speed limit tickets, cops never give them. The middle of nowhere.

I glance at Sally. A quick glance, one she might not notice. I do that a lot. Can't get past her beauty. Her preternatural beauty, my gaze sticks on it. Hard to keep my eyes on the road. My luck. It was better with Sally by my side, on my side. Much better.

"I met Princess Diana once," I say, tossing the words, little rubber toys in a bubble bath. "And Charles, the guy with her."

"Really? For real, really?"

"Yeah, for real. Venice. I spent some time in Italy, years, the mid 80s. Must have been about '84. I knew people there. A few. Artists mostly, a couple of writers, models. A shrink who introduced me to Anna Fendi. I stayed at her house in Rome. A safe house. Peach brown walls. Evergreen trees. The shrink knew how to throw parties, Venetian parties. Seriously decadent parties. Always a couple of Yugoslavian ladies willing to strip for cash, do favors. Met a girl, Eva. A member of Britain's Royal Society of Portrait Painters. 'With the Society's permission, and gratitude,' as she put it, the Society president asked her to invite The Princesses of Wales to become a Society sponsor.

"The Britannia, the royal yacht, had docked in Venice. Charles and Diana were aboard. A state visit, very formal. Eva had no direct means of talking to Diana, just the name of someone at the British embassy. I agreed to help her sort it out.

"Eva Julia-Maria Angolini. Her name. She was beautiful. Soft. Born in Naples. Spoke fluent English but with a heavy accent. She loved being Italian. Italian's love being Italian. She had a boyfriend. They married, eventually. I got a card, an invitation to their wedding, and Diana news. It traveled for over a year to find me. I missed the wedding."

"Do you miss our wedding?" Sally's toe. She knows where to put that toe. "We can stop. Skip the restaurant. Eat each other."

My young wife. Damn! Traffic is crawling. "OK. After Albuquerque. Would like to get through before dark. Maybe reach Amarillo. Let's see."

"Are you sure?"

"No, I'm not. I'm in driving mode. That's all. But we can stop."

"Later."

"Sure. OK."

I continue. "Eva had some friends. They were given invitations for drinks and eats on the Britannia's upper deck. Eva needed the evening invitation. A copy of one. Something. We called the embassy, left a message, never heard back. Walked Venice, walked for hours. All we got—an invitation for the morning's church event and a photocopy of the cocktail invitation. '8:00 p.m. The Britannia. Follow instructions.' She changed the name on the invitation and photocopied again, trimmed the edges, effective, without a close look.

"We got dressed. I borrowed a tuxedo from Eva's boyfriend, Alberto. Descent guy. His parents were born in Venice. Eva lived near the Guggenheim Museum, often derided its contents. 'Shit Pollock paintings oozing mayonnaise on hot days,' she would say. 'Novelty masquerading as genius, popularizing mediocrity.' She wore a light gray dress, lots of embroidery. Looked like a wedding dress skillfully renovated. We left the house at seven p.m. Very nervous. I asked her what the plan was."

I-40 began to open up. 50 miles an hour in a 75 zone. At least we were moving.

"No plan. She had no plan. 'We're going to walk in,' she said. 'Walk right in.'"

"A likable imbalance, Eva. We arrived early. Too early. Detoured into Vivaldi's Church of Pity. Venice was church-central. Churches everywhere. Big doors. We entered the main room. Stone walls. A heavy room. Cool. Two people in front of us, a young couple debating the need to settle some passionate dispute while telling each other to keep quiet. Lots of candles. Lighting of candles. People kneeling, crossing themselves. Crossing and crossing. Kneeling and kneeling. The binding comfort of tradition. Doing what they were told to do. Vacant humility. God and Satan listening to parishioner prayers. If people spent the time they spend praying to God, on being good to each other, there would be no need for God. No need for prayers.

"We left. Stood outside. Scanned the metal fence in front of the Britannia, an opening, the entry point, lots of cops, two British soldiers checking people at the gate."

Again, traffic slows down. For miles. Crawling, and crawling. Hate traffic. Open land all around us and I feel trapped. Asphalt borders. Highway claustrophobia. Can't see far enough ahead. Try. Open a Red

Bull. Drink it down, take a swallow of water. Love Red Bull, always drink it with a water chaser.

"Eva took my arm. We walked to the fence, along the fence to the gate. Got in line. A swarm of people held back by the fence were talking loudly. Mostly men. They came to see Diana's dress. An Italian designer had done the work. Very sexy. Princess flesh on display. That was the expectation. Diana dress stories led the news for days.

"We were next. I handed Eva the reconstructed invitation. She dropped her shoulder straps. Gave more light to her generous cleavage. The guards looked. The cops looked. Couldn't help themselves. I looked. Couldn't help myself. Eva waved the invitation. No one cared. Their eyes were full. We walked in. High speed trains rushing through windless tunnels. A summit view. Well, not quite. We followed instructions to another line that started at the gangway. Two more guards."

"This is a long story Ben, an old story. I love old stories. And hubs, I love you."

Sally—insatiable giving. An angel at play. I can't help thinking of her in multiple positives. Every moment I'm awake, something good in her lights up in me. She's a goddess. Certainly. What else? Alien. I think so. Rarer than Christ is popular. I'm sure of it.

"I'm trying to remember as I go, Sal, that's all. Takes longer to remember than it used to."

"OK, my ears are open. No hurry."

We're stuck in traffic. A big road, damn big. Open terrain with nowhere to go. Almost dusk. In the distance squat clouds in search of rain dim the sun and the far horizon with a welcoming glow. Beauty makes no mistakes. Beautiful women make no mistakes. Isn't true. Feels good to think it is. Sally lifts her skirt. Teasing. Planning ahead, heating the oven. Impossible to stay focused, to want to stay focused.

"Before reaching the gangway, Eva saw someone she knew. A local artist. His name was Giff. More plump than fat. He was moody. Sarcastic. Wore black overalls, neatly pressed shirts. Round, uninteresting face. A fantastic figure artist. Never asked what Giff meant. He was waiting by the gangway but not in line. We walked up to him, began chatting.

Followed him to the gangway entrance. Two guards were checking passes. Giff handed his pass to the first. The guy knew him. They began talking. We stepped in next to Giff. The second guard stopped us. Eva, still talking to Giff, said the first guard checked us. He waved us through.

"Eva continued chatting with Giff as we moved up the gangway. The point of no return. We passed it. A milieu of royal guests. And us. Forty or fifty all together, maybe more. Up the gangway to the deck we went, slowly. Then another wait."

High desert congestion. No different from city congestion... forward motion stops.

"Fenced-off spectators, people on the streets below. We were high above them, looking down. Royals are always looking down. No more check points. Couldn't be. That's what we thought."

Sally sneezes, softly, almost covertly. Shook my arm. "I have to pee."

"Now?"

"I've been holding it for miles, Ben. Miles and miles. Yes, Ben. Now."

I signal, tell the guy behind me I'm moving to the right lane. No trouble. A considerate driver. Traffic is almost at a stop. We go off road. A dog set free of his leash. A happy Jeep. Didn't go far. Found a good spot, haggard bushes, tall grass beginning to brown. Inanimate sound, can sound be inanimate? We wait for traffic to thin. Sally squats next to the open passenger door her white skin illuminating door details, the ground around her. Pee sounds. Sally's pee sounds. My wife. A melody in it. This time I hear the music.

Back on I-40. The road is clear, few cars. Doesn't take long to catch up with the congestion.

I continue. "We waited on the deck for hours. Felt like hours. Moved forward by the inch. Finally reached the next deck, and yet another stairway. Two guys at the bottom were checking passes. I looked at Eva. She at me. Convicts, we were, certainly. She smiled. 'Exciting, isn't it.' *Fuck, no.* That's what I thought.

"A man next to us, a bellboy type, asked to take our outerwear. We removed our coats. He took them, gave us a ticket. About ten feet from the stairway, we stepped forward. A big lady, tall–looked like someone who used perfumes you can't smell–she replaced one of the men at the bottom of the stairway. When we reached her, she asked for our invitation. I looked to Eva. Padded down my pockets. "Did you leave the invitation in your coat?" Eva acted distressed. Began checking her purse.

I rechecked my pockets. Pulled out the used church invitation. "I have this." I said. "Very sorry. Can we call the coats back?"

"No," the big lady said. "They've gone down. Go ahead. Just show them what you have at the top."

"Up we went. At the top, after entering the main room, there were two more guys, both in suits, one checking the invitation, the other announcing the name on it to Charles and Diana. Charles was first, a plain, mousy man living in discomfort in comforting routines, forgotten disinterest in his eyes. Friends told us there are four rules to follow when meeting members of the royal family. "Bow to them. Do not touch them. Do not speak first. Address them as Your Highnesses."

"I stepped forward with Eva next to me, walked past the two men bewildered and confused by the jumbled invitation I gave them, put out my hand to Charles. 'Hi. I'm Benjamin Mamott,' I said. 'A pleasure to meet you.' Perplexed, cautious, Charles, extended his hand. Royal blood. Dumb as fuck royal blood. Lucky, I didn't have any. We shook. I turned to Eva, introduced her to Charles, introduced myself to Diana. 'I'm with her,' I said. 'She has something important to ask you. She's a great artist. She can explain everything. I'm just helping out.' Diana, appearing delighted by my informality, smiled, and said, 'You'll have to move forward, I'm afraid. We can talk later.'

Her voice, it was sweet, tasted sweet. That's what I remember.

"I moved off. Visualized her dress in my mind. Looked at it in more detail than I could publicly. The dress was unexceptional. All the press coverage, all the fuss. Couldn't see why. Eva was behind me. Not sure if she bowed. I couldn't. Americans, we're like that, we're not programmed to bow. The room filled with a low buzz. The push and pull of conversation became louder as people relaxed, milled about, filled vacant spaces, acted unimpressed by the gathering.

"We took drinks and snacks from the waiters, began to feel a piercing discomfort. Eva waved, walked over to Giff. One of the waiters came to me, began asking questions. Where was I from? Was I enjoying Venice? Who did I know in Venice? No immediate answer. I just looked at him. Nothing to say. Diana walked up. The waiter backed off. She smiled. A nice smile. Attentive inquisitive eyes. Alert. Alive. I understood why people loved her.

"'Now tell me,' she said. 'What were you trying to say?'

"I began explaining the work Eva does. "She paints portraits, which, at times, appear more real than the sitter." Thought I shouldn't have said that after I said it. Diana was unfazed. We continued to chat, five, maybe seven or eight minutes, talked about art, the long-rowboat race, what it would be like to be Italian. Then she put out her hand. I shook it. Thanked her for sharing time with me. She turned around. Like that. She turned around. The dress. That's what it was, what all the fuss was about. The back of her dress. It split from the shoulders, narrowed as it plunged down her back to a neat black bow. And just beyond the bow, the beginning split of her butt, her very fine, clearly visible royal butt. I wanted to dive in. Right there. Grab her ass, both hands, and dive in. Beauty and the beast frolicking on the upper deck, looking down. Royals, they're always looking down.

"Eva came back briefly, then walked away again. Said she talked with Charles, then Diana. Charles held forth, hesitantly she thought, on the virtues of playing polo and fiddled with his left cuff. Diana was fully animated and cheerful, clearly stated how much she would love to be a Society sponsor but not at this time, and that she would be honored to have Eva paint her portrait. It was good. Eva was happy. I was happy for Eva. She did what she could for the Society and had a bit of luck herself.

"The waiter returned. He wasn't a waiter. 'We need to talk,' he said, and he took my arm. Didn't draw attention to us but he was quite decided that I should go with him. We walked to the edge of the crowd. Close to an exit point.

"I don't remember his rank, but he referred to it when he introduced himself. I looked at him. 'Why are you here?' he asked. I told him.

Explained everything exactly as it was. The color of his skin turned noticeably red after my explanation. 'You're not supposed to be here.'

'I know,' I said.

'You have to leave,' he said. I told him I wasn't going anywhere without Eva. He told me not to worry, she would be joining us shortly. 'You have to leave.' He said it again, more strained this time. Suppressed anger.

'Yeah, I understand,' I said. He straightened up, raw displeasure coating his eyes. 'You're making waves in my department. Please. Leave.'

Two military looking men, waiters, along with Eva, came to escort us off the boat, discreetly. 'We have coats,' I said, and I handed him our tickets. He took them, turned his back to us. 'They'll be waiting for you.'

We got into an elevator with the two waiters. Young, devoted, following orders. No 'think for yourself' orders. Never are. The elevator dropped abruptly, metal begging for oil. Low, stretching sounds. I imagined myself taking down both men, a James Bond moment.

"At the bottom, we were let out. No coats. We waited. Elevator doors closed. We walked down the last of the gangway. No coats. Waited. No coats, no tickets. We walked away from the boat shivering. Cold. Grand misbehavior. There was something intoxicating about it and concerning. Was anyone following us? We exited the last gate, walked along the *fondamenta*, (the walking bank along the canal), past the Vivaldi church. Walked at a brisk pace until we reached Eva's place. She poured glasses of wine. We sat down, stared at each other.

"How long we sat there? I have no idea. A long time. We sat, drank, emptied two bottles. Kept thinking, without talking about the big boat. Getting on it, getting off. We sat until Eva's boyfriend arrived.

"Alberto. He seemed unattached. I considered making a move on Eva. Imagined it. Wanted it. Settled for a gondola ride with benefits. We took the same route Diana and Charles took the day before. Eva wore a light black shawl over something like a smock. No underwear. Her eyes sparkled, sucked humidity from the air. She was into it. Eager to misbehave. I wore gray stretch shorts. A gray vest, six buttons.

"Eva knew the gondolier. He was instructed to look over us. He did and he sang as we meandered through the canals, light splashing off strokes of the oar, day warmth radiating from the walls–Venetian canyons rising between waterways and a thirsty sun. Eva threw her shawl over us. We disappeared from sight, from being seen, a good time to die, definitely.

"Ben..." a long pause, "Is that a true story?"

"It is, yes."

"You're sure?"

"Yes."

"And you didn't get arrested?"

"No."

"And Eva, did she paint Diana's portrait?"

"She did, yes. And they briefly became close friends."

"And the Royal Society of Portrait Painters? What did they say?"

"They removed her from their roster."

"They did?"

"She said they did. But. It didn't happen that way. The ending. Not exactly."

Traffic came to a stop. A solid stop, brake lights bake the night in a red glow.

"What? But I was into it, Ben. A great story. Impossible, but still. I saw myself in Eva's place. I like her, very bold.

"OK, whatever, hubs. Tell me. What 'really' happened?"

"No arrest. No apology. No fifteen minutes of fame. I stayed in Venice a few more days, three or four. Loved Venice, a city walking on water. Reflections. Boats. Children riding bikes in the compos. Street side storytelling, grappa, cheese toast, fizzy water, girl-watching. After the Britannia, I never saw Eva again, neglected to get her number. No return address on the note received at my Paradise address.

"The day after Eva left, I met a couple of writers, Erica Jong, and Ken Follett. Went to lunch together at Harry's Bar. Expensive. Hemingway's Montgomery. Three rounds. Good food, better conversation. Cults. Religion. Wealth abuse. Fame. The end of insignificance. Illusion. Went to dinner with Erica. An engaging mind. Infectious foresight.

'The zipless fuck.' Everyone read it. *Fear of Flying*. Ringo and his wife Barbara were sitting at the table across from us. Celebrity city. Everyone comes to Venice. I walked over to their table. Asked Ringo for his autograph. 'For a kid I know,' I said. 'She would be thrilled.' His wife, Barbara, asked me to sit down. Ringo scribbled on a menu. Almost too drunk or drugged to pen the last letter in his name. He made it. His million and one autograph. Maybe two million and one, or three. Very considerate. Felt improper urges looking at Barbara, talking to her. Normal improper urges. A one-time Bond girl. She was beautiful, an anomalous variant of mature innocence. Unusual. Should have requested her autograph, as well. For myself.

"The next day I took off for Pisa and the south of France. Topless beaches. Montpellier. Had friends there. Rained for days. Heavy rain, crop-killing rain. I stayed inside, happy I wasn't in jail, and I drank, watched movies, wondered if I had been arrested, if we'd been jailed, would it have been a British or Italian jail?

"Let's do Venice, Ben, take a gondola ride. At night."

"OK."

Sally in Venice, walking on water. She could. I was sure of it.

I hit 80 miles an hour, 85. Felt good. After miles of traffic, speeding was justified. An empty big wheeler passes us. Must have been empty, the driver in no hurry, just tired of sitting in traffic.

Hate traffic.

# THIRTY SEVEN

Food. Past due for a pit stop.

We cross the Rio Grande. Full moon over Albuquerque. A highway view. Homes. Stores. Warehouses. Buildings. Broken yards. Stray animals. Empty lots. Flagpoles. No need to stop. Plenty of gas. 288 miles to Amarillo. Three-plus hours, maybe more. A clear sky. The first biped to realize the night sky was not a roof. Hard to picture the moment, what it felt like giving birth to imagination, the first vision of eternity. Roadside bars, restaurant bars. Eat, drink and truck-stop bars. We pass them. Lots of them.

"Let's eat on the other side of Albuquerque."

"I'm hungry now."

"Me, too, Sal, but we have a lot of road ahead. Two thousand miles. Probably more. Would like to get past Albuquerque."

She agrees, relaxes, reclines her seat. Rolls up her window. Smiles. Blows me a kiss. Hints at the reassurance she needs but never asks for. Closes her eyes, fades from reality.

After Albuquerque we begin climbing. Almost 7,000 feet. Then down again to long flat miles. Very long, very flat miles. Sally's sleeping, breathing softly. We pass Clines Corners, Santa Rosa, Tucumcari, on into Texas, Glenrio, Adrian–towns filled with people who don't exist for most of the world's nearly eight billion people. They didn't exist for us.

A slight bump. Uneven road. Sally wakes up.

"Where are we, Ben? What time is it?"

She yawns, stretches.

"We're about 30 minutes from Vega. We can stop there. Eat, clean up. Then another 30-plus to Amarillo. It's about 5:30 am."

I'm not tired. Something complete about driving–the familiar hood, the view over it, the comfort of being in control.

"Sal, while you slept, I was thinking...."

She rolls a joint. Takes a long slow hit. Passes it to me.

"An idea," I say. "I have an idea. A theory on how we got here."

"How we got here?" She laughs, threatens to bite my ear. "You know how we got here." Another laugh, softer.

"Not how we got here, here as in where we are now. How the country got to where we are today."

"Bad cards, hubs. We were dealt bad cards. That's all. Was probably God. God the dealer, the house. Or the planets...could be misbehaving planets. Planets, they misbehave just like people do. Why else would you make gods of them? But really, what I think. Ego binging, that's how we got here, Ben. Ego is at the beginning of conflict, and failure, always." She pops a raisin in her mouth, several.

"Yeah, Sal, that...can't disagree with that."

Sally, my beautiful, profound, ever insightful wife. Impossible to keep up. No need to make it possible.

"There's too much ego gluttony in the world, Hubs. The 'I need to validate my self-importance' ego market. The greater the ego, the smaller the world we live in. Everyone is feeding ego, selling it, making money off it, shrinking our minds, magnifying the subjective, our vulnerability to deceit. That's how we got here. But the rich, if they don't start spending money on the poor, what money can buy won't be enough for them, for anyone. Our future, to survive we have to make more money, get rich off what we know. We can do it, Ben. Must do it, for our baby."

Baby!

"Look at the Kardashians...brainless body entertainment, sex people imagine having. We can do better than that, more than that. Want a Coke, candy bar, raisins?" Sally clicks on the radio.

Country Western music. Don't mind, mostly. Loath rap, Mozart, Heavy Metal.

Love rock and roll, Rachmaninov, silence.

Silence is best...the purest music.

# THIRTY EIGHT

A cluster of lights ahead. Signs. Pilot truck stop two miles ahead. Intersection of 385 and I-40. Food. Drink. Air conditioning. Menus. Bathrooms. Flush toilets. We get off the highway, onto old 66. I like 66. The road to adventure. Pull into a restaurant and bar in Vega. Half-dozen vehicles outside. Trucks mostly. An old Chevy. Rusting bumpers, paint peeling off the roof edge, around the door handles. A couple of bikes. A BMW sedan. Gray. Clean. I drop Sally at the door, gas up, park on the far side of the restaurant lot, opposite the propane tank. Well out of range of door dents. Hate door dents.

Sally's window is still open. The freshness of early morning; a dry fragrance mixed with leftover heat from the day before, drifts through the Jeep, reminds me of something I can't remember, a place I can't remember, don't need to remember. I roll up the windows, step out, stretch, lock the Jeep, head for the entrance door. I'm in a grand mood, relaxed and happy. Sally walking on water. Christ with tits, who would have guessed it? Christ's brother, I feel like I am, and I'm married to her. That, and I'm about to empty my bladder, fill my stomach, look at Sally, watch her eat, imagine things about her...Bonnie and Clyde things with a more salacious nature, a life worth living...absolutely.

Thin, white painted rails ran along the sides of the building. 4x4 poles hold up the awning. Roof could have been red. Difficult to make out. An unexceptional building. White and gray. They allow smoking. I look for slot machines, scantily clad cocktail waitresses, call girls, old men on sagging stools, big cigars. There aren't any. Isn't Nevada. The restaurant's bar is meaningful, accommodating, worn. Stale temperature throughout, dull, recycled, no air conditioning. Low maintenance chairs and tables are scattered unevenly across the main room. People eating, waiting to eat. Several turn to look at me. Their minds churning. Rapists, murders, thumb suckers, peeping toms, escaped convicts. How do we know? People, they can be anything. Two guys at the bar... they're disappointed Sally isn't alone.

I follow signs to the men's room, empty my holding tank...need a bigger tank.

Sally took a table next to a couple of kids, and their parents. They have a dog. *In the restaurant!? Odd. I think so.* Rodent class. Small, yappy. A useless thing. I favor big dogs with big teeth. Teeth that can stop a mountain lion. Dogs without pooper scoopers.

"Good choice, Ben." Sally hands me the menu. "I like it here," she says, mischievous lines accenting her lips. "Very friendly."

I pull out a chair, sit down, read the room. 'Friendly' didn't come to mind. Tentative, in some way, maybe. "Have you ordered?" I ask.

"Not yet. I'm looking for something naughty. A chocolate banana, topped with candied cherries, a hot berry and brown sugar muffin, smothered in warm honey butter and whipped cream. That's what I want."

"Christ Sally, how am I to keep up?"

"Think of me, hot and sweet, and you'll do just fine." She blows me a kiss, laughs elatedly, innocently.

My wife. Sally Isabel Mamott. How much the heart can love, and be loved? I'm going to find out. "I like it when you laugh, Sal. Everything about you makes music. You should laugh more often."

"I'll try," she winks. "I'm ordering bacon, pancakes with maple syrup, a glass of milk, jumbled eggs, a banana. How about you?"

"Steak, Baileys Irish Cream, and a doughnut."

"Yum," she says, poking me.

One of the kids next to us, the girl, drops her plate. Plastic. She's very thin. Pallid. Ten years old, maybe. Streaked brown hair, long, down to her mid-back. Plate doesn't break but her food splatters across the floor. The father shouts. "Damn you, child! Clean that up! And no breakfast!"

The mother raises a hand. Puts it down.

"Meat," I say, shouting the word, almost shouting... I think shouting it will help calm the parents, calm Sally. With good reason Sally hates the abuse of children. I hate it. "Meat. I'm having a steak. Steak, Bailys, and a doughnut."

Our waiter's Polish. Anya. Naïve, unassuming. We place our order, hold hands, think nasty thoughts. Feels good to think nasty thoughts. The Olympics of Nasty Thoughts.

The nastiest of nasty thoughts taking home the gold.

I can see that, sure.

# THIRTY NINE

Along time before our meals arrive.

"People believe in God because they can't imagine objective intelligence. Anthropomorphic vision, it's all they have, all we have. Very simple. No confusion. People are good or bad because they're good or bad. God has nothing to do with it."

"That's interesting." I say, half yawning.

Sally scoffs.

"Really Sal, what made you think of that?"

"The people behind me. I can hear them. They're Creation Evidence Museum pilgrims."

"They're what?"

"They believe man and dinosaurs coexisted."

"But that's not factual, Sal. Not even close to factual." I'm confused.

"Doesn't need to be to be believed."

Still confused.

The two bar guys are staring at Sally. She gets that a lot. Celebrity training. A heavy blond girl joins them. Minutes before she was sitting a few stools down, watching a wrestling match, talking to the bartender, throwing darts. The first thing she says to one of the guys, after he asks her to sit closer, is about a family he thought she knew.

"Sure," she says, "I know them. The Andersons. Hot tubs and refrigerators on their front porch. All year round. They have strange pets."

The guy puts his hand on her leg.

"Yeah," Sally continues, "believers envision humans having baby dinosaur pets, feeding Tyrannosaurus juveniles grapes and peas by hand." Sally holds her voice down, softens it. Checks to see if anyone can overhear us. Fear of insult. Of being insulted. Public humiliation. We all have it. How to get rid of it? Blunt. Have to be more blunt.

I raise my voice.

"There's no such thing as dinosaurs. All the bones? They're manufactured, an Area 51 cover-up. Alex Jones, Limbaugh, Hannity. Ask them."

Sally grabs my arm. "Benjamin Mamott. You shut the fuck up. Here's the waitress. Eat your steak."

A man from the other side of the room walks by us. He'd been sitting alone. He's big. A gutter face, sandpaper skin, badly dressed. Sally gives him a look, mean, gouging. Very unlike her.

The kids next to us begin playing a game with their soda straws. The dog yaps. Gutter face returns to his table, a beer in each hand.

The girl, or maybe the boy, knocks over a soda, splashes the dog. No leash. It runs toward the door. More yapping. Louder yapping. An irritating animal. Something to eat if you're a bear, lynx, raccoon, a big dog, anything with more teeth.

The mother smacks the top of the girl's head. The father leans forward, his hand in a fist, arm back. The dog runs toward the kitchen. I leave my chair, catch the man's arm midair. Hold it, squeeze it, think to snap it, how good that would feel...to me.

"Lay a hand on that child," I say, "I'll break your fucking arm." I can do it. Want to do it. The devil in me.

The woman screams. "You have no right, mister. No right. We will discipline our children however we want!"

"Lady," Sally turns toward her. "You don't know this man. Best if you don't get to know him."

The woman looks at me. At her husband. Her kids. The rodent. Adjusts her hair, her bra, her lipstick. Turns away, begins eating.

I sit down. Cut into my steak.

Dinosaurs in the Garden of Eden. Lies...the sacred fruits of our appropriated labor; nutrition-less lies. We live on them, believe anything to keep them alive. Why? The man from the other side of the room comes back to our table. My side, not Sally's. She glares. Cat-people eyes following his movements, his breathing.

"You're an asshole buddy."

"I know," I say, without looking up. "I don't like people." I swallow. Take another bite of steak, very juicy. The Creation family focuses on their food. Bartender begins drying a glass, flirts with Anya. An average looking guy. Typical guy. Typical bartender.

"Mind if I sit down?"

"Yes!" Sally spoke first. "We mind."

"I could use an asshole. Want a job?"

"No!" Sally spoke first.

"I am curious," I say. "What kind of job?"

"A five-thousand-dollar job. Five minutes. Easy."

"Ben, let's go." Sally grabs her plate. Takes it to the waitress. Asks for the bill. I study the guy, consider my options.

**Something about bars. Roadside commerce. Grease pits. People eating whatever and whenever they want. Roads. People live on roads. Road people. More and more road people every day. Everything out in the open. Shitting in the open. Pissing. Washing. Eating. Fucking and dying in the open.**

"Another time," I say. "But thanks for the offer." I stand up.

The guy isn't just big, he is huge. Not sure how I missed that. A foot taller than me, Over a hundred pounds heavier. Damn.

"Fine." That's all he says. Doesn't move.

I walk around him. Calculating. Watching. Waiting. Do I know him from somewhere? My DEA days, maybe. A long time ago. No connection. Couldn't be.

"Do I know you?" I ask.

He looks down at me. Cocks his head like boxers do in movies.

"No. You don't."

Sally pays the bill, walks out. I turn to follow. The man puts out his arm. Blocks me. Pulls out a Glock. Points it at the waitress. "Strip," he says.

"And you, you kids. Take your dog. Go to your car, put on some music, eat chocolate, and chips. Whatever. Your folks will be along shortly."

The kids turn to their parents. The mother nods. They leave... very excited. The guy points to the mother. "You, too. Strip. And you, father-man, you get to do the waitress. Your wife can watch. The rest of you, all of you. Watch if you want."

I push against the guy's arm. Doesn't move. Need to get to Florida. Christ! Gunmen in public places. Mass shootings. Just another day in America. Tomorrow's news. A killer. He could be. I push again. He lowers his arm. Pulls a second gun. Presses the muzzle into my forehead, between my eyes. Forces me to take a step back.

*Deja vu.* A pause, very pleasant. I've been here before. Suddenly, everything's clear, everything in its place. Purpose. There is purpose. Knowing that felt good.

Anya wastes no time stripping. The mother, too. No sound or movement from the other people. All eyes are on Anya, the mother, the father.

The huge man. He watches them. Directs with his eyes, the little show he sets up. Lights. Action. Camera. A guy in the back is filming everything. Impromptu porn flicks. It's a rising industry.

Blocking me. Restricting me. Anger, it gains strength, gnaws at the leash in my mind holding it back, breaks free. The guy vanishes behind memories and images of those who wronged me, wronged good people, plundered innocence for sport. The moment. The right moment. I grab the big guy's left hand, the one holding the gun to my face. Bend it back, kick his right gun hand toward the ceiling. Neither gun discharges. I snap his wrist. Sidekick his knee. Bring him to the floor, knee in his chest, pull my knife, press the flat edge against his spongy forehead.

Anya gets up, shouting. "Christ! Mister! For God's sake! What are you doing?" I look at her. Keep my knee and knife in place. "You aren't even supposed to be here," she screams! "You've ruined every-thing. No bullets. They're blanks, asshole. It's just a fucking movie." She goes over to the big guy. "You broke his wrist. He's, my father."

"What!"

"And that's mom." She points to the lady on the floor.

"What!?"

I stand up. Look at all of them. Inhale. Exhale. Rub my eyes. Shake my head, shake, and shake it. Walk to the door. Open it. Walk out.

"Finally, Ben." Sally's waiting. Has been waiting. Impatiently. "What took you so long?"

"Had to use the bathroom. You know, traveler rule number one. Pee when you can."

"Right."

I turn over the engine. Pull back and onto I-40 East.

'Money for nothing. Sex for free.' Was that ever true?

# FORTY

Greying day. The faintest hint of early morning. It may have been there but lights from Amarillo overthrew it.

"Want to stop at the Creation Evidence Museum?" Suddenly animated, Sally begins flipping through images on her phone. Turns toward me. "We could recreate Adam and Eve in the dinosaur tracks. Buy a bunch of apples. I'll feed you bad apples. Green apples, red ones, blue ones, and orange, and purple. Sinful apples. Would be fun. A California thing to do. It's on the way."

"We can do that, if you want, sure. But we need a snake. A rubber snake, a rubber Satan with rubber horns. A snake with horns."

"No snakes, Ben. Not even a rubber one."

"OK." Lots of OKs in life.

Sally hates snakes. Dead ones, rubber ones, movie snakes, painted snakes, even cartoon snakes. I say "OK" a couple of times. Feels good to agree with Sally.

"We can tag Amarillo, take whatever highway south and pick up I-20 East toward Abilene. See where to go from there. We've eaten, gas tank is full, windows washed–we're good. We can sort a rest stop after Amarillo."

"You always have a plan, hubs. Don't you."

"No, not really. I'm old. I have more scenarios to refer to. Looks like planning, I know, but I'm just lucky if experience makes a difference. That's all."

"Oh…" she opens a box of raisins, drops several on her tongue. "You were saying something, what was it? A theory you have on how America got here?"

"That? Right. No theory, Sal, not really. Just a thought, a collection of observations linked together without becoming a complete image."

"Sounds interesting, let's hear it, we have time."

A wise man marries a woman wiser than he. I did that.

"OK, sure. Before, when I was a kid, a young man, things were simple. Life was simple. Sex was simple. Right and wrong behaviors were clearly defined. Clear lines were drawn. Rules were simple and there weren't many of them. Guys did girls, married girls. Girls did guys, married guys. A man. A woman. Children. They made up a family. Fat people were fat because they ate too much, knew they ate too much. They didn't blame the food for making them fat. Meat was meat. Veggies were veggies. Now we don't know what the fuck we're eating. Torn, worn out jeans were torn and worn out. We got new ones. No one tried to make rich look poor, depravity sacred, sodomy ritualistic, same sex liaisons family friendly. There were no 'safe' spaces, no pronoun extremists, no mass deaths from Opioids and guns. Fashion was simple. Expectation was simple. Playboy bunnies didn't shave. Social media nudity, instant nudity, didn't exist. There were no never-nude-again tattoos robbing girls of their nakedness. No barcode girls. '60's girls were all skin, all girl. Big guys. Tough guys. Bikers, military guys, truck drivers, they had tattoos. Ugly tattoos, most of them. Tattoos added meanness to a guy's look. Simple. An out-of-tune piano was heard as being out of tune. No one tried to convince us it was music. People with poop bags and scoops, we never saw them. Dogs were dogs. Construction workers. Army guys. They wore helmets, everyone else wore hats. Simple. Everyone understood English even if they spoke a different language. Now we need translators at the Miami airport, every airport. Blacks were gaining civil rights, beginning to recover from decades of abuse. Growing their minds, their inherent power, bettering their understanding of the white man's weaknesses, his failure to rise above them. Lifestyle choice was just a choice, not a civil right. Sex was sex. Everyone did it. No AIDS. No orientation confusion. Just sex. Simple. Most of visual art was honest, self-explanatory, professional. Didn't require writers to give it meaning, the CIA to amplify its monetary value." I stop. Take a breath. "When

I was a kid? Sal. Christ! Every old guy says that 'When I was a kid.' Shit."

"Ben, that's your thought on how we got here? Life stopped being simple? Sounds more like what happened than why it happened." She looks straight at me. "Needs work."

"I know. I'm still thinking."

"Good."

Sirens. Far away, muted. They're getting closer. I begin checking the mirrors. We'd just skirted Amarillo, picked up 27 South. More sirens. Flashing lights far ahead. Fire. A building fire in the distance. A couple of cops and a fire truck pass us going 85, 90 miles an hour. I pull over. Never saw a fire truck move that fast. Another truck sped by. An ambulance.

Sally lights a joint, tosses raisins in her mouth. "I think we should get a cat, Ben. A Jeep cat. A pot-smoking Cheshire cat."

I like cats well enough. Don't dislike them. Can't imagine one living in my Jeep. "Yeah," I say. "We could. Let's see."

I get back on the road, right lane, hold at the speed limit, 70 mph, make a game of keeping the needle on the 7. My lucky number. More fire trucks. Flames are clearly visible now, looks like a block of buildings. Helicopters shining lights. Lights everywhere. Lots of sirens. We drive past. Hear several explosions. Blasts of light brighten low hanging clouds. Disaster frequencies. They're speeding up.

"I'm glad we don't live here."

"Ben. We don't live anywhere."

"Right."

# FORTY ONE

We keep on; the road keeps on. 'Life in penniless underwear.' I think that, seems silly, but I like it. Makes the drive feel bigger, not sure how.

Homelessness. The state of the world. Bread-and-butter Americans vying for fascist rule – an end to free speech, self-determination, freedom as we know it. "Sal."

"Hum."

"I'm still thinking."

"Sure, Ben. Good. We have time, and I'm still listening. I love you."

Damn. Every time she says that, it means so much I don't know what it means. It feels good, that's all. Every time. I continue with my theory.

"In the late '40s, early '50s, the CIA set up the International Organizations Division under Tom Braden. Tom's job was to stem the flow of talent leaving Europe and America for the Soviet Union. With the help of CIA money and power, Abstract Expressionism was converted into Freedom of Expression. The CIA funded shows in America and Europe. Nelson Rockefeller lived behind the Museum of Modern Art, and he contracted MoMA to put on shows and bought paintings to establish market value; the novelty market: the novelty lottery. Nobody called it that, but that's what it was, what it is. The anybody can play; anybody can win market. With money to be made at home, the talent exodus came to an end. And with it, fortunate or not, the professional standards that legitimized artists, legitimized professionalism itself.

"How do you know that, Ben?"

"Read about it."

"You read about it! Where? When?"

"Playboy. First time was Playboy. When they had real centerfold nudes. The kind we used to steal to wallpaper our tree houses. No tattooed girls, colored hair, tongue studs. Anyway, it was a long article."

"No studs for me, Hubs. Just you."

She pokes me, humors herself, takes out her phone, opens Google. Her screen begins flashing. Looks like she's signaling someone, sending a message to some distant world where albinos are born and fused into reality by pre-human imagination. She found several stories, articles, clips, begin reading. I continue.

"That the CIA significantly influenced the accepted perception and value of art and artists, reengineered how people think about professionalism, that professional standards are not essential to success, self-expression, social wellbeing–that's the home run that got us here. The long con that led to the PC gay-agenda con, to the Trump con, to we the people taking it up the ass for a fake orgasm."

"Ben, please, no need to be vulgar."

"Right. That is vulgar, it is, sorry." I pause, think, 'I like being vulgar.' Left the thought, take a hit, two hits, open a beer.

"Diminished moral expectations," I say. "The freedom to con without negative consequences, equivalence manipulation, that's where we are." Beer is warm. I skip it. Take a drink of water, cool my throat. Swallow slowly, imagine waterfalls and beautiful girls bathing beneath them.

"How I see it, Sal, and I might be wrong, but the removal of professional standards from art played a significant role in how we adapted to advances in technology, to how we became internet addicted to personalized wants...lost sight of what the whole needs for us to coexist within it to our own benefit. Absent professionalism societal wellbeing thins, shifts from reason and logic to opinion and narcissism. I'm still observing, studying the idea, but that's what I think. Old masters, modern masters, there's no equivalence. Trump administration, Obama administration, no equivalence. Civil rights, gay rights, no equivalence. Everyone, so many people, they're worried about artificial intelligence taking over, no point in that if eradicating the image of man is the aim. Modern art, con art…the novelty market has already removed human likeness from much of our visual footprint."

An abrupt change. Suddenly I feel sad, not sure why. Listening to myself, maybe that. We continue south on I-27. Almost straight. Transmissions, bearings, pumps, belts, tires, they know the road. I listen to them, analyze them. Sally leans against the door. A thin strip of the morning sun lights her face, the fresh crease in her clean blouse, her shifting skirt.

"For most people," she says, as she relights the joint, opens a coke, takes a hit and a sip before speaking. "How we got here doesn't matter. No time for it to matter. Not for young people. And the old people, most of them," she looks at me, "*many* of them, they don't care. Not anymore. People are decided, Ben, little chance of change. Look at you." She moves, reaches over, runs her finger across my lips. My still-dry lips. "I've told you. You're a man in a world that no longer belongs to you, and never belonged to me. We're on the outside orbit, Ben. And that's OK. Where is my world if not with you in yours? Where is your world if not with me in mine? Whatever and wherever that is?"

**Tracks on the beach, long slow whispers in the sand as waves recede.**

I want to pull over. Right there. Grab Sally. Strip her. Ease her onto a blanket in the warmth of the rising sun. Slow rub oil massage her entire body, every cell, love her, slowly, deliberately, bury myself in her body, in a world of sensation vital enough to survive the afterlife. I will. I'll do that. I'll find a spot, treat my Sally to a full body oil massage. I continue.

"Have you been to the Met? The Metropolitan Museum?"

"Once," she says. "A long time ago."

"Love the Met. A friend of mine, Thomas Hoving…he directed there. 1967 to1977. A dear friend, a good man, a great museum. Anyway, visualize a room full of old master paintings, the High Renaissance. Put yourself in the middle of the room and rotate 360 degrees. Look at all the people walking through, and ask yourself how many would have the ability to produce what is hanging on the walls? None, I would guess. Eva could, if she were there. Next, go to MoMA, take the center of a room, any room, rotate 360 degrees and ask yourself how many people walking through would have the ability to produce what they see hanging on the walls, from the ceiling, stuck to the floor. Most of them, maybe all of them, even guys in wheelchairs, blind people, monkeys in polka dot pajamas, kids on roller-skates."

"So?" Sally pulls on my ear.

"So, that's how art changed the world. How it went from highly skilled masters that knew how to draw, to anything goes, genius is novel, so novelty is genius, art. Anonymous, abstract, sterile."

"So?"

"So, nothing," I say, "No people. That's all. In most of modern art there are no people. Just stuff. If I dig up an ancient Mother Goddess statue, I see a person. Pick up a piece of modern art from some future ruin, what will there be in the rubble that points to us, that distinguishes us from the rubble?"

A window breeze tosses Sally's hair into a blur. She play's, tries to catch the breeze. "I'm thinking," she says. "You could be right. It's possible. I can think you're right. You can think you're right. Do we need anyone else to think you're right?"

I stretch, push against the steering wheel. "I've been thinking. An idea I have."

"Another one?"

"Yeah. A relaxing idea. You'll like it."

The town of Lubbock. Another ten minutes. Crop alley. Bushes, mounds, dunes, no place to pull over. Sally's slow rub oil massage—I have it all planned out in my mind—it will have to wait. I keep driving. Key West. Miles to go. I want to get there.

"What idea? Tell me more. Tell me more."

"As soon as I can, wife," I say. "As soon as I can."

Wife. I have a wife. Amazing.

Crops.

All around us, crops are everywhere. People watch crops. Crops belong to someone. Deserts. Barren worlds. Few want them. They're freer. You can say whatever you want in the desert.

# FORTY TWO

**H**ours. Driving hours. The sometimes-glorious monotony of repetitive sound, of space bending into shapes, absorbing time, a sense of things. All around us. Land at rest. Expressionless, untrodden earth. Always something growing, something breathing just beneath the surface, making nests, searching for food. Surviving.

Crops. More crops. Crops are good. Crops work for us.

We skim Tahoka, turn east on 380 toward Post. From Post, south on 84 toward Snyder. A drop in elevation. Dry. Private. 84 to Sweetwater next, then I-20 east to Abilene. That's the plan. Sally's overdue outdoor oil massage. The perfect spot. It's out there. I can feel it.

Justiceburg, the next town ahead. We pull in, look for a place to eat. A little sweaty. Hot. Cold beer in mind. Ice cold. Plenty of shrub, always shrub; tree's poorer cousins, grass, the odd cactus, dirt roads. Jeep roads. Roads less traveled. They tell better stories. Nothing to eat. No restaurants, open stores. Almost noon.

We leave Justiceburg. Hit the main road, what there is of it. A dust fog erupting behind us. I put my foot on the gas, pick up 84 toward the river. Forward momentum. It feels good.

We cross the river. Mud green, slow moving; remains from the last surge of a sudden storm. Another derelict bridge, potted road, rusting guard rails, America in need. A crashed car protruding from the river's surface, looks like a broken nose. Water pooling around it. Not that old. Partly burned, rusted, vandalized. An old news item — some deranged mother trying to kill her kids. She jumped the rail, cut her seatbelt, saved herself. A crazed teen selling drugs, running from the cops, craving his father's attention. He spins out of control, flips over the rail into the water, dies in the flames. A drug bust gone wrong. What else? Nothing. A car sticking up in the water. That's all it is. Blue sky. A beautiful day. Cruising highway 84. Tenantless terrain. Stingy land struggling to hold onto itself. Green-brown mounds, mound after mound. Spent oil rigs. Dozens of wells. Roads leading to ravines, low hills.

The beginning of an old road. Sally time, oil massage, an exit point. I take it. Very promising. We leave the asphalt, the lane markers, the shoulder cutouts, the shared space. Hit the dirt. A small service road. Doesn't go far. We keep on, go off road. Fresh tracks, we begin leaving them. Hate leaving tracks. The unseen world watching. Always watching. I want to be in it. Was trained to be in it. Tires dig in, pull. We leave tracks, keep going. Plain horizon, runt cactus, a brittle land, tarnished, patina memories in alternating reds, browns, dull yellows. A ravine. Jagged walls, sloping twisted crumbling walls. Lots of sun. We stop. What to do with the cat? If we had one. Roll up the windows, lock it inside? Put a leash on it? Let it run away? Dust smells, warm smells. I open my door, jump down, walk ahead of the Jeep.

"Here!"

Sally's out, already, studying a bright pink cactus flower, looking for the cat. She waves.

"Here! Sal. This is the spot. Come!"

Love. How do you define it? Really.

I go back to the Jeep, grab a blanket, pillow, bottle of water, a couple of candy bars, body oil. Set the stage, arrange my props. Sally's lithe shadow walks onto the blanket ahead of her, stays ahead until she lies down.

"Undress me, Hubs."

Who says that? *Undress me.* In human history, how many times has a beautiful woman laid down on an open blanket in some meadow, on a beach somewhere, anywhere, and said to some happy John, "Undress me?"

I do. Casually. Deliberately. Button by button. The side zipper on her skirt, I slide it down. Slowly. Run my hands through her hair, remove her open blouse, that's it. I toss my trousers, shirt, no care for where they land. Naked in the sun. We are, and happy, happy, and naked in the sun. I reach for the oil.

Stop…

Snake. Fuck! A rattlesnake. Diamondback, over four feet long. Gliding. Slow, smooth gliding toward us. Directly toward us.

"Sally," I whisper her name. "Don't move."

"What?"

"A snake. Don't move. They have shit eyesight. Shit hearing. Don't move."

She froze, her eyes bulging with fear. Fear that frightens me. I whisper again, and firmly, "Don't move."

A perfect spot, warm, private. Sally, her supple body tender to the touch, ready to be loved. Suddenly it isn't. Light turned to stone. All doors closed. Terror overtakes her. Panic. She struggles to run. I press against her. Hold her down. No change in direction. The snake keeps coming. Straight. Straight for Sally's head.

"Don't move." An uncompromising command.

Closer. A foot away. Same speed. Steady. Direct. Eyes, the stare of an empty mirror. Tongue flicking. Fuck! It stops, begins to compress. No time for analysis. My left hand, not as fast as my right but a better angle. It shoots out, grabs the snake just behind the head. I jump up, the snake whipping the air, searching for leverage. It has none. My grip tightens. I shove my thumb into the soft pocket beneath its jaw. Squeeze. Squeeze harder, choke it, take its air. Take its life. Look for a rock. Grab one. Crush its head. Throw it to the ground, kick dirt over it. Spit, throw the rock. Dead. It was dead.

I look up. Sally. She's running at me. Screaming. A rock the size of her head in her hands. White hair ablaze, damp skin reflecting, tits bouncing, muscles flexing. Nothing to compare it to. She smashes the dead snake. Smashes it again, and again, and again, over, and over until nothing more than a red blur remains to define what it was. She drops the rock. Collapses. Hands shaking. Body shaking. Tears racing from her eyes. "Never again, Ben. Never." A deep, trembling breath. "Never ever again are we laying down in the open."

# FORTY THREE

About one o'clock. Maybe two. We get dressed. Leave the ravine. Drive in silence. Very hot. Earth acclimating to its human infection. Mid-July. Too hot even for a hot month. Windows down. All but Sally's.

People who have never been cold. How many are there?

Snyder came next, and windmills. Giant, power-generating windmills...village girls on a hill waving their arms, looking for ships, sailors, pirates, spectators sensing adventure, vicarious loin-soaked dreams splashing on prehistoric shores. More oil rigs pumping. Some rigs not pumping. Fracking towers–invaders. Fences. Broken fences, old fences, new fences. No gates. Few road signs. No rain. Never rains. Not when you need it.

A record spinning. The needle broken. A hissing wobble. Don Quixote, his lance holstered, staring straight ahead. The open road. No one on it. No Voices. No arguments. No one ahead. No one behind. Nothing to lie about.

The band days. Rock and roll. No road can dream without rock and roll.

One day in the summer of 1969. A hot day, thin with dry air. Cutting across highway 270 to Bodie in my old top down. With Gilda Jones.

Bodie was a mining town. Deserted now, deserted years ago. We hit a long stretch of road. Straight and long. Wide vistas. Arid earth, few trees, no homes. I stopped. Got out. Put my hand to the road's hard surface; the crushed gravel, packed dirt, sun hardened. It felt human. Smelled human.

Gilda Jones on a Bodie day, right there in my top down, feet on the dash, sixteen years-old, my neighbor's daughter, Jumpin' Jack Flash blasting loud. Cracked speakers. Didn't matter. Couldn't fuck her. Wanted to. She did, too. We didn't, but she went panties down to Jumpin' Jack Flash. Let the bald wind lift her skirt. Gave me a grand tour. Her bright flaming puss matching her red hair. Her slender frame. It was a good ride. A desert ride. A hot day.

All the pebbles, the road dirt, the dust, sticks, bits of road grass, everything that made the road real, they all remembered the summer of 1969.

And Gilda Jones.

Snyder. Hermleigh, Roscoe. We pass them, turn east on I-20, drive through Sweetwater, head for Abilene.

Sally doesn't talk. Doesn't look at me.

Night falls. It's heavy. Empty. A beast from beyond, inaccessible to imagination. Fangs digging in, buried nightmares, bubble corpses rising from submerged memories, retired heartaches seeking new employment. My chest heaves, fights suffocation. Fear of abandonment—that hole in a child's heart happiness falls into and he struggles to escape from for the rest of his life, the claws, the dark that never sleeps.

Sally puts on her sunglasses. What can I do? My wife. The single spark that keeps me connected to life. Fear. I sink back into myself, into the depths. Go deeper as the miles slip by, as darkness thickens and curtains on the scenery draw to a close. Life's churning merry-go-round. How to get off and stay on at the same time? Aware of my life but no interest in living it. How to change that?

"I'm hungry…"

She speaks.

"Hungry!" So surprised to hear her voice, I almost shout the word.

"Christ Sally! I'm near suicidal. Sitting here, driving in the dark, assailing memories racking my brain, flaying my thoughts. It's too much. Where have you been? Just sitting there. Saying nothing for hours. Hours. Then abruptly, suddenly, you say, 'I'm hungry.' And that's it!" She ignores me. Then blurts out.

"Ben. You saved us. Saved me." Her toe digs at my zipper. "Snakes terrify me. You know that. I can't be near them. I can't. It's like they're elsewhere creatures."

"Elsewhere, meaning not from Texas. Not from Earth?"

She's back. Wife is back, shimmering, her luminescence, so pleasing to behold, fills me, expels the tangled horrors angling for my throat.

"Consider where we are in the universe," she says. "If there is a species more advanced than ours, they would likely be capable of entering our thought stream at any time, from any distance. And while they may have craft and means to defy gravity–proof of which is more abundant than proof of God–they would not need ships to come here to influence us. What we should be concerned with, is when they first entered our minds, how long ago, and whether or not the thoughts we're thinking now about them are their thoughts thinking about us. Watching us.

"Fucking snakes."

She loosens her belt. Stretches a hand over. Begins finger spooling hair on the back of my head. "I love you, Hubs."

"I know you do, Sal. And I love you, but Christ. You don't talk for hours. Dark hours. Then you pop back. With what? Fear of snakes, conjured by aliens watching us through our thoughts, living in our minds, toying with us. Maybe they are. Who knows? With how little conscious access we have to our brain, that some punk-ass alien juvenile may be getting in, mucking with the levers, pulling the strings. It's entirely possible. Why not? And it could be good, or not."

She unbuckles, throws her arms around me. Kisses and kisses me. Sits back. Sighs with relief. "Enough with the drugs and booze, Ben, and vegies. It's time for steak. A big-ass Texian steak."

"Yeah, a real breakfast."

"Breakfast of aliens."

"Do aliens eat?"

"I wonder."

"Do they pee?"

"I'll ask next time we talk.

"They talk?

"No, not really, they're well beyond language, religion, God, war, all the things that chain man to the human yoke."

"And jokes, are they beyond jokes?"

"I'll ask."

# FORTY FOUR

"Sally...."

"Ben, keep your eyes on the road. We're looking for meat. I'm looking. You're driving."

"The lights ahead, Sal. That's Abilene. We're maybe two hours from Glen Rose. Do you still want to go there?"

"Of course. Absolutely," she says, almost laughing. "The guy there, can't remember his name, he has what looks like a human footprint next to and partly overlapping a dinosaur footprint. One fossilized print claiming to speak for all fossils. One word in a book claiming to speak for the whole book. Easier to read one word than a whole book. People believe him, follow him..." suddenly serious, unexpected, she holds her fingers to her lips as if to prevent words from escaping. "Anything can be believed, Ben. Nazi style concentration camps in America. Blacks, Indians, Hispanics, Jews...locked up. Me for God's sake. Locked up. An end to interracial marriage, abortion, freedom of the press, free speech, travel, the right to vote. An America where only Trump approved businesses, laws, beliefs, education, news, relationships, and skin color, are allowed to prosper. Sabotage capitalism, communal spying, an unholy inquisition. It can happen, Ben. Will happen. If compromises are not made, the rule of law made to rule, the great American dream will fail."

Politics, when did Sally talk politics? Never. I thought, never. But she could, she just did. Damn. She could even be a politician. Imagine that. An albino president. Sally in charge. Why not. Madam President. Extraterrestrial Town Hall meetings, wings for all the children, pets in every pocket, free parking, an end to poisonous snakes, spiders, ticks, mosquitos, wasps.

"I hear you, Sal. Humans behaving badly. When do they not behave badly? How to live together without changing each other. Can we do it? And. If we can't…?"

We switch to B-20, drive through Abilene. Traffic. Hate traffic, stopping, starting, stopping, starting. Bumper talk, no interest in it. Row houses. Houses you find anywhere. People living in houses, watching TV, eating dinner. People who never talk about their parents. People who do. People who don't have parents. Houses in rows. Lives in rows.

"There! There! A steakhouse sign. We can make it. Take this next exit."

A big looping turn. Signals. Streets. A mall. Movies. Stuff to buy. People becoming people. We park, walk arm in arm, a cozy walk, enter the restaurant. Mostly a flat look, potted cactus on each side of the door, plastic trees, dark wood floors, no windows. A long glass case on our right, a crisp white tablecloth running its length. The case is filled with steaks beginning with a small one. Palm size. Then bigger, and bigger. Each steak has its own plate, an embossed card with gold trim detailing the weight and price just above it and a plastic cow next to it, highlighting where the cut came from. The cows get bigger as the steaks get bigger. They get bigger and bigger as you go down the display. At the end, sitting like Henry VIII, is a massive steak, huge, four pounds. No price. The sign reads, "Eat the whole thing. It's free."

Texas.

We eat. Drink. Laugh. Fall in love over and over again. Pay our bill and walk out. I hold the door open.

"Cactus." Sally, looks down, pulls me closer, pokes one of the pots with her toe. "What kind of company are cactus, what kind of friend? Daffodils, orchids, sunflowers, they're good company, friendly, one can see that, but cactuses? Cacti?"

We walk to the Jeep.

"Christ, Ben. That snake. It scared the hell out of me."

"Hell?"

"Yes. Hell. You know. Screaming sinners, lava flows, a red guy with a spiky tail and pitchfork smack talking God"

"OK. Then hell is otherworldly, like snakes?"

"No," she says. "It's too small."

"Small?"

She taps me on the head. "There, Ben. In there. That's where hell lives."

"OK." I think. And I think to think about it. Sometime. At some point. At some point I'll think about it. Or not.

# FORTY FIVE

Road trips. On the road. Off the road. That's what they are, on and off, stop and start, here and there. Anywhere on them we're coming or going. My 1998 Grand Cherokee. One of America's all-time best of the best 4x4s eating up the miles. Big V–8. Lousy gas mileage. Worth it. I named mine Jill. Guys. We do that. We name our cars, trucks, guns, dicks, whatever makes us feel capable, we give it a name.

Sally flips open the glovebox, keeps thumbing through directions on her phone, looks for candy, a stick of gum, a joint. Closes the glovebox, opens a box of raisins.

"Here! I've sorted the route." She's good at directions, most of the time. "We stay on B-20, pass Baird and Cisco. At Eastland, we could take 389, a big road. Or 570. There's not much difference in the scenery. Except for the lake, Lake Leon. A couple of small towns, then Stephenville."

"I've heard of Stephenville. The Amish. They have a community there, or near there. I think so. Amish aren't big in Texas. Have no interest whatever in the West Coast. Maybe the Rockies scare them. The Rockies and Sierras combined."

"Remember the Harrison Ford movie, *Witness*?"

"I do."

"I've wondered how accurate it was. If they really raise a barn in one day? We could go see them, Sal. Take a buggy ride, wave like royals to the rhythm of hooves clopping down on hard pavement. Maybe they'll talk to us, try and persuade us to live like them. Could be interesting, informative. Maybe their way of life is better, maybe we should join them, skip the Keys, embrace modesty, obedience, servitude. Remember the girl in the movie, she was bathing. Sponging herself down, I think it was a sponge. She gave Ford a welcoming breast shot. He struggled. She had great tits. And the Italian girl in *Godfather II*, Pacino's wife, her tits were straight up salutes. I'm definitely a tits man, Sal."

Sally jabs me. "I know you are."

We kiss.

"I'm good for a stop in Stephenville," I say, "Sure. We could learn something. The modest Amish. Maybe they screw through a hole in a sheet like the Satmars."

"Really? Satmars. They do that? A hole in the sheet. Can't see any fun in that."

"No, they don't. They never did. But they're big on modesty. As they define it, somatic pleasure is immodest, evil. Compliance, submission, and sacrifice are divine. Voiceless "unmarried" women pumping out population invasion babies – modesty slavery, an invasive rule driven cult hiding behind legitimate Semitic suffering. I don't like cults, Sal. Satmars…that's what they are, an authoritarian belief system laying the foundations of its own country; a state within the United States founded on religion only. I call them Hats. Uninformed block vote automatons isolated from reality (and the incidental "common" people around them) by Grand Rabbi dictates bloated with the power of suffocating archaic laws and rules. The power that binds their people to the rabbinical yoke. Man's yoke, not God's. Children taught what to think before learning how to think. I feel sorry for them, for us, for the loss of human potential inflicted by dogmatic overlords. Hats, a great loss, they have only the past to look forward to…a "chosen" life, robotic, isolated, unforgiving. Belief bondage. Slavery in America. It still exists."

"Hats, Ben? Isn't that like calling homosexuals fags?"

"No. It's not. Not at all. Hats don't like fags."

"Of course not." Again, she pokes me, but not for fun.

No rush to get to Glen Rose. I light a joint. Take a couple of hits. Pass it to Sally. Road trips. Long dates. That's what they are.

"OK, we'll try the Amish," I say. "See how deep they'll let us dive. All closed societies, the us–versus–them, cult types. They can be very addictive, trick you into believing the self-image they give you is better than the one you already have. The grand "chosen" self-image. That's what they sell, most of them, maybe all of them. The best way to be thinking, if you're in a cult, is how to get out."

She ignores me. I do as well. Memories, they pop up, whenever. Not much you can do with them.

"Here comes Cisco," Sally the tour guide. A lyrical voice. "There goes Cisco. Eastland up next."

We take exit 343 just past Eastland, pick up route 570 to Lake Leon.

"I could live in water, Ben. I feel like water, love water."

"I know you do."

She does. Sally loves water, she loves long distance swimming, both of us do and we're good at it. Perhaps, when I'm not watching, she transforms into an albino shapeshifter, runs back and forth between her human form and that of various cetaceans. Why not? In the water, she is a fish, an actual fish. A mermaid. A topless manatee with a good figure. A Siren calling out to shipwrecked sailors, merchant marines, virgins.

We pass a couple of Indians walking alongside the road. Beautifully fierce faces. Heavy walk. Slow. Deliberate. Forgotten. Cowboy hats. Boots. Worn denim shirts. Trousers. Shadows of a defeated nation. A lost world. Our world.

Highway 570. Southeast. Day's Inn. The Budget Host Inn. We pass them, stop at Exxon for gas. Lake Leon, up next.

# FORTY SIX

Rounded cupcake trees. Skinny trees. Little white flowers. Purple flowers. Double yellow lines. A country road. Still warm. Still hot. Too hot. Sweating. Not as much. Early evening…feels like midday. More trees. Bush. Few houses. Long driveways. Flocks of birds sorting a night's roost. Clouds changing colors, shapes, density.

"There's a lake," I say, "Lake Tanganyika in Africa. A big lake. They have fish there. Cichlids. The males collect shells. Make a mound as big as possible. Part of their mating game. Saw a documentary. One male cichlid steals shells from his neighbor, again and again. The neighbor is working so hard collecting shells he doesn't notice the guy ten feet away is robbing him when he's gone. The robber fish ends up with a bigger horde of shells, better odds of getting the girl. And he does. The thief gets the girl. Not sure why I told you that."

Sally brushes something off her shoulder, lifts her eyes, no comment.

"Cichlids in suits, Epstein, Trump. Guys like them. Maybe that. I saw a sign earlier. A big grinning man with a MRGA hat, a 'Make Russia Great Again,' vote Trump hat."

Despite open windows Sally's hot. She strips down, drapes a damp handkerchief over her breasts, parts of her shoulders. A lucky handkerchief.

"The lake, Ben. It was the mention of a lake. That's why you thought of the robber fish. We do that. We associate. A thought, an image, a sound, a stimulus of some kind strikes us and we associate to something we remember or imagine that helps us connect events together. That, and you don't like bad guys winning."

"Right," I take a hit. "Exactly. The bad guy's part, especially that. But who thinks of himself as the bad guy? I don't. Never have. Maybe I should."

"You're a lot of things, Hubs, but bad isn't one of them. Misbehaved, yes. At times you do misbehave, but you're not bad."

"Are you sure?"

"Yes. I'm sure."

"Why are you sure?"

"I have cousins."

"Cousins?"

"Relatives, data broadcast managers working behind the scenes, not just cousins. They keep me informed."

"They do? When? I've never seen them."

"They're not made to be seen, only heard. All I do is listen. Whenever I have a question, I listen. You know, a "those who have ears to hear," listen."

"That's all?"

"That's all."

Alien, she is, definitely.

And the "those who have eyes to see," part?

Route 570 is a friendly road. Welcoming. We connect to 2214 at the bend. Take 2214, head southeast. Lots of sky. Bleached telephone poles. Seventy miles an hour. An occasional mailbox. Cattle. The smell of cut grass. Dropping elevation. More mailboxes, clusters. Several attached together. Huddled like penguins in an arctic storm, flags bent out, twisted. Disfigured wings.

"And Ben...." Sally wags her legs. Pours water over her face. Floods the floor mat. The handkerchief, completely soaked, it clings to her, grabs hold like a suckling child. A great look. Better than a wet T-shirt. "I've been thinking about modeling," she continues. "Like you said before we left Paradise. I look young for my age, and I like showing off my body. With clothes, without clothes. I could model, like you said. And you. You look forty, act forty. You could model. We could model for Key's tourists and residents. Model nude, make sex tapes for the internet like that girl. The one that got her entire family a TV show.

People will follow us, Ben. For sure. They'll love us. Multiple streams of income. That's what we need. We're porn people. We know porn, the pleasure over pain industry, a vibrant industry. A never fails industry like drugs and alcohol. We can make it big, really big. But what I want most is to write. A diary maybe. A record of our adventures. Maybe a children's story. What do you think?"

What did I think? A children's story. All stories are children's stories. A search for meaning complete with demons running loose on dark windy nights, ghosts, witches, and goblins vying for story prominence, for a hand on the hand of fate. And good ferries, cute animals, magic potions…the healing allure of innocence doing all it can to sustain the illusion of goodness…of life never growing old.

"I can do it."

"You can, Sal, of course you can. It's a great idea. Have a look in the glovebox. Should be an old pad in there. At the bottom. Underneath the cards, the flashy ones from the Bellagio. And a pen, ought to be a pen as well, several pens. Maybe you should start with a title, a couple of first lines, and go from there."

"Right, "It was a dark and stormy night," she laughs, delighted and delightful. My heart overflowing, I can feel it. Sally, she's magic, that's all, pure magic."

Hot. We're almost to Lake Leon, a couple of miles. Sally sorts through the box, finds the pad, a pen, writes something, puts both back, slips on her mini bikini, keeps wagging her legs, holds the handkerchief out the window. It dries, instantly. Almost instantly.

Lots of almosts in life. Lots.

# FORTY SEVEN

"Lake Leon. Maybe it's a reservoir?"

Sally Googles it. Not the same as blunting it. Can't Google 'blunting.' Not its real meaning. Blunting is what you do to set up the next cockerel in the hen house romp, the next carrot and bunny joust. Google won't tell you that. But that's what it means, what we were doing, blunting it. Right there. The Texas countryside. Ranch Road 2214.

Sally begins reading off her phone. "Lake Leon. Location: On the Leon River in Eastland County, 68 miles east of Abilene and 10 miles south of Eastland. Surface area: 726 acres. Maximum depth: 55 feet. Impounded 1954."

"Impounded. What the fuck does that mean? How do you impound a lake? Take over its shores, surround it with barbed wire fences, make sure it can't escape. Terrible how lakes escape. When they do, they run around naked for years, scaring all the birds." Sometimes I like to sound like what I know is important. Probably normal to think that.

"Texas, Ben. It's Texas speak."

"Yeah. Must be."

The lake comes into view. A light blue spill reaching into the distance. We stop at the entrance to the public boat ramp. "NO GLASS CONTAINERS," written in big letters on the entrance sign. Beyond the sign, a dozen picnic spaces are cast between tree clusters. A few cars at the far end, a couple of trucks. Lake access. No one in the water. Lots of dead trees stippling the lake surface, gravestone trees, soldiers of another era leaving their armor behind.

We pull in. Park as close as we can to the lake's edge. An accommodating public facility. Very clean. No litter. No hippies.

Our arrival dust thins as it filters over the lake. We sit in the Jeep for ten, maybe fifteen minutes. Anticipation increasing, silently absorbing each other's breathing, our presence together. The want to touch, to run naked in the sun, to saturate our senses, flush life in all its glory down our open pores into the bloodstream. Never much for doing what other people do. Following. I don't like following. Don't like anyone telling me what to do. Can hardly tell myself what to do. I'm hot, inside, and out. Feel like a raging bull about to escape the ring. Bulging veins, tongue swollen. I wipe my forehead. Turn to gaze at Sally. To enthrall my eyes, satisfy lascivious poverty. No keeping a man from being a man.

"Damn Sally. You're so beautiful. I keep saying so, I know, but I keep seeing it. From every angle. How do you do that?"

"I'm not from here, remember," she laughs. Kicks up a leg, snaps her bikini bottom, opens the door, and jumps out, runs to the grass, bangs out some jumping jacks, cartwheels, squats, behaves like a three-year-old child, maybe five.

I pull off my shirt, pants. Slip on a pair of boxers, the poor man's swimsuit. Check the environment, every angle. Check for a shooter, thief, animal. Ears listening, eyes watching us...are they? A couple of people down by the boat ramp. Tiny people far away. No threat. No visible religion. No worries. Religion, the guilt market. Could we live without it? People doing and being as they wish without causing each other harm. What would that be like? Can't imagine it. Sally, she stands there. A Greek goddess carved from Egyptian alabaster, glistening like monument stone overlooking a deep sea and far horizon. She fills my eyes. I go to her, take her in my arms, carry her to the lake.

"You're strong for a little guy," she says, taunting me.

"Be nice." I taunt back, press my face into her belly. The warmth of it, baby making warmth. An unexpected sense of comfort.

"OK. But wash me."

"Wash you?"

"Yes! With soap and shampoo. Biodegradable shampoo. It won't hurt the environment."

Right. The environment. Hard to convince a guy sitting in a hot tub, girl on his arm, drink in hand and money in the bank that he has anything to do with some starving kid in the Congo, marine life choking on plastic, his fellow citizens dying from disease, falling through decaying bridges. More difficult to make things right than it is for one lowlife bully in the White House to fuck things up. I walk into the water. Think to drop her. A mean thought. Trump, his petty atavism, he does that to me. I turn and set her down on the beach. "I'll get the soap," I say. "The shampoo. A couple of towels."

My Johnny package, partly hanging out on the walk back from the Jeep, reminds me of a dog wagging its tongue to cool down, elephant ears flapping. It works, I feel a bit cooler, just a bit. Daylight dims slightly, thickens with warmer colors, drifting clouds. Sally is lying on her back, half in the water, half out, her feet making waves, splashing. The bright bits of blue cloth that make up her bikini, are magnified by her white skin. Look like they're going to leap right off her, begin matting with leaves, reflections, any wayward thoughts cast aloft by migrating butterflies. A happy girl. Gusts of warm air send ripples across the lake surface, tussle Sally's hair. I drop the blankets, toss the soap and shampoo on top of them.

"I have an idea."

Sally tilts her head. "Of course, you do."

"Let's race to the opposite shore. Looks like a half mile, maybe. Could be longer, probably is. Would be good. Some meaningful exercise to keep us in shape."

A porpoise with green eyes, eyes that see. She smiles. "A race. Great idea, Ben. Exercise will make us horny."

"Sal, we're always horny."

She laughs. Dives in.

I dive in.

Warm water. Gliding through warm water. Sally slows down. Swims alongside me. We time our strokes to look at each other when we take a breath. Perfect synchrony. That's our routine. How to be more together while together...we make a game of it. Doesn't take long to reach the far bank, lots of sand, the odd patch of grass. No people. We lie down. Light heaving. Air reaching deep, filling our lungs. It feels good. I roll my head to look at Sally. Gravity has no interest in her, I keep seeing that, no indentation in the sand. And she can be a fish when she wants to be a fish. She can, definitely.

Stranded on a desert island. We weren't, but it feels like it. A good time to die. How to control that? Must be a way. And how many 'good time to die' times are there in life?

After a light rest, we wade back out. A warm day, warm water. A slow wade. Once deep enough, we dive in, laugh excitedly, no one listening, race all out, lose our suits, keep racing, closer to the shore with every stroke. Closer and closer. We keep looking at each other between breaths, keep kicking, closer and closer to the shore. The shore. We look up. The shore is no longer empty. And we've lost our suits. A family. No, several families. Baby in a stroller. Couple of barking dogs. Two grills. Big, checkered blankets. Lots of food. Drinks. Orange sodas. Plastic bottles. Coke. Beer. Wine. Something harder. Litter...lots of potential litter. The closer we get the more we can see. Three cars, two trucks and another Jeep are parked next to Jill. A birthday party. Happy Birthday! written on all the balloons. Flashy balloons. Dogs notice us first. Bark louder. Everyone turns to look. All they can see is our heads. Fathers, grandfathers, wives, girlfriends, godmothers, bright kids, dumb kids, teens on their phones. Lots of kids. Dogs. Balloons. Grill smells. Laughter.

Too shallow to swim any further. We stand up. Everyone there—fat bellied adults, balding heads reflecting, sagging boobs stretching buttonholes, dismissive teens, summer faces, carnival stares, mouths swallowing, slurping. We feel them gasp. Oh, the horror of it all. Two naked bodies. More treacherous than a gun fight. Cover their eyes, protect the children, even the tit-sucking baby.

They all stare.

At that moment, looking at us is all they have in the world.

We walk out of the water. Deities of the lake. Aliens on the White House lawn. Don't bother to cover ourselves, make eye contact or say hello. Nothing. We just pick up our towels, soap, environmentally friendly shampoo, and walk through them, past all the protuberant eyes, protuberant mouths full of half-eaten food. The many flavors of surprise, horror, amusement. Calorie saving stares, surprise weight reduction gasping.

At my Jeep, I beep it open, we get in, toss our towels and toilet bags in the back, stare at each other, try hard not to laugh. Can't stop ourselves. We laugh. It's funny. Really. We keep laughing.

"Turn on the radio, Ben."

"Yeah."

I turn it on, back out, drive away.

Sally's biodegradable bath...it had to wait.

# FORTY EIGHT

Lake Leon is behind us. No sirens. No photos. No videos of the tall naked albino and the short old man. No internet stampede.... So far.

We drive on. Stephenville is close, thirty miles or so. I begin looking for a place to park. An overdue night stop, a rest stop. Drive past Desdemona. Shakespeare's Desdemona. Othello's wife, a Venetian stunner. Beautiful. Othello killed her. Killed himself. A very strange place to live. Could be. We pick up Farm Road 8 to Lingleville, drive past. Find a turnout. Few cars passing by. Seems like it. I pull over, stop. A wonderful night air envelopes us. Cars pass. Two more cars, then another.

"Lots of cars, Ben, not sure if I'll be able to sleep, if we'll be able to sleep. Too many lights."

"And car sounds."

"What should we do?"

Nothing.

We climb in the back. Still naked. Crawl under our black sheet, our black bedspread. Sex sleeping pills, take two an hour before bedtime, three if you don't plan to sleep.

Night rubber-stamping the dawn, signing receipts, paying bills. Nocturnal animals retreating into holes beneath the grass, tree holes, cracks in the rock. Fences struggling to stand erect. Cows. Mules. Old farms. Standing for hours on empty corners. Empty streets. Hitchhiking days. Hitchhiking Nights. Sleeping under freeway overpasses, behind bushes, on dividers, in open fields. I did that. It was all very normal. At the time, very normal.

# FORTY NINE

Dew, the remains of night. On the road, it's the first thing you smell in the morning. I like the smell, open my eyes. Remember *Witness*, the part when the bad guys come looking for Ford, backlit by an insipid pre-dawn light. They park at the top of a hill, the bad guys. Sort their guns in the trunk. Confident. Certain. Criminal. Rubber ducks. Toy heroes. Blow up dolls.

What's it like to wake up in the morning with established value? With being someone, with having something others value, value you don't have to fight for every day. What does that feel like?

Sally's still sleeping. She never snores. Few cars. Still dark under our sheet. I pull the sheet back. Just enough light to see the sky. Beautiful.

"Sally. Wake up. I just figured out how to stop global warming."

She moans softly, not really a moan, more like a vibration without sound.

Flashing lights. Colored lights. All around us, very bright.

"Christ! Now what?"

I sit up. Lights. A cop. He pulls in behind us. The windows are down. He walks up. Looks in.

"Good morning, sir."

A kid. Mid-twenties. Very proper. Nice face. Formal, relaxed.

"Yeah. Good morning," I speak slowly. Scratch my face, an itch under my nose.

"Just checking, sir. Need to make sure the Jeep isn't stolen. Been a long night. Some crazy behavior at Lake Leon." He doesn't sound Texan.

"Yeah? What happened?"

"Oh, just a brawl over some kid's phone. Two guys, best friends. One shot the other."

"Damn, what makes a phone that important?"

He shrugs, "Dunno. Phone was thrown in the lake."

I nod, a thankful nod. Sally stirs, slightly.

"Can I see your driver's license and registration?"

"Yeah, sure." I lean forward. Open the glovebox. Keep my bare ass covered. Take out the insurance, the registration folder. My wallet. "Here." I hand them to him. He stands there. Doesn't walk back to his car. Just stands there, sorting the data. Sees my sniper's badge. One Shot One Kill! Crossed rifles. Skull. Something of value. Maybe.

"I thought so," he says, and he laughs. A thick, a masculine laugh. Very friendly. A slight lisp on his s's. "I guessed you were from the North. I was right. I'm a Big Sur kid, born and bred, a coastal fog hound. That's what my brother calls me. Just moved to Stephenville. It's an OK place." He flips my license over. "You're from Paradise." I nod. "I've been to Paradise. My aunt kept a house there. It burned with the others. She died. Too old to run. Too old, period. Almost a hundred. Man, she loved the booze, loved it. Auntie Maze, an amazing woman, but too stubborn. Neighbors think she was drunk when the fire came. Maybe she was. My wife thought so. She's from here, a Stephenville native."

Startled, Sally sits up abruptly, stretches. Gives a full-on tit view to the cop. Her perfect female body. Her shoulders, breasts. The line of her jaw. The arch of her neck, smoothness of her skin. Hope we don't get arrested for nudity. A young cop, he stares, can't help himself, begins to melt. I'm sure of it. If I don't cover her immediately, he'll end up a little pool of goo on the road, very hard to explain.

"Sally. We have a visitor. This is…." I wait for him to say his name. Sally begins rubbing her eyes.

"What time is it?"

"I'm Deputy Steadman, ma'am." He points to his tag "It's six a.m., and ma'am, apologies for staring. I've never…."

"No worries, Deputy Steadman. Everyone stares."

Sally raises her hand. Waves at him. Throws the sheet over her head, lies back down.

"Maybe you can help us," I ask. "We'd like to visit the Amish community. Do you know where we can find them?"

"No. No, I don't. Sorry, sir, I'm too new. Might try the churches. Ask around. Someone will know." He hands me my papers, my license, runs his finger across the brim of his ten-gallon hat, maybe twenty-gallon, a big hat, very big. "Have a nice day."

He goes back to his car. Turns off his lights. Revs slightly, kicks up loose stones as he pulls out, drives by us, taillights flickering in the moist air. Tiny red suns setting in the distance. He's gone.

Fields all around us expand in the morning stillness, ripen with vacant moments. Grand, vacant moments.

We get dressed. Open a bottle, splash water on our faces. Empty our bladders, discreetly. Kiss. Eat a Mounds bar. Take a couple of hits. Finger-brush our teeth. Crank up the Jeep. Pull out, leave that space. That patch of space. Wonder, a thousand years ago, a million years ago, what was it that filled that space?

Nothing like Sally. That's for certain.

Space doesn't travel.

# FIFTY

"How are we to think about ourselves as we never have before? Is it even possible?" Sally rubs my cheek with the back of her hand. Heard what I said. The idea rolls around in her eyes, a little white ball circling the roulette table.

"Hubs. I have lady rituals to tend to, prime time calling, can use a shower as well. And you owe me a scrub."

"I do, definitely. And shampoo."

"Biodegradable."

"Right, biodegradable."

"There's a gas station coming up on our right, Alon. And there's a church on the left. First Presbyterian."

I pull in, stop at pump number 3, closest to the Minimart. Get out, stretch, yawn. Rub my eyes, blow my nose. Sally walks off. Quickly. Never want to come between Sally and prime time.

Sun feels good on my face. Around the world, how many faces have sun on them? No idea. I fill the Jeep. Middle grade. Add injection cleaner. Wash the windows. Think to light a joint. Don't. Pull over to the edge of the lot, away from other vehicles. Door dings, they're like the measles, like a disease, a plague. The door ding plague...it attacks when no one's looking, infects thousands of vehicles every day. Hate door dings.

In the Mini, Sally's at the counter, a big bag of chips in her arms. Two small boxes of Cheerios on the counter, milk, sliced meat, cottage cheese, soda, candy bars, raisins, some plastic cups. I go straight to the restroom. Clean for a gas station. No toilet paper. I carry some with me. A traveler's rule. Not sure which number.

Sally's waiting in the Jeep.

"I feel better, Hubs. Much better. And we have food. What do you want?"

I look. "A cup of Cheerios, slice of meat and a candy bar."

Christmas. Every day with Sally is an opening presents day.

"Here," she says, and she hands me the food. "Want a beer, a soda?"

"A beer, cold, if you have one."

She does. I take it, and the food. Road food, there's a flavor in it, a kind of illicit flavor like you're enjoying yourself too much over something average. Pets feel the same, especially dogs after they've had their faces in the wind, eyes watering.

Had a dog once. A German Shepard named Pound. Pound was a great dog. He played piano and whistled at girls when I asked him to. And he barked, mostly at squirrels.

"Thanks, Sal. I'll eat, then walk over to that church. Ask about the Amish."

"Right. Churches. I've checked, Ben. Stephenville is ground zero for churches. Over forty churches within thirty miles of town center, more or less. All with different names like Pony Creek Church, Cowboy Church of Erath, Riverside Baptist Church, Alive in Christ's Fellowship Church.

"Damn. Christ himself, what would he think? What would any non-believer think? Hollow rituals. Pedophile priests. The deceit of faith. Manipulative lies...Believing them doesn't make them true. A lot of tax exemption going on. Nothing Amish, though. You should ask. I'll wait here.

"With the cat."

"We don't have a cat."

# FIFTY ONE

The First Presbyterian Church of Stephenville, Texas. Early on a Thursday morning. Light in the sky is timid, hesitant to thin the blues. No one home. Doors are locked. Looks more like a storage facility, a center for senior bingo nights, cockroach races, ping-pong. Couple of wooden chairs along the outer wall. Not antique. Aged as if they were. An old bench. An old man sitting in one of the chairs. Crusty. Fragmented. Somber. Not sure if I like old men, nothing in them to look forward to. I walk up. Put out my hand.

"Hi. I'm Benjamin Mamott. My wife, myself, we've driven here. We're from Paradise, California. How are you today?"

He raises his head. Not that it was down. Looks at me, adjusts his gaze, tallies my pros and cons. Judges me average. Unexceptional. Safe. He shakes my hand

Guys meeting guys, even old ones, the first thing we want to know, is the guy we're meeting bent or not. First thing. Is a girl wearing a bra? Is a guy bent. We want to know. He's straight, white, but looks more brown than white. Tarnished, a tarnished look. Thick glasses. Face stubble, dry skin, bruised, sagging. Big scar down the right side of his jaw and neck. Swollen, a yellowish red tint. Sturdy gray shirt, frayed cuffs, faded black pants. Dirt under his fingernails, in the cracks in his hands. Dirt or dead skin. I can't tell. His shoes shine. A military polish, a military man. A magazine in his lap. Is he worth talking to?

"How old are you?" he asks.

"Sixty-four."

He winces. "Young. Very young. A pup. Where's home, where are you from?" He cups his ear to funnel the sound.

"California," I say. "Paradise, California."

"The fire?"

"Yes, sir," not sure why I said sir. "The Paradise fires. Not much left. We moved on." I take the other chair, sit down, remember my childhood Paradise. There were days, paradise days, welcoming days, hours in those days when my cousin Sophia and I played touch me here, touch me there games. Exciting games. Robust childhood games. *Lord of the Flies* equivalence, not at all. It was a time in life when fond memories outnumbered pitiless ones.

"Do you know if there are Amish people around here?" I ask.

Amish. He recognizes the word. Turns it over in his mind. A fisherman looking under rocks for hellgrammites. "Could be," he says, almost stutters, swallows hollow sounding air in gulps, fights to breathe. "There were some. In the 80's. Migrant Amish. I didn't like them. Nobody did. They came here, did odd jobs, mostly dairy work. Something of a community. They left, though. A few still here. Could be."

Have I met a man older than him? I can't remember. His hands shake. Glaucoma. Memory fading. A good thing. Maybe. Prosthetic leg. He had one. I can tell. I know guys. My brother, Anderson James Mamott. He served, paid dearly. Everybody pays.

The old man blurts abruptly, "World War Two. Atrocities. Nazi's." He pounds the words, spits them, shifts in his chair. "The killing. The fires. Lots of fires, flesh fires." His eyes, his look, it shifts, sinks. "I was there," he says. "I fought for my wife, Azura. My family. Came home, what was left of me. Got old. You see son, see what I am? This was a man."

He makes me look him over.

"What remains of a man."

"Still a man," I say.

He straightens up, an inner command. "I'm alone," he says, slowly, flatly. "Every morning I come to this Church and sit in this chair. I watch people, the cars I can't buy, will never ride in. The changing streetlights, the flag waving, saluting, dying. Dying is what I live for. Nothing to believe in anymore."

He's right. A long slow river sliding toward the sea, gradually falling. America abandoning its greatness.

"I fought, I killed. I killed men I didn't know, men who didn't know me. No one remembers the killing. Feels it when they go out to the movies, sit down for dinner, smile at themselves in the mirror."

I struggle to hear, lean toward him.

"Couldn't save the family...family meals, values, generational wealth, shared benefits. No one could." He slumps over. Tilts. Has trouble breathing.

I reach for the magazine, fan him, pick up the bottle next to him. Offer him a drink. Rum. Smells like rum. He drinks, inhales, sits up, continues.

"We beat Hitler, the Japs, Mussolini. Came home, got married, made babies, backbone families. Didn't matter, all of it, all of us. 'The Greatest Generation.' So what?"

Time to walk away. Felt like it. I want to. Can't move. Broken men. Broken people, there are too many of them. Too many like me, like him. A slight wind comes up. Stars and Stripes and the Texas State flag catch some air, smack the rope against the wood flagpole in front of the church.

I look at the man. He's crying.

"Shot in the head," he says, his tone sagging, thickening. "The bullet took off a big chunk of his face, the side of his head. I was standing next to him. Jason Benjamin." He looks up, a sudden small light in his eyes. "Benjamin. Like your name. Everyone called him Ben. We went through boot camp together. Ben was a happy man, big, never without a smile." He tries to spit. Mouth is too dry. "Like today, it was hot. Our platoon stopped at the edge of a small French town. Landscape looked painted, like drying paint. Didn't hear it. The shot. Nothing. Ben turned toward me. The left side of his face was gone. All of it. He fell over. Dead. On the road, a nowhere road, his smile seeping into the dirt."

Silence, blood silence, terrible images taking shape in my mind.

"So many," he struggles to keep erect. "They died on land that was not their own. They died. We died. With every death we died a little more, became less of who we are, but we kept fighting. Little Boy and Fat Man finished the job. Bigger bombs. We had bigger bombs."

He takes the bottle. Heaves down deep swallows.

"But…." He holds the word in his mind, waits. "What we left you—everyone who came after our Greatest Generation," He coughs. Congested. Wipes his mouth. "We left you, gave you the illusion that freedom is secure. Secure. Freedom is never secure." Again, he coughs.

I stand, begin to walk away. Not sure why.

"Sonny, wait."

He didn't shout, didn't even raise his voice, sounded like he did. I turn around, sit down again.

"The illusion," he threw the word. "Confidence in the illusion made people careless, greedy, self-absorbed. Turned families to ruin, devalued marriage, guiding institutions, freedom. That's what we brought home. A lesser future. We were not 'The Greatest.' Not even great. No. In the end, we survived, lived long enough to watch our victory die in the hands of those we fought for. A mockery of purpose, that's what we fought for, died for."

I want to interrupt him. To make him stop. Old wounds still festering; hidden crevasses in the chest splitting the heart, they were calling, screaming. Sally. Where is she? What is she doing? What am I doing?

Every species has a blind spot. Something about themselves they can't see that becomes the cause of their extinction. People have blind spots. Groups have them. Families have them. Old men have them.

He stops talking. Sags.

Two men sitting. That's all we are. No words. Just watching. Watching time eat away the day, the moment, our lives.

"Son. I'm old. Don't listen to me. No one cares what I think. Never did. Even when I was young."

Ancient trees, riverbeds, old men, old women. We see them, know they exist, know we have more to learn from them. No interest in learning, no time. The old man. Older than ninety. Had to be. Shaky hands, thick glasses, glaucoma, prosthetic leg, forgetting himself, no name. The last real Republican. He could be.

"'If men repeat often enough their hatred the evil comes to pass.'"

I stand up. Think so. I'm no longer sitting. The old man doesn't look up. Child of a deceased mother, barren memories, hope adrift on a bottomless sea. The greatest generation. They were. Still are. Clouds cross overhead, dimming the sun. A shadow over the land. One party government, it can happen. I stand there, listening. Thinking. Will we make it? I want to crawl inside myself, weather the uncertainty in my absence.

Sally. Children. Raising children, our shop, a home.

Better planning.

We need better planning.

# FIFTY TWO

I walk back to the Jeep. Feel disconnected. Utterly.

The man, his story, how he sees the world. It's real for him. He made it real for me, his world, not mine. But I am in it, can't separate from it, from the smells war etches into sense memory, the putrid failure of lives. Nam. It never stops being real. Each step feels like progress going nowhere. Boots on the beach, enemy fire, nowhere to hide. I cross the road. Cross the double yellow line. Step over an uneven row of plants, walk across the grass, hear the worms moving under my feet, feel them fear me, the weight of my footsteps. Life, her rules, not ours.

A warm breeze. I imagine myself in a faraway place. Not a vision but like a vision. Sally in my arms, a pair of swans drifting on some idle air. I imagine a world without me in it. Feels no different from the one I'm in.

Sally sees me. Waves. Paws the air like a cat. A relief to see her.

I open the door. She grins. Wide. Blows me a kiss.

The Alon parking lot. Stephenville, Texas. Clouds. They're growing, crowding the sky. Doesn't matter.

"You know, Sal, earlier. What I started to say. The warmer it gets, the less need we'll have for clothes."

"I don't remember."

"No?"

"No. You may have said it, said something about it. I don't remember."

"But you're young. Young people remember everything."

"Younger than you is not young, Ben. Mind if I put on some music?"

"Sure."

"Sure, you mind or sure it's, OK?"

"Sure, it's OK."

She pokes me, likes poking me, laughs, begins flipping through stations.

"Lots of preaching stations."

"Texas."

"Lots of followers, the Uncreatives; people fearful of exclusion damnation. Learning to follow before learning to think. Don't need a human brain for that."

"Texas."

"Right."

"And Florida."

"Right, Florida, but not Key West."

"Right, not Key West."

She sits back. Uses her toe to turn the dials, picks up BB King.

The old man. How to pull my mind away from him? And why did he talk to me anyway? His last words, were they? The last to be remembered. Maybe. BB King, "The Thrill is Gone." I listen, smile inside, turn to Sally.

"Longer, warmer days, Sal. Global warming. Here's my thought. All that's required to make clothes and the sale of clothes. That need will decline the hotter it gets. Clothes will become cheaper, unnecessary. Underwear sales. No one will wear underwear. Heavy jackets. No one will need them. We'll save money on clothes, maybe enough to need them again. It's all over, Sal. There's no backing up. We're not going to stop global warming. It's not in our nature to stop it. We're ego-addicted, anti-enlightenment-oriented creatures. Parasitic consumers, takers. Better to plan for surviving our failure than trying to correct it."

"Damn, Ben. Hubs. That church. What happened to you? Why so grim?"

She smiles, a whimsical invitation. "I can cheer you up. If you want. Should I?"

The cichlid thief. Changing the rules, being changed by them. The old man. Tell her? I want to forget him. Why? Self-portraits–people we relate to, people we hate, love, fear, envy–concealing what we see of ourselves in them... was I doing that?

175

# FIFTY THREE

Pliers. Screwdriver. Hammer. The tool trinity. Used to be we could fix anything with the trinity. And WD-40. Not anymore. The big three died. Computers were born. Need to fix my Jeep's hood release latch. The passenger door needs oil, the radio clock works intermittently, Jill is getting old. Wear. Is wear the same as aging?

Cars passing. Mid-morning breeze squeezing through the windows. Sally rolls to her back. Sticks her feet out the window. Toes the air. Beautiful, sensual toeing.

I sit up. Drop my arms over the steering wheel. Check the time. Ignite the engine. Big V8 kicks in. The roar. A controlled brawl. Dragons, bulls, big-ass bears. Acoustic muscle. A working sound. A sound that can take you anywhere. I can feel it, even in my bones.

"At the church." I try to talk. Can't. No energy to harm myself. Too relaxed. Feel like going to sleep. Too early. A full day ahead.

"Yes?" Sally sits up.

"At the church," I say, "I talked to an old guy. A World War II vet. Asked about the Amish. He said we could check around, but he thought they were gone. Weren't many of them to begin with, he said. I think we should move on to Glen Rose. Take a hotel. Get drunk. Stoned. Watch some porn, 69 the dinosaur walk."

"You do, do you?" She likes the idea. "Need directions?"

"Yeah. Guide on."

The corner gas station, the church. An old man. All old men. The old men we're going to become. The old women we're going to become. No old children, old babies, old tweens, old teens. Men and women. Only they get old. And my Jeep.

I pull out, turn right. Red light. Stop. A long red light. Wait. Insects. A grasshopper clinging to my wiper. Long spiky legs. Flat wings. Bulging abdomen, spiky mouth. Why did insects have to be so creepy? Puppy insects. Kitten insects. Koala insects. Why not? Could have gone that way.

Little red lights in the desert. Red light districts. Good red lights, bad red lights. Good red lights people think are bad. Bad red lights people think are good. Dessert red lights are more like lighthouses. A lot of lighthouses in Nevada, Bangkok, Amsterdam.

Finally green.

We drive on.

*On The Road Again*. Willie Nelson. Every time those four words come together in my mind, I hear Willie Nelson singing them. Maybe everyone does. Everyone old enough. Willy Nelson. John McEnroe, Princess Di, Mandela. Who we grow up with – they become a part of us. The Beatles, the Stones, the Dead, I can feel them bouncing around inside my head. And Coke, and Pepsi, they're there. I can feel them as well, and Fig Newton fig bars, wheat thin crackers, the forest, and horses, and Nixon…and Trump. Trump, the lying fuck. Which part of me was he? I try to think. The scared little boy looking up his mommy's skirt for cookies part? Not him. The draft dodger fearful of a real fight; the honesty of real men. Not him, definitely not. The big man, the bully, the narcissist con. Nope. The petty insecure whiner desperate for attention? I didn't have that part either.

# FIFTY FOUR

"Ben. A change coming up."

"Yeah. That's what Black folks have been waiting for. Sam Cooke said it would come. Still waiting. A wait too long."

"About a mile. Might be more than a mile. More like two miles. We stay on 67. 67 all the way to Glen Rose. Not that far. Then we take 205 to Dinosaur Valley. Amazing.

She almost laughs. "Imagine, Ben. Dinosaurs used to walk here. Giant creatures. Where we are, they were. And what came before them? You have to wonder. And what comes after us? Footprints in the sand. The next chapter. The next giant leap for mankind. Will it be the Electro-Sapiens – an electric version of man's bio-electric self? Something human that leaves no tracks? That's my guess."

I like it when Sally talks like that. The way her lips move, the way she forms words from her thoughts. I can almost see how she does it, smell it. She's smart. Never worries about convention. Never burps. All those, not albino things, she doesn't do them.

We find a place. Glen Rose Inn and Suites. Reminds me of places I never want to go back to. Pool. No one in it. A midnight swim? Maybe. Clean enough. We never do fancy hotels, fancy anything. Don't have the money for fancy. We do clean. When clean is clean, more money can't make it cleaner. We check in. Take a big double. A ground floor room. Drop off our bags. Walk over to the restaurant. Big Cup something. Cup. I think breast size. What else are cups for?

We take a table by the window. Prefer the window. Order lunch. I have a Big Cup burger. Want a steak and potatoes, lots of garlic, butter, and a beer. Have the beer. Sally chose a club sandwich and milk. Food. My primary interest in it…don't feel hungry after eating. That's it. Flavor was optional. Usually. After lunch we drove toward the river. The state park. After the park, the Creation Evidence Museum. That was the plan, and we were on our way. It changed when Sally saw a Creation Evidence Museum sign saying, "I SAW JESUS IN GLEN ROSE."

"Stop, Ben! Stop!"

"What!" I jam on the brakes.

"Let me out! I just saw Jesus."

"What?!"

She throws open the door. Falls out, scrambles over to the museum's white stone entryway, gets on her knees and begins to pray.

"Sally, What the fuck!" I walk over. "What are you doing? People are going to notice."

"Jesus. I just saw him. Look. There! See. Right in front of the museum. Right there. The light of lights."

"What? I don't see shit."

"No? Neither do I."

She laughs. Gets up. Gives me a hug. A wet hug. "I don't. You don't. But a lot of people walking through those doors over there, they do. They see Jesus in Glen Rose. His footprints are right there, next to the dinosaurs. He was here earlier, to save the dinosaurs, to save dinosaur souls. The Christ we got, our Jesus, he was the second coming.

"Maybe there's a third."

Church. Fuck. It wasn't Christ's idea. 'Do unto others as you would have them do unto you.' That was good. The instruction to look past what offends us to something higher, something of greater value…that's good. Making people pay and pray to be good. Jesus didn't do that. For sure he didn't. Ask Sally.

Entrance gate is open. We drive in. Unfinished driveway. A working parking lot. Clean, not tidy. Find a corner spot. Few cars. A slow day. We get out, sit down on the grass in front of the Jeep. Sally takes out a candy bar, raisins. A new box. The museum. A decent enough building. Lots of windows.

"We're not welcome here, Ben."

"I know."

"Then why go in? Remember that diner family?"

"I do. I remember. Actors, they were making a porn flick. I talked to them after you left. Not a real family. Lots of money in porn. Why would they come here, those people? Bother to tell anyone about us?"

Sally exhales dramatically, sweeps the air with her arms. "They're exactly the kind of people who might come here. Dinosaur porn, Ben. Maybe aliens lent them a camera. The dinosaurs. A long time ago, of course. Fossil pornography. Imagine that."

"Yeah, right. The porn market, it might be older than we think. But you're right. Nothing in that building would convince us that humans walked next to dinosaurs on muddy riverbeds with God gazing down at what he made, thinking, 'It is very good.' We know that. Anyone in the museum would know that about us. And it's six bucks a head to go in."

I begin digging a hole in the grass with my boot heel. (It's a boots day.) A laid-back day. Sun is out. Feels good.

"Ben, people who believe this fairytale, how do they imagine the man-dinosaur thing went down, living day to day with big animals with big teeth. How did that work exactly? Man for breakfast, lunch, and dinner?"

"People believe whatever they want, Sal. You've said it before. It doesn't matter, what they believe. How they behave, that's what matters. A lot of power in getting people to believe a lie. Any lie."

Sally gets up. Stands over me.

"Man lives with dinosaurs," she says, blocking the sun. "Dinosaurs go extinct. Man lives on. And on, and on, and on."

"And...."

"Nothing, Ben. Man lives on until he doesn't. Energy into matter, matter into energy, nothing defined.

"The end."

We leave.

# FIFTY FIVE

Park Road 59. A pleasant drive. Dinosaur valley. Lots of bugs hitting my window. Need more window-washing fluid.

"I like your Jeep Ben. Have I ever told you that?"

Sally. My wife, Mrs. Sal. The sound of her voice. How does it still sound new after hearing it so many times?

"Maybe. Maybe you told me. I can't remember. You did tell me to sell it."

"I did. Yes. Glad you didn't. Do you think I'm pregnant?"

"You don't look pregnant. You look…" I glance over. "Wet."

She leans forward, a thin, sleeveless T-shirt barely covering her.

"Well, hubs…surprise, surprise. You're going to be a father."

*Father!* "But how do you know that, Sal?"

"Albino, Ben. It's an albino thing. A female albino thing. For thousands of years, long before the pregnancy test, we engineered and installed the gestation koala. It's a tiny grain size organ lodged in the pineal gland, something of a pregnancy third eye, very unusual but normal for albino women. I have one. That's how I know."

"I see…OK." Teasing an old man. "And the babies eye color?"

"Green," she says, poking me. "Radiant green."

We arrive at the park. Dinosaur Valley State Park. Typical park entry. Park format. A good format. America has great parks. Magnificent parks. Glacier, Yosemite, Zion, Niagara Falls, Grand Canyon, Yellowstone. Great parks. Standard brown and yellow park signs. Very orderly. Well laid out. Lots of hiking trails. We grab a map. Try several roads. Follow signs to the Blue Trail. A good place to park. Empty parking lot. Smells warm. A forest smell. The usual small trees, shrub, grasses. The woods. I dial in, feel at home. All the silent, listening trees living their stories. The grand, passive awareness of every leaf, branch, stone, flower, blade of grass. Trees, vegetation becoming human, absorbing human DNA through urine, excrement, decaying bodies. I give way. Relax. Feel, for a moment, as a weightless reflection of myself shimmering on a still pond. Imagine Sally feels like that all the time.

"Ben, let's pitch the tent. Skip the inn, pick up our bags on the way out. Look! It's beautiful here. All the trails. The river. Blue sky. Let's camp."

Blunting it. That's what we're doing. Camping blunting. Lining up our next lascivious romp. Someplace new, something we haven't done before. Sex warriors, pleasure thieves, Bonnie and Clyde with a more salacious nature. That's us, who we are...fuck here, fuck there, fuck anywhere Bonnie and Clyde.

Snakes. Snake tracks. I check, don't see any.

We get out. "Let's try the river first. See where we are."

Sally grabs my ass. Pinches me. "Race!" She takes off. I watch. Mesmerized.

What makes Sally, Sally? I have no idea, but her effect on me is incessant. I never tire of listening to her, looking at her, of feeling no need to escape her presence. In the shower, asleep in bed, across from me in the Jeep, at meals, next to me in movie theaters, on top of me when she takes control. Even when she evaporates, her whiteness causing her to lose all distinction in the glare of the sun, she captivates, endlessly captivates.

I follow her. Run along the river trail. The great outdoors, being outside. I love being outside. Living in an open window. The river, water sounds, bird sounds, forest sounds. Dinosaurs must have loved it, too. Not the ones that got eaten, the rest of them. And all the people. And Jesus.

The trail leads to a sand bar at the river's bend. A large, bleached stretch of sand and rock. Warm under foot. We walk it, look up and down the river. Look for people. No one around. An invitation moment.

Smoke.

"Sally...."

She ignores me, lies down in the water, spreads her legs, her arms. Makes a water angel, splashes, a fish thing. Lots of Sally fish things.

"Sally. I smell smoke."

She sits up, hair dripping, her wet translucent skin reflecting the blue sky.

"I smell it too."

We look, kept looking as we cross the river. Warm water. Not too deep. The smell is growing stronger. Just above the rocks opposite us. Light puffs of smoke. We climb the rocks. Slip. Bushes scratch us. A fire on the trail. It's just started. A cigarette filter at the trails edge is still burning. We put it out, grab handfuls of sand and dirt. Throw them on the fire. Isn't enough. It keeps burning. We take off our clothes. Use them to beat the fire. Sally climbs back down. Gets hers wet. Her sweats. Her shirt. Throws them to me. I wring them out over the fire. Kick dirt, slap the flames, throw them back. Back and forth. We're winning. Two kids walk up. Twenty-somethings. What they think. Two naked people. An albino. An old dude. They stare.

"Help," I shout. "For Christ's sake!"

They drop their daypacks, begin kicking dirt and soil on the flames, the embers. Very expensive hiking shoes, sunglasses, fancy running suits. Lots of dust. Sally's getting glances. From both of them. I get a couple from the girl. Feels good to have her eye me, still strong, flexible, tanned. I like the attention. Sally notices, smiles. Throws me wet sweats. My sweats. I wring them out over the fire next to the girl. Stand close to her. The guy takes off his shirt. Beats down flames trying to climb the bush. We work together. Up and down the bank. Mud. Dust. Sweat. Cuts and scratches, dried blood.

The fire. We beat it. Whiffs of indifferent smoke twist into vacant air, a final breath, a parting signature. About ten to twenty feet of charred ground. No rangers. No surprise. Paradise following us. The cigarette that started the fire has lipstick on it. I hand it to the guy to put in his pocket.

"I'm Ben," I say, and I point to Sally. "That's my wife, Sally."

He put out his hand. "I'm James, she's Amy."

His girl. She's attractive. Lively facial expressions, smooth skin, wide succulent lips painted the color of the lipstick on the cigarette butt. Careless kids, possibly. Her blue eyes, I can feel them hiding, questioning. Black hair, thick and young. Amy. Family money. She has that look. That heedless to consequence I can afford it look.

James is lean, an athlete. The girly ponytail look. Neither one has tattoos, no never-nude-again barcodes, not that I can see. We take one last check of the fire, slide down the bank to the river and into the water. No judgement. No soap. We wash anyway, as best we can, the char, grime, and dried blood. Amy and James: The kids. I think of them as kids. They strip down as well. We search for deeper water, find a clear pool. I take Sally in my arms. James takes Amy. Summer love. Summer in love. Can seasons love?

We blunt it, take leave of our wants right there in the Valley River. The four of us, no dinosaur interruptions, no screaming people running for caves. The mind, it can imagine anything. God, Satan, elves, hobbits, flying reindeer, angels dancing on the head of a pin, peace on earth, ancient rituals to ward off dinosaurs. Dinosaur tracks…we forgot them. Forgot to look for them.

# FIFTY SIX

James and Amy walk with us back to the Jeep. We put on fresh clothes, offer them a beer, a hit, a glass of wine, remember but don't focus on what everyone looks like nude. Difficult.

Amy takes Sally's hand, first cousins, inmates, friends from long ago newly reacquainted.

"You guys want to go to a party?"

"Party!"

"A strip blackjack party," she says. "My friend's house. We can hike to it from here. A big house. Pool in back. Small group of people, mostly girls."

Florida. A little more than halfway there. Key West breezes. Comforting shade. An answer to life's relentless absurdities. Not yet.

"Sure."

An easy decision. I lock the Jeep. We cross the river. Look for dinosaurs. Pick up a trail. Amy takes the lead. James, then Sally. I'm last.

Following the one ahead. Always a line of some kind. A post office line, unemployment line, DMV line, doctor's office, grocery store, airport line, movie, or theater line, hiking up a hill line. Someone ahead, someone behind. Always someone ahead, someone behind.

A meaningful hike, several miles. An hour or two before sunset. Two guys come from the opposite direction. Big guys. Backpacks, serious hiking boots. Brim hats. Safari. New. They're moving fast. We step aside. They pass us, glance, linger. Amy. Sally. However exceptional they appear at gatherings, social events, parties...on the trail, cast against the darkening woods, their amatory appeal can't be missed.

The two guys stop, turn around. One shouts. "Wait! Stop! What would it take? The price. How much to do the girls?"

We stop. Amy rushes forward. Pushes past me. Begins yelling.

"Andrew Jason Smith. You piece of shit. Billy Anderson. Fuck you! Think of me like that? Talk to me like that? Ever do it again? Even *think* it and I'll have your jobs, your cars, your trust funds, your lives." She turns back to us, yells over her shoulder.

"Fuck you! Fuck you both!

I like her.

The two guys stand there. Shocked. Scared. Unfazed. What? Did they fail to recognize her? Can't tell. Don't care. We continue on. Less than an hour of light left.

When we look into the night, into the blindness of time. What we can't see is the future. We can't see ourselves in the future. That's what scares us, not the dark.

"Come on, folks. Keep up."

"We are, Amy, we're right behind you."

Walking in the woods, being in the woods, the daunting calm of slow-growing trees, it feels like skin to me, what it's like to be in my own body, a bigger body. Mountains, I am one, a mountain I keep climbing, never reaching the top.

Trails. I prefer trails to roads.

No trails, to trails.

# FIFTY SEVEN

A big house. Really big. Forty thousand square feet at least. Six car garage. New barn. Stables. Training grounds. Lots of white fences. A pool. Looks like a big pond, waterside plants, fish, a wooden raft floating in the center. Chairs all over. Umbrellas. Lots of places to sit. Lots of booze. Amy knows everyone, introduces us to her 'favorites,' as we walk through the house. House tourists. Worldwide, everywhere, people walking through other people's houses. Tourists, that's what they do.

A guy, mid-thirties, probably, big smile, lots of teeth, energetic, bright orange hair, he takes the mic. Taps on it. They always do that, people who start things, they tap on the mic. Wasn't a stage, where he was. Just a space above the pool, chairs moved aside, tables, small potted trees. He taps the mic, again. We look. Everyone looks.

"Folks. One and all. I'm Andy. Chief Happy Hour on the rocks. Mr. Fag to the initiated; confederates with elastic minds. And, as you know, my parents, the generous overlords of this Texian castle, are away to the land of milk and honey, for a month. A whole fucking month, and tonight, tonight is pin the donkey on the tail strip night!"

He's a little old to be living at home. I think so. Some guys never leave home, never marry. Not sure why. Odd. It's odd, that's all. Big applause, cheering, a joyous calamity and laughter. Could be getting his age wrong. Probably getting it wrong.

"Who wishes to play Strip Blackjack?" He says, and he hums into the mic, reminds me of San Jose de la Laguna Mission, the clerk, the bible, the cat. "Players, raise your hands!"

Most of the girls raise their hands, a couple of guys. The rest of us watch. If Sally plays, she'll win. She's good with numbers, cards talk to her, everything talks to her – the house, the just-cut lawns, the forest edge hunched on its furless legs watching us, its roots sensing our music, our dancing, our heartbeat, our thoughts. I get a beer. One for Sally. She takes it, turns to walk off with the others. She's going to play.

"Sa-al," I coo. "The guy, Andy, did you hear? He said 'fag.' He likes saying it."

She stops, looks at me. Those never-ending green eyes. One could fall into them so easily. A green hole, the female half of a black hole. I hover at its edge waiting to fall in or pull away.

"You're right, Ben. He does like it."

Spectator chairs are arranged. Tables set. Everyone has a good view. Bets are taken. I put fifty on Sally. Each player who loses, after removing his or her last item of clothing, has to pick some guy (there aren't many of us) or girl, swim to the raft and engage, with full abandon, in whatever impious exertion they can conjure until the next player to lose replaces them. The winner, at the end of it all, has to strip on the raft to Joe Cocker's song, "You Can Leave Your Hat On." No donkey mention.

Andy begins the countdown. "Tell me girls, boys, who am I?" Everyone shouts. "Mr. Fag!"

"That's right, you know it. And ten... nine...eight...seven..."

Two dealers standing back-to-back facing half-circle blackjack tables, not the pro version but nice enough, ready themselves to deal the first card. Both are tall, Nordic-looking blonde girls, naked but for a little yellow happy face covering their hairless nests. Eight seats at each table, seven girls, one guy. The excitement. The thrill. The nudity of it all.

"Six...five...four...three...two ...and one!"

The game begins. Nice looking girls, all of them. Eights, nines, several tens. And Sally. No number big enough. Couple of guys. Good student looking guys. What money can buy—first class seats, a daily massage, expensive wine, other people, votes, parties, parties without rules, parties immune to judgement.

Both tables, the cards go down, bets are placed. Players bet with their clothes. Sally takes off her top. Tits out right away. Bang out. Only two pieces of clothing. Shoes are left at the door. A clean party. Silk carpets, Kashmir greens and golds. No empty glasses, bottles, or napkins lying around. No house litter. Two maids keep it clean. Very busy maids. Attention focuses on Sally's pliable albino looks, her long legs, firm thighs, belly, her happy breasts, chatty nipples. She loves being naked. Other players take off shirts, a belt, earrings, a skirt. After each set, items bet by those who lost the round are removed from the table. Winners' items remain with the player to decide to put the item back on or leave them for the next round.

A second card set is dealt. Two players (one at each table) split their hands. One has two eights, a spade, and a club. The other two sevens, hearts, and spades. A good bet. They hit those pairs. Everyone hits, too many times. Sally. Sally holds, takes no cards. She wins. Three other girls win. The rest lose.

Sally puts her top back on, her sleeveless T-shirt.

Oh, the nudity of it all. The roaring nudity of fact. How do we live without it?

A few more rounds. The cards are shuffled. Drinks poured, joints and hookahs lit, Nepalese hash. Lines of coke appear. Never tried coke. No interest in trying it. Sally's barely drinking. Thinks she's pregnant.

Couple of people wade into the pond, go swimming. Not exactly swimming, something like swimming. A hot night. Just under a100 degrees. Dry.

With every deal, the dealers change places. Bets are placed. A couple of bras, several shorts, a shoe, hat, pair of pants, blouses. More flesh. Beautiful girls. I like it. All the skin, all the drinking, all the laughing girls playing with each other, teasing the guys, joking with the dealers. The smoking, snorting, blunting, wonderland of wealth. I like it.

The second card is dealt. Everyone but Sally overplays their hand.

"Time for the raft!"

Applause. The first loser, a happy loser. She jumps up, waves her arms.

Andy hurries back to the mic.

"Everyone, for those who don't know, this is Yuliya, our previous Strip Night winner. Yuliya dear, remember last time, we coated the raft in warm chocolate. Remember?"

"Yes," she shouts, and others shout, "Chocolate! Chocolate!"

"Not tonight, kids. Tonight, we're doing honey and butter. Lucky losers get to play in it, ramp up the romp, the warm honey and butter Mr. Fag romp!"

Applause. Shouts of joyful anticipation, big spoons stirring the loins, preparing participants for a sex sunrise.

Andy knows his people. They know him. Yuliya is designated the evening's first swimmer. She leaves the table. Very cute, peach colored skin, white peach, long flirting curls, blond. She walks around. Inspects the goods, checks out available guys, available girls, who is most ready to make her night. Decisions, decisions, thoughts waiting in line. Thoughts ahead, thoughts behind.

I want in, a romp in warm honey and butter, but with Sally. I glance over, catch her eye. She looks at me, smiles, wants me in the game. How? I wait with the others. Yuliya is in no hurry to find her fun. One after the other she pokes and pulls at each contestant and observer. Pauses to listen to the music wagging in our ears, to watch the lights strobing the permeable air, the secrets of our place in destiny flowing by without notice, we're hot, barely dressed, the night still young.

Yuliya stops in front of me, looks up and down my not so lofty frame, a smile begins to drift across her face, she steps away, then back. A full-on smile. She picks me.

A swim to the raft with Yuliya....

Cool.

Glad I know how to swim.

# FIFTY EIGHT

One a.m., maybe two.

Sally in my arms, we fell asleep on a big sofa in some corner room of the house, not that quiet. Wake up disheveled and happy, refreshed. New experiences do that, they widen the river we swim in, expand sense reality. And some, the most memorable, so enrich self-worth, that we use them to our craft our visible nature; to define who we are, who we think we are. Not sure if I'm doing that, but I think so. It's two a.m., a little after. A morning to reflect on a night to remember. Time to go. Time to find Andy. Always have to thank the host. He's sitting by the pond. Fishing.

"Any luck?"

"I'm always lucky," he says, and he holds up a stringer, three trout, cavern eyes staring. "I keep the pond stocked."

"A good idea, "I say, "and Andy, the games, the last act. The Cocker bit. Any chance you shot some video? I can't remember it, but I remember liking it...if that makes sense?"

"No, buddy, sorry, no video. Leave your address with Amy. If anything comes up, she'll sort you out." He turns to Sally. "You are stunning, woman. You have 'climax leverage,' the King James edition. If everyone could see you, just see you. All the eyes in the world, if they could see you, desire for anything else would come to a stop."

He cast again, looks back at Sally. "Where are you from? What world?"

"I'm not from Texas," she says. He nods.

"And you?"

"Paradise, California. Cinder town. And Tahoe. Spent a lot of time at Tahoe, and years out of the country."

Andy is older than many of his guests. Late twenties, early thirties. And he's younger and more serious than he first appeared. It's like that, isn't it…with people…how they look is not their story.

"If you're going to walk back, you'll need a flashlight." He nods to one of the maids. "We've had cougar sightings. Make noise when you walk."

"Sure," I say, "we'll do that." A good guy, Andy, not the kind to punish people who care for him. A man of leisure.

"Thanks. And we appreciate your hospitality. A memorable euphoria. Wonderful. And, may I ask," I am feeling more polite than usual. "The wall by the fireplace, the one with the medals, are they yours?"

"The purple heart. That one's mine. Afghanistan."

Fighting for lies, with lies. Andy's story. My story. Every soldier's story. War stories. People grow up with them, live on them, forget them.

"We have a big family. Multi-generational. Lots of cops and military guys. And you?"

"Me, yeah. I did 'Nam. A short stint with the DEA." Nothing I want to talk about. He knows that.

"You voted for Trump?"

"No." I say. "No, I didn't."

"I did. That lard ass pill–addicted fuck, all his lies, he's ugly. An ugly man draining the country into his own pocket. A gutter fag. He's no Texan. My neighbor's 98-pound wife could kick his ass. I regret it." Andy's pole dips, a sudden bite, he starts reeling it in. "Not everyone walks with dinosaurs here."

"Of course. And Andy, another question, if I could?" Way too polite.

"Absolutely. You're a guest."

"Why do you call yourself Mr. Fag?"

Sally nudges me.

Andy grins. A big wiry grin. "The joy of contradiction," he says. Then he pulls out the trout, a nice one, pan size, takes it off the hook.

"There's more life in contradiction, and life is too short not to live it fully." He pops his lips, weird, looks directly at me, picks up the stringer. "Do you agree?"

I want to disagree. Can't. "Sure. Makes sense."

Sally nods, smiles, he stares at her, she catches him, reels him in, swallows him whole, makes him happy. Nothing else to say. We thank him again, take the flashlight from the maid and head for the trees. Amy runs up, hands us her card.

"Either of you ever need a little extra heat. Let me know. I love to travel. Anytime, anywhere."

The two guys on the trail. Maybe they did know her, of her.

Sally takes the card. "We'll stay in touch. Certainly." She's genuinely interested. "Maybe you can join us in New Orleans."

Amy throws her arms around Sally, gives me a cheek kiss. "Maybe," she says. And she walks back to the house. A Texian castle, definitely.

We cut across the grass, into the trees and down the trail. Doesn't take long, no cougar, no biting insects, an easy hike back. At the Jeep we find a note tucked under the wiper, a handwritten note.

"Please, park in designated parking."

We purchased the $15-dollar primitive campsite ticket. No running water, no electricity. That made it primitive. Most of what I know is primitive. I'm primitive, a man made of basic parts. No need to change. No desire to change. Good people. Bad people. That's all there is. I know my place. Think I know.

We find our spot, no different from the one we were told to leave, crawl under our black sheet, decide to sort our route later in the morning. Let the cat out. The one we don't have. Go to sleep.

I picked up one-hundred and eight bucks betting on Sally.

# FIFTY NINE

I'm awake. A calm night. Trees at ease, comfortable in themselves, in the place they're in. A conscious or unconscious presence? How are we to know? The erratic purr of night sounds, forest lullabies, the air drifting. We chose sleeping in the back of the Jeep over the ground, windows are open, the day remaking itself in darker hues, bugs are out, animals, night stalkers. We drift away, as all humans do. Daytime reality slips into dreamtime, reshapes the day's events…toys of the mind under new ownership. Travelers and roads. Roads create travelers, weave the world's many lives into one. Traveling since my mid-teens. The traveler's handbook etched in my mind; guidelines handed down over millennia. 'Every night, if you wore socks, throw them on a roof of some kind before bed, let them air out. Traveler hygiene. Empty your bladder, aka, the holding tank, whenever you can. Never know when the next toilet will turn up. Wash whenever you can, streams, hotel tubs, gas station sinks, ponds, lakes. Wash at night what you wore during the day. Never sleep too soundly when you sleep. Carry three wipes worth of Kleenex or TP in your pocket. Always assume someone is watching.'

Dinosaur Valley, Texas, the USA, North America, the earth, life on earth. I close my eyes. They don't want to close. I force them to close. Cover my head, try to go back to sleep. Can't. Too awake to sleep. Too tired to get up. Need to relieve myself. Andy had bathrooms, his big house, his big bathrooms. Bathrooms with two sinks, a toilet and a bidet, marble floors, Italian tile on the walls, spacious. Our campsite, we have spacious. No bidet. I crack the door, stretch, relieve myself without getting up. A good trick.

> In India they don't eat with the same hand they use to urinate or wipe their butt. The right hand, thoroughly washed, is used for eating. Fecal jobs go to the left hand. What do left-handers do?

Lying next to Sally. She smells like candy, the candy we eat in dreams, remember eating when we were kids. I pull back the sheet. Morning rays light her up, her flawless skin crying for attention, demanding it. Radiant, self-illuminating. A tattoo, even a dot tattoo and she would never be nude again. A terrible thought. Tattoos are clothes of a more personal nature, but still clothes. They hide things–things people think they lack. What they think other people lack.

She opens her eyes, blows me a kiss.

"You want to play dirty?"

"Yes."

We do. We play dirty. A light frolic between opaque sheets and rolling drafts of morning light. Never too old to be in the present, never too young. Every touch evokes laughter, the want to touch again. Opening the doors, closing them. Pubescent merriment. Our little window in the world, we look through it, live in it, take great pleasure in living in it. A beautiful sunrise. We dress, eat a couple of candy bars. The last banana, some nuts. Drink a beer. Sort our route. Back up. Shift into drive.

Procreation, intercourse…chatting with God…the richest thing poor people can do.

We feel rich.

# SIXTY

**B**ack to Glen Rose, we pick up our bags at the hotel and press on. Texas 144 and 6 south to Waco, then US 190/290 to Houston, the ring road around Houston to pick up I-10 east. I've been on the I-10 before. The 10 to New Orleans. About 600 miles to go. Maybe we can make it by nightfall.

Not much else to say about Texas. As a state, it's like someone with a big face. Something you notice, but don't really want to think about.

In my mid-twenties. A lady I knew, Martha Murphy…I met her in New Orleans, the French Quarter. Is she's still there? Martha was a young woman at the time, a high-end Southern Belle, ultra-feminine, crisp, fragile, smart, the sweetness of fresh corn. Her grandmother told her, before she died, the worst thing is to die with regrets. Is it possible to die without regrets? Maybe. Lots of maybes in life.

"Micro-climate-shelters!" Sally sits up, abruptly. "That's it."

For days, she's been reading and rereading a special report on climate change in Scientific American magazine. We both read it. Sally understands it.

Texas144. Scrub grass. Squat trees. Tattered wire fences. Cows… grazing steaks. Deer, beaver, elk, bear, dogs, and puppies, if you live in China. Meals on feet, all of them. Not a lot of cactus. Forlorn things, cactus, a life separate from the herd – Mars offspring with no money, no ticket home. Hawks overhead. Birds of prey. They make the sky grand, give it a haunted dimension. Land smells. Fertile earth. The taste of it. How old is it? Do smells age? Few cars in either direction. It's already too hot. Sally puts her knees up, feet on the seat, spreads her legs, slaps them together, applauds her glorious invention of a fanny fan, relaxes, leans her head back, the rolling air. Could there be another one like her? Impossible.

"No more clothes."

"Sure, Sal. I'm good with that. More than good, but..."

She puts her finger to my lips, presses them, "Ben...you're a sweet man."

"Am I?"

"You are."

"Are you sure?"

"I am, yes." She pulls my cheek, kisses me. Albinos, ageless creatures. Have to ask her about raisins and cats. She likes them, I know that, but I kept forgetting to ask why. Forgetting more than I remember, everyone does.

"Really, Ben. There's no stopping us from exhausting the environment. Micro-climate-shelters. That's how we survive. Self-sustaining climate pockets. They'll pop up all over the planet as climate degradation overtakes the world. A slow-moving extinction event, that's what we are. We humans, we're like trees in deep winter. Too cold to die, we won't know we're dead until the spring thaw, when it's too late."

"Damn Sal, that's discouraging. Seriously."

"It is. Yes." She drops her head, covers her ears, uncovers them. "Christ, Ben! Our kids. After we have them, after they leave home, how will they survive?"

# SIXTY ONE

New Orleans ahead. The Big Easy. Sun is up. Sally is up, a beautiful morning. Bright. 72 degrees. Wide, flat spaces sweeping the countryside, and more farms, more houses. Houses with porches and plants and potted gardens. Big, well-attended gardens. And small ones. And partial ones.

Cruising, it feels good. A relaxed 55 miles an hour. Lake Waco. A big lake, dull brown, wind kicking up waves, chopping the lake surface, two lanes each way on the bridge. We keep on. Drive over the lake through Waco. Waco Texas. David Koresh. The Davidian tragedy, more like a massacre. Fuck.

Terrain monotony follows. Fields into fields, brush into brush, crops into crops. Driving memories. I have them. Dozens of countries. Always the same rules. Don't kill anybody. Don't get killed.

India. New Delhi. The monsoon season. Sheets of water filling the air, racing across the ground, down the streets. Warm, uterine water raising the river, flooding roads. I was driving a small Jeep truck, a Gypsy. That's what they call it. Made in India. The road was four lanes wide, not far from India Gate. I was in the far left lane. Some guy, 18, 20 years old, on a scooter, he came out from a side road, cut across all three lanes to end up right in front of me. I hit my brakes. Pulsed them. No luck. Rode up on the water, hydroplaned. The guy went under my front bumper. Disappeared.

"Fuck!" I shouted the word, many times. Let go of the wheel. Coasted to a stop. People came rushing out. Surrounded me, began shouting, "Back up! Back up!"

I clutched, put it in reverse and backed up. Slowly. The guy popped up in front of me. Popped up like a fucking jack-in-the-box. Lots of teeth. Face grinning, head wobbling from side to side.

I got out. People said, "No. Please go. He has no driving license." I left.

We make Houston. I-60, a loop road. More humid, a thick sense of things, congestion. Lots of changes. Can't remember how it was before, but it looks different. New buildings, bridges, overpasses, stilted highways. We're crawling. Ants on a lunch break. Lots of red lights in front of us. Twenty minutes. Thirty minutes. Forty. "Waiting and waiting and waiting for, can't wait any longer, can't wait any more." A line from an old poem.

I hate traffic, vehicular strangulation. Tires around the neck, babies crying, dogs barking, the crawl chokehold, it pulls you down to street level, to living on the street—the feel of sewage looking for drainage.

Lanes open up. A relief. Onto I-10, heading East. Always feel like speeding after being made to grovel for road crumbs. Trinity Bay came up on the right. Can smell it. Just above sea level. A few feet. Much of I-10, and the surrounding lowlands, all underwater in thirty years, maybe sooner. Lots of green. Three lanes. Guys with blue-green bags picking up litter. Sally puts her foot out the window. A sexy foot. Same role as a dog sticking its tongue out.

More traffic. Lots of trucks. Big trucks. Hate driving behind trucks. I move to the fast lane. Don't feel like it. Semi's. Single rigs, double rigs. Dozens of them, shiny boxes on wheels. Sally keeps her clothes on. Good idea. Truckers, they look anyway. They always look, look and look. If she raises her blouse, they'll drive off the highway, crash into the swamp, get eaten by alligators, snakes, something ugly. Lots of crops. Wheat. Maybe. The working world. Few miles before Beaumont. Cheap food, fast food. We take the exit, the drive through, pick up two hamburgers, everything on them, fries, small cokes. Get gas, cut back to I–10.

"Hubs, are you planning to make New Orleans before dark?"

"Not sure," I say. "I feel like driving, just sitting here behind the wheel looking out the windows. Road history, travelers' tales, all the stories we drive over to tell our story. It's a curious process. Sometimes it seems we're as much the people who came before us as we are who we are now–that what we're experiencing is a continuation of what they experienced. From the moment pavement goes down and the first car rolls across it, we're there as much as we're here now.

"It's going to be hot today."

"I know that, Hubs. I do. Why do you think I keep taking my clothes off?"

"Why you keep taking your clothes off?"

"Because it's hot. That's why. You want a sip of Coke? Want me to feed you?"

"Feed me! Sure. Food and a striptease. Great."

Sally loosens her seatbelt, gets close, slides in. Food is hot, the hamburger, she presses it against her breast. Makes it talk, "Hi, Ben. Eat me. I'm Betty the Burger. Sexy Betty."

She unwraps the burger.

"Let's have a talk, little Betty burger, a nipple-to-bun–heart-to-heart. Kosher, that's kosher, how I define kosher."

Sally puts a bite into my mouth, drops a hand to my crotch.

"Take a bite, Ben, take a bite."

I do. I take a bite, began chewing, and another bite.

"Chew faster."

I do, faster. Sally's hand finds its pace, a romantic combination of blues and classical rhythms. My mouth feels good, my crotch feels good. Removing her blouse, playing her song, our song. Sex. We love sex. We do. That's all. It's simple. It's healthy. It's positive. Sex is good for the soul, good for the body, good for the mind. But why is seeking pleasure a vice and war is not? Who made it so, and for what reason? I swallow my last burger bite, delicious, then bang…missiles away, cannon fire, small arms, semen pops the cork, exits the theater. A simple, wonderful escape.

"The fuck of fucks, Ben, that fuck. Where would it be?"

"Only one place, Sal. The Top of the World. An Everest fuck. A Nobel Prize fuck."

Cock would freeze—a top-of-the-world dickcicle. A final hard on.

Had to think about that.

Texas fast food. Jack-in-the-Box.

They make a damn good burger.

# SIXTY TWO

A slow-moving dance hall. The Big Easy. That's where they got the name. Catering to the human pace, human needs. Blunting in New Orleans. Kicking it down the road. Louisiana. We roll in, pass Lake Charles, Jennings, Lafayette. No hurry.

Already in New Orleans in our minds.

Benches. Wood benches, concrete benches, metal, and plastic benches. Benches with a view, benches without a view.

Thought too much of myself as a young man. With good reason. People told me I had something special. Could be a real somebody. They said things. Made comparisons I wanted to believe. The confidence of youth. I had it. Was it? Why not? After breast milk, youth is the next big inhalation, the tree upon which pubescence ripens.

One day, The Beverly Hills Hotel, before a lunch invitation, I was sitting on a bench along one of the hotel walkways, reading Chaucer's *Canterbury Tales.* Probably the only guy in L.A. doing that. An old man walks up. Stops. Stands over me. An old man with massive sunspots, some more brown than others. Layered wrinkles ripple across his neck. He's well dressed, an ultra-thin mustache did little to separate his nose from his upper lip, squint brows, ridicule in his eyes, his voice.

"Look at you," he says, cackles. "You think you're so sharp, alert, so aware. And you haven't noticed the duck sitting under the bench beneath you."

He laughs–scoffs–walks away.

I bend over. Take a look. There is a duck. I reach under. Grab it by the neck. Pull it out and look at it. It kicks, flaps its wings, tries to get free. It was sitting on eggs. Four of them. I brought its eyes level with mine.

"What kind of mother are you?" I scold. "Laying eggs under a bench! I could have broken them with my feet."

She keeps struggling, flapping.

"OK," I say. "You can live, I'll let you live but only if you move your nest. I'm going to come back and check on you. Don't be here." I squeeze her neck tighter, a little tighter, put her down. Walk away. Remember the old man. His thin mustache, squint brows.

Never thought about what to think of him.

Construction cones. Road work. Painting the shoulder white. Why do that? A few miles from Henderson. Signs for airboat rides. Kayak adventures.

"Airboat rides! Look, Ben!" A billboard up ahead. "Let's do that! Airboats. I've never been on an airboat."

It's warm. Humid. The thin satin of Sally's blouse clinging, scripting her inviting curves. All her curves. Women, how do they do that... the girl thing, a slight drop of the hips, twist of the shoulder, move just a little to the right, a little to the left, move just so, turn just so... and a rush of visual scenarios run through a guy's mind, a fine amatory rush and the match is struck, he's done, the guy, cooked, his focus overthrown. All he can think of is "sex." Like that, a slight twist, a sigh, a pause, and he's done.

"Sure," I say, recalling past experience. "It's fun. I chased alligators in the Everglades, crocodiles, maybe. Twenty years ago, more. Can't remember exactly. A thrill. Gators are fast, like fish. When we see them in zoos, anywhere on public display, they look dull, slow moving, without ambition. In the swamp, except for python encroachment, gators are king, or crocs. OK, sure Sal. Airboats it is."

"Great! The Atchafalaya bayou is coming up. It's a swamp. They have airboats. Here! Here! Exit 115. Cecilia Henderson! Take the exit!"

Road signs. Green with white letters. Every state in the Union has them. One country, like it or not. Signs don't lie. We take exit 115, make a couple of turns to Henderson Highway. Two lanes. Sagging telephone poles. Hardly a highway. Boat dealership on the right. Some boats covered with white tarps. Others are not. A bunch of illegal Mexicans hiding under the tarps, in the boat's shadows, under the boats themselves, their bare feet sticking out. And there are others standing in the open, bent over, pretending to be boat motors, or upright, posing like adoring statues pointing at some sale item…a special deal sign taped to the windows. Immigrant phobia, shadow phobia, tit phobia, mermaid phobia, underwear phobia, swear word phobia, insult phobia, belief phobia, they're real, ask anyone–stuntmen, third graders, prostitutes, bankers, zookeepers, guys who fold pizza boxes, anyone.

We pass the dealership, yellowish grass, weeds mostly, grow along the road. Needs a mow. Runoff trenches need cleaning. On the left, a billboard. Uncle Sam. Top hat. Finger pointing, as it always does. "We Thank You. Honor Our Vets."

Politicians. Fuck. They're good at lying, but why are voters so good at believing their lies? Another thought to think about. Our defenders, military grunts, the guys who do the dirty work, the real work of securing our freedom, the job that makes all other jobs possible. Vets. Without them there is no us. Christ. I hate politicians. What benefits them, what they can use, who they can use is all they think, when they think, if they think.

I pull into a gas/mini. RAM-something. Go through my usual fill-up routine. Try to keep the tank half full. Hate running out of gas. Hate lots of things, certain people, places, behaviors. Hate comforts the powerless. The 1973-79 gas shortages, I remember them. Sally heads for the store. She loves shopping. Doesn't matter what for. Earlier she changed into a longer skirt, summer cotton, very light, a yellow flower pattern. Her blouse, more like a shirt made of the same cotton, is also yellow, but lighter, no flowers. A vision. Always a vision. I watch until she slips behind the door.

The guy who opens the door for her, a "cool" dude, his pants, hanging below his hips, drop lower as she walks by, he stumbles, trips and falls. Some girl kicks him, knocks him down as he tries to stand, another girl does the same. A "cool" dude. Very "cool."

I finish the fill. Pull up for Sally. Rude to sit at the pump after a fill. Sometimes I like being rude, being someone I despise. Not today.

She comes out. Two bags, full of goodies. Cookies, bananas, apples, three bags of Truly Southern Pretzel Crunch. A bag of almonds. Water. Beer. A jar of peanut butter. Chunky. She knows I like chunky, extra chunky. More beer.

"The girl inside says we can get ice up ahead."

"They don't sell ice?"

"No. They have cold drinks. Not ice."

"Mini marts without ice. How often is that true?"

"True?"

"Mini marts, how many have ice? How many don't have ice? We don't know. We assume they all have ice. It's a question."

"Ben, did you take something, smoke something?"

"Maybe. Probably,"

A quarter mile down the road an ice shed came up. We stop. Our chest takes one bag. We buy two. Expect the second bag to melt before using it, doesn't matter. Abundance, having more than we need. It's a rare feeling.

Lots of boats in people's yards. People pulling boats on the road, off the road. We cross a bridge at the end of Henderson, cross another muddy river. Seriously muddy. More boats. Boats are the second car here, ice sheds the third. Lots of ice sheds. We turn left at the lighthouse. Looks fake. Wonder if they use it. Drive straight through the intersection, over the levee to the water, take another left under the overpass. Feel the weight of the overpass shadow as we cross under. Probably imagined that. Drive past a derelict pier. Something beautiful, even cruel, in how water pulls on the pilings thrust into it. A hundred yards further, an open space. A rutted, overgrown turn-out. I pull in, feel my tires grip stubborn earth, gnaw it. And viscous swamp smells. Alluring. Soothing. Dangerous smells. They fill the air.

An old man and a kid are standing in the turn-out some ten feet in front of us. The man is wearing blue overalls, a brown T-shirt, leather brim hat, snakeskin hatband barely attached, leather chin strap, blue eyes, trampled skin, goat hair, goat eyebrows, goat beard. The boy is wearing the same, except for the hat. No hatband. No goat hair eyebrows, beard. Next to them, a sign, big letters painted black on bare plywood held up, I imagine, by a stick wedged in the ground behind it.

*"Pro Airboat rides. The biggest bang for your twenty bucks! Free beer!"*

"Free beer!" Siren words. Words more important than other words. Words that get more attention than other words. Sex. Money. God. Free beer. All siren words, words you can't avoid hearing.

Beyond the sign there's an airboat tied to a stake. Gray mostly, rusting gray, dry moss embedded in the rust. A big-ass house fan stuck on the back of a big-ass shoebox lid. It looks like that. The blade is screened in. All but the exhaust end. An old boat. I imagine the man getting it for his tenth birthday. He's seventy, seventy-five, eighty? Far from new, an antique now, the boat has a certain charm. Wooden seats. Stained and faded life vests, frayed straps, they're sitting on the seats, a cooler next to them, and two long poles, a spotlight, rifle case, a rifle inside. I know the difference. Don't care.

I turn off the Jeep. Get out. Sally gets out. We walk over.

He's old, the man, like I thought. Older than me. In better shape, maybe. He throws his arm across my shoulder, one of those "We're going to be the best of friends, even if I rip you off," moves. Sally goes over to the kid. Says something to him. Stands next to the boat. Seems they've been waiting.

"Swamp sliding," begins the old man, his attention directed at me, the guy he expects to pay him. "That's what we do, swamp sliding. The Melancon alligator dance. No one else can do what we do. I'll tell you why. You want to know?"

"Yes, I want to know."

"I'm 81," he spits. Isn't chewing. Just spitting. "And I can still get it up." He lowers his voice. Not sure why.

"A fucking Swamp Cowboy," he says. "That's what I am. All Spartan. One hundred percent man plowing the bush from cradle to grave. No Viagra for me. A good-looking woman, half my age, if I see one," he says, "my ol' Charlie jumps right up. Like my boat, Mister. It will get you out there and back, no worries. And the kid. He's twelve. We're taking him with us. You coming?"

I look at Sally, she smiles, steps into the boat.

He never answered why he does what he does.

# SIXTY THREE

I climb in, stand next to Sally, the old man after me. They have a cat. A real cat. A coon cat. Purebred. Healthy. Looks wealthier than its owners. Faking poverty. Maybe they are. The kid pushes the cat off our seat, steadies the boat. Sally hesitates before she sits, a butterfly hovering, white rain in search of dry earth, the kid looks, the old man looks, I look. Eyes, any eyes, Sally controls them.

I sit down.

The old man, after adjusting his rifle, flares, rope, several other items, climbs into his seat above us. Leans forward.

"Sorry mister. Ma'am. Forgetting my manners. My name is Abe, Abe Melancon, and the kid there, he's Junior. That's what everyone calls him. Don't know what we'll call him when he grows up. He loves cats.

"Junior...push us out, boy. And get in."

"I'm Ben," I say. We shake hands. "My wife, she's Sally." Marking my territory, good fences. Sally shakes his hand. Quickly. Detaches.

"A pleasure, ma'am. Ben."

Junior leans into the boat. Pushes, moans, slips, falls, a knee in the mud. Tears his overalls. A new tear. Cuts his elbow. Hat falls on Sally's feet. A faulty chin strap. Greasy hair. Matted. He gets us out, rolls into the boat more than climbs in, falls into the water covering much of the boat's floor. Sits up. Apologizes meekly, begins splashing water on his cut, on Sally. Her clothes stick to her, share the contours of her perfect anatomy, Junior stares, fumbles for words to apologize, she waves him off, offers to help clean his injury. Maternal. Comforting. Twelve years old, the boy, his eyes tracking Sally's every move. Easy to imagine what he's thinking.

Abe turns the key. Click. Engine doesn't start. He pauses, counts. Would do well to spend more time brushing his teeth.

"Folks! The original gator capture tour is underway! We're goin' dancing," he crows. "Swamp dancing. The great Melancon Mamba."

"Capture!"

"Oh," he goes on, "that twenty bucks? It's twenty every half hour. You OK with that, Ben?"

He yanks a wire with a plastic handle, opens the cooler. "Have a beer!" he shouts. Grins. His mouth is missing lips, real ones. He tries the key again. The engine swallows hard. Rattles. Coughs. Lights up. Loud. Too loud.

"Go!" I shout.

"Go! Put the sound behind us."

He throttles down. We're off.

Alligator hunting on the bayou...The plan?

Abe spins the boat around. Heads out. A wide channel. Double pole telephone poles line the channel. Concrete and steel stick men paralleling the highway. Crane legs. A race to collect their wings. Can't see the highway, trees along both sides are too thick. A dense mass of vital green. Our wake rushes toward them, the water's edge, the brooding shallows.

Abe punches it. Straight out. Poles begin clipping by. Wonderful. The air rushing, pushing against the face, the body, pushing harder, defining the limits of sensation. Making it personal. Junior grabs the cat, sits down on a pile of rope in front of us, crosses his legs. Hat flips off his head. The chin strap holds. Can't see his face. I'm sure he is smiling. Sally's skirt, all but the part she's sitting on, catches updrafts one after another.

The old man, wearing a pair of WWII pilot's goggles, scratched, smudged, and his angle of view limited, can't see. Surprised he can see anything at all.

"Yo Santa! Jolly ho!" I shout. Not sure why. Can't hear my own voice, can barely feel it. Abe hits the throttle, lays it down full on.

Sally's bare waist lights up. Striking, always striking. I put my arm around her. Discreetly slip a hand over her right breast. Hold her close. She cuddles. A balcony view, all shops are open. The scent of a woman. Sally's scent, it's something I smell with my body, not just my nose. Not sure what anyone else smells.

The sound is behind us. A relief, but still loud. An old engine. Powerful. Surface water ahead is flat. Static. No bumping as we skim across it, accustom ourselves to the hard pressing air, its informality, its indifference. I open a beer for Sally. She skips it. Pregnant. I drink it, guzzle it, open another. Try to light a joint. Can't, even with Sally's help. Her clothes, flapping, they keep getting in the way. I eat the joint, take a couple more swallows of the old man's beer. Blonde Ale. A local brew. Solid purple and yellow graphics. Color choices, who makes them?

Trees. Lots of trees. Haunted trees. They look haunted. Foot traffic. Strolling sentinels. We pass between them. Single trees. Clusters. Trees without trunks. Swamp trees feeding simultaneously on the ground, water, and sky. What's that like? What does it have to be like? Humans. We're almost three quarters water. Breathe air. Can't live under water. A shit design, adolescent. Purple and yellow. Is God a color? Red. Maybe red. Little red lights in the desert red. No alligators, not yet. Beer and the joint are kicking in. Nice. Inside smiles lighting the way. I'm enjoying myself, utterly.

# SIXTY FOUR

Pushing material certainty, pushing with purpose. The boat is straining. Old, well made, straining all the same. Crossing the water. Snakes do it. Bugs. The Christ lizard runs on water. Junior and the cat haven't moved. Abe's trying to whistle "Country Road." Can't do it. Keeps trying.

Full bore. Moving fast. The metal towers stretch out ahead keep going east. Headless sprinting legs. We turn north, the tree line indents, breaks apart, gives way to open water, halting beauty, an odd mist lingering among the trees as if it had forgotten something and is waiting to remember.

"'Gators are in the north! The north!" Abe bends over, cups his mouth, shouts louder, "'Gators are in the north!" He barks the words. Likes barking them, and he keeps hitting hard left, hitting it. Beginning to like him. A rocks and dirt man. Fresh fish for breakfast, venison for lunch, alligator for dinner. Or steak.

More trees, myths with branches and leaves, a dense world, little room for error, minimal light, then open water again. Abe keeps shouting. Can't make out the words. Just noise, human noise, and he keeps leaning forward, bending over us, further and further forward. Far enough, he makes it, finally gets the look he'd been waiting for. From the moment he saw Sally sitting next to me in the Jeep, he's been waiting for a look, hoping. Both breasts are out. Success. A wind rapist sharing his prize. I catch Sally's blouse ends, help her button up and tie down. She pulls her skirt in, tucks it between her legs. Still moving fast. We slip out of sight. In an instant, ancient trees surround us, examine our purpose, our worth. Their awareness of us thickens the air. They're hundreds of years old, maybe, they look older. Wise trees, they must be.

"Here! This is the spot!"

Abe's voice. A torn voice. We barely hear it. He cuts the power. Engine jerks, spits, the fan stops. We keep moving forward. Drift silently into twisted shadows, dappled light, a tentative calm. All those National Geographic clips, BBC clips of animals sensing the presence of a predator, fear in their eyes, anticipation, unease. They are in this space, somewhere. Eyes watching us. Waiting. Attack or run. Abe's rifle in reach. My knife. We keep drifting, straight and forward. Change in the stillness follows. Water bugs, swamp mosquitos, flies, they follow. The boat edges between the trees. Giant, bearded trees. May not be as old as they look. Two cranes take flight, movement in the water. An alligator. Maybe.

We emerge from the dark. The dense green, into a narrow opening sided by thin trees. Stop. Just ahead of us, a couple of hundred yards, a small island, little vegetation, few logs, gray green scrub, a beach. An alligator on the beach. A big alligator. Massive.

Abe pulls on my shoulder, Sally's.

"You see him?"

Junior sits still. Motionless. The cat's asleep.

"Yeah. I see him."

Sally sees him.

He sees us.

Abe drops his voice to a whisper, "That 'gator killed my brother. Junior there, he's Doug's kid. He saw the whole thing. Paralyzed his mind. He's not dumb." Able puts a finger to his lips. "That gator. He knows we're here. He's watching. We make a move toward him, he'll drive. He's smart. Real smart. Tricked my brother, baited him, got him to come in close. Rangers don't believe he ate Doug. They tagged him, don't want him shot."

"What?"

An eruption. Sally grabs Abe's chin, pinches it between her white finger, her white thumb. Keeps her voice low, yells with her eyes— bright green flares scolding.

"You lied!" she demands. "I heard you. You said we were going to chase alligators. Not kill them."

"Ma'am, yes, ma'am. I did lie. I'm sorry." Tears begin to well up, used tears.

"Everyday ma'am, we go to that spot. Where you found us. That spot. We put up that sign and wait. Wait for someone. That one person. The shooter. Your plate frame has 'Paradise' on it. We took it to mean you folks were sent to us, the answer to our prayers. We want to bury that 'gator in my brother's grave. Our family graveyard. The whole family. Four generations are buried there. Not Doug. He's in that beast."

Silence. It's not the death of words. Feels like it.

"OK...."

"I watched you," he says. "Your eyes are sharp, trained, mine are near gone for distance shots. Junior shakes too much. We need a shooter. The way you looked at us. You saw everything. My rifle didn't concern you."

Nights alone in the woods, in the cells of memories I can't forget. Hidden nights. Thoughts of abandonment, disownment, betrayal. A perfect shot gave me purpose, vicarious revenge. A family of one, that's what I was. Before Sally, it was just me. War, manipulative rules, dogmatic correctness, small-mindedness, they took my friends, my sister, my childhood love – the corner girl with curly brown hair. Corrupt teachers, religious leaders, greedy businessmen, political leaders stealing our identity, our lives, lying to make us believe they can give us a better self-image than the one we have...man's most gifted extortionists. Can't kill them. Want to. Want God to do his job or seek work elsewhere.

"OK. I'll help," I say. "Sure. Make the ride free. Like the beer."

Abe. It looks like he is aging right in front of me.

"Ya Ben. OK, ya."

"Sally. Hands me the rifle."

She knows guns, Sally. Doesn't like them in the wrong hands. She unzips the case, slowly, pulls out the rifle. My mind runs with the zipper sound, all the times she unzipped me, handled the goods, ate me alive. The rifle. A bolt action Winchester 308. Clean. Stock is gouged, charred in spots.

"It's sighted." Abe drawls. Wobbles in his seat. Steadies himself.

I think, "Sighted by who?" Don't ask. The weight of a rifle. It tells you something. What the rifle can do. What it's made to do. Felt good to feel familiar. Weapons, microscopes, telescopes, cars, phones, they extend our reach. Make us bigger, more demanding on ourselves, on the environment, on God. I lift the rifle. Shoulder it. Snug it. Open sights. Sort my barrel rest, a low branch. Abe steadies the boat with his pole. Air is still. Utterly. My mind focuses, strengthens my eyes, shrinks the distance, enlarges the target. The indifferent hunger in an animals' eyes, the gator's eyes. I can see it. Predator eyes, they're all the same. A thousand rehearsals, the need to get it right. Fate. Every shot begins with fate, a moment's vacancy in time. And silence. I squeeze off a round, follow it, imagine how it hungers for the air, the impact. A dime shot between the eyes, clean. Blood spurts. Vigorous spurts. Junior has binoculars, passes them to Abe. The 'gator doesn't move. We watch. He doesn't move. Blood spurts continue, thin, slow down, come to a stop. He doesn't move.

"Wait," Abe whispers, puts up his hand, as if to stop us jumping in the water, swimming to the beach. "I know this beast."

We wait. And wait.

He doesn't move.

Abe gets down. Goes to Junior. Puts a hand on his shoulder. Squeezes it. Junior doesn't stand. They both stare, keep staring. A heavy boot pushing down on the alligator's head, holding it down. Is it over? One shot. Is one shot enough?

Abe gives me the nod. I take the driver's seat. Reload. Hold the rifle in my lap. Turn on the engine, move into the open, head for the island. Slowly.

The cat gets up, stretches, yawns, licks, and scratches itself, walks to the front of the boat, climbs up a slanted bucket to get a better view. Junior stands up. Low engine sounds, coasting, gliding forward. Water talking to itself.

We touch ground a few feet in front of the 'gator. A huge body. Massive. Easy to see how he could eat a man.

Stillness, a placid simplicity. Windless trees, grasses, surfaces of time. No one moves. We wait. No one moves.

The cat moves. The 'gator goes for it.

Junior falls forward, toward and into the oncoming jaws. The cat jumps aside, leaving space for a shot. I take it. Blow out the back of the 'gator's head, still driving forward, its teeth close on Junior's right arm. Doesn't bite, too dead to bite.

It lands hard, tilts the boat when it hits, bounces, exhales what death takes from all living things. The weight of a violent life pushing down, water splashing. Eyelids open, lifeless eyes staring beyond themselves... windows on an empty future.

Lots of blood.

# SIXTY FIVE

"In Hemingway's *Old Man and the Sea,* Santiago–that's the old man–he catches a big marlin. Too big to be believed. He ties it to his boat and heads for shore. Sharks eat it, otherwise, it was a good idea."

"No sharks in the bayou, mister." Junior's voice (the first time we hear it), has one of those kid sounds that make you think future actor, announcer, auctioneer.

"You're right, Junior," Abe adds. "Lots of teeth but no sharks."

We tie the 'gator just like the old man tied his fish. All of us together. Difficult. Takes almost an hour. Doug's body inside. His skull, hip bone, something. We feel something. Ropes are tight. We have our package. I take the driver's seat. Throttle forward, accelerate slowly, hold a steady even pace. Follow the path we came by. My memory isn't photographic. Can't say that, but I never get lost. Not in the forest. Trees are good listeners, and they share.

A good day. I feel good. Important. Accomplished. It won't last, I know that. Think too little of myself, too little of the world. For the moment, though, as we slip between light and shade, fill our lungs with the air of a place we've never been before, caring for people we don't know, justice favored the little people. Two old men, a kid, an albino. Junior can bury his father. Abe, his brother.

Sally goes to Junior, holds him, examines his wounds. I watch her, how tender she is. His hurt goes into her. She takes it. Absorbing other people's pain is part of her beauty, part of what she does, what makes me want her, what makes everyone want her. She isn't a whore, but she gives like one. Always gives more than she receives.

The white Buddha. There is one. Arya Tara. Born of the tear of suffering.

Sally is the white Christ. The girl version. Who knew it? I'm feeling good. Very good.

Abe sits down next to me. Removes his hat. Still wet, muddy. Wipes his nose. Leans his head back. Exhales deeply.

"Take us back, Ben. We're done here."

"Yeah. No worries," I say.

My second time driving an airboat. I like driving. Prefer tires and road wear to water but water has something. Depth, something that can pull you in, cause you to disappear where roads would expose you.

Sally tears off part of her blouse, uses it to wash and dress Junior's wounds. We killed the giant, a coffin brute. Grief could rest now, and the dead. Very warm. Very humid. Humid fragrances. After 1 p.m., closer to 2. A guess. Time flattens out ahead of us, loses its way. The shot. All the effort needed to tie down the 'gator, the blood memory cannot dissolve. Gone. Done. Revenge. Revenge *is* sweet, but never final?

Forward motion. Slow enough for small fish to nibble on the gator's head, the shreds of meat moving water has yet to wash away. The engine purrs, shares our mood. Hisses veiled obscenities at the dense air, the clusters and rows of trees, low bushes, island clusters on both sides, movement under the moss. Distance feels like it is pulling us, more than we're driving toward it.

After bandaging Junior, Sally rocks him in her arms. The boat water no one bails soaks into her dress, into what dry spots were left on Junior's overalls. He collapses in her lap. (Heroines in movies. There are too few, too seldom.)

We reach the telephone poles. I bank right into the channel. A boat passes us on the left. Moving fast, giving his riders a thrill, hands waving. Lots of shouting. The 'gator, tied on the right side, the tree side, they don't see it.

I beach in front of my Jeep. A relief to see her, an old friend. We get out. Abe hands us a beer. We hand him fifty dollars, don't have to. He hands it back. Won't take it.

A good day.

All days should be good days? Why aren't they? Junior's crying. Life. Life is so difficult to understand that whoever does understand it is misunderstood. Sally goes to Junior, takes him in her arms. Holds him, a white Krishna, Buddha, Christ, no real difference between them. Fuck. How easy it is for gods to make humans happy…if they want to.

Sally kisses Junior on the forehead. We watch, a Lazarus moment, Junior matures suddenly, stands erect, certain, his face bright, a grand smile covering half of it. "Dad's happy now," he says. "He's coming home. Finally coming home."

Abe opens another beer. I join him.

A good day. Definitely.

# SIXTY SIX

Sally brushes the wind from her hair, lights a joint, hands it to me... leans back.

"Do you ever think, Ben, that sometimes, when everything about life feels so perfect–the company you're with, where you are, the time of day–that you wish you could die right then, right there, in that place, at that exact moment?"

"Sure. A good time to die. I think about it. I do. I have. A lot."

"And what do you think when you think about it?"

"About the perfect time to die?"

"Yes. The perfect moment to meet, for the first and last time, that person in you who dies for you. What do you think?"

"I think we have too few perfect moments."

"Me, too. Just now, a second ago, felt like a perfect moment. Did you feel it?"

"I did, yes. Justice. Reconciliation. Healing."

She spreads her toes apart like a normal human spreads his fingers.

"I didn't want it to pass, Ben, but it did, instantly. And right after the perfect moment passed, I began to wish every moment would be like the perfect moment. And I think, if any perfect moment I've already had, had been *the* perfect moment, and I died, all the perfect moments which came after the perfect moment would not have happened."

"Right, I can see that."

"You can?"

"Well...no, not really, but it's fun to think so."

"Ben!"

She smacks me, not hard, bites my ear, a little. I hand her the joint, put the Jeep in reverse, back out, wave over the roof at Abe and Junior, they're pushing out. Sally waves. We drive away. Don't look back. Sally. Pregnant. Really? Something to think about, but not now.

Almost 3 p.m. Plenty of daylight left. Sally Googles our route back, through Baton Rouge all the way to the French Quarter. I gear down, turn onto Main Street, Henderson Highway, the same road. Two rights at the top of Henderson and on to I-10. A clean entrance. Feels good to be off the water. Hadn't thought it felt bad while we were on it. Definitely not a boat person.

Travelers are never on time, never late, never follow a fixed route, they just pick a direction and go. I've been doing that all my life. Most of my life, what I remember of it. Can't remember half. Don't want to. My mother, what I remember most about her is meanness. Not sure how much of the half that was.

Not enough Sally's in the world. Need to fix that, sit down for a man to man with the big guy, with the 'I'm everywhere, know everything, am every answer to every question,' guy. That guy, *the* Guy. "Hey," I'll say, as he pops the cork of a fine burgundy. "How about more Sally's, you know, like my Sally. We could use millions like her, save the race of man, colonize the solar system over night, fly to Mars from JFK in under 24 hours. How about it."

"So, Ben. What do you think?"

*Think? Again?*

"I think Junior is going to spend the rest of his life looking for someone like you, Sal, never find her, settle for less and live unhappily ever after. But. Maybe. Maybe he'll be lucky. You never know. Christ, before we met, I thought shopping at Goodwill, eating tuna out of a can, cheap prostitutes and box wine was the best life had to offer. A man without a wife, he's less than what he can be. Hope he makes it. Poor kid. You did him a favor, Sal. A lifetime favor. He'll never forget you. Amazing. You're amazing, perfect. You'll be an amazing mother. I love you, Sal. That's all you need to know about me. All I need to know about myself."

"I love you, too, Ben," she says. "And I'm hungry. And Ben...."

"Yeah."

"You still think I'm pretty?"

"Pretty? Yes, I do. Absolutely. From the moment I saw you I couldn't…."

She interrupts. Winks.

"What are we going to name our first baby?"

The look. She does that. Anytime she knows I have no choice but to agree with whatever she's going to say, even before she speaks, she gives me that look. That, 'I know I've got you, fight if you wish, but I'm holding a straight flush and all you have is a pair. A low pair, at that.' That's it. The low pair look. The two twos,' two threes, look. It's possible to win with two twos. I can think that. Don't bother.

"I like Ida," she says. "And Calypso, Irene, Michela, and Sue, if it's a girl. And Alexander, Joseph, Claudy, and James, if it's a boy. I can tell, Ben. I'm pregnant. No doubt.

We'll buy a kit. Do a pregnancy test just to be sure. You'll see. We'll need a name. You need to pick one, two."

I-10 lifts off the ground on concrete columns, stretches across the swamp. Intense straight lines cast against the irregular shapes of trees and water. Hours earlier we were on the other side of the trees. Miles from the highway. We were in the swamp, part of some mythical land where ancestral spirits, long ago departed, weave their story into the swamp on the wings of chirping birds and insects.

A perfect moment. It was. Somewhere, for someone.

# SIXTY SEVEN

Sally leans over, kisses me on the cheek. "Remember, hubs, the first time we met, our first real time roll?"

"Of course. The hairdressers."

"Yeah, Jane Ireland's Wig Wum Wow snip shop. All the pink and white stripes.

Remember, she always wore pink, drove an old Chevy Malibu with pink stripes, dyed her

poodle pink, and her goldfish."

"I remember. No choice. And I try not to remember, but she's one of those people who

casts an image so indelible it never leaves the mind."

"Never?"

"Never, exactly, as in it will always be there competing with fossils for millennia to

come."

"Ben, you exaggerate, really. Jane was sweet, a near blind wobbly little woman everyone

loved."

"You're right, Sal...absolutely."

Holding a pair of twos. I stop talking.

All lanes are clear, road sounds echoing large. Wheels spinning. Jill the Jeep plowing through time. Back on the road. The travel goddess giving life to high expectations. Legs wide open. Windows down. Hot air pulling moisture from our skin. Big V-8 guzzling fuel. Bugs smashing against the windows, mixing with blue washer fluid.

"The back room," she smiles, a quicksand look. "Remember?"

"I do, Sal. The room with all the panda toys, paper cups stacked on the cooler, the empty water bottles, boxes and boxes of shampoo, cleaning fluids, canned goods for emergencies. Jane was a hoarder, is a hoarder. Not exactly normal. Was she was trying to feel rich. Maybe, but she didn't care much for money. Preparing for the next war, possibly, or something worse...much worse."

"And the old *Godfather* poster, Ben. Remember, it was black and white. Brando wore a tweed coat, hands forward resting on the desk, his mind concentrated, thinking. 'Who to kill, when to kill, why killing is good, when necessary. Remember?"

"I remember, Sal, happily and clearly. And I love hearing you tell the story."

A mustang passes us. Fast. Red, shiny rims, top down. I check my mirrors, my speed, relax. Cruising I-10 just west of Baton Rouge. I know the road, all four main highways crossing the US. I know all of them.

Sally continues: "He watched us. The Godfather. Blessed us. Watched you pick me up by the waist, rip off my panties with your teeth, watched me wrap my legs around your neck. You remember.

"You do. Yes." A quick smile. "Exciting, isn't it, just the thought."

She pauses, downs a handful of raisins. "There we were, standing. You seemed bigger at the time, taller, heavier, there's so much man in you it's easy to exaggerate. I knocked off your hat, began rocking on your shoulders. Cradled. Felt safe. I let you in. Gave your full access. You were such a turn on. Such a fucking turn on." She waves her hand across her face like a fan. "It felt good, so good. Always feels good with you, Hubs. Christ! It was wonderful. A top ten hit. Utterly grand."

The need for spontaneous pleasure, we have that in common. Then and there, we fell in love, on that day, in that room with Brando's blessing, we fell in love, left the room, the shop, began a life together. I felt like a hero. Still feel like a hero. Every time Sally tells that story, I feel like a hero.

I like feeling like a hero.

Every man does.

# SIXTY EIGHT

A long causeway. Minimal traffic. Another "Begin Higher Fines Zone" sign. Three lanes. The Horace Wilkinson Bridge. Ego Art: Rich people buying memorial gravestones, attempting to immortalize their names on highways, bridges, parks, buildings, walls. Making sure we don't forget they're better than us.

The Mississippi. A big river, an artery, a snake struggling to digest industrial waste; the rot of human negligence expanding its territory, wending its way to an imbalanced ocean, transient seas, life without living. Loading docks on both sides of the river. Oil drums, several. A couple of big ass white balls on the left. Some kind of storage tanks. Defying nature is not controlling it. More loading docks. We drive on. Muddy water, Mississippi water. Not what one expects after so many songs, stories, photos, and scenes in movies have eulogized it, made it more beautiful in our minds than reality. Each time I see it, the Mississippi, big comes to mind, not beautiful. Each time. Lots of muddy water in the southeast.

More signs, signs too big for the messages written on them. 12 East to Hammond, 10 South to New Orleans. We fly past Baton Rouge. Hello, good-bye. Soft scenic. No all-out porn skyscrapers dicking squatting clouds, like New York, Chicago, Dallas. Low key. Orderly businesses and housing, trees, hints of swamp close by. Always. Another causeway. Easy riding. More trees, signs, ubiquitous signs. Caution signs. Weigh In All Trucks signs. Uneven road signs. A left over "Last Chance for Fireworks sign." An Exit 187 sign. Talking signs. Laughing signs. Happy signs. Ugly signs. Signs in signs. One country whether we like it or not. One people. Cell towers. Power lines. Some clouds. Very warm. A world free of clothes on sweltering days. Why not? I glance at Sally. Love doing that, try to imagine what she's thinking, what she's imagining, remembering. Raisins...I have to ask.

"Sal, why do you like raisins?"

She throws me an albino glance. An elfin kind of scolding.

"Really. I'm curious."

I stare; forget I've asked a question. How is it that she keeps becoming more beautiful?

"My uncle," she begins, "he followed us from Africa. Loved wine. A sweet and simple man, cheerfully rotund and generous. He always talked to me like I was older, closer to his age. He made me an equal in his company. We had wonderful loving conversations over wine and raisins. And he had a cat that knew how to fetch raisins. We'd play word games, not always, but often. Every time Uncle won a word, he took a drink of wine. Every time I won a word, the cat brought me a box of raisins, raisins Uncle made from a special selection of his harvest. They were good raisins, much better than what I buy today. But the cat, Ben, that cat knew sign language, and he could fetch. I swear. Every time I won a word, he asked if he could have a couple of raisins before he brought me the box. I'd nod, and off he'd go. And when he came back, he smiled. Really. That's why I love cats, and raisins. They make me smile."

Sally can read cat sign language, came from Africa? Didn't know that, the sign language part, or maybe I did, but forgot. The kind of forgetting that wipes memory clean away, that kind. Did she just make it up? Could have. Makes sense she'd be from Africa. Birthplace of man. The real Garden of Eden. Sally. I can't decide if she's human or not, if I want her to be human, or not. If what I want makes any difference, or not.

Cats with talking paws, smiling, eating raisins. Of course.

"A McDonald's coming up. Exit 206. I have to feed the baby."

"A Mac and fries for the baby? Is that a good idea?"

"My body will clean it," she says.

Christ with tits. Definitely. A lot of people think the Ganges cleans itself, makes itself pure. A lot of people think that. Sally does it.

Another memorial gravestone bridge. The Spencer Chauvin "remember me" Bridge. Sally Goggles it. Rarely occurs to me to do that. Not the usual vanity memorial. Chauvin died on the bridge working an accident.

Good men. There are always good men. And too few good men in power.

"Wait! Ben!" Sally shakes her phone. "There are two McDonald's! Skip 206. Take the next exit. Exit 209. It's closer to the highway."

We veer right off 209. Down the ramp, right on US 51. Signs. How would we manage without them? A couple of blocks. McDonald's on the left, Burger King on the right. I look. Think, "Burger King's spicy chicken sandwich nice and hot. Very tasty."

"I want McDonald's, Ben."

"I know," I say. "Me too."

Albinos. She knew what I was thinking, felt like she watched me think it. Burger King's spicy chicken sandwich tastes like it has life in it. I think so. Maybe not.

A short line for the drive through. Usual arches, windows, tables. What I can see of the floor and the outside grounds, all is in good order, clean. Must be clean. Clean tricks us into believing junk food is good, even healthy. A corporate ruse. They all do it. Government corporations, corporations themselves, the big guys. They find ways to increase product price with no addition to product value. Monetary instruments. That's what they call them. Add a little more water to packaged meat, make it heavier. Decrease the length of bottle droppers and spray bottle straws, make hand creams a little thicker. Leave more product in the container, buy more off the shelf. Gas pumps that fail to print receipts bring people into the Mini Mart where they see things, buy things, spend more money. Ads on the phone while waiting on hold, free advertising; means of stealing our time with redundant questions when one prompt asking what we want, searching, then connecting us, is all we need. Consumers, the more we spend, the more control corporations have over us.

We get in the drive through line. A pickup truck ahead of us. Dark green. Shiny. Two kids and a dog in the back. A Doberman. Young. Mean dogs, even when they look cute. They're playing in a tub of water. An inflatable pool of some kind. Laughing, splashing, throwing toys, breaking toys. No one in the world but them. A warm day. A massage day. I lean my head out the window. Relax. Feel like I am getting used to swamp time, southern time, black people time, a comfortable familiarity in it, a lazy calm. Relaxing. Putting my guard down.

Turning my back on the sea.

Was I?

A girl. Dark, curly hair. Plump. Baby plump. Nice feet. Her nipples, three-inch areolas introducing them, were always hard. A Hawaiian girl. Her dad was in the Navy, stationed in Hawaii. He drank, forced her to watch him disgrace himself in front of her mother's photo. She was eighteen. We went all in on the beach between waves. Sand in my eyes, ears, hair, every orifice. Indecent grit, primitive sand, it was rough, but fun.

I stayed in Hawaii for five weeks. The girl, I did like her, but she wanted to marry. Wanted me to take her with me when I left Hawaii. She said, "Never turn your back on the sea." I did. Once. I was walking the edge of a lava flow on Oahu. Yards above the breaking waves. High enough not to worry. I turned my back on the sea, squatted, reached for something on the ground. A wave caught me, knocked me down. Tried to drag me over the edge. I put my feet out, pushed against the slide, tore my feet on the lava, came to a stop. Five, six inches from the edge. Took weeks for my feet to heal. I left Hawaii, unaccompanied.

Time and place...it makes a difference.

We order three big Macs, two fish sandwiches, fries and two big Cokes with lots of ice, an extra cup of ice.

Nothing for the cat.

A beautiful day on I-10. No hurry, no rush, gulls riding air currents, minimal exertion. That's what we are, gulls gliding, the world below a serenade of color and contrast.

Need to buy Sally a wedding ring, a real wedding ring.

# SIXTY NINE

We cross the last of the causeways. The long road. All around us a desolate green, a desert green. Miles of it. Short trees. Dense bush. Always lots of bush, and shrub. America. I love America. Great roads. Intoxicating roads. A beautiful country. Grand.

Sally changes into a one-piece dress/skirt, dark yellow, large wooden buttons. Jeep's windows are open, a reveling air catches her attire, loosens the buttons, shares the goods, stunning. Fags, poor fucks, what they're missing. Fags and vegetarians. Tits and meat, life without tits, without meat, without bacon…what's the point?

We keep on 10 into New Orleans. I've been there before. Memories, they rush in, hover, struggle to complete themselves. Memories always struggle. Lunch at Antoine's with Martha. I remember being there, the need to be there. To be anywhere. It was humid. Like today. Very humid. Hot. The kind that makes you want for ocean breezes and cold drinks. Sweltering heat. Thick. Oppressive. Demanding. Cathartic.

New Orleans is a skin place. A medieval flesh hound sniffing out weaknesses in moral proprieties. Challenging them. The French Quarter is all I know of New Orleans. What I think of when I think of New Orleans. It has a place smell more than a people smell. Lots of bars, carry-out drinks, antique stores, galleries, ornate wrought-iron balcony railings, wood shutters, historic arches, and columns. Streets immortalized by the wild libations of libertine souls. Streets lined with glittering, candlelit windows, freshly painted facades, bewitching buildings that confine you, shrink you, harness your nothingness. Big or small, I dislike cities. Even the ones I do like. Cities are where the human race turns to relieve itself of insignificance, to self-defecate. Human outhouses with no Haitian Bayakous to clean them. That's what cities are. Automaton environments consuming more than their share of resources. Relentlessly wasteful. The brutes in charge, the privileged big guys, they know that, and rocks and fish know. People don't. Not yet.

We find street parking. "Thank you, parking gods." Never certain of how to please them...sacrifice quarters, fill the meters for other people, bolt cut the quarters and stuff them into meter slots, break the meters. Parking gods. Who knows what they want?

Four blocks from Antoine's and Jackson Square. Andrew Jackson Square. Lots of tourists. Everywhere you go, tourists look the same. The look of careless impermanence. They all have it. We walk. I hold Sally close. French Quarter necromancy...there's always something frightening about it...a treacherous past that may come to life, reach out, grab you, pull you into the walls, through the walls into bedrooms, brothels, drunken brawls, murder scenes, robberies, ritual orgasms. The ruthless romance of myth. I can feel it pulling, calling us, "Drop your guard," it says. "Turn your back on the sea. Free your mind. Have nothing to protect, no opinion you cannot do without." Can't remember who said that first, if anyone said it first. Fuck. I like my opinions. Would rather have my own than someone else's. Sally likes hers. I like hers.

Most of them.

"So, what do you think?" I say, unfolding my arms. "This is New Orleans!"

"I love it, Ben! Love it. Makes me hot inside and out. Feels like we can fornicate anywhere. Street corners, in front of stores, restaurants, bars, wherever. Do you feel that?"

"Yeah," I say. "I do. I feel that. Definitely. But why use fornicate?"

"I'm teaching you how to be less vulgar, Ben. Fornicate is a soft ball word, not a hard ball word. People can't take hard ball, not for long. Primitive egos are like that."

Primitive egos?

No real order to life. Only looks like it because we can't imagine a world without order.

"Wait!" Sally puts up her hand, the most beautiful traffic cop ever. "There's a food store. Compac Groceries."

She goes in. Comes out.

"No pregnancy kits."

We continue walking. Easy streets. Living in the Quarter, I could do it but not without a life raft stashed in the attic, and not for long. Too flat. Too close to the rising sea.

Antoine's. I open the door for Sally. Not much of a gentleman. Few men are. I like thinking I am.

"Thank you, Ben." I continue holding the door. Three more people walk through.

"Thank you, mister." One of the girls, there are two, she likes that I held the door. The other girl didn't. The guy they're with, he doesn't even notice me, is wholly unaware that he entered a room, that it's daytime, that his shoes squeak, that his shirt is stained. That he's still in diapers.

"Yeah, sure," I say. "Sure. I work here, they pay me to look like a customer being nice. Makes people feel welcome."

"What?"

"Nothing, nothing at all. Just happy to be back in New Orleans. You wouldn't understand, enjoy your meal."

They take a table, the two girls and the guy. A big guy, too big. We remain at the door. Look around. White tablecloths High ceiling. Wood furniture. Polished. Nice. Too rich for us. We go to the bar. I order a craft beer. Sally picks it up, takes a swallow, asks for a fizzy water, hands me the craft, cold, very cold. A cold beer on a hot day. One of the greatest little pleasures in life. I drink from the bottle, always drink from the bottle. Stays cold longer. Glasses are for girls, hard drinks, wine. Bartender tells us the beer's name. Don't try to remember. No room in my head for memories I expect to forget. Sally. Pregnant? What does that mean, exactly? She does know things, still, she may not be pregnant. If not, what would that mean?

Early evening. Not many people, diners. They look at us, the diners. Scan us. Weigh and measure us. All of them. Even the heavy ones with spandex shorts, swollen feet, shade umbrellas, fanny packs filled with snack food. Nothing to do with the beer, drinking it from the bottle. Maybe my cargo shorts and shirt—un-ironed. Maybe we look unwashed. It's none of that. It's Sally. Her alabaster attraction. Her dress. Thin cotton, big wooden buttons down the middle, open to show just enough cleavage. Very sexy. She's wet with sweat. AC isn't working or isn't on. No one else sweating. Unusual for Sally. Pregnancy sweat, a baby thing. Could be. New Orleans, the unexpected ever lurking about, cleaning its coat, licking its paws. Sally feels something, slides off her bar stool, a tall chair more than a stool.

"I have to pee."

"Everyone does. Hurry back. I'll order another beer. Two. Maybe three!" I nod to the bartender. Female, black, a good figure, attentive, tall, soft face, white shirt, black apron, Christmas smile. Black people still make white people feel important, some white people, too many white people. Predatory racism. A lot of whites addicted to that shit…Trump and his Nazi-supremacists: Trumplicans. They're wholly addicted. A Klan state, that's what they want. No end to human pettiness. She pours for a girl at the end of the counter, a barcode girl, tattooed head to foot. Bright red hair. Freckles. Large nose ring. Brass. Shiny. Put a rope though it and you could lead her around like a Swiss cow. Novelty addiction – a mental disease of unknown consequence reformatting perspective, crippling realities hold on the evidence of fact, infringing on rules that punish – it's spreading. Jesus. Buddha. Muhammad. What would they say? What would the cat say? Blazing red tattoos on her ear lobes, wrists. Some kind of snake. Beautiful?

She was, once. Easy to imagine what she looked like before the tattoos, the body graffiti. Not anymore. Something happened to her, took something from her. She drinks from the bottle, lips it, wears a bra, panties, a toy chastity belt, maybe. Her dress is short, light blue satin, very tight. A prostitute? Actor? Teacher? Single mother? All four?

I empty my bottle. Drink Sally's, order two more, take a moment to wander through Vegas memories, and life with Sally, a life made more wonderful with every touch, spoken word, look of affection.

From behind me, a body coming in close. I can feel it. Was trained to feel it, sense it. Two hands reach around, cover my eyes. Soft hands. Fragrant.

"Surprise…. Guess who?"

"What!"

"Guess who I am."

"I'm trying," I say. "I'm thinking."

A girl. It isn't Sally. Surprises. I don't like them. In the woods, the jungle, surprises kill you.

"Come on, Ben. Guess! One guess. Only one. If you get it wrong, you buy me a drink. Get it right, I give you a blow job. Here and now."

She knows my name. I take another swallow. Want to light a joint. Where's Sally?

"Can you say something more? A hint?'

"Raft," she says. "Raft."

Raft? Andy….

Yes! Her voice. It goes with black hair, blue eyes, wide pink lips. "Fuck. Amy! Where…how the hell did you find us?"

She sits down. Pours the fresh beer I ordered for Sally into a new glass, a cold glass slid to her by the bartender. She drinks it. All of it. Doesn't stop, orders another.

"I arrived yesterday," she says. "I'm staying with a friend. Saw your Jeep. Thought you would come here. No reason why. I just thought it, came in, and here you are. Where's Sally?"

"The bathroom. She's… Well, she'll tell you."

Amy. Andy's place. Sex, drugs, and rock and roll. Ecstatic memories. Sometimes I feel closer to my Jeep than people. Wonder what that says about me.

"Where are you staying?"

"We haven't decided yet. Arrived a couple of hours ago. Sally's first visit."

"Stay with me. At my friend's, Simbana's. She's fine with guests. It's a big house. Old, grand. Half an acre on a corner, set back from the street. High cast iron fence. Two stories. Attic windows. Columns. Wraparound porch." She scribbles down the address on a cocktail napkin. "We're having a party tonight. A *Game of Thrones* party. Very private. Hop on the streetcar at Jackson Square. A buck fifty each, with one transfer."

New Orleans, something in the way it breathes. Images of whale sized porpoises with almond eyes, no discernible tattoos and three extra fins fighting for the dorsal position, really tiny puppet dogs chasing giant bear cubs up dwarf trees, aliens that look like people but with skinny feet, shrunken heads and hands, begin coursing through me, drifting across my mind, waving profane banners, calling for erotic attention. New Orleans casting its spell, dissolving reality. It does that.

"And here's my number. Call me if you get lost."

"You're not going to wait for Sally?"

"No time, Ben. Sorry. See you there."

She runs out.

No blow job.

# SEVENTY

aiting for Sally. Beginning to worry. I finish my beer. Pick up the glass Amy ordered. Drink it, what's left of it. Watch the red headed nose ring girl adjust her bra, pay, and leave. No tip. No parting thank you. A single mom in need of better luck, maybe. Black bartender, I like her, who wouldn't, she's mesmerizing, a dancer's grace. She's not happy with the barcode girl.

Sally? Where is she? I get up to look.

"Mister. Please pay before you leave."

"Oh! Sorry...I'm coming back. My wife, she's been in the bathroom for a long time. Too long."

That look. The two twos' look, lots of girls have it. The bartender does. I put down a twenty. "To guarantee I'm coming back," I say.

She nods. I turn to go. Sally walks up.

"Damn, Sal. What took you so long? I was getting worried."

She smiles. Kisses me. "Sorry, Ben. Sorry. I was playing with my tummy. My baby tummy. Trying to feel something. Too early, I know, but it was fun. Got a little too excited. Are we going to eat here? I'm not that hungry. I'd like a beer though, two beers, three."

"And the baby?"

"I know, Hubs. The baby. I've thought it through. Pregnancy is too restrictive. That's all. I can't be restricted, there are reasons, necessary reasons...besides, my body, it has certain assets; Lucullan attributes other bodies don't have, even albinos. I don't talk about it. You know that. But it's true. I make the world I'm in more than it makes me. Regardless of what goes into my body, there's no place here, no environment on this master earth, safer than inside my body. I'm not her only mother."

Her what? A she? Were we having a girl, a mini-Sally? A mini alien? Are there others? Mothers?

I order two more crafts. I'm feeling good. Even happy. A clean alcohol high. I like drinking, that nicely rounded buzz which follows the first few swallows. It's like morning, the relief that accompanies the first yawn. We finish. Pay the bill, leave a tip. More than expected. Compensation. Bartender smiles. New memories. Humans. Memory collectors. That's what we are. Trash collectors, memory collectors. Not much difference between them.

Very humid. Looks like rain. Feels like rain.

"Hey!"

Sally finds something.

"They have a pharmacy museum here. Maybe some old cocaine, opium, weed. Chartres St. About two blocks."

"Let's have a look," I say. "It's a Lewis and Clark thing to do...drug hunters primed to open new territories for discovery and plunder. Once you're in I'll guard the door, watch for police."

"Ben, you're too serious. It will be fun."

"I know. I'm trying not to be." I smile. Lots of teeth.

Tourists. I feel like one, don't like the feel of careless impermanence. Tourists are inattentive, bumbling things who dress badly, spend money, talk too loudly, return home with photographic proof of grand adventures they failed to experience.

We make the pharmacy museum. It is interesting. Surprisingly. Happily. Especially the smells – anonymous information in a forlorn search for means to express itself. The myriad stories never told, what they smelled like, looked like, felt like. Old labels, old cabinets, old jars trying to speak. The fraught murmurs of diminishing value, I hear them calling...something hears them. Opium-soaked tampons is a hit with Sally, and the cocaine toothache drops. The leech jars put her off. We don't stay long. Hunger, the gnawing stomach; our apex predator within. We can't ignore it. No matter what, it catches up, demands payment. Homer wrote about it. An old story.

We walk up Toulouse to Royal, up Royal to St. Peter. Street musicians playing jazz. A whole crew. Tuba, trombone, trumpet, keyboard, percussion, voice, guitar. Blacks and whites. A jovial mood. Loose fitting clothes. Everyone's relaxed. Big buckets with dollar signs on them. Rouses Market. We stop to listen. Not a bad living.

About to rain. Definitely. Rouses, something of a catch-all food and drug store, we go in. Buy a couple of salads. Chicken. Dry roasted cashews. No pregnancy kits. Didn't look for one. A clean store. No point in buying umbrellas. Too warm to care about getting wet.

"Oh! I saw Amy earlier."

"Amy! Amy from the fire, the card party?"

"Right. That one. She's here, in New Orleans. Saw the Jeep. Invited us to stay with her, a friend of hers. It's okay. She said they're having a party tonight. An 'exclusive party.' A "Game of Thrones" party. We're invited. I have the address. And Amy's phone number."

"Damn, Ben! Great. All that while I was in the loo. Will be fun to see her."

# SEVENTY ONE

According to myth, and all those stories scout masters tell around campfires to scare young scouts spending their first night in the woods, Orleans people, French Quarter people, they feel their skin more than any other part of the body. On the streets, in the windows, the shops. Exposed skin sampling the environment for hints of pleasure, that's what you see, skin with its tongue out, lots of skin. Some great to look at. Some not so great. Some better kept covered, buried, jailed, wacked with a flyswatter. An old lady...at least 75, 80. Maybe older. Always difficult to get age right. Platinum hair, brittle, sagging shoulders, face lifts (more than one), unnaturally perky tits, nose job. She's wearing a miniskirt—green with pink dots, gray, short sleeve top and running shoes, miniature toy poodle on a leash, poop bag in her left hand. Chasing youth, some version of vitality. It isn't working for her. Not from my point of view.

"Hubs, I think it's going to rain before we finish our food."

"We haven't begun yet." I hold up the salads, the chicken.

"That's my point."

It does. It starts to rain. Deep, gray-purple clouds. Light wind. Street artists frantic to collect their work. Ants running from jumping spiders, bug spray, anteaters. Instructions, ads, directions chalked on paving stones begin to blur and dissolve. Lots of people, a few dogs, all running. Almost all. Umbrellas, bobbing flaps of color, they collapse as people enter buildings, stand under balconies, awnings, trees. Rain. Plants like the rain. Sally likes it. I like it. We duck down an alleyway toward the front of St. Louis Cathedral. Many people going in, rushing, pushing. Too many. Seeing the cathedral is not a high priority. Not for us. San

Jose de la Laguna Mission. We have a church, our church, and our chicken's getting wet. Wet food. Wet air. Wet clothes. Every curve of Sally's body is no longer hidden by loose fabric. A goddess. Absolutely. Athena with a better body. Venus with a better body. Hera, Nemesis, Sunna with a better body. Equally real as unreal. She is incomparable. Do girls ever feel like that about guys? That we're gods. Incomparable. Zeus. Shiva. Amun-Ra. The better part of creation?

Doubtful. Guys, we know how fucked up we are, and knowing it, rather than give us cause to better ourselves, we think better of ourselves because we're fucked up, which is worse than how fucked up we think we are. The limits of patriarchy…when we care less for our children's safety than aggrandizing male self-importance, we hit the limits of patriarchy, and we are hitting those limits today. Ask the weather, ask plants and animals on the extinction list, ask all the people who will be dying of thirst in ten years.

"Jackson Square, Ben, let's go."

Food's getting wet.

"Why not, sure, Sal. No cars allowed. No bikes, skating, skateboarding. No unicycles. Golf carts. No fucking on the grass. Don't see a sign for that. Never do. Must mean it's OK."

"Of course, it's OK, everyone knows that."

We walk into the square. A square with a circle in it. Benches all around. More rain. Warm rain, bathwater warm. Intense. Major General Andrew Jackson high on his horse in the center of the circle in the center of the square. A neat and tidy park. I don't remember it that way.

We find a place to sit under some trees, a bench in front of a goddess statue. Venus. Warm Italian marble. Probably not. Breathing is not living. We have to breathe. Living is doing what you want to do, being where you want to be. We feel at home under the tree, embers of early man awakening our senses, memory of primal savannas, jungle. We're in them, alert, engaging our senses, enlarging them, growing the human brain, raising the bar.

We eat from each other's containers. Laugh. Roar! We're soaked. Few people around. Heavy rain. A suckling rain, a New Orleans's monsoon, relief from the heat. It pulls the weariness from our bones. The long hours of sitting in the Jeep, the days.

"Open your mouth, hubs."

I do.

Sally feeds me. I feed her.

After the salad and chicken, we eat the wet almonds. Delicious wet almonds. A perfect moment, I reach over, unbutton her two top buttons, slip my hand in. Check to see if anyone is looking. A few people hurrying by. One or two that are not. We're visible without being seen. The streets empty. Very heavy rain. An exciting heavy rain. Sally. She moves onto my lap. Begins to channel forbidden pleasure. Most of what gives us pleasure is forbidden by someone, some group, religion, tribe. Make another baby to keep the first baby company. We do our best. We pamper the wet, waves of passion swallow us, hide us, give us new life. Secrets... there are none between us. Not that we know of. There are things we don't know about each other, there are always things we don't know, but there are no secrets, things we're afraid to say to each other.

"Ben, that was great!" She eases herself off me. Throws her hair back, a cloud burst dressed in white. It rains harder. But for us, the square is deserted. The streets deserted. Very heavy rain. Wet can feel so good. It does. I do, and I'm happy. How rare to feel happy, that it's safe to feel happy.

Our clothes, as they cling and sag, splash against us with every step after we stand and begin to walk away, remind me of all those western movies where people act like it's not raining, when it is.

We leave the park. Skip the riverboat. No one in line for the Jackson Square streetcar. We wait. It rains. We stand. It rains. We keep checking the tracks, as it rains. A small speck in the distance getting larger. A red speck. The car. It comes toward us, slows before the stop. Drifts. A dance move, streetcar ballet. It's red, the car. I remember them being green, dark green-brown-with-wear green. Love the wood seats, mahogany, polished rails, brass hardware, pull-down curtains.

Almost six. A little cooler. The rain stops. Lots of standing water. We head for Amy's.

New Orleans.

It's better than what I remember.

Better than what I forgot.

# SEVENTY TWO

The first car drops us short. We need another ride. More rain. Still warm, the middle of the tracks, a track/street intersection. Sally removes her dress, wrings it out, puts it back on, her body beneath the dress remains visible, visible but not illegal.

Waiting. Standing in the rain. Standing between the trees. Big trees. Old trees. Old houses. Beautiful old houses. They line both sides of the tracks. Old streets. Nice streets to live on if you like people around you.

"How long before the next car?"

Sally checks her phone. "They say ten minutes."

The next car arrives. Ten minutes exactly. An accurate schedule. A smooth stop. For a moment I feel like I'm inside a clock, what the world looks like from inside a clock.

The conductor, a lady, she leans from her seat, "You're wet, kids. Bone soaked."

We are. But somehow comfortable. Looking down before stepping on the car, Sally sees a broach on the ground, picks it up. We climb in, take a seat several seats back. I offer Sally the window. No one else on board.

"Thanks, Ben. In a minute. I want to talk to the lady."

"Wait!" I whisper, "She thinks I'm a kid?"

"Immature, hubs, she thinks you're immature. She's being nice."

The second car (this one *is* green) has a Chinese Mexican woman at the controls, always think I know where people are from. Her hair is straight, dark brown, curled at the ends, high hairline, middle-aged, wholesome. She sounded black. Words evaporated off her lips when she spoke, a Southern drawl, heavy. Love the Southern drawl, how it shaped her syllables.

Sally pauses, gives me a kiss, turns to the lady.

We begin moving. I sit down, dripping, look out the window. Worlds waiting to happen, worlds that have happened. Wide, long lanes. More trees, massive trees with huge branches, dense leaves, old friends out for a stroll that stopped to chat and forgot to move on. Elaborate gingerbread homes. Grand old homes. Homes that raised families. Homes that built America, made us what we are, what we imagine ourselves to be.

Sally and the conductor begin talking.

"Name's Bonnie," she says. "Where are you from, young lady? And you are young. A never-grow-old type. Women like me, right? Oh, what we'd give to look like you."

"Albinos," Sally responds. "It's an albino thing, I used to be a mermaid."

They both laugh. I don't see the humor.

"Ben." She turns toward me. "That's my Ben. We're from California. The North. Paradise. I'm Sally."

"Paradise? The place that burned?"

"It did. Yes. That place."

"And look at you. Don't they teach you to use an umbrella in Paradise? And girl, I can see every part of your anatomy. I'm just say'n. Eye candy tends to get eaten in these parts. Cover up some. Sorry, miss, sorry. Mean no offense. I'm not much on taking advice and I don't like to give it, but you're beautiful. Too beautiful. Had to say something."

Sally blushes. Looks like it. A little more red in her color than usual, always fun to watch her glow change hues.

Two kids get on at the next stop. 16, 17 years old. Could be older. Whitish-brown color, a mixture. Sharp features, long hair. T-Shirts with big tongues on them, shorts, buckle down sandals, sideways baseball hats. They take seats in the back.

The conductor and Sally continue talking. Sally shows her the broach. They talk about it, pass it back and forth, Sally pins it on, turns to show me, waves. I fantasize about life in old time New Orleans.

Dainty women with parasols, children in school shorts, school caps, neatly pressed shirts, dogs without leashes wetting car wheels, chasing cats.

We make a turn, a slight turn, just enough to lose balance. Sally grabs hold of the overhead bar, the line of her bare arm, shoulder, breasts, stomach, hip, thigh, leg, the complete line from hand to foot is visible. Can't take my eyes off her. Have to...the two guys...they're boys, really, younger than I thought. As we approach the next stop, our stop, they come forward, hesitant, then run past me when the door opens, tear the broach off Sally's lapel, knock her to the floor and run out. With the broach.

"Fuck! Fuck! I'm too old for this crap." I say that like all old guys say it. Heave an incomplete sigh and get up. Bonnie helps Sally, takes her to a seat, makes a phone call. Not to the police. I kick off my sandals, jump down and begin running, feels good to run. "Old but fit," I say that, often, have to prove it. Can still see the boys. I'm moving fast. A deer racing, the sound of rifle fire hammering his ears. My muscles take over, remember jumping from rock to rock across streams, down hills, mountain life, running all out, young legs taking the bumps, leaping, jumping, getting in shape for ski season. I love running, love it. Closing the gap, sprinting, gaining on them, they cut through some houses, down a side street, split up. I follow the bigger one, the guy with the broach, he's slowing down. Anger fuels my eager muscles, I speed up, imagine catching him, grabbing him by the throat, choking him, squeezing until his eyes blow their sockets.

An angry old man with a bone. I am one, have always been one, from the day I was born.

I'm nearly on him, he cuts left, crosses the street, a car almost clips him, almost clips me. At the next corner he turns right, meets up with the other kid, keeps running, a business district, small, a few shops. We run past them, past people watching, people not watching.

Christ! They take some stairs, outside stairs, at the top both jump down to another outside stairway, another building. I skip the jumping, go through the building. Catch up with them on the other side. They're not expecting me. I clothesline the bigger one, crack his nose, he fell to the sidewalk, got up and ran into a dress shop. The other kid went in right behind him, me behind the kid. We all stop in front of a big, tattooed, man. A massive, six-foot-plus Samoan-looking guy standing in front of a massive garment press. Steam frothing from its sides, lots of clothes on racks, a couple of women trying on skirts and a Chinese woman at the cash register. All the windows are open, and the door. Still raining.

"Dad, we can explain!" The first thing they say. That was it.

"No need," says the Samoan. The big guy. He takes the broach, hands it to me, turns to the boys.

"Unbuckle and bend over. Both of you."

Distraught, they say nothing, drop their pants.

"And kick off the skivs. Your bare asses are all I want to see. Give 'um up. Now!"

They drop their skivs, all the women look away, not all, maybe none. He walks over to the cashier counter, pulls open a cabinet drawer. Owns the place, seems like. Owners have a thing they do, an owner thing. He had that owner thing. The way he took out the wood paddle. It was an owner thing to do. And the paddle, it had holes in it like the paddle my grade school principal used on undisciplined students, irresponsible stubborn students…could never remember their names.

"Bend over," he says.

They do, they bend over, grip their ankles tight. Calfless juvenile legs, bare cheeks, timid flesh hoping for clemency.

Whack! Solid, the first kid cries out, the older one, the bigger one.

"Quiet! My own breathing is all I want to hear."

Whack, the younger kid. He cries out, louder.

"Quiet! Every sound I hear adds a whack."

They fell silent, took their hits. Took and took them. In the end, they were tough. They kept themselves whole. Something to respect.

"And what do you say?"

They turn, look at me.

"We're sorry, mister." Almost in unison.

"And what do you do?" Says the father, the big guy, his voice carries authority when he speaks but somehow sounds half his size.

"We return the broach, Papa, the man with the broach. Apologize to the lady."

"Good," he put the paddle down, turns to me. "They're good boys," he says. Almost involuntarily, my eyebrows raise, but I agree. "Largely good," he adds, smiling.

"Yeah, I know," I say, feeling relaxed, no longer angry. I enjoyed the run. "Boys will be boys. Fuck, men *are* boys, boys with bigger egos, that's all. What's your name?"

"Abraham Graham."

I know the name. Not able to place it. Dignity in a man…skin color can't define it.

"Pleasure to meet you, Abraham. And thanks." I open my palm. The broach. The first time I actually look at it. It's beautiful. Looks real. Hadn't thought it could be real, that the fates would give us something of value beyond our means. It was the boys stealing from my Sally, hurting her, that made me chase them…and pride, and ego. I know that. Everyone knows that. Ego needs attention, can't be ego without attention. "My wife. Gotta get back."

"Of course, the boys will take you. Drive you."

"Good, that works. Thanks."

The boys pull up their skivs, their trousers, very slowly.

Abraham walks us through the doorway to the curb, to his car. A 60s convertible, a Chevy. Beautiful, red with whitewall tires, white top, white fins, polished chrome, no rust. Clean interior. A Gilda Jones ride. The older kid gets in, takes the wheel, the younger one jumps into the back. I take shotgun.

Stops raining. Pauses. Nice.

Doesn't take long to get back to the streetcar. The kid pulls up next to it, parks partly on the grass, partly on pavement. Bonnie is waiting, standing outside. She appears bigger than before, puffed up, hands on her hips, a mean face, hard for her to make a mean face, but she does it.

Meek, humiliated and bruised, the two boys walk up to her. Drop their heads.

"Sorry ma'am."

"Not to me," she snaps. "Her."

"Yes ma'am."

They turn to Sally. She's sitting on the step, regal, something shining, an image of innocence in wisdom. How could anything negative ever touch her? The boys apologize, Sally accepts. They shake hands, turn back to Bonnie.

"Auntie, we didn't know it was you…."

She smacks them. "Don't talk to me. I hate callin' your dad on you. Damn kids. You're runnin' thin now, very thin!"

"Can we go?"

"Yes…go."

They get back in the Chevy, pull away, slowly, a cautious exit, distance between us increases. Rain suddenly erupts dissolves them. Gone. The street takes over, the trees, all the history of lesser events, worse events, they take over. I sit down next to Sally. She's shaking. I hold her close, very close. Warm her, feel my love for her flowing, filling her veins. She stops shaking, we sit. We sit until she moves, gets up, puts a hand on my shoulder.

"Thank you, Ben. My Ben. It's a good luck broach. You'll see. And Bonnie, thank you."

After adjusting her dress, and a modest preening, Sally picks up my sandals, passes them to me, reaches for Bonnie's hands, holds them. Bonnie smiles, a beautiful smile, pinches her lips together, gives Sally a hug, gives me a hug.

Time to go.

We stand back as she rolls away, a big, wind-up toy unwinding. A clock's world.

# SEVENTY THREE

Rain intensifies. Endless wet. The end of days. Maybe. A full bladder. I look for a tree, a corner, an obscure spot. There aren't any. Cities: privacy poverty, expensive poverty. Already wet. I turn from Sally. Embarrassing if she notices, if anyone notices. I let go, feel better as the warm release escapes my body and runs with the rain.

Chicken Little's sky is definitely falling. Rain. Lots of rain. We walk in it. Slog through it. Walk longer than expected. Another intersection. Flooded. I feel like a fish, not the first time. Won't be long before we grow gills, begin to speak, and walk like fish, shrimp, octopus. Two more blocks to the address Amy gave us. A rich part of town.

The house is a corner house, white with blue trim. Grand, manageable. Tall, latticed windows, shutters, columns with carved crowns. Ornate attic windows with all the lights on. Two chimneys, Greek key and grape cornices, a large wide wrap around porch with sofa swings on both sides of the front door. Big pillows. Inviting. No one swinging in them. High see-through fence all around. Iron. Freshly cut grass, soggy grass. Flowers. Manicured hedges. We check the address. 376. Yep. We've arrived. Wet, spent of enthusiasm, holding each other. We hesitate at the gate. Stand there, thinking.

A good idea to go in, or not?

Sally nudges me. I ring the bell.

A long slow chime, melody filling empty spaces, creating them.

We wait. I ring the bell again.

The gate opens. Graceful, the sweeping flow of a matador's cape. Granite footpath led the way to a light blue staircase, enamel finish, white rails unfolding at the bottom. Sally takes my arm. We ascend the stairs. Door is open. Rooms well lit. Music playing in the background, something African. People inside moving about, talking. Fifteen or so. Maybe twenty.

Dripping on the entry matt. Looking in. Who are we? Why are we there?

A girl taller than Sally, historic beauty, very attractive, covered in a white tunic (mostly covered), she's carrying a tray of drinks, joints, pills in colorful containers. She stops. Smiles softly, nothing unusual in our appearance, our condition.

"Would you like towels, a drink, drugs?"

Sally's eyes light up. "We would, yes!"

"All three," I add. "We'll take all three. Thank you."

She hands us some pills and two thin champagne glasses filled with clear liquid. A champagne glass does not guarantee the presence of champagne. We don't care. It's time to change pace, to reassess determinants of human value, entertain the possibility that everything we believe to be true, is not true.

"I'll be ba-ack," she says, tries to sound like Arnold Schwarzenegger. Too attractive.

"I need to change, Ben. This dress. Look. One of my favorites. It's a mess. What can I do with it?"

"We'll get it cleaned Sal. Cleaned and pressed. Make it new. It's a beautiful dress. Petals on a flower. That's how it looks on you. Tomorrow we'll find a cleaner."

She kisses me, leans into me. "Thank you, Ben."

*Not her only mother. Still thinking about that, and the Ganges.*

The tall server girl returns carrying two big towels. "If you wish to shower," she says, "There are two available. One at the end of that hallway." She points. "Another up those stairs." She points again. Sally picks the hallway. I go upstairs.

Up and up, eager to bathe I move quickly. At the door to the bathroom, my hand out, about to turn the knob, I pause. Don't know why.

It opens. A girl comes out. No, a woman. Striking features, present features. Light green dress, tight, small opal colored jacket, long pearl earrings, a pendant with an eye in the middle of it, beaded necklace, thin wire glasses. She's South American? One of the Andes tribes? Colombian, maybe. Women like her, that look like her, I've seen them in the Santa Marta Mountains…years ago…hash trips.

She's beautiful. An informed smile. Light brown skin, golden brown. Dark eyes, long black hair, thick, glossy, inviting. She gives me the once over. A pro of some kind. I straighten up.

"You're dripping wet," she says. "Would you like me to dry you?"

"Sure, thanks, but you'll need to be quick. My wife's waiting for me downstairs."

"Of course," she says. "Come."

I follow her. Two doors down. A bedroom. A big bedroom. Bigger than our two Paradise trailers put together, and the Jeep. Silk carpets on the floor. Framed mirrors. Marble fireplace. Several Frederic Church paintings. Originals. Must be. A grand canopy bed, mosquito nets tied to each pole. An interesting mix of heirloom amenities; personal treasures.

She leaves me standing at the door. Comes back with a bathrobe, towel, and a glass of wine. Rose´.

"It's Domaine Ott," she says. "And please, take off your clothes."

"Here?"

"Why not? It's my house."

Her house.

Shirt, hat, shorts. I peel them off. Drop them. A thick splash. The sound of wet cement landing on dry dirt, ladles of stew filling empty bowls. She hands me the robe, the towel. Holds the glass of wine, keeps it from spilling, takes a sip, cups my prime with her free hand. Weighs it in her palm, gives it a good squeeze, a slight pull. "Nice," she says.

"Your wet clothes, I'll have them dried and sent to your room. Dutch door at the end of the hall, key is in the lock."

Over her shoulder on the way out, "See you downstairs."

New Orleans! No answer for how familiar it makes me feel.

# SEVENTY FOUR

Alone. Naked. Wet. Standing in a bedroom I've never been in before, in a house I've never been in before…the lady, her palm, how she held my prime. I want more. More of the house, more of the lady, more unconditional stimulants. More, more, more. Something wrong with me? Probably. Definitely. Explosions. Background memories rising. Flares lighting the night sky. Viet Cong everywhere, assembling themselves into known shapes; tree trunks, rocks, walls, doors, masks to hide behind. Strangeness becoming normal. Might be. Or is everything strange all the time and I just don't notice? Would it make a difference if I did notice? Pills asking questions, Champagne talk, contents of the tall glass exciting the blood, opening lines of indirect communication with altered states. Drugs…man's first wireless call to God.

I dry myself. Put on the robe. The door, a knock.

"Yes?"

A maid comes in. Could be the owner's daughter. She's young. Looks young. Maybe not. Curly hair, dimples. She picks up my clothes, glances at me. One of those no-rules glances that can fit anywhere, mean nothing at all, or something very important. I can't grasp it. Don't need to. She leaves without saying a word.

I wait a moment, a couple of moments. Walk downstairs.

Fragrances. Sally has one, a Sally fragrance, it's becoming stronger. I see her. She's lingering, waiting for me just beyond the bottom of the stairway, has on a robe like mine, a towel wrapped around her hair. Amy's with her. They're holding hands. I join them.

"Damn Amy. The people you know. What can I say? Thank you for the invite, the roof over our heads. Much appreciated."

Amy pulls me toward her, gives me a hug, pushes against my chest, yanks my robe open, lets the dog out, pats him on the head, puts him back.

"And so…" she giggles, cinching my robe belt. "The night begins," and she skips off, drifts off, flutters. A happy girl.

Blunting it in New Orleans. Everyone is. Restrictions collapsing. Peremptory rules falling. No fear of transfiguration, of insult, or failure. Failure. Whatever it is, I've been afraid of it my whole life. No longer living my own life, feels like that. Can't fail if I'm not me. Fears that diminish an exchange of differences, gone, no more God, no need for God. Music. The mood taking hold. The place taking hold, the pills, the drink, the comfort of becoming unrecognizable to oneself, to memory. I'm doing that. We're doing that. The people I see. All of us. We're following multi-world breadcrumbs, tempting excess, sniffing, becoming the mood–a mix of fragrances, the weight of the air, the smoky haze drifting between rooms shifting as people walk through them. The lighting, separate from its source, moves with the haze, a hypnotist's wheel captivating us. Not a house, Simbana's house. A lifeform of some kind. That's what it is. Feels like a living thing, something absorbing us. Something, but not a house.

Two elves in extra high heels, with drug and booze trays, walk by. They're elves, real elves, not girls made to look like elves. I reach out, take another glass of wine, a couple more joints, pop a pill. Not sure what it is. Sally, too. She took several, downs them with red wine, tugs at my robe, pulls me to her, "Hey, buddy, want to see what's under *my* robe?"

I did. I do. Every second, every minute, every hour of every day. Sally is the drug of my life, the strongest drug I've ever taken. We kiss. A long, moist, mint, and cinnamon kiss. I begin untying her robe knot, the split widens. People walk by. Colorful people. Colors that look like people.

"Shall we wander, get something to eat? Or?"

Drugs and alcohol coming online, the front lines…nothing between us and all lies we tell ourselves to convince us we are who we think we are. Rouse's lunch is fully digested, whisked away to Wasteland: a planet on the 'yet to be discovered' list. Good idea to eat.

"The dining room, Ben. It's over there. I'll meet you. Simbana wants to chat. The owner."

"Oh, Simbana. I met her upstairs. Gift of God. That's what her name means. Not sure why I know that. I'll get you a plate."

"Thanks, Hubs," she walks away, excited.

The dining room isn't really a dining room. No plates, chairs, tables. Just pillows and baskets, baskets with tall handles sitting on the floor. Baskets with an assortment of foods, exotic meats–kangaroo, water buffalo, reindeer, elk, iguana, mammoth, giant sloth. Lots of fruits and vegetables, many varieties. And sandwiches, pastries, cheeses, candy, drugs…all in baskets. People pick them up, pass them around, carry them around, set them down and move on. Different rooms, venues changing from room to room. A strange group, and not strange. Unusually usual. Can't see why Amy calls it a Game of Thrones Party. I think about it… not for long. A party. A place to spend the night. That's all it is.

I'm the oldest guy there, one of the shortest. And all I have on is a robe.

# SEVENTY FIVE

"I'm Adam."

A guy. Late twenties, early thirties. He's wearing a business suit. No Game of Thrones in that. Fine, gold rimmed glasses, painted goatee, looks painted. He walks up to me.

"How are you this evening?"

How the fuck did I know how I was.

"Have yet to decide that," I say. "About to get a bite to eat. Have a look around."

"I'll join you," he hesitates. "If you don't mind. And I'm fine with massaging your shoulders while you eat. Only if you want, of course."

"My shoulders. Why?"

"A first and final offer," he says. "You eat, I massage. We get to know each other. A fun start. Then you massage my shoulders."

"Why?" I try to focus, can't quite get what he wants, how he sees me. Reality shifting gears. Buses driving in different directions simultaneously. My mind goes blank. He stares at me...very serious... then winks.

"Oh, yeah. I get it...yeah. Sorry, bud." I say, "I'm a tits man. A girl's-only John, but thanks." Polite. Why am I being polite? I don't feel polite.

Adam saunters off. I pick up a basket. Cheeses. A nice brie. Spicy crackers. Pour myself more wine. Drink half, pour again, pick up a bottle of water, sit down in the middle of the main room, rotate 360 degrees, slowly. The house is getting bigger. Certainly, clearly getting bigger. Learning to fly. I'm sure of it.

Two girls come by. They're dressed in peasant Game of Thrones garb. Bosoms bulging. Grand curves and laces. Big, grinning faces. Jovial pub girls.

I hold up my glass. "Cheers ladies."

They laugh with one voice, ask, "Would you like a shoulder massage?"

Shoulder massage. What's with the shoulder massage? Was I missing something?

"Later," I say. "Maybe. Thank you." Too polite. Something wrong with me…definitely. I light a joint. Take a bite of cheese. Wonder where Sally is. Look around, look for her, decide to go upstairs, see if she's in our room. Finish my wine on the way, the joint, feel light, see-through, as if a separate self has stepped in, taken my place, convinced me it's me, that everything about me is public knowledge.

The Keys. A long way to go, miles to go. I want to be there.

Sally isn't in our room. Her robe is. Her sandals. Don't see my clothes. My hat, shirt, shorts. I walk out, leave the door open. Go back downstairs. All around me people begin appearing in costumes. Throne's characters. I'm wearing a robe. Missed the character in a robe. Must have been there. My ass. Hands on it. Surprised, I turn abruptly. Takes a few seconds for my eyes to catch up.

"Sally!"

She's made up, braided to look like Daenerys. Silver dragon necklace, sheer light blue gown. Isn't really a gown, more like a shawl, tied to cover small patches of flesh. Beautiful.

"Want to dance, Hubs?"

"Now? Sure. A slow dance?"

"Yes. Slow and close."

Just us on the edge of time, the beginning of it all. Feels like it. Her heat into mine. Mine into hers. Dance floor erotica. Slow moving. My robe belt, she unties it. My robe, she takes it off. I feel like it's still on, strange. The real Daenerys. Sally could have played the part. Slow dancing. People mingling around us, pulling up chairs, finding partners, smoking, drinking. The house, the mood playing. The Orleans's tenor taking us, winding us up. People diffuse into groups and stray individuals, some working themselves, others letting someone else work them. Drug fog rolling in…diming judgment; the need for criticism to define value.

Two aliens, eons ago, the tall skinny kind with fishbowl eyes and squat noses.

"Hey," says alien one. "We've done our job here, haven't we? We followed the instructions on the box, built herds of believers, like it said…dependable material processors. Like it said. Humans, the lot of them, per the instructions, we've programmed them to think they have a choice; the right and ability to decide their fate. It's a major accomplishment."

"It is. You're right." Says alien two, and he lights a hookah tucked under his arm. "They do think that, the humans."

"They do, without hesitation," returns alien one. "However, because choice is not theirs, and they will likely find out, we need to give them something, something to pit them against each other and not us, something inaccessible to fact."

"Of course," agrees alien two, and he put his hand to his chin. "I know," he says, his fishbowl eyes lighting up. "Remember that childhood story, Godlinger. The one where the little female Belliwader catches a big fish, a wizard of some kind that talks to her, tells her, reveals to her, all the secrets of the universe. The Godlinger fish story. Remember. It's a good story. Let's give them Godlinger, focus their attention on the fish. That, and other humans, the several we can program to say they talk to the fish. We can call taking to the fish, religion."

"They'll never go for that," says alien one. "Too obvious. And Godlinger, it's too long"

"They will, trust me, they'll go for it. And we can shorten Godlinger to just God. Make it easy, make them believe God is good for them."

"How?"

"We lie."

"Right," says alien one. "A good idea. Damn good."

"Definitely," agrees alien two, and he passes alien one the hookah.

Nothing attached to definition. Model citizenry evaporating with the tide…does getting lost in reality, make it real? My thinking…was I thinking? The room heating up, the house global warming, everyone connected, sperm rising, vaginal juices steaming. Joy to the world! Fuck! We were on, all of us, whoever we were, whatever we were, we were fully loaded, separate worlds melding onto something more complete but less definable. Multiple sighs of high relief reverberating throughout the house. Dozens of simultaneous eruptions. People exhausting the bounty, losing touch, exhaling contentment, sitting down, laying down, collapsing, many of them. A few still eating, trying new positions, waiting their turn.

Sally sighs, stretches her wings, lies down on the floor. Amy lies down next to her. I squeeze between them.

Feminine warmth, it pulls me in, takes me home.

Still early.

I cover us, fall asleep.

# SEVENTY SIX

You're under water, holding your breath, the bottom of a blue lagoon. It's been two minutes. How much longer can you last? Thirty seconds, forty? A minute more, two, three more minutes. Are you less than halfway through your air supply? More than halfway?

Holding it, that's all you're doing, for as long as possible. Finally, you must breathe. Too far to the surface, you inhale, take in water, it floods your lungs, a cool feeling, almost inviting, then...you begin to breathe normally.

It finally rained so hard for so long that coastal residents, in order to stay in their homes, grew gills, webbed feet and webbed hands. Lots of web variation, different sizes, thickness, color, length, agility.

Aquatic Sapiens, that's what they named themselves. Competition for Electro Sapiens, robots, smart toasters, smart clothes, smart lawn mowers, fridges, ankle bracelets...

A white bunny rabbit, just like the ones we see in the movies.

It hops by.

Almost 8 p.m. I wake up, pull on my eyelids, they feel stuck. Evening light, pallid, a dim glow taunting darkened corners, private alcoves, the conscience of sinners feeling no sin. Sally and Amy are gone. Cleaning up, getting to know each other better, I think so. Very different girls. Amy's more human.

I put my robe on.

Dazed people lying about, shirts open, skirts up, assorted levels of undress, of eating, of kissing, of fondling, of libidinous fantasies exchanging vows. A calm disorder. The hum of equilibrium. Women walking back and forth, a couple of ultra-10s, models, tall, slender, they're wearing body paint; clothes painted to look like they're alive and trying to free themselves from the girl's bodies as they walk. Mesmerizing. With each step the clothes reach for me. They do. The painted clothes. Very hot 10s, very weird hot 10s.

I hunt for a bathroom, find one, take a leak, wash my hands, rarely do that. Splash water on my face, rarely do that. Think to chuck it. A hint of nausea. To chuck or not to chuck? How often is that a question? Something to consider? Mind feels like it's filled with air, some kind of hollow echo speaking in tongues. A pleasant temperature. I go outside, walk the porch, evening mist dismissing the rain, errant patches of light taking their final bows across open doors, walls, furniture, shifting bodies. A couple of chairs, a small table between them, a hookah on the table, ready to smoke. I sit down, strike a long wooden match, a pilot light match, the kind that gives you splinters if you're not careful. Take a hit, look for anyone carrying drinks, bottles. See one. A young man. Ivy League. Crisp movements, an oddly long neck. Probably got bullied as a kid, called "Giraffe-ee," "Giraffe boy," "Long Neck," some dumbass name. I wave him over.

Adam follows him.

"I'll take one of those wines," I say. "A bottle."

The boy lowers the tray. I pick a bottle. A red cab.

"Thanks."

"Myself as well," Adam says, and he eases in, takes the chair across from me.

"Mind if I sit? Is this seat reserved?"

Polite people. Never trust them.

"No worries," I say. "I'm waiting for someone, but it's not reserved."

He sits down, crosses his legs, adjusts the chair, the cushion.

"Ben…it is Ben, correct?"

"Correct." I scratch my head. Did I tell him my name? Can't remember.

"You're a tits guy. You said that, of course, but you're prime man, Ben. I have to tell you. Very prime. I'd love to work your shoulders. Have a long chat. There's so much two men can share. Just say the word. Angels work in mysterious ways."

Again, the shoulders. Was I supposed to respond? Say what? I thought about it. Didn't think, said: "Yeah, sure, have to, massage away."

"Really?!" His face lights up.

"No. Not really!" I say. "And you're Adam, right?"

"Right."

"Listen, Adam, no offense, but I have no interest in guys who have no interest in girls. Never have had. Never will have, but I get it. You want your happy endings, your own dance routine, that's cool. I want mine. Every guy wants his rod jolted. Right. That's what guys want, every day, when and wherever possible. Right."

"OK, right."

"So, here's the thing, Adam. Here's the thing, the essential point, an essential point." I scratch an itch behind my ear, rub my eyes. "Tits work for me, for guys like me. For you, for guys like you, it's not tits. The want for happy endings is what we have in common, but that's it. We live in different turn-on, turn-off, worlds. That's the story, the whole story. Splat. You want men in your world. A world dominated by male sounds, male looks, male smells, behavior, activities, male on male sex. That turns you on, gets you off. I get that. Doesn't work for me, don't get how it works for you, don't care. Female flesh, touching it, tasting it, seeing it as often as possible—that turns me on, turns on guys like me. Movies with nude girls in them. Here's what I'm saying, Adam, here's the point, a point. Tits guys, we love watching female actors remove their clothes, especially the really beautiful ones. Puts a nice bit of heat in the pocket, gets ol' Henry out of bed. Today, too often, when I click on a movie, a regular movie, a cop movie, an action film, a comedy…no homosexual content warning comes up in the ratings, something telling me what to except, giving me a choice to watch or not. Nudity does, and smoking, and swearing, and drugs, and violence. I'm ok with those, of course. I like it when they show tits, but along with tits, and pardon me, Sally's trying to get me to stop using the word fag, I get fag scenes, fag themes, fag innuendo, even sodomy, without warning. Does nothing but put me off. Yours world is not my world and I have no interest whatever in making it my world. It feels like manipulation, the covert gay stuff. It is manipulation. Like I said. I need to feel like it's my decision to do anything, really. I'm old. That's my program, like it or not."

Adam smiles, in a way. I pick up my wine glass, take a couple of swallows.

"I'm thinking," he says.

"OK."

"Sure. I see, Ben. It feels unfair, like making a Christian pray to Allah. Right?"

"Right."

"And we homos, we have our own movies, so why should we be in yours? Especially without telling you. That's what you think?"

"Right."

"Fucks with your foreplay game."

"Right."

"And I'm gay."

"Right."

Adam slaps his leg. Takes a hit, a drink, starts laughing. I laugh. Not sure why.

"A joke Ben. Just having a little fun, wanted to see how many times I could get you to say…right."

"Fuck!"

Why am I having this conversation? I check myself. Am I still me? Do I look like me? I do. I think. Maybe it's the robe. I knew fags but had no fag friends. No reason to, so far.

"Bob. Can I call you Bob instead of Adam?"

"Hobnob Bob?"

"No, just Bob," I say.

"Why? What's wrong with Adam?"

"Nothing, just thinking."

"What?"

"Adam and Eve. The Eve bit, how does that work in the homo world?"

"It doesn't. You're right. Where I come from, Eve has a rod."

"Oh…so you're alien, is that it? Born gay…that's what it means. All of you, you're from some far-off world, a guys-only world.

"That's right, Ben. A guy's only world. Everywhere you look, guys are there, strolling in the park, walking the dog, buying food, feeding baby guys, guys watching guy tv guys, guys playing guy football, guy medicine practiced in all the hospitals. It's great. And there must be a guy heaven, a gay guy heaven. Just imagine." I can't. He stretches abruptly, sits straight up.

"Interesting," I say, and I take a long draw on the hookah. Exhale toward him, into his face.

He takes out a cigarette holder, a bone handle, carved, something elaborate. Pulls a Marlboro from his pocket, offers me one, I decline. He lights up, takes a long drag, leans forward, a toothy smile from certain angles, blows smoke in my face, grins.

"I like the word 'fag,'" he says. "The way you use it. Nothing personal, just a word for something that sounds right to you. I like saying it myself. How it sounds, how it spreads out in front of me when I say it, clears the way. It's a word people notice, I know that. I know they'll hear it. In all you just said, the word 'fag' is clearest in my mind. Most words aren't heard, and they're forgotten immediately if they are heard. Not 'fag.' The word 'fuck' as well. It has gravitas. 'Fag' has gravitas. 'Nigger' has gravitas. Blacks, some blacks, they love 'nigger,' use it all the time. It's not a white word. Whites don't know what it means. It's a black word, their word, they don't like whites using it. Money is a white word. Was a white word. 'Fag' belongs to us. We say who can use it."

Enjoying himself. Half listening, still, I hear him, keep eating, smoking, drinking, looking. Looking for girls to look at. Looking for

Sally. I'm feeling good. Simbana. There's something kept about her, but not by a man or woman.

"Think about it, tits man, words. We make them mean what we want them to mean. 'Queer,' 'gay,' 'faggot,' 'closet,' 'queen,' 'partner,' 'marriage,' 'dyke,' 'fairy' 'rainbow'…they're our words now, trophy words. 'Marriage' comes to mind, you think 'gay.' 'Queen' comes to mind, you think 'gay.' 'Rainbow' comes to mind, you think gay. 'Closet' comes to mind, you think 'gay.' Anytime you see two girls together, two guys, especially young guys, you think 'gay.' We're in your heads, modifying and normalizing lifestyle variation, lifestyle choice. Gay sex everywhere. In movies, like you said, every program and ad we can get in, we're in. Minority suffering leverage. Sympathy leverage. AIDS leverage. We've made impressive gains for just a few percent of the population…we're…."

His every word becoming gospel, he's rolling it, spinning it, a whirling dervish reaching for nirvana.

I put up my hand, "Whoa, OK. OK…whoa, Adam. Sure, but what does all that have to do with me, with this pipe I'm smoking, the tasty wine in my glass, those girls over there dressed like the three muses. Or undressed like the three muses. I don't know. Impressive gains, yeah, but I have to think about it. Sodomy; the consummation of homosexual union, that's the problem, Adam. Pumping gas up the tailpipe. Is that a good idea, something to popularize?"

"Right," he says, turning away as he speaks. "You're right. Shit for babies, it sounds bad. You make it sound bad. Fags, we never think like that. You're missing out. That's what we think. All you breeders, you vagina guys, you think sodomy is unnatural. It's not. Caged is what you are, by false modesty, modesty slavery, self-righteous overweening. You think submission, prayer, and resignation; being stepped on, is what it means to be good. Might as well be Muslims, Moonies, Tom Cruise Scientologists, Hasidim, any dog in a cage. You're missing out, a long way from feeling like you're free to do with your body as you wish. You want a massage?"

"What?!"

"Kidding. Just kidding. I'm no homo, Ben. It's an act. I'm an actor. An audition coming up tomorrow, early. I love women, adore them."

"What?"

He sits back. Lights a cigarette, grins like a child certain he'll get paid for a job he didn't do.

"Nah...I'm a fag, all fag. Just playing, a little jerk-off sleight of hand, that's all." He starts laughing, slaps his chest. "All fag, full on and full blown, that's what I am, no looking back. The dicks have it in my world," he said. "Hallelujah, sinners."

I scratch my ear, always doing that, dig out a piece of earwax, flick it off my finger, take a moment to clear my mind. No luck. Propaganda wars, the power of deceit. Doctor visits, I think about them, about having to piss in the clear plastic cup, carry the cup for everyone to see (kids, old ladies, fat men) from the toilet to the waiting room.

A couple of joints on the table. I pick one up, take a hit. Too much, cough, keep coughing. Adam gets up, wants to slap my back, I put out a hand, stop him, stop coughing. Clear my throat, empty my glass of wine, fill it. Clear my throat again.

"You talk like this to everyone?"

"No," he says. "Actually, just you. Not sure why."

I take another hit. More room opens up in my mind, room to get high in. Two more hits, and two more. Pot, good pot, there's a certain comfort in how you inhale and exhale good pot.

"Me neither," I say. "I wouldn't consider myself a conversationalist, not that. I don't like people, generally, and I'm not crafty with words. I never talk to fags, never. I'm scared shitless of them. Afraid that someday a guy like you is going to tase me, grab my Wally, take him away to some kind of bat cave and feed him to something that lives in the cave, something with pitcher plant eyes so big dinner plates falls into them, and Wally's. Eyes that dissolve Wally's, lots of Wally's, my Wally. Gone, down the drain never to return. I'm sure that would happen. Without question, sure as sure."

"Damn Ben. Damn. You do, you've got it bad, man. Really bad!"

"I do, I know. Bad, since childhood, lots of fights, school suspensions, punishments."

I hit the wine, the hookah.

"Sorry man, really...."

"Me too," I say, "for myself. I feel very sorry. It's the way I am, that's all. Can't stop myself from being what I've become."

"And there's nothing I can do?"

"Right, Adam, nothing you can do. But thanks."

"Are you sure?"

"Yeah, I'm sure," I say, and I halt my words, lean forward, blow smoke in his face. "Kidding, Bob. Just kidding."

He flips me the bird, both hands. "Asshole."

"I am. Absolutely. People say that. Not all the time, but they say it." I continue.

"What I don't get, Adam, and I suppose it's obvious to you, but how a John, any John, when he sees a beautiful, naked woman–perfect breasts, ass, face, skin, figure–how he can have no desire to slip it to her. How he can skip having tits in his life, I don't understand that. Vaginaphobia–fear of women. You guys afraid of women? Is that it? Whatever. Very sad. I think so. A life without tits. Can't imagine it."

"I like you, Ben. No reason to. Most people only feel unrestrained when drugged or drunk. Not you. Drugged, drunk or not, you're out in the open. One of those, 'am who I am, don't give a fuck what others think' types. A refreshing change. And that shoulder rub? I have moves, Ben, moves."

Shoulders. I never really think much about shoulders. Sally's shoulders, I think about hers. Ignore his question. "Like you said, Adam, I don't give a fuck. I have no interest in faggyness, if that's a word, and I don't want faggyness forced on me. I'm not difficult to understand. And why all this interest in me. I'm just a guy waiting for his girl, enjoying the party. You're an OK looking guy, guys that like guys must like you."

"It's a fag thing."

"What's a fag thing?"

"Beginners, virgins, no matter their age, guys that have never had a man tryst. We're always looking to pick a cherry. Gives us bragging rights, you know how it is, how you straights talk. 'So, man, how many virgins have you done?' 'Ten, fifteen maybe, hard to keep track.' 'I've done twenty.' 'Only twenty?' says another guy. 'I'm over a hundred virgins, all from different countries. Love virgins. But they tend to attach.'"

He smiles. "Wouldn't want you attached to me, Ben. A horrible thought."

I cringe, demonstrably, blow my nose.

Each table has a cigarette box, I open mine. A half dozen brands. Don't smoke cigarettes. Adam hands me his Marlboros. I take one. Light it. Inhale. Smooth. Flavorful. Difficult to believe it's bad for me. Light rain again, about 80 degrees. I pick up my wine, swirl it, watch the purple deepen in color, think I watch it deepen. Empty it, one swallow. Not the way to drink wine, a fine wine. Want to get back to where I left off before falling asleep. To feeling what it felt like with Sally on one side and Amy on the other.

A 64-year-old virgin. Never thought of myself that way. No interest in thinking it.

Sally walks up, her Daenerys hair and attire still in play. A big smile.

"So... gentlemen, what are the two of you talking about? And hello." She reaches out a hand. "I'm Sally. Mrs. Benjamin Mamott."

Introducing herself as Mrs. Mamott. Mrs. Benjamin Mamott. It's the first time.

"He's Adam," I say. "A fag juiced to the gills. We're talking."

"Really! About what?"

"I'm not sure, not exactly. Stuff."

"A conversation most people are afraid to have, Mrs. Mamott."

"Exactly," I say. "Stuff," and I swirl my wine, take in a heavy from the hookah.

Sally pulls my legs apart, sits on top of me, lights a joint, finishes the wine in her glass, what there is of it, lifts for a refill. I fill it, fill my mine, fill Adam's. A full night yet to come and all I want is to curl up with Sally and go to sleep.

"We were making light of weighty topics, unnecessarily weighty topics," Adam says. "That's what we were talking about. Overweight topics that need to go on a diet, to live on less attention. Ben would agree."

I nod.

"And you don't mind being called fag?"

"Ma'am. Mrs. Mamott. I'm from New Orleans." He leans back in his chair, makes it seem kinglier, picks up the hookah, pulls a long hit. "Seriously, what do I care? People can call me whatever they want. As long as we're not under water, I'm good."

He keeps his gaze on Sally. "Ben. Would mind if I took Sally, you know, to my room?"

"What?!"

"Kidding, guy. You're too easy."

"I'm old."

"He is," Sally says, blows the words with a kiss, "but damn good."

"Am I?"

"You are, Hubs. Can't imagine a better man."

Cool. A smiling heart, I have one.

# SEVENTY SEVEN

Dark outside. Light rain, marauding breezes shifting the curtains, errant napkins, garments, candle flames. The moment rushing by. Impossible to grasp it.

Adam lifts his glass, cheers us, stands up. Bows slightly, the male curtsy. Kisses Sally's hand, holds it, lingers. Looks at me, expects something. Not sure what. Can't decipher it. Too stoned. I nod. A friendly nod. New Orleans underwater. It will be…again. Very high odds.

Ivy League; the boy, balancing a full tray of guest beverages. Adam sees him, smiles, feigns rubbing his shoulder, gives us a parting glance, slips away.

Sally takes his seat, tops off her glass, puts her elbows on the table, her chin in her hands. "What next, Hubs?"

"Nothing, I'm just here. Looking at you, thinking. These people, this place. What it all means or doesn't mean. Is being good a bad idea?"

After a swallow, a hit, a yawn (which makes me yawn), she says, "How can being good be a bad idea?"

"Not sure. It's an incomplete thought. A lot of haze at the moment, a nice haze, but still…people who are good, because they're not always good, do bad things. Right?"

"Yes."

"Is doing one bad thing cause enough to classify a good person as a bad one? How many bad things have to be done to make someone bad? Who decides what is bad, what is good? How bad can you be and still be good? How good you can be and still be bad?"

"And…?"

Sally. I have to reach a little, focus my thinking. "Religion, Sal. Religion scares me, it teaches so little of what there is to learn. Herds people rather than guides them. Drives the mind, like Adam said, into thinking being stepped on—openly manipulated to personal disadvantage—is what it means to be good."

Quiet. She sits there. Doesn't blink. Doesn't speak. Beautiful. I look around.

Simbana's house. A surreal wishing well. No one doing what someone else is doing, being what someone else is being. A home feeling bigger on the inside than the outside, like a brain turned inside out, exposing the concubine wheels of the master clock...the limits of our creation.

"Ben...Simbana has a Jacuzzi in the prayer room. Want to soak? Relax? Have prayer sex, invent prayer sex?"

"A prayer room, really?"

"Joke, Ben. Wake up! You know, be here now or be nowhere."

"Right."

She takes my hand, leads me through the house. Her house. Feels like it. She knows everyone, everyone knows her. A lot of people. Seems like a lot. Only twenty, twenty-five tops. All manner of Game of Thrones attire—Wildlings to White Walkers. Very cool. We veer left into the central hallway. An antique display case centers the wall, rosewood, beautiful tooling. We stop. Several fossils in it, coins, a discolored letter on velum, strange script, maroon ink, a bone hairbrush, two very fragile cups and saucers, several rare books, and photos. A little gold cat.

"Ben. Have you ever stolen something?"

"I guess. Sure. Can't remember. Well...yeah, bike parts, Playboy centerfolds. Years ago. I needed bike parts. I raced. No money in it, not for me, a kid's place in the world. I worked for a bike repair guy. He had one lung. A skinny, brittle looking man, smelled like new rubber most of the time, bike wheel rubber. And cigarettes. His name was Henry. When a shipment came in of something I needed, a new derailleur, say, or brake pads, pedals? I'd open the box, lift one and say we were short if Henry asked. He never asked. Maybe he knew and didn't care. Couldn't race himself, said he was Olympic material once. Something happened, he gave up racing, gave up sports. Started drinking, smoking, then drugs. Hard stuff. Opium, heroin, meth… fucked himself up. I raced for him. Lost one race. That's all. He liked that about me. That I won races."

Sally's green eyes, looking at me, amused.

"So, yeah. I did steal."

"The cat." She points with her little finger. "I want the cat."

"Of course, you do, dear."

Simbana. She's standing behind us. How did I miss that? Near shit myself. Not very alert, not myself, was I anyone's self? The mood, it had me. The fog. It had me good. A cold beer. I want one.

"It's yours," says Simbana, running her finger along Sally's jaw line. "I bought it for you, on safari, a long time ago. Please, take it."

She leans forward, opens the case. A bouquet moment—the combined fragrance of a woman lying naked beneath clean sheets, and a gourmet meal requiring immediate consumption. How could a case smell like that?

Sally reaches in, picks up the cat, reacts as if it begins purring.

Simbana shifts her gaze, reminds me of women who get paid well for satisfying men they find repulsive. Tips her head slightly and vanishes down the hall. A mile-long hall, the inside of an animal, something big, bigger than an animal. Could be.

Lots of walls. Lots of wall candles, candles on tables, counters, in people hands as they prowl the Game. Lots of orphan church candles. Maybe they're lost. The candles. The Church…fuck. The Church is not Christ, it's anti-Christ…might even be *the* anti-Christ. The pedophile capital of religion.

"Let's go to our room, Ben. Sleep, make room for more drugs."

Still want a beer. Look for one as we retrace our steps to the bottom of the stairway. Two young women, Chinese. Eighteen, nineteen years old. Red hats, transparent red shits, and skirts. No underwear. They're pulling a small red wagon full of red apples toward the next room, a red room. I can see it. The doors open. People inside the room are wearing red. They look happy. Love Chinese women. Guys are OK, but they're guys, just guys. The women are fantastic. We walk past them up the stairs to our room, toss our dried and pressed clothes off the bed, collapse on the cotton bedspread, hold each other, close our eyes, and fall asleep, the little gold cat safe between us. Purring.

A lone trapper, rifle over his shoulder fading into the trees, tall trees, sleeping under tall trees, living under them, endless sky above, the future hiding somewhere known, somewhere frozen. Meadows of snow. Wind. Siberia. The Tundra. The trapper. He's certain his world won't change. That what was left behind for him he will leave behind for those who follow. No population refugees. No fear of extreme climate. Climate is already extreme, has always been extreme. Wilderness government overseeing all. Nature. Still bigger than man. He's sure of it. As sure as he is of the cold.

# SEVENTY EIGHT

"Ben...what time is it?"

I open my eyes. Are they my eyes? Am I seeing for myself or someone else? A low rumbling downstairs, steady bass notes. Deep, full notes. Still dark. Sally's breathing softly, her heart pumping alien industry through her veins, albino translucence texting heaven. A cold beer, very cold, more than cold. I want one.

"Not sure," I say. "It's dark. Late, early. Could be either one." The feel of Sally's body next to me, what it does to me. The comfort in it is impossible to explain, nothing in my experience compares to it, and it's so simple, all I'm doing is lying next to her. A man lying next to his woman. That's it. The beginning and end. Christ! I was going to be a father. How? Wasn't even sure how to be myself. If I needed to be myself.

Knew a cult leader once. Years ago. A know-yourself-find-yourself cult leader out of Northern California. His name was Robert Britain. A fat fuck, thick eyebrows, glassy egg-like eyes, rubber band lips. Bald guys with fat noses, food stuck between their teeth, beer-stained shirts, guys with their flies open, their tongues out, wandering around looking for attention. Britain wasn't one of those guys, but I thought of him that way. The Teacher. That's what he called himself. Said he was a female goddess trapped in a male body. Right. More like the embodiment of "conscious" evil playing God. A pedophile rapist piece of shit hiding his diseased fantasies behind hierarchical refinement; music, wealth, fine wine, classical art, exclusive knowledge. A sick fuck. A lowlife con. Trump's secret guru. Could be. He got young guys to tally his John, said it would make them pure, make me pure, open the doors to heaven. Cult mind control, thought reform: thinking another person's thoughts as if they are your own. I went for the virgins. Seventy-two of them. At least seventy-two.

Awake. Difficult to remove ourselves from the sheets, too comfortable. Waking up happy. No need to get up when you wake up happy. Better to stay in bed. The world in bed. Waking up happy. Imagine that. Nobody getting up. Nobody going to work. Nobody making money, paying the bills, putting food in their mouths. Everyone dying in bed. A happy ending. How life should be, and how it is…not sure if they know each other.

We get up, shower, put our party attire back on. My robe, her long scarf. She adjusts her hair, slips on her sandals, pops a couple of raisins in her mouth. Our bedroom door is open. Has been open, must have forgotten to close it. A piece of litter in the hall, a small coin size scrap of paper, light brown. I can see it from the bed. A woman walks by. Naked, tall, lots of tall walking around. I like tall. Long dark hair. Dimples at the top of her butt cheeks, stunning. Stunning women. The benevolence of mankind's radiant beauties, can't imagine living without them. The paper sticks to her foot, grabs hold. A tick thing to do.

"Nice tits."

Sally nods. "Nice tits, ass, and legs. Very nice."

"You want to meet her, Sal? We can ask."

Sally loves sex, everything about sex, everything. Whatever gives greater life to the senses, makes reality more real moment after moment, is sex for her. She loves it, wants everyone to love it. A full-frontal world, no attachment to clothes, no secrets. That's what she wants, how she lives.

"Later," she says.

"And my beer, I can use a beer?"

She takes my arm, escorts us to the door and down the stairs.

"One Hubs beer coming up."

# SEVENTY NINE

People talking, new people arriving, the same people with different looks, but for a few candles here and there, rooms are lit without an apparent light source. Music fills the air without speaker amplification. Guests are walking about, mingling, searching each other's bodies for visual toys, erotic delights, opportunity to defy the expectations of the harnessed masses. Early morning at Simbana's. Still dark. Waiters are calling people to a pre-sunrise event in the main room.

A big room, the main room, wood paneling, glass chandelier, wall sconces, dream catchers, prayer scarves, silk carpets, decorative statues — Indian, Chinese, something else, Persian maybe. Cushions to sit on, big pillows, trays of food, weed, pills, hash. All are laid out in colorful plates and bowls on the floor.

No beer.

Sally sits down, crosses her legs, assumes an impossible yoga position. A black couple sit down next to her. Maasai. Look like Maasai. Beautiful skin, regal posture. Blond twins sit across from them, one male, the other female. If they had a baby, would the baby look like them... exactly like them?

"Sal."

"Yeah, Hubs."

"I'm going to the kitchen. I need a beer. Cold. Very cold."

"When you say that, Ben. It sounds like 'Bond. James Bond.'"

"Really!"

"Yes, really. I like Bond. Go, find your beer."

Always feel like I'm doing something wrong when I lose sight of Sally. Still. I walk away, wander about the house, touch things, look, watch people without clothes do things. Lots of things. Things that don't look like things and do look like things. The fog has me. The soothing fog. It takes me by the nose to the kitchen. A kitchen I remember. How? Where the special plates are kept, a favorite cup, I know where they are. Is it my memory? Difficult to tell. Except for a midget girl sorting through drawers and cupboards, there's no one there. I poke around, find a six-pack, Turbodog, not my favorite, not cold enough. They should make beer cans that keep cold on their own. I pop the cap, three caps, put the cans in the freezer, check the bins for meat.

The midget gives me a look. I give a look back. She's thin, long blond hair, a stout face, slim nose, soft red cheeks, straight legs, a seasoned little woman look more than a midget look, but still midget.

"There's a roast in the oven," she says. "Have some."

"Sure. I'll do that. Thanks." I find a plate, a knife. Cut a thick chunk, feels good, the smooth slide of the blade through flesh, very sharp. Not much of a knife if it's not sharp. Then...an overwhelming sudden break in clarity. An abrupt stop. My mood jumps, pitches, feels like I hit a wall. A giant marshmallow wall moved from place to place by thousands of rat-tailed ants and pink-eyed mice. I hit it face first. Squash. My life, it's no longer mine alone. Not that God is at work, but *something* is, something's watching. The walls, the air, objects in the room, the floor, Sally's albino relatives, the ones flying around in UFO's...is it them? Drugs...maybe the drugs. Drugs with eyes. An odd moment, agreeable, but odd.

I eat. The meat is hot, juicy, a hint of spice, no idea what. Fetch a beer from the freezer. Ice cold. Drink it. Take another beer, drink it. Take the third and join Sally in the big room.

People, some are sitting, standing, some leaning. A small stage, circular carpet on a slightly raised platform, lots of pillows, rolling fog machines mixing vapor and hemp smoke, vases of flowers, a fountain behind the flowers. The fountain is made of brass. Two monkeys playing on a small, tall table, a glass of wine lying on its side, water for the fountain flows from the glass over the table and down to a pool with yellow fish in it. The water changes colors as it flows.

Next to Sally I relax, take a swallow, offer her one, she gives me a kiss, puts her arm around me, leans into me. An ice-cold beer or Sally, which to drink first?

Simbana appears on stage, missed how she got there. Her hair, tied in a bun, appears crown-like. She's barefoot, with a sheer, jade-green dress split in the front to her navel, on the sides to her hips. Her lips are bright red, her lashes long and white.

"Friends. Welcome to my home. To this hour, this moment, this stage. I have two unforgettable acts for you. Mesmerizing acts. *The Big Tiny*, and *Put In*. Both will leave you speechless."

She bows, people applaud, not loudly. "But first, I have question," she says, and she motions to a small man on the edge of the gathering. Like everyone else, he's fully invested in the glories of hedonism...his face, plump with expressions of revelry, his mood elated. He's wearing, sort of wearing, a leather blacksmiths apron, dirty and worn, nothing more, and he's visibly unstable as he stands, steps toward Simbana and hands her a paint brush, the kind used to paint house trim.

"Thank you, Jackson," she says, and she holds up the brush. Lights focus on it, give it a candlelight look. "What is real? What is not? You think you know. Do you?" she asks.

Of course, we know, that's what we think...all of us. All the people in the room, and what a menagerie of people we are, every height, weight, color and blend you can imagine humans made into appears to be represented, and there are no more than thirty of us, if that.

The music stops, light is sucked from the air, all we can see is Simbana. She takes the brush in her right hand and brushes it across her left shoulder. Her shoulder disappears. She bends over, brushes her knees. They disappear. She brushes her stomach, the top of her head, her waist, across her breasts, they all disappear. She keeps brushing until all we can see of her is her eyes and mouth.

I take a hit, finish my beer, pull Sally close, slip a hand under her gown, imagine laying naked on a beach in the Keys, watching clouds drift by, and birds.

Simbana's mouth smiles. Her eyes brighten. She brushes her breasts back, nothing covering them, she brushes her stomach, thighs, her shoulders, they all come back with no clothes on them. Standing before us, utterly naked, she again asks. "What is real? What is not?"

I whisper to Sally, "That's the best striptease ever. Vegas would love it."

She puts a finger to my lips. "Shush, Hubs. Quite."

"At this moment," Simbana continues, and she brushes parts of herself away again, "you can't decide if I am here or not, real, or not. I'm thinking the same as I look at all of you. All that is real is present. What is not present...what is in the past, what is in the future...is not real. Right now, if the attention in your mind is focused on what you remember I look like or imagine I will look like with the next brush stroke, you are not here, not awake, not alive in this present moment.

"You are, we all are, that which we give our attention to moment by moment. If attention is given to images evoked by memory, images evoked by future imagining, all the past and future chatter running through your minds, then you are not here. Not real. Not alive. I am not here. Not real. Not alive." Within seconds she strokes herself away entirely. We can't see her, not a finger, an elbow, a hair on her head. "Now," she says, "now you can't see me at all, but I'm here because my attention is focused on my being here and not on the imagery in my mind running back and forth between the past and the future. And you are not here if you are looking for an image of me that you remember being attached to my voice." She then brushes herself into view again. "Life takes place in the present," she continues. "We are alive or dead to the extent that our awareness is self -aware in the present. Be here, or be nowhere," she says, and she bows, walks off the stage and into the arms of her Game of Thrones party.

"I want that brush, Sal."

She pokes me.

"Really. Imagine what we could do with that."

"Ben. There was no brush. That wasn't the point. You missed it."

"Be here now or be nowhere. I got that." Thought I did. I always think I get it, whatever *it* is.

"No brush?"

But for a few candles, the room goes dark. Feels warm, the darkness, like the soothing hands of a skilled masseuse easing warm oils into weary skin. A complete emptiness filling nothing. Then change, transition, the crew returns. Incrementally the lights come back on. Small lights directed at the stage center. The carpet. The pillows swelling and contracting like refulgent bubbles in thick soup. A lady, she's middle aged but looks like a teenager. Could have some Sally DNA in her. She takes the stage, begins undressing. The lights focus on her, behave like hands unwrapping presents. Feels like all of us in the room are equally lit even though lights are not directed at us. She has a way, the lady, even before speaking, she has a way. There's something non-trivial about her that captures the imagination, the desire to ask questions. That's what I think, what I think Sally thinks. Intrigued. We are. Everyone is. Nudity explains a lot, but not everything. I take another swallow, a hookah hit. Leave my mind to graze, to find its way. Drugs, without them many new ideas would never escape the servitude, fear, and conformity laid down by puritanical asceticism.

Holding a small mic, the lady drops her last clothes item, a red scarf, and smiles broadly. I like her. Have no idea why she's there but somehow her being there makes sense. She has a complementary figure, not a model vision of beauty, more the farmgirl look. The wholesome, milking cows and feeding mice to cats' kind of farmgirl look…the, I can bear many fine sons look, you see in the women in Indian villages.

"*The Big-Tiny*," she says. Her voice is sweet, something you can taste in the air. "Are you ready for it?"

Cheers erupt, and applause.

The lights shimmer and dim as she picks up the little pile of clothes at her feet with one toe, and tosses them into the crowd, a bride's bouquet looking for new employment. Don't notice if anyone picks up the red scarf. Too stoned to care, I lean back, lean into Sally. Want to laugh. Not sure why.

I sigh an inside sigh, feel like all life on the planet is flowing through us, through the house, the stage, the carpet, the trays of pills, the colored pills, weed, eatables, beer, sex, nudity – evangelical bareness raising the dead. Spontaneous life, it comes from us, I can feel it growing. The earth, what it feels like to the earth to roll in space along a course dictated by a hungry sun. I can feel it. The earth's fate (mother earth). She's not talking about it, but she knows her fate, where her rotations are leading her. I feel her, know it. Something feels her.

Music.

An Indian tabla. Light tapping at first, finger tapping, then deep, gouging moans pressed into the drum surface by the heel of the hand. A taunting rhythm fills the room, invisible nymphs unmasking carnal intrigue lead the mind down narrow alleyways to a band of gypsies known for casting spells, faith healers, snake charmers, and tarot mavens – keepers of an ancient religion kept captive by its failure to foresee future renovations of faith.

The kitchen midget. She steps into the light, walks toward the stage. A spokeswoman for midget rights, she could be. At the stage, she finds the brightest spot on the carpet, shades her eyes, waves at two men by the stairway. They call out. "We love you, Abby." Abby gives them a crotch thrust, blows kisses, begins to dance, to sway, to loosen her gown, a sheer, turquoise dress, split in the front to her navel, on the sides to her hips. She's graceful, her bones liquid, her hair strands of silk drifting in a blue surf.

Abby in charge. The midget. She's got our attention, self-aware or not. Then, behind her, something big begins to emerge. A shadowy thing reaching, followed by a man, a very big man. A giant really. A Game of Thrones giant playing his part. How did he get in? My first thought. That big. A guy that big, every door is too small, the roof too low, but still there he is. He sits down on the carpet next to Abby. (A visual comparable to an elephant sitting next to an ant, grasshopper, a mouse, something very small.) Makes a sound that giants make, picks up Abby with his thumb and forefinger and drops her on his shoulder. (She's going to ask if he wants a shoulder massage. I'm sure of it. She doesn't.) Instead, she takes a sprinter's pose next to the giant's neck, counts "1, 2, 3," then takes off, sprints from his neck, along his outstretched arm, which is way out there, to his hand, then she turns around and sprints back to the opposite hand. Back and forth, and back and forth. She runs, runs, runs. Watching begins to make me dizzy, and what sense does it make anyway. Everyone's watching. Maybe that was it, all that was expected of us. She stops, jumps down, lands in the giant's lap, drops to the floor.

Do we applaud? Is it over?

Abby walks off the stage, takes a drink of some guy's beer, goes back, rubs her tidy midget hands together, sits down next to the giant, shoves her hand under his ass, and lifts him up.

"Whoa...Wow!" Everyone there. "Wow!"

She does that, nothing to it, just like that. And she keeps holding him up. The giant. It looks like he's floating. Maybe he is. And somehow, he stands up bent over, takes off his shoes, damn big shoes, and runs on the tips of his toes, the very tippy tips, back and forth from one of Abby's hands to the other as she stretches out her arms and begins rotating like a ballet dancer. Then, little by little, as the giant tiptoes back and forth, she pulls in her arms until the only place the giant can pace is on the very top of her head. And he does, he begins running in place on the top of her head. Her very tiny head. No visual for that.

"Wow." Again, and again. "Wow," is all we can say.

Then she stops. Lets the giant down, bows holdings hands with him, thanks everyone for watching, announces that *Put-In* is up next, that she would like to stick around but she and the giant are getting married. They just popped in to say hello. A favor to Simbana, they said, and they left, a Santa up the chimney kind of exit.

*The Big-Tiny* is over. The stage empty, the room dark, intermission. Well. Giants in wonderland. What would Alice think?

People laughing. We hear them. People in rooms above us, a game they're playing, something with a bouncing ball. Sally reaches into my robe, takes hold, feels like squirrel fingers with mittens on them, something thermal and pliable. She gives me a good rub, warms me up. A woman keeping a man warm. A man keeping a woman warm. Cavemen rubbing sticks together to make fire. A long time ago. Those bipeds. They knew nothing of us in their future, as we know nothing of those in our future. Well, not nothing. We know something, but what?

I slip a hand beneath Sal's gown, knead her right breast. The need to Knead. Very satisfying, always is. Our attention leaves the stage, the room, I'm about to mount Sally, or she me.

We stop.

Two guys walk onto the sage. Naked, sucking their thumbs, and carrying pink piggy banks with bunny tails.

The lights brighten. We sit up.

One guy looks amazingly like Putin, as much as one can imagine what Putin looks like naked. Not an arresting image, ruder looking than anything else. The other guy looks like Trump, as much as one can imagine what Trump looks like naked. Grizzly body hair, mostly gray, bubbling fat, sagging skin, knees that look like he kneels a lot, and not in prayer. Nauseating, both of them.

No tabla.

"So," says the Trump-looking guy, as he looks up and down the Putin looking guy, then looks at us, the audience. "I want what he has," he says, and he points at Putin's tallywag. "Here," he says, to the Putin guy, and he hands him his piggybank. "Put your tallywag in here, just put-in. That's the game. Don't worry, it detaches. You put-in what I want. And I put-in what you want. Together we fill our piggybanks and stay out of jail."

"Ok," says the Putin looking guy.

"Great old friend. Always know, I'm here for you," says the Trump looking guy. "I'm just saying. It is what it is. I'm here for you."

Where did Simbana find these guys? How can they look so much like Trump? So much like Putin? Drugs. Maybe it's the drugs. Maybe the two guys are not even there. Maybe they are there, and our imagining them being there, is taking place at the same time and we can't tell the difference between them. And maybe they are there, and that's it, or not there, and that's it?

Putin and Trump, naked, and butt to butt. Piggy banks nestled in their arms, keeping them safe while doing other's harm. Happy little pigs, keeping each other close, each wanting what the other has, having too little of what they want most.

"My turn," says the Putin looking guy. As he eyes the Trump looking guy's tallywag, less than grand, and says, "I'll take that tallywag, less than grand, put it in my piggy bank, transport it by hand, and let me say thank you to you Mr. Trump. You're the man. Anytime you need help winning elections, just let me know. I'll do what I can."

"And I thank you," says the Trump looking guy. "Rare men, and rare friends we are indeed. Men like us, by any means, must succeed."

"Corruption rules!" They say together, saluting the audience. "Hail corruption."

Done. Their last words. "Hail corruption." Then off they go, each with the other's tallywag in hand, off to conquer their countrymen to the rhythm of a marching band.

No one moves. Stunned, aroused, horrified, disgusted. Can't tell.

The tiger just before he pounces. The prey just before he pounces. Which are we? Both? Neither? A fly buzzing. I try to catch it. Miss. Try again. Try several times, miss each time. Zap it with my mind. Can I do that? Focus, compress my attention into a laser thought. Voodoo. Fly zapping voodoo. No idea how to make it work.

The Big Tiny. The Put-in Putin. Trump – defiler of a nation. Naked schoolboy stupidity, trading the nation's freedom for his own. Indelible images. The mind gasping, bending fact to make reality palatable, imaginable…livable. An idle haze fills the room. Pot smoke, candle smoke, cigarette smoke mingling with plant smells, body odor, food. I pop a pill. Sally, too. A green pill or blue, they look the same. People begin to stretch, whisper, glance about, mice sneaking crumbs from unattended grain bins. Though moving, the bodies all around us appeared still, like door stops, chairs, potholders, hat hooks.

The Tabla stops. Lights dim. The candles dim. What next? We're all thinking. "What next?"

# EIGHTY

Faint rays of morning light begin to brighten the sky, to nourish lingering odors and fragrances sent from the past, from the night before. Tactile reminiscence refreshing our shared contentment, the beat of our hearts. A new day.

Simbana removed the stage. Didn't notice when, wondered if it was ever there. Drugs. They work you, add dimension to routine, answer questions before they form. Love drugs. If I could, I'd choose to be reborn a drug. A kick-ass drug, one that gives conscious access to one hundred percent of the brain. A fucking god drug. Imagine that.

I can. The human population processing reality though conscious access to the brain, complete and total access. I can see that, sure. And it's not us, not our present population.

"Ben," Sally pulls my arm. "It's time to leave."

It was. It is. We help each other up. A semblance of clothes hanging on us, my open robe, Sally's scarf in disarray. We tidy up, somewhat, take the stairs…all manner of heavenly mischief taking place around us… pleasure feeding the senses, magnifying them…it's a finite happiness too little understood. Looking past what offends us to something higher. Christ did it. Pleasure is higher than pain. I think so. Enlightenment is higher. Sally thinks so. It's odd. Heaven is a pleasing place for Christians who fear pleasure.

At the top of the stairs. We ease into our room, get dressed, sort a path to the door, kiss Simbana, thank her for looking after us…for the cat. Sally takes her hand. They knew each other before the party, somehow. I'm sure of it. Sally places the broach in her hand. "It's for your next guest," she says. They both share a thought, eye contact. Simbana takes the broach, its good luck passing to the cat. Maybe. Never run out of maybes. We miss saying goodbye to Amy, walk out the inviting entryway, down the steps, down the road, across the divide to the streetcar stop.

Did we? Did we cross the divide, stop at the streetcar stop? How would we know? The difference between an outdoor simulation inside Simbana's house, and being outdoors…how would we know? Know for sure? Know anything for sure? Be here now or be nowhere. Right.

Sun. The sun is shining.

Feels like the sun....

# EIGHTY ONE

**H**appy to have dry shorts on, a dry shirt, dry sandals. We're tired but wide awake, animated by the afterglow of nascent revelation. Simbana. Her house. Reality. No real name for reality however extensive our efforts to define it.

No one else at the stop. Already warm, gripping warm. We wait.

"I'm pregnant, Ben."

She is. She says so. I step closer, cover her belly with my hands, can't discern the difference. She puts her hands over mine, presses down lightly.

"How does that make you feel? Us having a baby, a family...an extended family."

"Feel? I haven't thought about it, Sal, not much. Some. Nothing bad. Fatherhood. Family. Both are new to me. I'm excited, definitely excited."

"Across the street, Ben. Do you see her?"

"I do, yeah. Noticed her when we walked up."

"Why is she waving at us?"

"No idea."

A lady, owlish face, gray-blond hair, some white, dry, looks like a wad of straw...a nest of some kind. She's waving at us. Does she know us? Looks like she does, acts like she does. With each wave, she sways a little, first like a snake, then a ballerina, then snake, and her colored gown, what she's wearing; bits of different dresses, the bits move with her. She waves at anyone going by. Doesn't know us. Everyone who turns her way she waves at them. Entertaining herself, she's doing that.

No embarrassment – the freedom of insanity. Maybe she isn't insane, just making people think so, so she can act insane? America going blind, opaque ideologies eroding logic, invigorating discord. The woman. Is she homeless, one of the few whites living in the Ninth ward? Maybe, who cares. And if she is crazy, how does she live, get from one place to another, pay her bills, be taken seriously?

A guy on a bike rides by. He's wearing some kind of athletic suit, yellow and black, the wasp club…maybe. Nice bike.

She waves at him. He doesn't notice.

Sally waves. The lady stops, stares, but not at us, goes back to waving.

A streetcar pulls up, we get in, sit down.

The lady waves goodbye as we roll away.

Two stops later, a family gets on. A husband and wife, three kids. The smallest is a boy, very tiny, maybe half the size of his father's forearm. The next is a boy as well, all three are boys. The oldest looks to be five or six, the middle kid, four. Both parents are huge, not fat, they're gigantic physical things that jostle and bob like warm Jell-O every time one of them moves, lifts an arm, takes a bite of food. Can't imagine lugging all that weight up and down stairs, in and out of buildings, cars, busses, planes, waking up to it every morning, and making babies, how do they do it?

I turn to Sally, cup my mouth. "I want to ask them."

"Don't you dare Ben."

"But I want to know, you know, how they do it?"

"Shh, not so loud. Maybe they don't. Maybe they adopt, let people assume they do it."

"Right, maybe."

The car continues down the track toward the French Quarter. And my Jeep. I begin to visualize sitting in the driver's seat, turning over the big V8, feeling ready for more open road, fresh surroundings, the hum of tire wear.

The guy, the fat father. I give him a better look. About six feet tall, bald, the kind who looks like they're born bald, a big potato look. He seems nice enough, fatherly enough. Wearing a striped T-shirt, brown trousers, flip flops on his feet. His wife is wearing flops as well, and all the kids. She's reddish, a redhead with freckles, so many freckles they're almost a skin color, and she's wearing a red dress. Red on red. The radish and the potato. Happy people enjoying their world, winning life's lottery, lots of laughter, opinions, pranks. I turn toward them, the wood seats feel newly polished, shiny.

"Excuse me," I say. "Sir, ma'am, but I have a question. Something I've wondered about for many years which I'm hoping you will answer for me."

"Benjamin Jason Mamott!" Sally, a reprimanding look. Being told what to do, my first response, do it anyway. Can't stop myself. Want to, but not really.

"It's, well...my wife thinks it's a bad question."

They look at each other, the radish nods, the potato turns to me.

"Sure. Ask away. We're both teachers. What's your question?"

"There you are," I say. "The five of you, a family. I see three beautiful kids. They look like you, enough like you, so I imagine they're yours, then. Because, honestly, and out of genuine curiosity, I can't imagine how you do it. You know, how you plant the seed, water the lilies...."

The guy inflates his already massive body, scowls; the glare of a man certain he can dip his wick into any soup he wants, no matter how fat he is. He softens, his scowl bends into a half-smile, eyes twinkling, rubs his nose with the back of his hand.

I wait. Sit still, perfectly still.

"If I told you, you wouldn't believe me," he says. "And yes, Mr. Benjamin Jason Mamott, they're ours, our three tuggy bears."

Facing me, the guy grins all doughy-like. "But thank you for asking," he says, and he turns back to his family— his wife and children. Fat and happy. They are. No doubt about it. Fat and happy.

They got off at the next stop. Didn't answer my question. Might not be a question?

Sally elbows me, hard. I rotate, look out the window.

"You're pathetic, Ben."

"I know. Sorry." (Always being sorry for something, seems like it.) "But I had to, Sal. That question. I've wanted to ask it for years. They came across like good people, people who wouldn't take offense. You know, the kind that look past offense to something positive, something they can control. Happy people do that. They looked happy. I thought so. And, Sal, I'm, still thinking. Your pregnancy, our pregnancy. It scares me, a little. And it excites me. That's what I think, what I think I feel."

"What?"

"Your being pregnant. You asked how I feel. That's how I feel."

We sit. Bouncing on the car's wood seats. Bouncing along, no one else in the car. New Orleans, maiden of palatial devilry and divination etching her durables into our mind, street by street, house by house, tree by tree.

We get off at Jackson Square, watch the car disappear, adjust to the presence of more people, the sounds of more people. Big people, small people, cars, birds, distant instruments calling for attention, street music squeezing between pedestrians, buildings, signs. We walk to the Jeep. Not far. A beautiful day, few clouds, light breeze, slightly humid. A damp heat, something unraveling that pulls on our clothes, makes people dress down, girls dress down, expose more skin, amplifies social foreplay. Muslim women, no foreplay for them, the covered ladies. I remember one. And the heat that day.

A small town in Kashmir, Islamabad, 1989. I stopped to buy gas on the way out of town. It was hot, a nagging hot that melted the air, the thoughts in your mind. I got out, left the attendant to fill the tank, walked over to the road, hard packed dirt. Sat down on a rail, took out a cigarette, didn't light it, watched people go by. Slow-moving people, just a few. I watched them. Cars drove by just as slowly. To my left, in the distance, I saw a lady walking toward me. She was covered from head to toe. Proof that a woman moved beneath the covering came only momentarily when her hands caught the light. Her approach seemed endless, and she appeared to float more than walk when she passed by. Her head did not turn right or left; she faced only forward. But for her pajama leggings and sandals, which were spotted green and dark brown, she was covered in black. Heat-absorbing black.

# EIGHTY TWO

**N**eed to buy Sally a ring.

"All these shops, Sal, so many, let's see if we can find you a ring."

"Really, Ben?"

"Sure, really. Let's see what they have."

I like being the good guy. I'm not good, don't think so, but I like playing the part. The store is dark for a jewelry store, more of a pawn shop with some antiques.

"Can I help you?"

A guy comes up. I think he's a guy. Looks like a girl, acts like one, sort of. Gender games. The disinterested multitudes forced onto the field, handed bats, told to play.

"Can I help you," he/she/it asks again.

"We're looking for a ring...a ring for her," I add.

Very excited, Sally laughs, openly flirts with the guy/girl. Of course. Why not? Better our chances of getting a good price. He flirts back, or she does, whichever he or she is. A transgender moment, confusing. Ladies' locker room today, or men's'? Girls bathroom, or boys?

He/she brought out a couple of trays filled with rings. Opens the trays and pushes them toward us. Junk. Dime store rejects, that's what they look like. Sally doesn't care. She begins sorting them by size and color. She likes gold, all the golds are first. She examines each one, drops them if she doesn't like them, sets them aside if she does. Most are dropped, two are set aside. She gives less time to all the silver rings, sets none aside.

"Of these two, Ben, which do you like the best?"

The first is thin with a small blue stone in the ring's center, surrounded by gold leaves curling back to hold the stone in place. The second is heavier, a little thicker, another blue stone but no leaves, just little hooks reaching in from the sides to secure the stone. The heavier ring is less expensive.

"Three hundred and eight dollars, or two hundred and twenty dollars."

The jeweler holds them up.

I take the first ring. Lean across the glass. "I'll give you two fifty for this ring and a quick five with either one of us."

"I'm a girl," she says, but I like you both. Two seventy-five and I get the girl."

"I thought you said you are a girl."

"I am, but I feel like a guy today. Standing here, looking at her, I feel like a guy. My Wally's getting hard, and I don't even have one."

All my life I've had no problem determining the difference between a boy and a girl. Still no problem. Not with the basics. Guys carry a stick, girls don't. I put the ring on Sally. Pay him/her/it $300, absence the five. We walk out, grab a sandwich, make our way to the Jeep.

My 1998 Grand Cherokee, she opens her doors as we walk up, wages her tail, she's happy we're back. Parking spaces are lonely spaces. Cars know that, dread them. Jill knows. Jill the Jeep. Love my Jeep. We get in, start the engine, roll down the windows a, light a joint. A big-ass joint. A New Orleans going away present to ourselves. The day is hot, and just waking up. I take off my shirt, Sally unbuttons all but one button on her blouse, curls down the top of her shorts, exposes her lower abdomen, very sexy. The baby belly show, very popular on nudist beaches.

"Thank you, Ben," she says, and she gives me a kiss, holds up her finger. Smiles. "I'll thank you properly when we stop for gas. Sooner, maybe."

Two cars waiting for my parking spot. I back out, move into the intersection, turn north. Sally Googles Interstate10. The streetcar fat couple, and their three kids, are stopped at the corner. I wave for them to cross in front of us. An apology. Sort of. Thought about running them down, how much damage they would do to my Jeep. A stupid thought.

We leave New Orleans.

# EIGHTY THREE

"Ben. I've been thinking. If we have a girl, let's name her Diana, after the Princess of Wales. And if we have a boy, let's name him Obama."

"I'm fine with those. Sure. Might be odd though, a white boy named Obama."

"I'm not really white, hubs. Not by definition. I'm albino, and...."

"Yeah, he could be white or black, depending on how the sperm felt when he met your egg. Imagine it, that little sperm head, he stops right there, right at the egg's door, the rest of the sperm gang right behind him, and he thinks, before jumping in, am I white today, or black? We'll see in nine months. A White Obama! Could be interesting."

"No chiding, Ben. It's a good name."

"It is. I agree. It's a good name. Sure as hell beats 'The Donald,' whatever the fuck that means."

"You understand everything, Ben."

*Do I?*

*Only need Sally to think so.*

We pick up I-10 East off Dumaine Street. A few clouds dimming the sun. Still heating up. Yesterday becoming today. Windows are down, the road ahead inviting. Nowhere to be but where we are, no one to be but who we are. Free birds in a cage, life's rules before all others. Nature always wins. No matter the game we play, nature always wins. Water. A river coming up, an inlet. Lots of sea containers stacked on the ground. Tracks. Some kind of mining operation. Bums hanging around the tracks. Maybe they're not bums. We cross the water. Greater New

Orleans unfolding ahead of us, dissolving as we pass by, thinning into look-alike homes, look-alike driveways, industrial complexes, business centers, streets, swamp, bayou reserves, a final railway overpass just ahead of the small Lake Pontchartrain Bridge—Twin Span, to the locals. Another, please remember me, I'm better than you, memorial bridge.

Fuck. Everyone wants to be remembered.

Sky is clear, an effortless blue, water all around us. "Stairway to Heaven" playing on the radio. Sally relights the joint, takes a hit, passes it to me. Lots of smoke. Goodbye New Orleans smoke. I pull a deep hit, a chest hit, too heavy, begin to cough, take a drink from my thermos. A deep drink. Water's ice cold. Has to be ice cold if it wants to be real water.

Ice water.

I love ice water.

Sally pops open a Red Bull, enriches my view, both breasts, a bit of leg. Always feel like I'm seeing her for the first time. Every day is like that, feels like we're just beginning, even while years of memory disagree. But memory lies. It does. Most people are better at making it up, then remembering it.

Blunting with Sally on a big American highway. I like it. The feel of my knobbed steering wheel grip. The leather seats, the indiscriminate air rushing through our clothes. I like it. Love it. A great day. Sally leans back, almost slouches, puts her feet on the dash, pulls out a math puzzle book (brain exercises for mature minds). She loves numbers, talks to them, reads them, eats them, shapes them into verifiable benefit at the casinos, makes a game of filling out government forms like a sixth grader, never loses at chess. Her favorite season of the year is tax season.

After Lake Pontchartrain we hang right on10 East, the Stephen E Ambrose Memorial Highway. Memorials, fuck, without them God would be less rich.

Key West. We are close...in West Coast miles. No plan to stop driving. Sally kneads my man tools into a pillow, falls asleep in my lap, knees against the lower dash, her arms folded into her chest. A cat in her basket.

It's late. Streetlights are on, car lights, billboard lights, lights lighting lights. Night driving, the dark, washer fluid getting low. If it runs out,

I'll fill it with Johnny John fluid. Fill it right up. I've done that before. Works better than commercial brands, and a lot cheaper.

Always good to add a little water.

Our next big town is Mobile, Alabama. Barely above sea level. Always like the sound "Mobile Alabama" makes when you speak it. It's like warm water, something soothing. Talking to myself. Talking and talking. Repetition nausea, day labor. Fuck, fuck, fuck...how many times in a row can I say the word fuck, hear the word fuck, before tiring of it, before repetition nausea takes hold and I choke on the word... die from insult intolerance. I have no idea. Have no interest in having an idea, not that I can think of, not that it matters. I'm bored, no reason to be, can't admit it...no reason not to admit it. Whose brain was I in anyway? Can't tell. Simbana's house...are we still there?

Cars going by, cars passing me, cars I'm passing. Sally stirs, shifts her arm. Falls back to sleep. More cars passing, cars, cars, cars. A big semi, lots of chrome. He splatters kaleidoscopic reflections across my dashboard, across my windows and mirrors. A man in a hurry, he's driving fast, pushing it, well over the speed limit. An empty trailer, no freight, that's what I think. Or he could be carrying a bomb, a bunch of illegal girls primed to seduce high-level CEOs, or drugs for some covert government exchange with Peruvian witch doctor's adept at mind-control and money laundering.

Exit 13. Theodore Dawes memorial something. Two more miles. Gas stations...Pilot, Shell, Chevron. Don't want to stop. Sally wakes up. Doesn't sit up.

A coyote, a big male, it runs onto the highway. I don't swerve, catch his back legs, pull to the right. Sally grabs me around the waist, squeezes me as we begin to slide. I pump the brakes, hit the grass shoulder sliding, keep sliding, the grass is loose, damp, my wheels tear into it, splatter roots and mud on the doors, the windows. We come to a stop, few car lights on the opposite side of the road, no one notices our slide, stops to help us.

Mud on the Jeep, a slight dent in the front left bumper, maybe.

"Fucking coyote! You see him anywhere?"

"He ran off, Ben. Hobbled off. Something. He's gone. We can't park here. A cop will stop. Ask us questions."

"Yeah. He will. Christ!"

We drive on. It's still dark.

Night driving. Animals and accidents. Stars overhead, the universe; time reinventing itself, ceaselessly.

We pass Mobile, our headlights vanishing behind the wake of cars and trucks ahead of us. No one from Mobile knows us, knows we're here, that we're driving by. Sally returns her head to my lap, curls up, tucks in her arms, falls back to sleep. Innocence, sometimes it lasts. I finish her Red Bull, drink two more. I like night driving, the emptiness in it — a darkness desert — the absence of my fellow man. Pedophiles. Purveyors of iniquitous want consuming future light; the evil men can do. Hate pedophiles. And men who beat women, hate them, and rapists. Wouldn't know what to think, though, if people put a homo in the White House, gave us a dick for a first lady. Wouldn't know what to think. Sally would. Sally would know. Girls know things. Albino's know things. Alien albinos, they know more things.

Just past the George Wallace *please remember me I'm better than you* tunnel, we intersect the Jubilee Parkway. A little after 1 a.m., warm for 1 a.m. I can smell the water, the grass, the stale remains of low tide. I like I-10. Not that different from other highways. Getting hungry. Rural Alabama, Escambia County. Florida state line coming up.

We cross into Florida.

# EIGHTY FOUR

"Sally...we're in Florida!" I try to whisper, can't, too excited. "The Key West state, Sal. We're in it."

Sally shifts slightly, can't tell if she's still asleep, or listening without talking. We pass Brent and Ensley without pause, a clean, well-lit section of road. Wonder if the Ensley's were once Beusley's, Beasley's, Easley's? People changing names, clothes, countries, loyalties, beliefs. Why?

"Escambia Bay, it's coming up." No response. Should I wake her? The road rises gradually, a commercial elevator rise, industrial. A new county, Santa Rosa. A lot of Santa Rosas in the US, a lot of Delhi's, Dublin's, Moscow's, Baghdad's. 70 miles per hour. I'm doing 75. Slow down, no hurry, no memorial *please remember me* dedication for the Escambia Bay Bridge. Don't see one.

*The Sally and Ben Blunting It Memorial Bridge.* I name it after us, for us.

(Everyone wants to be remembered).

We stay on 10, pass Tallahassee, very little change in the surrounding fields, trees, building clusters, lights. Miles of the same. It seems so. Few curves in the road. Can't see much. Almost sunrise. We're a couple of hours from Jacksonville, and highway 95 south. I prefer 95 to all Florida's west coast roads. 75, 490, the small roads.

"Ben, Mr. Husband, I need to eat." Sally sits up, her hair rumpled, her person in disarray, still beautiful, more beautiful. She throws her head back, dry washes her face. Everything about her glows...her lips are moist, fresh, her eyes gleaming. Maybe she leaves her body at night, slips into some other dimension; the twilight zone, visits with her kind and comes back with a new body in the morning.

Maybe. Lots of maybes in life. Ubiquitous maybes, they're like mosquitoes, gnats, politicians.

"Sal. We're in Florida."

"Thank you, hubs. I know. I watched us cross the line. Very exciting, a big dreaming night for me last night, very big. Flying dreams, sailing dreams, wind and warm fluids washing over me, through me. I was in so many places at the same time. Dreams make me hungry, ravenous, especially flying dreams."

"How can dreams make you hungry, Sal?"

She adjusts her blouse, buttons a few buttons. "Every animate body needs to eat, even a dream body. Dreams are an experience, and anything we experience – because experience contributes to our reality – are alive, real, in our reality. Dreams, premonitions, déjà vu, they're all real. It's our interpretation of dreams that's unreal, not the dreams themselves."

No point in trying to keep up. Two's, one pair. That's it. "OK," I agree, "and good morning wife. We're in Florida…we made Florida."

She blinks, sends her hand on an errand, gives me a kiss.

"My ring, Ben, it's beautiful. Are you happy you bought it?"

"Happy? Absolutely."

"She unwraps an energy bar, opens a juice, pops a few raisins in her mouth. "When are we going to stop for food, hot food? Maybe we can find someplace to bathe, take a shower, a hot shower. Get the Jeep washed."

"Right, poor Jill. She does need cleaning, a serious wash and wax."

Hot water. Warm water. A big difference between them.

"Here. Look! A Best Western coming up, a McDonalds, a waffle shop with fast food waffles."

We take exit 343, US301 to Baldwin. Highway exit variations, there aren't many. Sameness, we love the mundane in sameness. Makes us feel like we're in control, and it bores us. The control, we like, the boredom, not so much. McDonald's is on the opposite side of the road, we cross over, take the drive-through lane, two cars ahead of us. McDonald's on the moon, Mars. One day, wherever we go there will be a McDonald's selling the same Big Mac and fries. Until the end of the universe, we'll be seeing Big Mac's everywhere. And even then, after the end, there will be a McDonald's at the gates of heaven. Heavenly Golden Arches offering a celestial Big Mac, some kind of voguish equivalent to seventy-two virgins, burning bushes, walking on water.

We order the usual, and an ice cream, get back on 301, miss the Best Western, find a Red Bar Inn next to Waffle House. The Red Bar isn't new. Looks like a big ranch house, the kind of building they use in movies when some poor sap, running from the cops, or bad guys, needs a place to hide. A nothing place, but it's clean, the water hot. We take a room, number 17. I unlock it (they still use keys), kick the door open with my foot. A small room, rectangular with a bed sitting in the middle of the room. A King Size bed. Two imitation wood nightstands with plastic lamps on them sit on either side of the bed, a flat screen TV on the opposite wall above a painted chest of drawers. The paint's peeling. The bathroom and closet are at the end of the rectangle. Closet space is defined by a wooden bar running between the wall and the bathroom door. A few wire hangers, suitcase stand and ironing board inside it. All the conveniences of home.

Sally drops her bag on the stand, lays down on the bed, removes her clothes, grabs the remote and clicks through programs and channels. Porn channels (too expensive), nature channels, history channel, the cartoon network, news, she stops at the trailer for *300*, clicks on it, turns up the volume just as King Leonidas roars, "This is Sparta!" and kicks the Persian messenger into the pit. All the messengers.

"And this is me!" Sally roars, spreading her legs. "Bonnie Elizabeth Parker with a more salacious nature. I need a quick one, Ben, then a shower."

The hotel door. We left it open, a habit...becoming a habit. Two people watching us, watching Sally from inside their parked car. Always happens, anytime of day, anywhere, all ages, sexes, even animals, bugs... eyes that see Sally want to keep seeing her.

Eye candy. Sally's the opium of eye candy.

I close the door.

# EIGHTY FIVE

W e stay one night at the Barn, comfortable enough, accommodating enough. Pack and leave early the next morning. Wash the Jeep (very lucky, no dents, no damage. Coyote must have hit the wheel). I loop around and onto I-10 just as the sun splits the horizon. All the sunrises in the universe. Right now. Eyes that can see them. I want those eyes.

"We're here! We're in Florida, Ben…Florida. We made it! Paradise past, Dante's Inferno, all behind us now. Your Jeep took us away, got us here. Amazing. Jill the Jeep." She pats the dash. "We made it! We made it Sea breezes. I can feel them, smell them."

All the windows are down, puttering in the slow lane, no hurry. Sally waves at the sky, designs the shapes of faraway clouds with her fingers, howls with delight but not a howl animals would make. It's more a howl like the sound trees would make if we could hear how much they enjoy the wind rushing through their leaves.

Thirty miles from the beach, we're at least that, probably more. How can Sally smell the Atlantic from here, feel it? She can. I believe her, smell it myself to feel closer to her.

"Hey, hubs. When do I get to drive?"

The big question. A bigger than God question. The driver's seat. Give it up. The controls, give them up? My Jeep? Too attached. Need to think about that. Don't want to.

My brother driving, a dirt road just beyond the ridge above Fallen Leaf Lake. He was testing new wheels, the engine he'd just rebuilt. We were hitting it hard. Invincible youth. Lots of dust, a sharp turn. We started sliding, a big pine tree coming up fast on the edge of the turn. A big fucking pine tree. We kept sliding, dust billowing. The tree. In my face. It was all I could see, all the variations in the tree's bark, they were clearly visible. Impact with that tree on my door, on my body next to the door, was imminent. Death imminent, everything I knew about myself gone, dismissed as incidental, then, abruptly, without apparent cause, we were back on the road. Have no idea what happened.

I wasn't driving that day, on that dirt road.

Giving up the wheel. It's risky.

"On 95, Sal. Maybe then."

She glares.

"I'm trying Sally, wife, I am. I don't know how not to drive, that's all, something like that. I'm not the best at just sitting."

"I don't just sit."

"I know. I don't mean just sitting like doing nothing. You know what I mean, what it's like with your hands on the wheel, eyes checking the mirrors, watching traffic, looking for cops, any kind of highway disruption. Driving is active, decisive, very difficult to let go of that."

"I'll take care of you, hubs, no worries. When I take the wheel, you can play with me, massage my thighs, slip in if you want, more than once, if you want. That's doing something...something for both of us, and the cat. Yum, yum," she says," smiles.

"OK, sure. Once we're further down 95, closer to the Keys."

"Deal." She puts out her hand. We shake.

"A choice, Ben. Decision time. Jacksonville, it's coming up, we have to cross over the St. Johns River on the *remember me* Fuller Warren Bridge into downtown or cut south just ahead on 295 and cross the longer, and likely more beautiful, *remember me* Buckman Bridge. The Henry H *remember me, please!* Buckman Bridge. Which one do you want?"

Everybody wants to be remembered.

"Why?"

I can't think. Something distracting me. A feeling not my own...
someone's feeling. Whose? Driving related. Maybe. Something odd.
Life is odd. Death on drugs, that's what life is. Sally behind the wheel,
self-driving cars, self-driving homes, self-driving meals, self-driving
pets, children, toys. All in a future coming our way, soon.

"No need for why, Ben. Just pick a bridge?"

"OK, the bigger more beautiful *remember me please!* Buckman bridge.
That one."

"Good, my preference as well. Let's take it."

We bank right, head south on 295. Goodbye, Interstate Highway
10, old friend. Roads for friends. Good to have lots of friends.

# EIGHTY SIX

More track houses, spindly evergreens, high school grounds, well laid out, track and baseball fields, night lights, a pool, everyone in Florida has a pool. Close to the bridge. Minimal traffic.

Concrete walls, lining the highway, stop at the river's edge. Water now. Lots of water. A big river.

"Ben, it's beautiful. I love rivers. Big ones, they're like moving lakes."

"Fuck!" I slap my head. "We forgot Amy."

"Did we?"

"I thought she was coming with us."

"Was she?"

"I can't remember."

"Neither can I."

"Does it matter?"

"I don't know."

We keep driving. Water. Wide blue water. Life without water, without air. Facts. We need them to survive. What happens when we don't need them? Don't need water, don't need air, don't need facts?

"I thought she was going to meet us at the Keys."

"I thought we were taking her."

"Maybe we're both wrong."

"Maybe."

Lots of maybes in life.

Once on 95, well south of Jacksonville, I pull over so Sally can drive. She's a good driver, I know that. But giving up the wheel. How

I feel...can't tell exactly. Driving gives me a lot of private pleasure, as long as I'm not stuck in traffic. Hate traffic.

She takes the wheel. I sit back, try to relax. The big pine, in my face, can't shake the image, take out my phone, begin researching towns along our route. Not in control. I feel lost, something lost...a bear cub caught on the edge of a cliff, calling for his mother.

"St. Augustine, Sally. St. Augustine is up next, it's the oldest city in the US. Lots of cannons and such."

"OK."

She's focused on the road. Doesn't turn to look a t me.

"After St. Augustine comes Palm Coast. That's what it says here. Palm Coast is a new city. Founded in 1999. Then Daytona follows, more or less. Fast cars. That Daytona. It was purchased for 1,200 dollars in 1870. After Daytona we have Cape Canaveral. Then NASA, the big picture show.

"And where are we now?"

Sally driving. Very excited.

"We're passing St. Augustine, only nine or ten hours to the Keys. Depending on traffic."

"Nine or ten hours! That's all? Wow, Ben. Cool, very cool!"

"Yeah. We're close now. After the Cape we pass Palm Bay, Vero Beach, and Fort Pierce. One of the oldest east coast counties. Then West Palm Beach and Fort Lauderdale. I have a friend in Fort Lauderdale. He travels. Over a hundred countries so far, has plans to drop into at least fifty more, maybe all 195. He has guns, a gun collection, an old infantryman's musket, shotguns, blow guns, a couple of derringers. You'd love him. We'll call, see if he's there, swap stories...travel stories, hunting stories, swim in his pool. If he's there."

About 30 minutes went by. 45, maybe. Browsing the phone. Scanning the view, occupying myself.

"Here. Listen to this. According to the CDC, the average height for American men is 5 foot 9 inches, the average weight, 197.7 pounds, and waist size is 40.6. For women, the average height is 5 foot 4 inches, the average weight 170.9 pounds and waist size is 38.4.' Our eyes are not mistaken, Sal. We're the fattest fucks in the world. Much easier to control people who can't control themselves."

"It's a rule, hubs. 'If the herd's going in the wrong direction...' Don't follow it," she says, and she glances over, smiles...she loves driving. Loves it. "Where are we now?" she asks. "We passed St. Augustine a long time ago. Feels like hours. How much further?" An eager girl.

"Not sure. Flagler Beach is either coming or gone. About four hundred miles to go, probably more, but not much."

Sally in charge. The wife. Nice. Being a passenger, I like it, like having the leisure to linger on a view, an idea. To take Sally up on her invitation. I loosen my belt, slide over, unbutton her top, take hold of her nearest breast, massage it, switch from breast to breast, try to taste them through my fingers, can't. Imagine I can. Makes my Jolly jump. I drop my hand to her thighs, a sweet and natural notion delightful to beginners and pros. Then...then it happened. Right then. It happened. The long accident on Highway 95.

Six or seven cars ahead of us, a big livestock rig, after passing two trucks hauling zoo animals, cut back into the slow lane too soon, clips the lead zoo truck, jack-knifes to the right at the same time the zoo truck jack-knifes left. The entire road ahead became a wall. The second zoo truck tilts, falls to its side and slides. Cars begin breaking, crashing, flipping over. Lots of red lights, dust, and smoke.

"Sally! After the guard rail, cut right, head for the trees."

"Yes! I will. I am!"

She just misses the car in front of us, a new Lincoln, black, nice, and shiny. The driver hits his brakes, spins off, we can see his face, his desperate, disbelieving eyes, as he hits the end of the rail and rolls over behind us. Sally punches it, our wheels grip deep, hurl clumps of dirt and mud, clumps of grass. Another Jeep follows us. A Wrangler, much smaller than Jill. Sally stops at the trees, keeps our distance from the barbed wire fence. The Wrangler passes us, follows the tree line, tries to pass the trucks, doesn't make it. The second zoo truck is still sliding. The cab broke free of its trailer, the trailer hits the Wrangler, bounces it into the trees like a tennis ball.

All is confused. *Bombs going off in my head. Bombs I threw. Bombs thrown at me. People screaming, lots of screaming, people running with their ears covered, frightened, emaciated flames slip between crashed vehicles looking for fuel, for food, for more fire.*

Sally relaxes her brake pedal, turns off the engine. A haze made of smoke and heat covers everything.

"Damn!" Not good enough. "Fuck. Fuck. Fuck!" I yell, scream, "FUCK!"

We sit. Watch. The horror continues. More cars crash, more fires break out, more people torn from their plans, their happy hour, illicit rendezvous, birthday party.

"Are you OK, Sal?"

"Yes. I am. But damn, Ben. Fuck!"

"I know."

"Fuck."

It goes national. The long accident on Highway 95. Makes all the news stations.

Sally. I pull her to me. Hold her.

We're still alive.

# EIGHTY SEVEN

The sky is no longer blue, our drive no longer enchanting.
People are hurt. The apathetic strings that manipulate life defying free will, shattering expectations. We get out, inspect each other, the Jeep, the cat. We're fine.

Lucky, very lucky.

"Sal, I'll get the First Aid kit. Grab a bottle of water. Vodka, flares, the fire-extinguisher."

"Yeah...."

We collect ourselves, hug, walk to the road. Cars are backed up beyond view. Both sides of the highway. The accident has crossed the divider.

Gawkers. Accident vampires, clogging the roads, rear-ending other gawkers, amplifying injury.

Hundreds of vehicles, looks like hundreds. A world in disarray, wreckage everywhere. Cows. Animals everywhere. All kinds of animals, even an elephant, a young elephant, a turtle on its back, legs aren't moving, head isn't moving. Two zebras. They wander, dazed, frightened. No room for emergency equipment and people to get in but they do. Somehow, a few. A fire truck, a couple of cops, an ambulance.

Animals run from them, from the fires, the sirens, the flashing lights.

Sally and I go from car to car. Debris everywhere. Manage minor injuries, shock mostly.

The Keys. Once again, are very far away.

By the time twilight falls, people have resigned themselves to spending the night on the highway. They make camp. Those most severely injured have been evacuated by air or in one of the few ambulances that made it to us. No one died. Somehow, no one died. The highway, blocked for fifteen to twenty miles in both directions, is home for now. I don't mind. Not really. I like being outside. Sally does as well. Road trips. Uneventful road trips are not road trips. They're something, but not road trips, not the kind that recreate how we define consequence.

"Want a candy bar, a Milky Way?"

"Thanks, sure."

Sally removes the wrapper, hands it to me. We're sitting on the Jeep, leaning back under the open tailgate. A clear sky for low elevation.

"Shall we go back out? See what else?"

"We should, yeah, immediate and temporary relief. That's us." I pick up our aid bag. "Let's try the other side of the highway."

"Looks bad."

"It does, Sal. It is."

It is bad. Fewer semi's but just as bad. Obscure shapes, people walking, fading into the dim, the smoke, the flickering lights. Plans disrupted; lives put on hold. Like that. A click of the dial, a turn to the right instead of the left, a pause before stepping out of the elevator, a second too late, a second too early, and everything changes. Reality: the beast of ages, taunting us, confirming it has no master, not even God.

Dark now.

We step over the metal rail divider, spot a young family huddling next to a yellow VW Beetle. The new model. The driver's side door is torn off, two tires blown out. They pulled out the seats, were sitting on them in front of a small fire. And they were drinking, drinking, and laughing. All down the highway and up, the night feels less cruel. Small fires burn, music plays, survivors are talking, making friends.

Sally steps forward, "Mind if we join you? We have medicine, bandages, disinfectant."

"Certainly. Please, sit down. I'll stand."

The father gets up. He's young, 27, 28. Black hair, a slight beard, strong, sleeveless shirt, dark red, Semper Fi tattooed on his upper arm. Powerful legs, sharp jaw, eyes are thoughtful. A soldier once, an athlete now?

Sally takes his seat, I stand.

They have two girls, three or four years old. They look like the wife, their mother. They're chubby, cheeky girls, curly blond hair, pink dresses. Could be twins, maybe they are. One throws her cupcake (no wrapper on it) for her sister to catch in her mouth. She misses, bounces off her lips. The cupcake is small, about walnut size, maybe strawberry. The other sister picks it up, throws it back. They miss again, might have been intentional. The cupcake rolls into taller grass. Both jump up to get it, happy for a chance to run, to spend their youth. I glance over, the father glances.

The girls freeze. Don't scream.

A panther. Black. More hungry than frightened, he crouches, his appetite wanting but hesitant, ten feet in front of them. I'm just as far away. The father a couple of feet closer.

"Girls. Listen, don't move. Listen to me, hear me, your father. Hear your father. Don't move. Keep staring at the cat. Eyes on the cat and listen. Listen to me. Don't turn around, just back up. Back up very, very slowly. Listen to me. Hear only my voice in your head. Back up, very slowly. Listen, listen to me. Back up, slowly."

Their father's voice. They trust him, begin to shift their weight. I remove a flare from our bag, pass it behind me to Sally. Hidden behind the man's wife, she pulls the cap, lights it, hurries it back to me, almost throws it. The father lunges, grabs his girls, I toss the flare at the cat's head, follow the flare with my knife. The cat spooks, turns, misses the flare, takes my knife in the shoulder, runs off.

"My knife! Damn! Damn!"

"Great move, old man, great move." He soft punches my shoulder, puts out his hand. "You're ex, right?"

"I am, yeah."

"Which branch?"

"Marines. Sniper. Rewards and punishments. A life better forgotten."

"I know. It's good, and not good. I know. Thanks."

"Sure." My knife...fuck.

"Sorry about your knife."

"Yeah, nothing to do."

Attachment to things, useful things, reliable things. I am...we all are.

Sally gets up. The wife also.

"Wait! Don't leave. Girls come; I have chocolate. Everyone, let's open a bottle of wine, eat some chocolate."

The wife leaves us, grabs a lantern, pops open the VW glove box, takes out a handgun, a .38, and walks toward several burned out cars and an upside-down trailer with 'Wine Wonderland' written on it. She opens the back, bottles fall out, several break. She sorts through them. We watch as the lantern bobs up and down, illuminating, her face, her ample figure. She's a small, big woman. Cheerful, embracing. Finally, the bobbing stops and she walks back, four bottles in her arms. Caymus, Opus One, Screaming Eagle, Harlan. All good wines, great wines, expensive wines, wines we can't afford.

"Don't worry folks. The trailer's ours," she says, and she extends her hand. I shake it. Sally shakes it.

"I'm Peggy. Friends call me Puddy, or Pud."

"Pleased to meet you, Pud."

"And that's Jimbo, my husband, the girls are Ruth and Anne. They're three and four but not a year apart."

"I'm Sally, he's Ben, my husband. We're on our way to the Keys. To live. We're from Paradise, California."

"The burned place?"

"Yeah, the burned place."

"You poor people. We saw the news. A terrible fire. Terrible. A broken world."

Silence. A cautious moment, migrant images passing through the mind. A broken world, indeed. Was made broken.

"Right. Well…here we are now. Which wine should we start with?" Pud holds up the Screaming Eagle. All smiles. We open it, find some cups, different sizes, materials, shapes. I take a small juice glass, Sally a silver baby cup, lots of dents. After one bite of chocolate, and putting their girls to bed inside the Beetle, a safe space, our hosts join us with plastic cups, one clear, the other with flowers on it. We finish the first bottle. Doesn't take long. A good time to drink, to drink too much.

After the fourth bottle Pud fetches three more. We drink them.

"Here's a question." I raise my glass. Sally raises hers; Pud and Jimbo raise theirs.

"How do we know we're not being watched? Not watched like in God overseeing the death of every cell in our bodies but watched by what we think we're seeing." Enlightenment off the rails, wagon. Does it have a wagon?

"Seeing?" Asks Pud. "You mean if I see a plant, it sees me?"

"Something like that. Yes. A good comparison."

Sally laughs, hugs Pud.

"And reflections, and rocks, I see them, they see me? And sounds, does what I hear, hear me? Is that what you're saying?"

"Yes, that. Don't you sometimes feel like you're being watched? *Déjà vu* comes when we notice we're being watched. That's what *Déjà vu* is, us being aware of being watched.

"I think so."

We drink two more bottles. Eat Swiss chocolate, three bags of Cheetos (the hot ones), cold hot dogs, no ketchup or mustard, drink bottled water, keep putting wood on the fire, finish the wine, stop putting wood on the fire, put the fire out, go back to the Jeep fully intoxicated, a few hours before sunrise.

No one died.

A Panther. Zoo animals hunting for food on US 95.

Unbelievable.

# EIGHTY EIGHT

Scratching sounds, clawing. I wake up, sit up. Listen. Nothing, a silent night crawling into itself. Sally lying next to me, loving me even as she sleeps. I lie back down, pull her close. She smiles, sighs.

Distant helicopter rotors, getting closer. The first filaments of morning light reaching from behind them. Three, four hours sleep. Still tired. News helicopters hovering overhead, cameras strafing the highway for images of transcendent misery. Frightened zoo animals, frightened people. Hundreds of wrecked and damaged cars and trucks, big rigs, campers, boats, bikes, traffic backed up for miles on both sides.

Google maps. People finding roads around the congestion. Not us... not today. The Keys...not today. Sally yawns, stretches. I love hearing her, a musical body. Sally sounds, inviting sounds.

"I'm hungry Ben, and I need a bath, a shower."

No hangovers. She doesn't have one, neither do I. It was good wine.

"Relax, Sal, have some juice, some raisins. I'll see what I can do about the shower."

A warm morning. One helicopter came in closer, then another. Sally leans out the window, waves, shouts, "We're OK everybody. Looks bad but we're OK."

A beautiful woman. Everyone loves a beautiful woman.

I turn toward the line of wrecks and begin walking. Miss my knife. A hundred yards or so down the line I find a truck. The cab is smashed but standing, a food truck, the kind that serves everything from coffee and soft drinks to hotdogs and hamburgers. The guy who owns it is open for business. A cheerful guy. Flat ears, stained apron, wide, round nose, a bit red from drinking, bright red. I buy hamburgers, drinks, chips, cookies, a couple of big jugs of water, half dozen chocolate-covered, cream filled eclairs. A good day for sweets.

Two minivans with tables in front of them on the other side of the road, they're selling fruits and vegetables. I cross over, pick up apples, bananas, a ripe mango. Love mangos. A lot to carry. Forgot I have to walk back. Manage well enough, don't drop anything.

At the Jeep, Sally is sitting up, an open nightgown look, talking to some guy with a mic and a girl with a camera. They don't look like news people. The novelty market infecting journalism. Maybe. Probably.

I walk up. "Sally, here's the food, water for your shower, and who are these people?" I turn toward them. "Who are you?"

The guy, shorter than me, lots of plastic surgery. Nose, chin, cheeks, he smiles the best he can. Some faces don't look like they work right. His didn't.

"Filmmakers," he says. "We make movies. *Magic Moments*. That's our company name. Here's my card."

I don't take it.

"Look us up. We saw your wife."

The girl focuses her camera on me.

"You saw my wife?"

"On the news."

"The news?"

"The News. Soon as we saw her. We immediately thought she'd make a glorious movie star. Talent we can take national, international. What do you think?"

I look at him, at the girl. She's beautiful.

"Ask my wife," I say.

"We did."

"What did she say?"

"To ask you."

"I see. OK. I'll take that card."

He hands it to me, a laminated card, white with a big pillow on it. *"Magic Moments"* written on the pillow, in a florid script. His girl gives Sally her card. I look at her again. Well above average.

"She's Desiree," the man says. "Des, for short. Means desirable. I'm Oscar. Oscar Maverick Dean. That's my stage name. Oscar M. Dean. OMD for short." He puts out his hand, an awkward gesture for him. We shake.

"What kind of movies?"

"Adult movies."

"You're a porn actor?"

"No. Not really. I'm needed sometimes, when they run short, but I mostly direct."

"Oh."

Desiree eyes me, gives a look. That only-something-girls-can-know-about-you look.

"We can use you as well, old man," she says. "You're fit. No sagging skin, a good head of hair, persuasive package in the basement." She eyes my crotch, steps toward me, her camera in one hand filming.

Sally smiles. They're playing a joke on me. That's what I think.

"This is all a joke," I say, "right. A joke. A laugh."

Des laughs, "Damn, you caught us."

They all laugh, I laugh. Feels good to laugh.

Sally looks at me, straight on. "It's no joke, Ben. Really. We can talk, maybe work with them. They know the business. We've thought of doing porn. Many times, and if...."

Desiree frames the camera. "Take one. Rolling..."

I put my hand over the lens.

"Now? Here? You see where we are?"

"Sure. I see where we are," Oscar gestures. "All this wreckage, it's great stuff, dramatic, compels viewers to stay tuned. Suffering and sex, an impressive combination. I know what people want, folks. I do. Look, all that smoke, and fire in the background, very marketable. We should begin filming, really. Why not? From devastation highway arises the Phoenix...the randy phoenix. That's it! The title. *The Randy Phoenix.* We can do it."

A strange little man. Can't settle on what to think of him. Desiree is different, an upper-level woman. It's obvious she's thinking. A dangerous woman. Maybe.

"Sally, you decide."

She tilts her head, begins purring...for a moment she actually looks like a cat. Maybe she is a cat, a cat without the vertical-slit pupils disguised as an alien albino. "Let's eat, talk, relax, make a decision later."

I empty the two bottles of water into a black trash bag, squeeze the air out, tie and hang it from the branch of a nearby tree. The water will heat up in the sun. Sally's shower water. Small holes poked in the bag releases the water, makes a fine spray. I pull a blanket from the Jeep. Des and Sally spread it out, lay down the food, drinks, the few beers we have in our cooler. A picnic. A Wonderland in ruins picnic.

We eat, drink, smoke and drink some more, fall asleep in the sun, on the blanket, choppers overhead, debris all around, abandoned vehicles. Accident litter. Almost noon on Interstate 95. The most dangerous highway in the country.

People say that.

# EIGHTY NINE

It's late, feels late. Still afternoon when we wake up. Worlds real and imagined occupying the same time and space. How to choose between them. Can we? Music playing, a variety – from several directions. An elephant rummaging through the back of my Jeep.

"Christ! You see this!"

They do, all eyes are on the elephant, a juvenile, maybe two years old.

"Flares, Ben, use a flare."

"Right." Flares. I have two left, scramble to grab one, behind the back seat, its cap's already broken, I strike it, climb into the front seat waving it in the elephant's face. He backs up abruptly, hits his trunk on the roof. I drop the flare, singe my leather seats. The elephant pauses, looks like he wants to ask a question. Eye contact, man, and elephant, we stare, wait for words, there are none. I throw the flare (becoming good at that), it hits the top of his head, he panics, runs, almost tramples Oscar. Oscar's trying for a clip of Sally, posing like Athena with the elephant raging behind her, rearing on its hind legs and roaring. Zoo animals free of their bars and chains. Wonder if there are snakes. Zoo snakes. Do they still have venom sacs? And what happened to the panther, to my knife?

"We got footage, everyone. Live footage!" A lottery moment for Oscar.

"The Albino Story, Part One. We got it."

"Right," Des is dismissive, but in a nice way.

"The porn scenes," Sal interjects, "the ones with me in them, my baby belly, when it begins to show, What then?"

Sirens, lights, equipment sounds. Repair and clean-up crews. They're few in number and some distance from us. Most of them disappeared a few hours after the crash. Odd. The four of us, standing now, adjusting our clothes, finger combing our hair, yawning, we look up and down the highway. Little has changed from the day before. Those who stayed with their belongings, their car, truck, bus, are wholly committed. A highway village, we're starting to look like one. Cooking fires, makeshift kitchens, bathrooms, stores.

"No worries, Sally," Oscar says, "we'll sort the belly later. For now, here, folks, here's what we should do. I'll tell you." A big grin.

"What, Oscar? What should we do?" Des put her hands on her hips. Glares at him.

"We should set up a stage. Put on a show. Tonight. The news cameras will spot us. No cost. They'll shoot us, light the stage. We can film at the same time. Des and Sally can dance, sure. Soft erotic, an enticing double striptease, nothing heavy. Porn-lite, we hit all the right visuals before the camera's blink, before they can blur the tits. Live on national TV. We can make a mountain of cash...a whole mountain range!"

"The powers that be fear nudity." You've said that how many times, Oscar? You want to get us in trouble, again. Is that what you want?"

They start fighting. Des and Oscar. Yelling. Feel like clocking both of them.

"Shut the fuck up! For Christ's sake!" I shout.

They stop.

"No trouble, Ben. Sally. Des. Apologies, many apologies. On my word." Oscar bows, raises his hands in prayer. "On my word, no trouble, just fun and profit. We need a stage. There, you see that truck laying on its side, we can make a ladder, climb up, use it for a stage."

Why not? Very few serious injuries. No one died. No emergency. Nowhere to go. Crews will get to us soon enough. A show. Could be fun, entertaining. Why not?

"Ben, you're down with this. Right. Let's make that ladder."

"Yeah, OK." I pop my neck, my right wrist, offer assurances to the ladies.

"We'll be back," I say, turning to leave.

Then, I hear it. My name–Ben. It's being called. Someone. Very faint and far away, more like the sound of a memory than real life. Coming closer.

"Ben...!"

Again. There it is. Yes, it is my name.

"Ben! It's me!"

No.

"Benjamin Mamott!"

Impossible. Can't be, can't.

It is.

"Amy!"

She runs up to me, hugs me, kisses me, looks for Sally.

"For Christ's sake woman, you're like a fucking homing pigeon! What is it with you?"

"I'll tell you in a minute," she says stepping past Oscar to Sally. "Found you! I knew I would."

"You did?"

"Yes, I did."

"Were you coming with us after Simbana's? We couldn't remember."

Amy pauses, puts her palm to her head. "I can't remember either. Simbana's house can do that. I just knew I'd see you again. That's all. Damn! Look at you. Beautiful, always beautiful. And you," she turns to Desiree. "Who are you?"

"I'm Desiree, Des."

"Nice to meet you Des, I'm Amy," she says, and they shake hands. Both are shorter than Sally, less exotic but tasty.

Des points, "I work with Oscar, over there. That odd little man. I do porn, we do porn, join us, why don't you. I mean, look at you. You're stunning. The three of us? Guys will lose it just thinking of what we can do for them, of what we can do for their girlfriends, their wives."

"Amy, I have a thought." Sally pulls her closer. "Let's talk, smoke, think and drink this through. Consider our options. At the moment, though, all I want is to take a shower. Ben showed me how. You can join me if you wish. And Des. There's plenty of water if we're quick."

"Oh, Ben," Amy turns to me, "I saw Sally on the news. That's how I found you. Everyone saw her, loved her. Simbana drove me, dropped me as close as she could, went back to New Orleans. I walked over a mile to get here, maybe more. They're doing a great job cleaning up. Traffic is flowing through side roads around 95."

Great. The three girls huddle closer, hushed voices, glancing, playful eyes, Botticelli muses escaping their canvas cage.

Oscar walks over. "What are they talking about?"

"Something," I shrug. "We'll find out."

Somehow, Oscar is beginning to seem normal, look normal. Not sure if that's good or bad.

We leave the ladies, go out for wood, more booze, snacks, material for our ladder, to find a band, speakers. We tell people the girls are going to perform, lots of flesh, spread the word.

Don't have to walk for long before we find what we need, divide the load between us and head back. Sun's going down, spending its light on the shadows, a daily deposit. Almost to the Jeep, we see helicopters at three different heights above our spot, blades whirling, crews hanging out the open doors, tongues hanging out, lights and cameras focused on the girls. The three of them. They're showering together, washing each other, playing in the bubbles, playing with the bubbles, with each other. In the strong light drops of water splatter across their bodies, shimmer; a kind of human bioluminescence casting spells, an optical chant making the desire to keep watching the mind's only occupation. Truth in beauty. It's always been there. Women. They're endlessly desirable, unexpected, magnificent creatures.

Lights are on them, the world watching, they move as one, as a waterfall cleansing itself, returning as mist to the river above at the same time it's falling. Breathtaking, that's what they are, coruscating, the three of them, every movement a statue for the sculptor, a glorious painting for the artist...beauty for eyes to see, all eyes. A better window on the world than watching bombs shatter lives, tanks crush cars, blast villages, destroy bridges. Better than watching blades leave their sheaths, bullets their casings, blood drain from lifeless bodies, tears torn from the eyes. The girls showering, better to feel their joy in pleasure than all the hate and anger, the dregs of crime and war viewers are exposed to every day.

Sally, Amy, Des. The thousands of eyes watching them, wanting them, remembering them. The newly famous, those last few moments before they can no longer be anonymous in public...they're in them. Muses with nine lives.

A wind gust scatters the shower spray. Chopper cameras zoom in, keep shooting. Oscar keeps shooting, begins running around the bag shooting. Shooting, shooting, shooting, around and around, with each revelation he gets closer and closer to the girls. Once close enough, he tries to get in between them, pushes his way, looks up at the choppers, tries to film himself being filmed. The girls kick him, smack him, push him away. He pushes back, no luck, three against one. He throws down his camera, goes manic, screams something obscene, probably obscene, difficult to tell. Confused, maybe, an act, maybe...he fumbles himself, slurs, shakes, stammers, loses it, utterly, starts ripping at his clothes, tears them apart, returns to running circles around the girls. In all his glory he embraces the dancing light from above, the unforgiving eyes of the many.

Embarrassing, maybe not. Sally looks at me. A wry smile tweaking the corners of her lips, she gestures toward Oscar, covers her eyes with her hand, speaks to no one I can see, removes her hand, looks at Oscar. In an instant he swells up, turns into a food item with legs, a walking cheeseburger (with bacon) waving its arms. All the chopper cameras leave the girls, focus on Oscar as he continues to run circles around them. And, as he runs, like waiters bringing out new dishes, he switches from a cheeseburger with legs and arms to mashed potatoes, then corn on the cob with the little yellow cob holders sticking out each end, then a hotdog, without the bun, the chopper guys loved that one. They filmed and filmed as he ran and ran, changed, and changed, then, when he turned into ice-cream and melted it was all over. Oscar dropped to the ground, mostly undressed, and began kicking like he was in a pool racing for gold, and licking himself, ran out of breath and passed out.

He's not dead. Could be if death knew how to animate itself.

A strange little man, definitely. Very strange.

And Sally, what the fuck...?

# NINETY

All manner of department vehicles and crews reach us before we got up the next morning. Down the line they're busy dismantling temporary structures, clearing away debris, burned out cars, broken toys, scattered belongings. No one died. A two-day long accident. Starting to hate cars. Not my Jeep. Amy, Des, and Oscar slept outside on a waterproof tarp, blanket, sheets, and a couple of pillows. Sally and I slept in the Jeep on the bare mattress, wasn't uncomfortable, not with Sally next to me. Sally makes everything comfortable, life, the afterlife, everything.

More and more noise. Rescue teams all around us. Freedom to move on. Freedom to speak freely without retribution…not yet I sit up. Two cops, husky types, Rottweilers, Dobermans, are walking toward us. Toward the blanket. They stop a few feet back, look down.

"Is that him?"

"Yeah. That's him."

The taller of the two cops, who looks like he's in charge–tall people always look like they're in charge–bends over, taps Oscar on the head. Oscar looks up.

"Yes."

"Are you Oscar Dean? Oscar, smile for the camera, Dean?"

"Maybe."

"The news last night, asshole. Remember? Everyone saw you. Everyone."

Oscar winces, "You don't have to be rude, officer," he says, and he sits up, pulls the sheet with him, fills their eyes with free Desiree and Amy upper body shots. Beautiful upper body shots. Doesn't help.

"See this photo?" The tall cop tosses it to him. "It looks like you. See what you're doing."

Oscar's eyes glaze over.

The shorter cop grabs the photo, slaps his face with it.

"That's not me," he protests, pouts, looks down. "I didn't do that."

"It is you. You did do that. Get up, get dressed, you're coming with us."

We stare. Say nothing.

The cop tosses us the photo. "In case you're wondering," he says, his voice contemptuous, his manner punitive.

Oscar pulls on his fashionable jeans, a tee, discolored moccasin loafers. The cops handcuff him, walk him away, push him into the back of their two-toned patrol car, drive off.

The villainy of stalking innocence, infecting and defiling it, all the do-gooder movements crying for the unborn that fail to protect living children. Pedophiles, death sentence therapy. Works every time. Hate pedophiles.

Des jumps up. "Shit! The car keys. He has the car keys! All my stuff, our equipment. The camera, they're in the car."

I open the Jeep door. Consider grabbing my monkey stick from the door pocket. An inlaid piece of mahogany with a bulbous metal head. Regal, beautiful. Used it in India. Wacked monkeys with it, a hawk once. Just in case, I keep it next to the driver's seat. A strong urge to break something. I leave the stick, walk over to their car, a tiny thing, smash the window with my elbow. Felt good and hurt at the same time, always think my appendages have metal in them, I open the door.

"Take what you want."

"Amy, are you coming with us?" Sally asks.

She smiles. "Yes Sally, I am."

"And you Des. You coming? We have room?"

"I'd love to, sure. Yes…happily."

She nips her camera, tripod, a few things, and a bag. We use the last of our water to wash our faces. Eat a few candy bars, some raisins, drink some juice, turn over Jill's big V8. She needs detailing, some interior work, sounds good. Sally takes shotgun. Amy and Des rearrange the mattress, the pillows, relax on our comfy bed. We pull out and back on the road south.

South to the Keys.

# NINETY ONE

Air rushing through the windows. Our clothes, outdoor tablecloths tossed by an afternoon breeze, billow, and flare. Feels like we've been dropped into an old movie, where a bunch of poor kids hop into the rich kid's new chrome-accented convertible and cruise country roads, waving at cows, smoking filter less cigarettes, drinking beer, music blasting from the radio, straining the speakers. We're on the move and making good time. No hurry. A warm day, full sun, few clouds, minimal traffic. Malls, lots of malls, shops, homes, gas stations, the glories of cookie-cutter sprawl, open fields, trees, some evergreens, palm trees, crooked streetlights with bulbous heads, a *War of the Worlds* look. We continue south, the Flagler Beach accident dissolving behind us, sinking into memory, losing strength. Lots of birds, flocks. Black-birds, thousands of them. I feel tired, no reason, turn to Sally.

"You want to drive?"

"Do you want me to?"

"I do. Definitely. We'll stop for gas soon. Eat. Clean up. You drive from there. Fort Lauderdale isn't far. A couple of hundred miles, about that. We can visit my friend Loki. Remember. I mentioned him. His name's Lokilino, we call him Loki, master of swear word therapy. Met him on a plane to Bangkok twenty years ago, maybe thirty. A bachelor considering marriage, an okay-looking guy...like most guys. He was born in Fort Lauderdale and he's Burning Man crazy. Caustic sense of humor, great fun, very bright. We can swim in his pool. Rest, stay overnight, if he has room. Hit the Keys tomorrow."

"Could be fun, Ben, sure. Loki's it is." Sally puts her hand on my knee. "Daytona coming up, a few miles, ten, maybe less, maybe more, not far."

"At our present pace, we can reach Loki by early evening. Would be nice. Swim a little, relax, eat well, laugh a lot. Ready ourselves for the Keys."

"A good plan. And Ben. Loki. That name sounds familiar. Have I heard it before?"

"You have, Sal. Must have, likely have...maybe have. Well... Loki is a mischievous shape shifter. An old Norse god, of sorts. Lokilino, my Loki, he's Italian, not much for shape shifting, but the mischievous part, he's got that bit right. Not difficult to imagine him chasing naked cheerleaders across a football field at half time, an air strip, a five-lane highway, up Everest. Mischievous, he's definitely that. Loki invented hysteria nudity. They sell it in small coke bottles to rovers and lonely aliens stuck on Mars...at a discount."

"We like mischief," Amy and Des speak at the same time, laugh at the same time.

"We all do," Sally says. "Life without a little mischief...a lot of mischief. What would that be like?"

"Yeah."

"No new ideas. No imagination."

"Right, no place to go you haven't been. Nothing to learn you don't already know."

"Rocks," adds Des, "rocks have no imagination. And human rocks. Rocks that are human. Statues, that's what they are, human rocks. Remember...the Pet Rock fad? Remember that? Maybe it was the rock's idea and not the human's, a trick to get humans to move them around. Some rocks like to travel, see more of the world, meet other rocks."

The road. We pause, listen to it. A silent surface, an asphalt drumskin waiting to vibrate. The sound of ideas learning to think for themselves, the time it takes for the mind to grasp them, or not...beauty in the absence of definition.

"Sal, remember when I asked you to describe the female orgasm. Remember what you said."

"I do. Of course, I do."

"Right. Well, you said, you said 'It's like rain in the desert.' That's all.

"It's more than that, Hubs, much more. We have girl words for it, how it feels to us. No guy words."

"An eruption of Saints, purifying." Amy cheers, throws up her hands, "that's what it's like, an eruption of saints, and goddesses."

"That' right," Desiree adds, "It's how you meet God, the only way to meet God, the only time his direct line is open. Absent orgasms people go through religion. Nowhere near as much fun."

I agree. Of course. Girls, they know things.

Exit 268. Gas stations, restaurants. We stop, gas up, clean up, buy more food, water, and raisins, a 12-box pack, order takeout breakfasts. They taste like someone's already eaten them. We throw them out. Sally takes the wheel, adjusts the seat, the mirrors, fastens her seatbelt. I slip in back, Des and Amy. A surprise of some kind. They're waiting for me. All smiles.

# NINETY TWO

The road, road trips. Before there were roads, there was a need for roads. How long from the awareness of need to satisfying need? I wouldn't call it evolution. Adaptation, some version of adaptation. "Ladies," I lean to my left, sit up slightly, "I'm having a thought, something interesting. I think so." Lying in the back, our mattress easing the ride, I'm feeling good. My head on a stack of pillows, Amy, and Des threading my toes with their hair. Hard to imagine, fun to watch, tickles.

"What would it be like," I say, "if we didn't have butts to sit on? A very different world for sure. Lots of pillow shops. Everywhere, everywhere people go, everywhere they sit, there would be pillows and pillow shops nearby, even small corner-of-the-wall shops in elevators for people who like to lean against the wall for long rises.

"Ben!"

"Yeah."

"This is something we need to think about?"

"No, no need. Of course not."

"OK."

"Still, Sal, there must be alternate designs, designs that got thrown out or used on some other planet. Take elbows. Imagine having no elbows or heals on our feet. Somewhere out there, way out, there may be a human race, a race just like us but with no butts, no elbows, no heals."

"Ben...hubs, you're still talking?"

"Yeah, it's the tweaks, Sal." Hooked on my own words, I keep talking. "There are so many tweaks. So many possibilities. How does nature decide? The laws of nature? Our eyes. Think about it, about how much of a reduction in pollution would there be if nature had made our eyes better equipped to see in the dark? If we could see as we do during the day, and also see at night with thirty to fifty percent less light than what we see now, we would use less electricity. Burn fewer truckloads of coal to make electricity, buy fewer batteries, minimize the use of nuclear power and the burden of disposing of nuclear waste.

"Just one little tweak, Sal, if nature had made that one little tweak a long time ago, everything would be different.

"Ben…"

"Right, I need help. I know."

Amy passes me the joint, I take a hit, several swallows of beer, awkward swallows, a difficult angle, nice taste, the weed, it's good weed. Amy brought it with her. Simbana's special blend.

Sally closing the distance, driving on, smoking cigarettes, drinking mini-Coke after mini-Coke, singing to herself, singing to us, she turns the radio on, turn it off, rolls the window up, then down. Behind her, my body, oiled and laid out like a fine meal, I relax, begin to drift. Miles goes by with miles to go. Lost miles, miles far from home, miles that get too much sun, miles attached to minutes…it's a race. Will the miles arrive first, or the minutes? Must call Loki. Amy and Desiree agreed to knock on his door when we arrive, to announce in sing-songy voices "Ready or not, here we are!"

Loki! "Oh, ladies, I just remembered, another thought. Loki shoots lizards. He's probably shooting them now."

"Ben!" All three speak at once, "Stop talking!"

I do. I close my eyes, focus on the afterglow of a happy ending, on a world free of suffering and shallow disputes, on empty space, on nothing, nothing at all.

Loki. Call him.

I will.

Later.

# NINETY THREE

wake up. An hour has passed, Sally thinks two.
Warm, a little damp, comfortable. A new body. Feels like I have one. Feels great. It happens. There are days, hours, even weeks when I feel great, invincible, fully realized, enlightened.

They don't last. They never last.

Washing up, paying bills, body maintenance, meetings, meals, parties, buying clothes, buying, and eating food, driving, walking. Interest in life fades with repetition, necessity takes over, then boredom, followed by moral insolvency. What to do?

More sex.

The first answer to every question is more sex. How many hours are there in a day? More sex. Can kangaroos back up? More sex. Is it time for another drink? More sex. Is Trump an electronically transmitted disease? More sex. Where do we go when we die? More sex. Is there a God? More sex.

I slip on my shorts, shirt, sandals, climb into the passenger's seat, attach my seatbelt, light another joint. Wonderful. Life. It can be. A beautiful day. Beautiful. Florida is good at that.

I dial Loki.

"Hi! This is Loki. You're crazy to call. Leave a number."

"Loki! Pick up!"

No answer.

"Brother, it's Ben. I'm headed your way with Sally and two beauties, Amy, and Des. Are you home?"

No answer.

I pass the phone to Amy and Des.

"Loki, I'm Amy."

"And I'm Des, short for Desiree."

"Ben says you're great, a good time roll, smart, experienced. We need proof."

No answer.

"He's not home."

"I take the phone. "Listen, Loki. We're not that far out. Will call again, knock on your door."

He picks up.

"Ben! Fuck man. Great to hear you. Sorry. Christ. I was outside. Stood my ground. Shot a lizard, a big one, at least three feet. Been trying to nail him for days. Planted new kick-ass flowers in my garden, beautiful flowers. That bastard ate them. All of them. I shot him. Looked like a mob hit. A sloppy mob hit. He ran to the neighbors, climbed a tree, hid in the branches. I tucked my gun under my shirt, walked over, waited for him to drop. He didn't drop. I waited. Too many branches for a clear shot. People passing by. Too many people. I went back in and watched from my front window, waited half-an-hour, an hour. Went back out. That prick was still alive, bleeding but still there sitting in the tree, part of his head missing. A monster lizard. I tried to knock him down, threw rocks at him, sprayed water. He's still there. That fuck. I came back for my speargun, heard the last of your message. Yeah. The pool's warm. Guest rooms are empty. See you in a few. Have to go."

He hangs up.

Gangster lizard. Yeah. I can see that. A movie, a series.

We continue on; the day remains beautiful.

Florida…an all the sun you can eat, hurricanes-for-free State.

I imagine Loki getting nabbed for animal cruelty, trespassing and disorderly conduct, by outraged social programmers, profanity police, clerics, and politically correct authoritarians with tiny heads.

Signs for Cape Canaveral.

Exit 205 A. A is for NASA's Port Canaveral and little green men directing traffic on and off the highway, dozens of them. Little green men waving their arms and erecting vote for Trump signs with Russian flags, and "MAKE AMERICA MINE" slogans, stuck on them. The signs are big, wall-size signs, dozens of the little green men get squished each time the breeze shifts and knocks one over.

A messy exit.

Exit 205 B. B. Orlando International Airport and Minnie and Mickey Mouse made infamous in the future for becoming the first cartoon characters to gain greater fame by selling sex tapes to under-aged adults, and fornicating in a feature length animation – 22nd century cinema – a Progressive Generation remake of *Porn 101*? It's a short mouse length film, very popular on a small scale.

Wondered how many people mix up exit A and B, go the wrong way. Somebody knows?

We drive on.

After Canaveral we hit sign after sign for beach towns.

Florida.

More beaches in the lower forty-eight than any other state, and oranges.

"Time for a pit stop folks. Anyone thirsty?"

Sally's driving, likes driving.

"I am," I say. "A cold beer would be great, very cold. I'll have one, two, maybe three."

"Me, too!" Amy squeals. She gets excited easily. Some people act more alive than they really are. Amy's more alive than she acts.

Des is good with water. "Maybe juice," she says. Sally wants a sip from each of our drinks, a box of raisins and a scoop of ice cream. For fun, during happier Paradise days, she'd press a mound of soft vanilla into her nipples, have me lick it off them before it melted.

She loves vanilla.

And raisins.

And cats.

# NINETY FOUR

A head and above us, the sky is blue, the day warm, accommodating, the road, for the moment, sparsely populated.

"The world we live in," I say, and I blew a smoke ring toward Sally. Her open window sucked it up instantly. "To change the world, we need to change in it. But how? The myopia of cultural, religious, social, and familial programs installed during childhood, for most people, have become who they are, who they think they are. To change that, for people to see themselves as not themselves, it's not going to happen." I pause, take another hit, open, and close the glovebox. No reason. Don't need a reason "What do you think, Sal, Amy, Des? Is anyone really happy?"

"We're happy!"

Des and Amy are sitting crossed legged, playing un-strip poker, exchanging gin shots and hits. No clothes, they're playing to put them back on. A Vegas act, I'd pay to see it. Body money. Lots of body money in Vegas.

"Intermittent happiness, we get that, "I say, "like we get so many things. To be happy, to experience complete happiness, that's what I'm thinking, and I think it's more aspirational than actual. But what if something changed? If something dramatic, big, and unexpected took hold, something that gripped us by the throat, captured our attention, reformed the rules?

"What if one day, wherever we are, whoever we're with, whatever we're doing, all clothes disappear, vanish as a stain bleached away and we return to our natural state. Naked and vulnerable. Everyone. Just like that. No clothes! All skin. Only skin. Nothing to hide, little room for pretense. Everyone in the world naked. What would that be like?"

"You mean would it make people happier?"

"I don't know. Maybe, maybe not. For many people, maybe most, there's nothing more frightening than nudity. Next to nudity, God is ant food, flea food, something smaller. Nudity, sex, and swear words. They scare the shit out of people. The big trinity; master deities with real clout. Having no fear of them should make people happy."

Sally turns to me, throws me a kiss with her eyes, "Makes people like us happy."

Des and Amy cheer. "Happy, happy, happy."

"OK," I say, "OK. Now answer this. "Do girls ever pee on toilet seats or is it just guys that do that?"

Des pats me on the head. Bad puppy. "You need help, Ben. Really."

"I know, I keep hearing that."

Christ. I always think other people think like I do. They don't, and they don't need to, even I don't need to.

"Another fifty miles to Fort Lauderdale. We'll be there soon. See if Loki survived his lizard hunt."

"Can't wait!" Amy says. "The lizard guy, I have a feeling about him, one of those inside itchy feelings."

A beautiful day repeating itself every second. The hiss of tire wear. Stretches and stretches of highway, long stretches. Cruising, windows down, deep swallows of ice-cold water, juice, big pipe hits. The heavies – heroin, opium, cocaine. Sally and I, no interest. We did cocaine once, ran to the edge, looked over, came right back.

Moving to the Keys. It's Sally's idea, indirectly, an article she read. We talked about it before the fire. It's a good idea. Sally's good at having good ideas. Girls, girls know things, girl things, important things, have little or no velleity toward sodomy, child abuse, rape. Women's rights. They're more right than men. Most of the time.

"Sally, you want me to take the wheel?"

"No!"

Wow. Into it, she's hooked. Driving. Lots of people have a driving addiction. I do.

329

We continue on; the day bright; a Jill the Jeep mood rolling us along the big road, both part of it; and not a part at the same time. Travel magic, new territories of untapped imagination igniting our endorphins. Joints and cold beer in hand, we're all smiles, even the Jeep smiles, and the cat.

A bus inching up beside us, slowly, doing a mile or two an hour more than Sally. A senior's bingo bus, old people who know they're old but don't think it, adult diapers holding it all together, the death sequence closing in. They look at us as they pass by, several push their faces to the glass, no teeth, big grins.

A big white pickup follows the bus, Southern Cross flying on one side of the cab, pirate flag on the other, cigarette smoke belching from the windows. The driver pulls up beside us. His shotgun is wearing a cowboy hat, faded brown, no hatband, twisted brim, a denim shirt, big red, white, and blue tattoo on his neck, two eagles fighting in the air. A rat face, whiskers coming out his nose. He lowers his window, waves, tries to get Sally's attention. She slows down, gives him room to swerve around the bus. He slows, instead, gives Amy and Des a long look, licks his lips, shifts his gaze back to Sally, then across to me.

He points, shouts, "You! Old man!"

I turn, lean across Sally toward him, quickly check the highway ahead and behind. Minimal traffic, no cops.

"Nice Jeep. Where are you from?"

Eye contact, reading intent, weighing risk, a pause. I shout, "California plates, dickhead!"

Sally gives me a dark look. Amy and Des sit back, remove themselves from view.

"What?" It's not a question.

Sally slows even further to let him pass. He doesn't pass. The driver hollers something, can't hear him. I shake my head. His shotgun repeats it.

"He says, 'What's an old hippy faggot like you doing with three beautiful women?'"

Sally ignores him, keeps driving.

My mood shifts, how to respond. No control. I shout. "Money! Bitch. They pay me. My tool, it's a massive faggot wonder. Pull over. I'll show you."

"You got it, asshole." He passes us, speeds ahead and pulls off and onto the shoulder.

Sally slaps me. Amy and Des too, they all slap me.

I deserve it.

Sally sped up, drove by them. They pulled out, pressed the road, caught up with us. The shotgun guy, he leans out the window, slams the palms of his hands on the truck door. A dull, flat sound, nothing beautiful.

"Pull over, fag! Or we'll run you off the road!"

I hear him, sounds like his voice is decomposing.

Another Sally look, fear in her eyes alarming me, loading my rifle, sharpening my blade, waking the soldier; the man I know I am, that all men know they are but few become. The angry man. Control him. Can I? Do I want to?

The pickup pulls ahead, stops in a turnout, lots of dust. Sally lets off the gas, breaks, downshifts sharply, stops yards behind the truck. Oncoming cars swerve out of our way.

'Road rage, do not engage.' Right.

"Sally, the monkey stick. Please...."

She reaches into the door pocket, hands it to me, holds it for a moment before letting go.

"Don't use it, Ben."

"I'll try not to, Sal."

"Do more than try."

No plan to try, none at all. I get out. My knife is gone, sheath empty. The monkey stick...it will do.

The driver and his shotgun both jump down. Eager movements, glaring eyes. The driver walks ahead, broad shoulders, fur-like skin, each step toward me is committed, deliberate. An interesting face, features appeared stretched, arranged to project authority, a man with bargaining power, someone I can like, maybe. Maybe not.

Few cars passing. Shifting air, birds, a light haze.

The driver stops two feet in front of me, his shotgun to my left. Both are bigger than me, but not much bigger. Farm workers, maybe, python hunters, drug mules, delinquent dads. Tough guys, maybe. The older one, the driver, he speaks first.

"They pay you. Why, look at you," he huffs. "Your faggot wonder. Show us."

"Sure," I say, and I reach for my zipper.

They step closer. I hold.

Shotgun licks his lips, wags his tongue. The driver spits, he's two feet away, close enough. I bring the bulb end of the stick up fast, catch him under the jaw, put all my weight into it, push up and back. He bent back, fell sideways, hit the ground. Shotgun threw a right, awkward, probably left-handed, grazes my cheek just under the eye with his watch, I bleed immediately, reverse the stick, take the bulb in both hands, and shove the handle into his belly, hard. He heaves, doubles over, drops to his knees. Paying for his sins. I kick him in the face, a vicious kick, split his nose, blood explodes, his jaw cracks, I know the sound. Like hearing it. I kick him again.

The driver sits up, a gun under his belt, white handle, imitation bone. He tries to reach it. I throw the stick. Not the best throw but it hit his arm. He pauses. I take a breath, step in, and grab his legs below the waist, lift and throw him down on the hard ground. He cries out, a loud cry, filled with pain, deserved pain. I lose it, go feral, kick, and kick him, kick, and kick. Abuse, too much abuse in the world, childhood abuse, caustic memories accelerating my anger, justifying it, contributing.

I pick up the gun, break it apart, throw the pieces into the bush twenty feet away, stand over the driver, look down. "I'm no fucking hippy, you dick. Never call me that." He lifts his head, starts to speak. I twist my heel into his groin, crush his balls, kick him again. Again, and again. I kick and kick, harder, much harder, go from one face to the other kicking and kicking.

"Ben! Ben! Stop! You're going to kill them. Stop!"

Sally is standing next to me, shouting, pulling on me. I stop, press the back of my hand to her cheek, curl a strand of her hair with my finger, pick up the monkey-stick, wipe blood off my cheek, walk back to the Jeep, sit down, buckle my belt, light a joint, take a long slow hit, lay my head back, exhale, close my eyes. Not in control. No enlightenment for me. Fuck.

Cars passing, trucks, a bus full of screaming schoolgirls, two busses, three. No one stops to see what happened, to help us. To help the two guys lying on the ground.

Rage, I know her, I know her well. We've been close my entire life. Sometimes we talk and I convince her to relax. Try to make her believe the world is a better place than she imagines it to be, a happier, sexier, less abrasive place. And sometimes, too much of the time, we don't talk.

Today.

We didn't talk today.

Sally pulls out, drives away.

# NINETY FIVE

"Loki, we're in my Jeep. You remember, Jill the Jeep. We're sitting in your driveway. Where the hell are you?"

"We should have called, Ben. You said you would."

"I forgot."

"You always forget."

"I'm old."

"Older people don't think so."

"Older than me people?"

"Right, Ben, older than you people." A bit snappy, Sally. Baby snappy. Could be.

Amy and Desiree are stoned, completely lit. Two happy smiles, not much else. Human smiley faces with great bodies.

A rap on the window.

Loki, a big grin, sunglasses, shirt, shorts, athletic shoes. Always wears a shirt, shorts, and athletic shoes. Never goes anywhere cold enough to change out of them. A big lizard, he has it in hand, spins it around by the tail.

"Got the son-of-a-bitch." He grins. "Come in, come in," he raps again, waves us on, walks off toward his garage, drops the lizard in a can, hits a couple of buttons on his phone, opens the front door.

"Are you coming?"

Loki's driveway is made of white rock, a big C shape with an island in the center of the C. Small palms, flowering plants and shrubs, a mix of boulders and grass populate the island. A ranch style home, lots of windows, good light, pool in back, five bedrooms, three car garage. Loki's doing well.

"So, Ben, how the fuck are you?"

"You're looking at it!"

He laughs, we laugh, shakes hands, he gives me a slap on the back. Sally, Des, and Amy, he hugs them. Holds Amy a bit closer, she allows it.

"And you are?"

"I'm Amy," she says.

"Aim me, Amy. Can you?"

They laugh. Loki and Amy, why not? They're a good match. He takes her under his arm, nudges me.

"How was your drive?"

"Uneventful, Loki. Uneventful."

We walk through the living room. It's something of a double living room, pull open the sliding glass doors, he and Amy step out.

"How's the water lizard man?" Amy asks adding transcendent meaning to her words.

"Warm," Loki replies, "salt water warm, 95 degrees. You want to play poke the bunny? Eel in the haystack?"

Amy, she's got him, hook is set." Of course, she says, why else would I be here."

A good match, definitely. They jump into the pool, kick, and churn the water. Big boat propellers, that's what they look like, churning propellers.

Sally and Des go to the kitchen. I follow. We find food. A well-stocked fridge. Nothing like a well-stocked fridge.

Fort Lauderdale. Loki's house. A day too warm for clothes. We remove ours, let the cat out, cats, and the dog. Leave our food on the counter, slip into Loki's 95 degrees saltwater pool, relax like rich people, pretend like rich people.

Nice to feel safe.

Loki voted for Trump.

I try not to think about it.

# NINETY SIX

Early morning. Sally wakes first.

Gunshots, not too loud. Three shots. We get out of bed, musty smell in the air, damp.

"Gunshots?"

"Yeah, small caliber. Very close."

"Loki?"

"Must be, I'll check."

I go to the living room, white marble floors, big totem poles with flat squished ears, frond paintings, gun racks, wine racks, books, Loki in his underwear, a .22 in his hands, the window open.

"Squirrels, the little fucks. Quiet!"

Two guys in their underwear, guns, girls. All American Pie. I walk to the kitchen. Loki lets off two more rounds, closes the window.

"Want a beer?"

"Sure."

Sally pops her head out, "Is it safe?"

"Yeah, we're having a beer. Want one?"

"Gin and tonic." She says, "I'd prefer gin and tonic, feel like celebrating. No reason." Stepping into the room, she runs her fingers through her hair. Her night shirt, an old shirt, a buttonless shirt, flew open as she approached. Sharing her beauty. She does, often. "OK, a breakfast beer," she says, "half glass to start. I can do that, and a banana."

Amy and Des emerge. Can't tell if they came from the same room, Loki's room, their own room. Both are barefoot, hair disheveled, inviting.

Loki eyes, them, eyes Sally.

"Ben. Anytime, brother. You can visit anytime."

We grab beer, fruit, bagels, smoked salmon, cream cheese, cottage cheese, boxes of cereal, milk, pork rinds, a nuts platter, napkins. Put everything on the kitchen counter. Take what we want, slide the glass doors open, go to the pool.

Loki picks up a bagel, salmon, beer, sits down between Amy and Des, takes a bite of his bagel. Amy and Des press against him, Amy more vigorously. He returns the pleasure. A good match.

I pull Sally's chair closer, grab my beer, take a long, slow swallow. Ice cold beer, smoked salmon, cream cheese, almonds.

A good day to be human.

I bite into the bagel and salmon, chew slowly, decadently (if one can do that), very tasty. "Anybody voting in 2020?"

"For whom?"

"President."

"Why?" Loki mistakenly inhales beer, starts coughing, all of us pound his back.

"Our last free election. Maybe."

The girls agree.

"You worry too much, Ben, ladies. Everything's fine. And will be fine. We can count on Trump to think of himself first in any situation. A congenital liar, he's predictable."

"That's good?"

"He's American, we're American, and we're in America. Whatever comes, we'll be fine. My guys: Trump's party, Republican leadership, they're no longer concerned with the strength of the nation beyond the profit they can make from weakening it. We know that. They know that. Corrupt government works. Corruption is good. Fuck, I forget how much I hate liberals when I see Trump's face, hear his pathetic drawl, I do, I forget, but hell, he's the guy in charge and it's two years away. Have another beer."

Not my point of view, why would it be?

We finish breakfast, clean up, brush, shower, check the news.

A lizard runs by the pool.

I hand Loki the rifle. His house. His shot.

"Ben, have you gone to see a doctor lately, need a check-up, to refill a prescription, anything like that, anything medical?"

337

"No."

He takes a shot, hits the lizard's back legs, spins him around, he almost flips over, starts crawling toward the fence, a bigger lizard attacks him.

Loki reloads.

"I have. Two days ago. My annual physical. Fuck. I signed in, filled out the paperwork and stood by the door. Waiting room was full, no place to sit. The nurse handed me a fat tablet, told me to update my information. A big fucking electric tablet, orange and white, page after page of questions. 'Where do you live? How long have you lived there? Have you traveled out of country in the last six months? If yes, where to? How many people are living in your home? Are they members of your family? Do you smoke? Have you ever smoked? Do you take drugs? Do you drink? If yes, how much? Have you ever been arrested? Has any member of your family ever been arrested? Have you had all your shots, recently been exposed to people with measles, bronchitis, Ebola, yellow fever, swine flu, dengue, AIDs, syphilis, gonorrhea, clap, crabs, herpes? How often do you brush your teeth? Do you floss? Are you registered to vote? Is there a gun in your house? Are you a felon? What is your sex? Male, female, other? Do you cross dress, wake up male, go to bed female, prefer same-sex sex to the opposite-sex sex, do you masturbate, if so, how often? Have you ever paid for sex? If yes, when, where and how many times? Does anyone pay you for sex, open your eyes for you when you wake up in the morning?' I couldn't believe that shit. I answered no for every question, threw the tablet in the trash, and walked out."

"I'm not much for doctors Loki, or checkups, rather stich myself than be stitched. The only time I trust a doctor is when I'm unconscious. Sally. She's never been to a doctor, not for herself. She heals doctors."

Loki continues...changes the subject. "A woman president, maybe it's time for a woman president."

"Could be. Sure."

"A pair of tits with balls. Mother America. Might be good. Girls know stuff."

"They do, Loki, girls know stuff."

Amy removes her towel, goes to Loki, takes away his gun, walks him to a big cushion chair, beige and brown stripes, a throne chair, and she does things. Girl things, things every guy wants girls to do. The surf pushing casually toward the shore, hissing softy as it melts into the sand, warm sun on our faces, covering our naked bodies with natural warmth, it's a long time ago, we're hunter-gathers taking mankind's first vacation.

Simbana's's drugs, we have a bag full. Amy's stash. Popped a couple of pills with breakfast, all of us. They're taking hold, settling in. We feel good, delve into obvious opportunity; a sense of things the mind imagines before they happen. Sally tosses her shirt, Des has already stripped, I drop my shorts, doors are open, we accept, walk out, wade into the pool, let the pool water talk to the water in our bodies, sharing water, we do, we share and share.

A fine Lauderdale morning, purrs all around.

The inestimable comfort of friends. We're all smiles. It's time to go. Jeep's packed (wasn't really unpacked), windows washed, tank full. The Keys are close. We're close.

Amy stops us at the door.

"I'm staying. Loki asked me to stay. He wants to marry me."

"He proposed!?"

"He did, yes. He proposed. I said yes."

"That's great, Amy, stunning! Loki's a good guy. He'll protect you. Really great."

Sal and Des grab Amy, hug her vigorously.

Sal takes her shoulders. "That's mad lady, stunning. We'll see each other soon. Baby shower." She rubs Amy's belly.

"Yeah." Desiree echoes.

Loki comes to the door, we congratulate him.

He winks.

Walks with us to the Jeep.

Amy begins to follow, forgets she's undressed. No Hasidim modesty poverty in Fort Lauderdale.

Passerby's stare, whistle.

Loki flips them off. "Kiss my tango," he says.

Floridians, they know what that means.

No one stops.

# NINETY SEVEN

Heart attack highway. I-95. Still on it, a couple of hundred miles to the Keys. We pray for uneventful travel, no traffic, no accidents, no altercations, no excitement, just the road ahead, the drowsy sky, the easy calm of contemplating sweet illusions, imagining impossible exploits. Windows are down, a clothes-optional day, a thinking optional day, stress optional.

Des made a seat behind the front seats with cushions, stretches her feet over the middle console, plays with Sally's arm, my shoulder. Back and forth, arm, shoulder, arm, shoulder, until I tickle her feet.

"How about Amy and Loki?" she says. "Pretty cool. Knights in shining armor. I want one."

Sally chides me. "I found one," she says, "not so shiny but a knight for sure. Definitely a knight."

Happy people. We are. I'm driving, feels good to be driving. Key West. Drinks at the beach with little umbrellas in them, Happy Hour days. Naked days, naked nights. Can't wait. A bus passes us, lots of clowns. Never saw a clown bus before. They're all different. All drinking and smiling, big smiles. A clown convention, if there is such a thing. Maybe they're going to one, or clown school, circus training, a costume party. They wave, all of them, as they pass. They wave and lift their glasses, bottles, cups. Their hands are gloved, hair tousled, lots of primary color. Red, yellow, blue, white, green, red mostly. They keep waving, drinking, smiling. We laugh at them. They laugh back. Gender? Wasn't sure if clowns had one. They'd make fun of it if they did.

The bus is big, feels like it takes forever to pass by. A long bus, bigger than usual, big windows, green stripes on a white background, new…expensive.

I pull in behind the clowns, pass a cattle truck, a truck carrying half a trailer home, and a Budweiser truck. Thought to wave the driver over, shout "Hey Bud, give me a beer!" Female driver, looks female. I'm feeling good. Stupid good, the kind that makes you think well of yourself even when you do something dumb.

Des removes her shirt, airs her bountiful bosom, stretches, pulls her hair back. "Sally," she says, "can I ask you something?"

"Sure."

"I want to know what it's like being so white. That's my question. When I see groups of people, I see in them people who look like me, most people do. Not you. How does that feel?"

Sally doesn't answer, doesn't move. She laughs, "I don't see anyone who looks like me, even when I look in the mirror."

"Oh!"

I turn to Des, "It means she's the second coming. The third. Maybe."

"Is that what it feels like, being so white? Like the second coming?" Des smiles, almost laughs. "I have lots of second cummings, as many as possible."

"Right, and third cummings."

"Right. Thirds."

"Cum, cum, cum. Cum all ye faithful."

"Well," Sally sighs, catches Des in the tide of her green eyes. "The first few years of my life began in Africa. My parents were black, but not one of their parents, parents. Mom's great grandmother was albino. We lived in Zimbabwe, a village near Gweru. You wouldn't know it.

No one does. The whitest woman in Africa. I would be if I grew up in Africa. If I still lived in Africa. Then, as it is now, Africa, like America wasn't kind to differences. Discrimination, social exclusions, they were rampant, cruel. I was sent to America to live with my aunt when I was eight. My parents joined me a few years later, we took a house. Dad worked for a vending machine company. It was nice, peaceful. Being albino and young was novel, people wanted to know me. I made friends, many friends. My parents divorced when I was nine. My mother got custody, then lost her job. She was attractive, but weak. People used her, and she used me. Rented my body to pay our bills. The police found out, forced me to live with my father and his new wife. I was fourteen. His wife didn't like me. Her name was Charlotte. She didn't like my father giving me more attention than he gave her, attention I didn't want. So, I ran away. Couldn't hide, cops found me every time and brought me home. Each time I ran away, they brought me back.

"Being albino, a rare full moon all day, that's what it's like. Impossible to hide, nowhere to run, ever. That's how it feels."

Des lights a joint, passes it to Sally. "Sorry, Sal. Damn. That's dreadful."

Sally takes a hit. "The trail of tears. While the Indians defined it, many others also lived it. Still live it."

# NINETY EIGHT

Time for lunch. Travel hunger is not the same as stationary hunger. We find something off the highway. A nothing, roadside lean-to and truck, a flatbed. A sprite old man selling fresh fruit and vegetables, age has injured him, taken what it always takes, but he moves well. Chews and swallows' bites of sweet corn as he serves us.

We eat, devour fresh picked apples, bananas warmed by the sun, grapes, celery, and fresh carrots, a couple of perfectly ripe avocados. Feels good to eat healthy, civil decadence. The man has a juicer, picks up power to run it from a wall of Tesla solar cells on the back of his truck. A well-organized old man. We like him. Several glasses of fresh-squeezed grape juice later, and several covert weed hits, we're done. The juice is delicious.

After lunch, Sally takes the wheel. Almost giddy to get behind it again. The driving bug has her. Something else to like, a new toy. I take shotgun, sit back, put my feet up, light a joint, open a beer. Too warm. Forgot to fill our cooler with ice.

Alone for years, a miner panning for gold in the high Rockies, his hands crusted with wear, face unshaven, unwashed, pants smelling of excrement, urine, smoke, dirt. He lays down his pan, bends, drinks the cool water, tilts his head, studies the undulating reflections of the sky on the stream's flowing surface, lights what's left of his last smoke, uses his last match. He inhales deeply, long, and slow, exhales long and slow, watches birds scatter in the distance, frightened.

A visitor, maybe, or an intruder. More likely an intruder. He leans over, picks up his rifle, a weathered Winchester 30/30, late 1800s, cracked stock tied with rope, well oiled. He slides a shell into the chamber, listens carefully. The pauses between sounds, he hears them. A man, must be. Can't see him, knows he's there, knows the sound the steps of a man would make, is certain he can hear the difference.

His pan feels heavy. He looks down, a small trickle of water seeping over it exposing a nugget, its rounded edges gleaming...gold! He reaches for it, a good size nugget, quarter-inch diameter, maybe more.

He looks around for the intruder, knows he's there, checks the tree line for expected shapes, and shapes that shouldn't be there, some part of the body, the face, shoulder, rifle barrel.

An elk, large, male, breaks from the forest cover, steps into the open meadow, a gallant animal, magnificent. The miner watches it, thinks to shoot it, gut it, skin it, eat it. Looks down at the nugget, sees two more in the stream, picks them up, sets down his rifle.

He pans almost a pound of gold, packs his burlap bag, and leaves the valley.

A red light. I-95 South ramp just ahead. Sally stops.

Megaphone voices, lots of banging and shouting. Des sits up. Throws on a shirt, one of mine, takes out her camera, begins filming. A protest. An anti-abortion protest. I've heard of them, first time seeing one. People with signs converge all around us. Dozens of people, grouping and regrouping, meandering across every corner of the intersection, mothers pushing strollers, a nurse, a couple of guys. Guys pushing strollers always looks wrong, like tall people walking tiny dogs. There are balloons, bouquets, kids chasing each other, kids chasing pigeons, and seagulls trying to steal snacks. Most protesters are badly dressed and smoking cigarettes. A lot of cigarettes, a lot of fat people. Always fat people, they're everywhere. Holding hands, chanting slogans, singing hymns, sanitizing fat, walking God's sidewalk runways, saving the unborn … they think so.

Several of them, maybe a dozen, are well over three hundred pounds. A protest weight-loss program. That's what it should be. Body shaming. It's not working on them. The gospel truth, it's not working.

"Christ, Sal. I can't imagine looking at all that fat in the mirror every morning, having no control over how much food I put in my mouth. Abort fat, go on a diet, exercise. Should be an abort fat protest. Abortions save lives, save women from ruin…and where are the protesters willing to look after the unaborted, once born? Are they to fat to care? Probably."

"Ben. That's not nice. Maybe they have medical conditions. Cushing's syndrome, a thyroid problem."

"Maybe, but they still look like dollar-an-hour dough boys carrying signs."

Big signs, to go with their big bodies. Cardboard painted white, stapled to sticks, words brushed on in red ink.

*BABY KILLERS ROT IN HELL!*

*GOD WILL PUNISH YOU!*

*HONK IF YOU LOVE JESUS!*

"Unbelievable. Look at them. No idea we're closing in on eight billion people worldwide. And God said, someone said God said, someone always says God said, 'Let there be abortion to keep humans from overpopulating their planet.' No one listening."

*Unitary Executive Theory hard at work so a government by the rich, for the rich shall never perish from this earth. Trump supporters, they don't get it. And Christ. Did Christ know how many people would be beheaded, burned alive at the stake, tortured, and butchered in his name? Did he foresee the Crusades,*

*Hitler, the use of his name as a weapon? Did he know, before he died, that his death would be the death of innocent millions? And if he did know, and still he came, what does that say about him, about us? At the voting booth...small, aborted minds should get a quarter vote, not even a quarter, an eighth. Maybe. Liberal PC inquisitors an eighth as well, and hippies half an eighth. Religion, fuck. We're born slaves... made to serve. And the master we serve, through the leaders that master us, is not God.*

Green light. Can't help it. I stick my head out, strafe their dull faces with my middle finger. Shout, "Make Russia great again, vote Trump."

Des sticks her head out the back window, shouts just as loud, "Make babies, not war. And ban fat! Send fat to hell! Fat is a sin. Punish fat! Take away fat's right to eat! No right to abortion, no right to gluttony. F–u–c–k Fat!" Des laughs, I laugh. Hysterically, too hysterically.

We feel the carnal nerve of those willing to challenge social norms without fear of consequence. Feels good, justified.

The protesters yell back, can't make out what they say. We zip by. They throw signs at us, cups, hats, shoes, rubber babies, anything but food...wave their arms, give us the finger.

### HONK IF YOU LOVE JESUS!

Sally honks.

We bank south onto 95. The last leg, our long drive coming to an end.

Was it?

Highways, roads to Wherever land, pavement sounds, fences. Travel smells, trees, bushes, rivers, fields, towns, and cities. The smell of a place smells different to people passing by than it does to people who live in it.

Roads, no permanent residents, no final definitions. The universe is made of roads, and the places they lead to.

I relight my pipe, take a hit, pass it to Sally.

"I'm driving, Sal. Later." Feeling a little agitated. No reason to. That's what's agitating me.

Sally smiles. "I know," she says. "For now, just sit, watch, and relax."

"I can do that."

"We'll switch at the next stop."

"Des...a hit?"

"Sure." She takes it, hits it hard, a subterranean voyage, hits again, hands it back to me.

"Want a beer?"

"Can't. No open containers."

"Oh. Right."

The rules. Nooses around our necks, locks on our minds. Too many rules. Too little of the fenceless frontier we stole from the Indians. Too many *Please-remember-me–I'm-better-than-you* memorial bridges, highways, buildings.

Wasn't tired of being on the road, but driving, however present it is, isn't where we're going. I'm ready to reach the Keys, park, turn off the engine, make a new life.

Sally blows me a kiss. I open a beer, take a swallow. Warm, a warm swallow.

# NINETY NINE

iami. We pass it.

We pass Homestead and Florida City. Lots of places with names, places that are not real places, people that are not people real people would recognize.

Card Sound Road, or Route One? The GPS giving us options.

"Ladies," I raise my voice, the professor, the teacher, not quite, tap my finger on the dash. "Time to make a choice ladies. Do we choose the faster Route One, or the slower Card Sound Road over the Card Sound Bridge."

"Card Sound, what kind of name is that?" Des is incredulous.

Sally laughs. "It's a funny name."

"Do cards make sounds?"

"The cards themselves?"

"I guess," I say, "if you tear them, attach them to bike spokes, light them on fire or crumple them, they make sounds, but that's not really the card making the sound."

"Right."

Several gulls flying low pass overhead, a scattering of small birds, a lone crane.

Never play the radio, almost never, prefer listening to ambient sounds, the life around me, the possible danger in it. I turn it on. "And today's weather, folks. It's going to be a hot one, hot and sunny most of the day with temperatures in the low 90s, few clouds. And our terrific traffic guy, Jim Sands, he says traffic on 95 is backed up. Again. Hallelujah Floridians. Keep those water bottles close."

Hate traffic.

"And, in other news. News of little joy," the announcer pauses, we can hear him breathing. "A Disney World alligator ate a little girl; parents couldn't save her. Disney killed the alligator. And another black man has been shot by white cops. Cops said he was running. The shooting's being investigated."

Almost impossible to punish cops…a good reason for bad guys to become cops, for cops to become bad guys. Last chance power. Never see rich people become cops. Radios. I turn it off. Humans, is ego all we are…me, me, me, the only mouth we feed?

Sally straightens up, grips the wheel. "OK. Card Sound Road it is."

The navigator, my job, a dollar, and a half for the bridge. I check the ashtray for coins, adjust our route. "Turn here, Sal, this left exit. Lucille Dr."

Sally makes the turn, a clean turn, tight, then a smooth right onto Card Sound Road. A small, country road, double yellow lines down the middle, forty-five miles per hour. Pine trees, ferns, bushes, all craving light, reaching for the open road. No one ahead. No one behind. Perfect. We're not hungry, or tired. A good feeling.

Bits of swamp, and a mix of greens expand on both sides of the road, lots of green. Love green. Love looking at it, tasting it. Watering the eyes like we do plants, that's what looking at green feels like. Sally's eyes are green. Is green for her greener than it is for people with brown eyes, blue, black, hazel? Probably not.

"Beer stop girls! Time for a beer stop. Alabama Jack's. It's coming up. A fish place, seafood, conch fritters, cold beer! Very cold. Let's stop."

I imagine a frosty Bud, deep satisfying swallows, multiple fermented swallows. Bud. If not the king of beers, it is the king of beer advertising. Definitely.

"On the right, Sal, it's coming up! Jack's! A hundred yards." I almost shout. Odd. Never thought of beer as being that exciting. It could be.

"Easy, Ben."

Sally puts on her blinker, no need to but she does it anyway. We pull in, park, get out, drift a little, absorb our surrounding, adjust our clothes, the little we're wearing. Too hot for clothes, too hot to even think 'clothes,' no choice, have to wear them. Adam and Eve. I think it was Adam that fucked up.

Jacks is basic, low roof, planters, metal, and wood-slat fencing, painted concrete walls, white plastic chairs, laminate tables, inviting fragrances, nice people. And the Card Sound Bridge, we can see it from the front of Jack's parking lot, it bulges up from the gray road ahead like a colossal snake filled with slowly digesting travelers and their vehicles.

Hot. Ninety-eight degrees, hotter than predicted, the air oozing with humidity, a clutching dampness. We skip eating. Order beer, ice cold beer, lots of it. Ice cold, really ice-cold. On a hot day, beer is food. Beer French fries, beer bread, beer salmon, prawns, cuttlefish. We drink all of them, run back and forth to the bathroom, inadvertently raise sea-level by six inches. A lot of beer. Des grabs our cooler. We fill it with ice, beer, fizzy water, and coke. Finish off our last round. Thank the folks working there and walk back to the Jeep.

Sally takes the wheel. She forgot I'm supposed to drive. I forgot. My life in her hands...it always is.

Des opens the passenger door, waves me in. Pinches my butt. Her body, my body, bodies in general, they're toys to her. I think to let her play, sit down instead, wonder if girls are as horny or hornier than guys, just a lot better at hiding it. We head for the bridge, the digesting travelers blob just ahead.

"That's strange!!!"

Sally's hands spring open. She jerks them from the wheel, puts them back. Keeps driving.

"What!"

"We followed the signs for Card Sound Road, the Card Sound Bridge. We did. I know we did. We saw the bridge ahead. We all saw it. Jack's, we were there, just now. We were there. Now we're not there. We're back on Route One. We just passed a Route One sign, but where's the bridge? How did we get on this road?"

Drugs, must be the drugs. Not enough drugs. Too many drugs. Drugs, alcohol, and aliens. Need more of all of them, and sex.

I sit up. Des sits up, picks up her phone. We check maps, Google Earth, the clock. Almost an hour since we left Jacks. A lost hour.

"You're right Sal. We are. We're on highway 1 for Key Largo. After we hit the Overseas Highway, Key Largo comes up. How can that be?"

Vacancy; space emptied of time, of material substance, what's left after vacancy?

"Alabama Jacks, Card Sound Bridge, they were right in front of us. Right in front. I can still feel the beer cooling my stomach." Des rubs her stomach.

"Where did they go?"

"Don't Text and Drive, Arrive Alive." More signage telling us how to live, how to drive, how to believe, how to think.

We enter Monroe County. No welcome banners, cheerleaders kicking up their legs. Didn't expect any. Don't care where we are, how we got to where we are, what happened, or how it happened. I feel good. Sally's driving, living, giving me life.

"Key Largo, really!" Des bites off the corner of a Mounds Bar, keeps talking. "The same Key Largo where Trump cheats on the golf course, lies about club size, picks up his balls, moves them to better spots, fabricates a fake score at the end of games?"

"Right. That Key Largo."

"A curse on Trump, has anyone tried that, anyone we've heard of?" Sally groans, an odd sound for her. Exasperated, she pulls over. We get out, stand back from the Jeep, the traffic. Hot. Very hot. Life fucking with us. We think we know life, that we understand, that what we know we know absolutely. We don't.

Des opens a coke, strikes her lighter, relights a joint. "Highway 1," she says. "How did we get on highway 1? I liked Card Sound!"

"Me too," Sally adds, waves at a passing school bus.

"Doesn't matter, ladies. Not now. Wherever we are is where we are." I kick a couple of idle rocks, imagine what it would be like to surf on a whale's tongue, pluck nose hairs from the inside of an elephant's trunk, throw darts at ticks from twenty feet away. Disposable thoughts. I have them, lots of them.

"Let's go."

"Right," Des concedes, sighs, exhales her disbelief. "Both roads take us to the Keys. Doesn't matter which."

Key West. The Keys. The sound of it. I like the sound. The chattering clink of distant wind chimes, a flute sound penetrating dense jungle foliage…the keys to primal happiness, that's what Key West, The Keys sounds like.

"Yeah, Des, either road will take us there. Hemingway, poor sap, he lost his shit in the Keys, killed himself, ate the raw end of a shotgun round. That's what I remember. And Sloppy Joe's. I remember Sloppys…and the free-for-all Fantasy Festival. I've done that Fest. Lots of painted bodies out for show, everything on display, every body part. A clothing-optional event, not many of those. Imaginative, fluid, unencumbered revelry. You'll like it."

Sal and Des, their eyes light up. Both have beautiful bodies, and they love people to see them, to want them, to give them what they want.

"And what should we do when we get there, the first thing? Find a place to stay. Swim, eat, drink, walk the streets? How say you mavens of the miles?"

"Take a shower." Sally and Des speak at once. That happens more often than one would think.

"Right, of course, as soon as we get there, we'll find a place, take a shower."

We turn south, pick up the Overseas Highway, pass a sign for the Key Largo Baptist Church, can't see the church. Florida the flat. Florida the will-need-a-snorkel-to-live-here-in-the-future kind of flat. A "Crash Ahead" warning sign spits yellow-orange letters at us. Caution, Caution…Caution. The sky is not falling, but it will."

Hot. I sort through the cooler, open a beer. Pass it to Sally, she downs it, most of it, one swallow. A thirsty girl. Des as well. Me too. Very hot. Cold beer, not enough cold beer. Do suns drink beer? Probably not, but they should.

A scattering of clouds array the sky ahead of us, far enough ahead to be visible over the Keys. Where we're going…the clouds are already there.

"The Card Sound Bridge. Really, Ben, Sally. Come on guys, come on. Doesn't it bother you that we missed it, that we don't know what happened?"

"No."

"No?"

"Yeah, when do we ever know what happens, what makes what happens happen?"

"Sometimes we know."

"Maybe."

Two hours, a hundred miles, about that, and we'll be there. Heaven. Not Paradise.

"Des."

"Yes, Ben?"

"While we're cruising along, just cruising, and wondering if somehow, we'll find ourselves inside the Card Sound Bridge snake, fighting off road wear, rusting brakes, flat tires, hallucinogenic digestive fluids. Tell us something. Your story, everyone, from their point of view, sees a world not seen by anyone else."

"My story," she says, and she levels her voice, "it's not much. Not really. People living their best or worst life. Wishing things were different than they are. A typical Midwest town, typical Midwestern childhood. Lots of Republicans, grilled meat, barns, churches and bars, horses, and tractors. My dad designed tunes for slot machines, worked for the mob. Well, the under-mob, if there is such a thing. All those people who support the mob, servicing mundane mob needs. He met my mom in Vegas. Brought her to the Midwest. Was difficult for her to adjust. The pace, it was too slow for her, uninspiring. In Vegas she worked as an escort, top of the line, very expensive. Not really the housewife type. She turned to porn after meeting dad. Didn't tell him. Sometimes, often, she took me with her to the porn studio. She's a stunner, mom, easy to sell. I think dad knew, knows, but didn't care, and doesn't care as long as she gives as good to him as she gives to the high rollers. Sounds bad, but it was okay, is okay. All the lights, the expensive equipment, the action. I fell in love with it, all of it. Decided to become a filmmaker. Porn was all I knew. When I met you, Oscar had just begun training me, he was giving me advice, the experience I need to begin making my own films."

"God. For Christ's sake, Des. It's not okay, not really. That you've made something of it, and Sal has as well, that's great but Christ, holy fucking Christ. What's wrong with people. Both your mothers? Fuck!"

The Overseas Highway. We're on it. The final stretch, the world coasting by, coming to meet us. Flat for miles. Fall-off-the-edge-of-the-world flat, mile after mile after mile. Bridge after bridge after bridge. Lots of bridges.

At times we're closer to the water, at times further from it. With every meaningful change in distance trees get thinner, smaller. Gaps between buildings get wider, fewer businesses, parking lots, driveways, and fewer homes. Island hopping, key to key, horizons drifting with the sun, boats writing stories with their wakes, people fishing, stubbled trees spent of their youth scratching at the sky for new life, gulls gliding, beaches calling, a naked world, nature is naked, always naked.

The drive is beautiful, everything about it inviting. Water, sometimes deep blue, sometimes light blue comes into and out of view, islands in the distance, boats, low flying planes, come into and out of view, more and more water in and out of view. Stretches, some long, of nothing *but* water on both sides of the road. Ocean views, varying shades of blue-green promise at rest, waiting, encouraging. A slight wind teasing surface reflections.

Florida. The Keys. Key West.

One last bridge, the Cow Key Channel, we cross it. Roll into the Keys.

Money. Time to make a lot of money…to have fun making it.

The richest thing poor people can do.

Plans. We have them. Big plans.

# ONE HUNDRED

We found a place in the Historic District, on Duval, a few clicks from Sloppy Joe's. An inn, a corner place, gnarly. Slanted staircases, railings, dark, musty red carpet, loose at the edges, frayed. The carpet runs through the halls, up the stairs and into an imagined attic space filled with old pirate weapons, bottles of rum, many of them empty, chests stuffed with fine clothes few had any interest in, cheap jewelry and books. Books no one can read, no one learned how to read. An old inn.

The manager shows us around. A brisk walk. We like her. A jovial, bread and butter dyke, quick to tell jokes, laugh at them. Could be a Hell's Angel, maybe she is. A fine old Hog tucked away in her garage. We take a room next to the pool, small but clean, secluded, lots of trees. A tiled courtyard at the inn's center, a bit lumpy but nice, authentic. Potted plants, benches all about and Fantasy Festival signs posted everywhere. A big deal, the Fantasy Festival. Used to be every October. An unrivaled unveiling experience.

Street parking. Very limited. We need to move the Jeep, find a lot-park for the night. An old hardtop Cadillac is blocking our exit. Sally's trying to get out. The car blocking her isn't moving.

I lean forward, like it makes any difference, and yell. "You dumb piece of shit. Moron. Move your fucking car!" Beginning to like yelling.

Sally honks, sits on the horn three times. Three long, loud presses.

Nothing.

Inconsiderate people baffle me. No one wants to be dealt inconsiderateness so why are there so many inconsiderate people? People who think more of themselves than the good they can do. Something to put more thought on. Maybe. I'm happy, but feeling older, like I'm draining out of myself, a clock ticking without sound, but audible. Very strange. Makes me defensive. Of what? Not sure. Don't really care. Don't care much about most things, everything, but Sally. That's what I tell myself when I'm not looking.

Sally pulls around the car, goes over the curb. A Jeep thing to do. I hang out the window, my mouth cocked and loaded with a bristling blend of ripe swear words. Can't pull the trigger, swallow the words. A little old lady behind the wheel, shriveled skin, spotted, pasty, cracked skin. Age eating her away, flesh-eating age, eyes eating age, gut eating age. A skeletal image, an X-ray printout, no teeth, thick glasses, seconds left to live. I smile, wave, feel younger. Reborn.

Sort of.

She doesn't look at us.

Desiree googles parking. We find a spot, grab our bags, lock the Jeep, walk back to the Inn, to our room, to our one big bed, small closet, fridge, TV.

The Fantasy Festival...they changed the date to late July, early August.

Only days away.

# ONE HUNDRED ONE

**H**ot chocolate chips, all squishy and warm inside an enormous chocolate chip cookie. A big, oven baked chocolate chip cookie, right off the cooking tray. Nothing like it.

Our first day in Key West. A sunny morning. A chocolate chip cookie morning.

"Ida...Calypso...Alexander...Joseph...Irene...Michela...Claudy... Sue. Baby names, Ben. Remember?" Sally rolls over, puts a bare leg across my rig, pulls in close. My mind fills with suspect thoughts, something morning does to you when you wake up in a new place but think you're somewhere familiar. I put out my arm. The right side of the bed is empty. Des is on the floor, she slept there, part cat, maybe. Dog maybe. An animal of some kind. She likes the floor. I wonder what her plans are, after the festival, what our plans are?

"Ben, are you listening?"

Too early to think, can't remember if I'm listening or not. Thought I was. "Yes, I am. I was. I am listening."

"If it's a girl, I like Ida, a little mystery in a girl's name is good. And a boy, Claudy. That good man you've talked about, his name. I like it. What do you think?"

My brain isn't logging on, I can't focus.

"Ben! We have to get up, sort out the day. Where are we going to stay through the festival? Here? We can try. It's nice. Maybe we can get a discount. And what are we going to eat? Where do we buy food? We need set locations and more girls for our film, a guy, and raisins, several boxes. Lots to do, Ben. Up-up. Desiree! Time to get up."

Sally in command, planning ahead, visualizing our future,

A docile, innocent flower, Sally, bubbly, and demur, all that—until the mood takes her and she rips into your shorts, tears away anything between her mouth and your royal. A semen hummingbird, she needs sperm to keep her in the air, hot male juice to get her through the day. I have plenty. I'm a virtual sperm pump cranking out millions of wiggle-heads every day. Ben and Sally, Sally, and Ben. Sally and Ben and a baby. Hum. Is three a good match, does it need to be? The Wizard of Oz, he would know.

Des gets up. I get up. Sally gets up, a bit of a belly showing. Is it getting bigger? Can't tell. I squeeze into the shower with Des… we play with each other, wash, play again, get hot, get off, she gets out. Sally takes her place, enters the shower lips first, kisses me with her entire body. She does that, have no idea how, makes me feel weightless, alien training wheels. Maybe that's what sex is, alien training wheels. She takes her time, has her time, we get out, dry each other off, play a little more, savor the afterglow, get dressed. Sally puts on a white, deep-cut sleeveless blouse, white skirt, white sandals. Des does the same but more revealing. I do nothing more than my usual shirt, shorts, sandals. A typical guy. I don't change much. Wear the same clothes for days.

On our way out we meet the manager. She's in the courtyard. Great smile, the kind you put on posters to cheer people up.

"Good morning, folks. A good rest, comfy?"

"Yes, very." We spoke at once.

"Glad to hear it."

"Would love to chat," I say, "have a drink together. When you can."

"Me too, you're an interesting trio."

"Later, then. We're out for an early lunch."

"A late breakfast, Ben."

"Yeah, a late breakfast, early lunch. Brunch, I guess."

"You folks plan on staying with us through the festival?"

"We'd like to. Sure. Do you have room?"

"I'll arrange it, kids. No worries. Enjoy your meal." She turns away and goes up the stairs. A man meets her. They hug, kiss, he grabs her ass, she grabs his. Dyke or not, hard to tell, doesn't matter. Never did matter, not to me, to Sally. They laugh, disappear behind some ferns.

Florida. The Keys…. How easy it is to have a good time.

We leave the inn.

Five, six blocks up Duval. Sloppy Joe's is open.

# ONE HUNDRED TWO

**D**uval Street.

Everyone in Key West knows it. Tourists know it. Roosters know it. Lots of roosters on Duval, roosters roaming free on every street, kings assessing their kingdoms. No need to wash their hands before dinner.

A bright sun, warm, lively. People ambling, drifting on the Keys, blunting without knowing it.

Shops are open, many of them world famous shops, open and busy. Bicycles, people riding them, leaning on them, some people carrying them. An array of art galleries, mostly novelty art, globes and such, vendors selling purses, postcards, maps, fast food outlets, famous candy stores, famous bars, famous corners. Hookers. Three of them. They have college girl looks, sassy, not too pricey. I can tell they hook. Sally can tell. Des can tell. Like recognizing like. We expect to see them again.

Alive. We're alive and we know it, all our senses reeling in life... life at its best. Pleasure, damn to hell and eternal curses upon those who made pleasure sinful and pain virtuous.

A beautiful day on Duval. We stroll unimpeded by any kind of necessity, fear of being late, concerns over inadequate looks, social standing, unfulfilled dreams. No rush, no rushing, we are where we want to be, where weeks of travel and years of hope have brought us. A new life, starting over. Well beyond my teens, a gray man, doesn't matter. I have Sally, she has me...what there is of me age has neglected, failed to mature.

Duval is magical, surreal in glances, animated, talkative, every corner, every pole, tree, road sign, street sign, every product on display, all of them are telling the story of their lives, their doorway stories, window stories, postcard stories, litter stories. There was litter, some, and there were children, children walking with parents, walking without parents, playing with pets, chasing birds, and losing balloons, their plaintive, doleful eyes watching as the balloons drifted away, shrank into the sky, and disappeared over the highest palm trees, the highest roof tops. And roosters. Ubiquitous, brightly colored, they occupy the sidewalk like people, walk like people, read Playboy magazine, carry cell phones, trade feathers for cheap beer in the bars, sell pot and bikinis to pigeons. A very Duval thing to do.

Sloppy Joe's Bar is just ahead. A squat building, brick, black/white lettering, nothing fancy. A small crowd obstructing the entrance. We wait until they move on, not sure why. It's warming up. People begin removing extra layers of clothes, nothing extra on us. We walk into Sloppys, Sally in the lead. Following her, it's like following a breeze, something you know is there but can't see.

Big doors, six maybe, they open onto two streets, make a welcome entrance, a casual blend of privacy and exposure. Floor is tiled, smells like a place we've been before, like many places we've been before. Native paintings on the walls, wood tables, wood chairs painted red, sturdy but comfortable for hardwood, dozens of hanging flags, framed photos, citations, stuff.

Lots of stuff. Friendly.

The bar itself is beautiful. A grand, looping design, wooden draft beer handles and wood stools. We seat ourselves, settle into the famed allure, wait for menus. For time to stop. It never does, but if it did, the moment we're in would make a good stopping point.

Bar noise is low, no band, just a few people, the bartender (tending to several customers) is a young woman in her mid-twenties, maybe late-twenties, a slight twist in one of her front teeth. She wears a bright orange, sleeveless shirt, faded jeans torn in both knees, frayed cuffs and pockets, bar codes on her shoulders. A trash-age girl.

Trashagers, that's what I call them, all the tattooed people who like the vagrant look, the trashy, depraved tramp look. Millennial's, Gen Xer's, whatever else, punks, hippies, they're all trash-agers. How to make looking like you have nothing mean you have everything. Advertising agencies figured that out long ago. Designers figured it out, religious leaders, McDonald's, modern art promoters, and the CIA, they figured it out. A good trick makes pots of money. Novelty sells. Makes people feel special. We plan to make people feel special ourselves, make money, lots of money. Designer sex films, that's what we're going to do, make films so erotic that even our cameras get hard, strain their cases, do unnatural things. Sally's plan, with enough production success, even fame, is to petition for a woman on American money. A hundred-dollar pussy bill with Pocahontas on it, or Gal Gadot, (doesn't matter that she's Israeli), or Marilyn Monroe. Marilyn Monroe, that could work.

The bartender, "Hello folks. I'm Sally. I'll be taking care of you today."

"Sally." Sally claps her hands, waves them, pops a couple of raisins in her mouth. "Me too!" she says. "I'm Sally, a Sally." She extends her hand. The other Sally shakes it. Shakes Des's hand, shakes my hand.

"Are you folk's thirsty, hungry? You look thirsty. What can I get you?"

We smile, feel like our lips leave our faces. "Beer, beer and menus."

"Right," she slaps her forehead, not sure why.

"There," she says, pointing to a sign behind her. "Those are our beer choices. I'll get the menus."

Sloppy Joe's Island Ale...too expensive. Yuengling, maybe, we like Yuengling. Standard Buds, Coors, others. Guinness was there and Blue Moon, Corona, and Fat Tire.

Sally the bartender comes back, menus in hand, a wholesome face lighting her dimples, her full pushy lips, wide cartoon eyes, long legs. She could do well in porn.

"I'll have a Blue Moon." Sally says, her favorite beer...compliments her green eyes...she thinks so.

"And you?" She looks at me.

I like her, very attentive, cute, and Sally likes her.

"Yuengling," I say. "I'll have a Yuengling. And Desiree," I turn toward her, "a Yuengling for you?"

"Sure," she says, adjusts her blouse, pulls her hair back

"Your name is Desiree?" Sally reaches out, puts her hand on Des's hand.

"Yes...it is," Des answers.

"I love your name, Desiree, love it. Desire with an extra e. E is for edifice...of the male kind. You know." She laughs.

Des likes her.

"I'm going to use your name throughout the Fest. Desiree. The Fantasy Fest, nothing like it. And this year, people have no idea. Nothing like it. It's our first no rules year, mostly no rules. I'm going near to naked as I can get. Transparent paint. I'm going to get painted in transparent paint. Really. I know someone who does that. Imagine my luck. Very exciting." She turns. "Be right back."

Two Sally's. Is there another Des around? Des watches Sally pours our beer, over pours, cleans up, pours some more.

A couple sits down next to Sally, my Sally. The guy is tall, the girl too. Both are drunk, cheerful drunk, lots of laughter. They shout for drinks. No one notices, a laid-back bar, a laid-back town. No pushing, no hurry.

"This is good," I say. "I like it here, the slow-bake pace. It feels more human, aboriginal. Maybe we should skip renting and buy a house. Pretend we're real people."

"We will, hubs. We'll make lots of movies, buy a house, have kids, raise a family.

Premiere porn films. Performance Film's, Inc. That can be our name. We'll use day-to-day people, train them like we said. Tell real stories, hire actors that make viewers believe they're in love. That the sex is long-awaited, emotional, life affirming, wholesome. Fear of the body, immodesty, shame, censor...our films will reassess those fears, free people from them."

"A nice house on the water, you think so?"

"Yes, a very nice house on the water. A home."

"OK."

A new life. It is possible.

Sally returns, our beers in hand, her youthful rack pushing hard against a thin, wireless bra. They want out, I want in. Guys, we always want in.

Key West. Sloppy Joe's. We're here. Ready and eager. Sally takes our order. One original Sloppy Joe Sandwich, for me. A South Carolina Mustard Barbecue Sandwich for Des, and a famous "Full Moon" Fish Sandwich for Sal. Lots of fame in the Keys, and roosters.

"To us!" Sally raises her glass. I raise mine, Des hers, our beer frothing, spilling, having a say. "To all good things to all good people."

"Here, here," we say, and we clink our glasses together, down their contests with ease, plop our empties on the bar, laugh, hug, wait for Sally to refill, to bring our food.

A warm breeze gusts through the open doors, very pleasant. Des turns toward the entrance, delighted by the caressing air. Two boys, eight or nine years old with curly hair, freckles, plaid shirts and faded trousers, Huckleberry Finn types. They're standing in the doorway staring. Gawking at Sally or Des, I can't tell which, or both, both require multiple looks. Frequent multiple looks.

The couple next to us huddles. Looks like a huddle, like they're planning something, want us to think they're planning something. They talk. Slurp and talk.

"Look at this light," Des, waves her hand. "The humanness of this place. Maybe I should start filming," she says, and she picks up her camera, removes the lens cap, clicks the on switch.

"Can't, Desiree." Sally interrupts. "So sorry. Very sorry. You need management permission."

"Right."

Des sets her camera back on the bar.

Next to her: "You … lady. Were you filming me?" The tall guy, he's tall, he pushes at the camera.

"Me?" Des responds, incredulous, takes no offense. "No. Not me," she says. "Not filming you, not filming anyone. I was going to. I want to, but no."

364

The girl with him, hops off her stool, addresses Des. Not as tall as I thought. "He's famous," she says. "It costs money to film him. Everyone pays."

I roll toward the man. "Might be best if you just lift your glass, have a long satisfying swallow, and get on with enjoying yourselves. You're drunk, and that's OK, that's what we're here for."

"Not drunk, my friend. Drinking."

He raises his glass, the girl raises hers, we raise ours.

"A toast, folks," the guy says. "A toast to getting drunk at Sloppy Joe's. To endless Key West days. And to good health. Cheers to good health, and a good fucking day for all. Cheers!"

We salute him, down our refills, call for more.

Food arrives.

Sally pokes me. She likes them. "Hey!" I say, "You folks want to join us? We'll take a table."

"Sure," they speak at once. "We're Bonnie and Clyde."

"Really!" We speak at once.

"Yeah, really. Bonnie Selfridge and Clyde Hart. That's us."

"We fuck for money."

"Great!"

The world is only confusing if you're confused in it. Christ said that when he was asked about Mary Magdalene.

No one wrote it down.

# ONE HUNDRED THREE

We take a table nearest the street, next to the open doors. Began talking, lots of girl boy talk, sex games talk, sex games merchandizing talk, sex stores talk. Storyline and plot talk. No baby talk. No 'not her only mother' talk. No what the fuck happened to Oscar talk. Another round of drinks, we throw them down, refill and throw down some more.

Bonnie and Clyde are fully loaded. Sally, myself, and Des are gaining on them, working it. Tortuga pirates on a binge, elephants staggering, bumping into each other and their Marula tree. Getting sloppy, all of us. We order dessert; the key lime pie, frozen, covered in chocolate. Clyde eats his in two bites. A big guy, Brad Pitt hair, heroic self-image, cube chin mooring his face, a sad look, sort of, maybe contemplative. Well built, fast when he isn't drinking, I think so. A difficult man to fight. Some guys are easy. One punch, one kick. Others, the Clyde types, better to just shoot them. Miss my knife.

"More beer, Clyde?"

"Sure, mate. More beer," he holds up his glass. Calls to Sally, his voice rolling big, MORE BEER in capital letters. Sally waves, she heard him.

"Gentlemen, ladies, please...." Two couples sitting at the next table. Nicely dressed, expensive watches, jewelry, clothes, tidy people, tucked in people, the kind you see in ads for new kitchens, living room furniture, at the bank borrowing money, opening new bank accounts. "Can you hold it down folks?" One of the men, mustache, sharp eyebrows, a split in his chin, he continues. "We're talking quietly, not bothering you. Less volume, please."

Clyde responds, tries, throws out whatever comes to mind. "No worries, friends. Ladies and men. Sitting there. All sitting there. Happily sitting there. Nice people. It's all good. All good. Dining next to us, it's OK. We're OK. You're OK. Everyone getting along. The girls," with a wave of his invisible wand he introduces Sally, Des, and Bonnie, "these beauties, they are about to remove their clothes. For you, right here. You see them, imagine that. What do you think folks? These three beauties, utterly naked. Imagine that. No charge for imagining."

He laughs to himself, raises his glass. "Cheers!" Drunk. Definitely.

"Sorry. I know, I'm talking too much. Too loud. I know it. OK, I won't say a word more. Not one word. A little mouse, that's me. Little mice, all of us, quiet little mice." Clyde opens his eyes wide, exaggerates the look, takes out a cigarette and lighter, lights the cigarette, drops the lighter. Just misses his glass.

"You can't do that, mister. No smoking!" Indignant, justified, the woman sitting closest to us waves her hand, clears the air, repeats herself, "You can't do that."

"I know, ma'am," Clyde says. "I agree, I do. I'm not smoking. The cigarette is smoking. You see." He holds it up, smoke rising from the hot ash drifts into the air between our two tables.

"The cig smokes, ma'am. I just inhale. That's all." He pauses, inhales, too deep, begins coughing, coughs on the woman, blows smoke across the table into her face, her partner's face. Air from the open doors blew it back over her, over them. Clyde leans toward them, wobbling, his chair beginning to slide.

"You're drunk, sir, vulgar, and rude. Disgraceful!"

Clyde stands up, sort of, he stops sitting, bows as one would with a cape and top hat.

"Yes. Yes, I am, ma'am, ma'ams, sirs. I am drunk, and happily so. I'm sloppy drunk in Sloppy Joe's with every expectation of becoming drunker. He bows again.

"Thank you very much."

A sudden smell, mordant, vitriolic. Gross flatulence. Someone forgetting under the hood manners.

"Christ! That's disgusting. You're disgusting people." The man closest to Clyde turns his face away, grimaces plaintively, pinches his nose. An odd look next to the Gucci tie.

"She did it!" The other lady at their table stands up, points at Sally. "That albino there, she did it. She made that smell on purpose and directed it at us."

Flatulence directors, pros in gray rubber suits, a fan in one hand, fire extinguisher in the other. Equal pay to retirees holding stop signs at school cross walks, directing kids, cars, other retirees. Can't imagine it.

"Listen, lady," I say to the woman. I'm calm, feel calm, relaxed, slightly intoxicated. More than slightly.

"That albino," I smile. "Her name is Sally. She's albino inside and out. White skin, white blood, white intestines. I know her, we're married. I can tell you. It's odd. I know, odd as hell, but she never flatulates, she can't. Gas can't escape her because she doesn't create it. She's alien, comes from a fartless planet. It's a fact. And if she did fart, if she did, they would be white odorless farts, guaranteed. She's fartless, always has been. It's an albino thing."

Getting more difficult to fit thoughts into words.

Her husband, he acts like her husband, stands up, kicks back his chair, steps in front of her, gets in my face. Right there, provocative eyes, pushy nose, mouth hovering. Standing over me, looking down, unsure of what to say, what my response might be. Bad breath, weak posture.

Out of the corner of my eye, I see Sally. She's hurrying over with a full pitcher, her loose blouse waving at on lookers, legs smiling through torn jeans. A horny girl, trashager horny. She glances at us, nervous, pours both tables. I pick up my glass, take a swallow. Cold beer. A hot day. I take another swallow, several. We all do, even the folks at the other table, all but the guy standing over me.

Clyde laughs. Not sure why. Neither is he.

"Mister," I say. "Sir. The mood I'm in, it's a good mood, hard-earned and easy going, and that's good, because it could be, sir, that you're implying – not saying so, just implying – that I have told an untruth. Lied to you about my Sally." Eye to eye. "Which is not the case, right? You're not saying that."

"No, I'm not...." He hesitates, swallows. Reddens.

"Yes. Yes, I am." He bends lower, gets an inch more in my face. "I am saying that. Yes."

I like him. Almost.

He points at Sally. "She farted. That white creature there, she farted at us, insulted us. I want an apology."

Everyone wants an apology for something.

"OK," I say. "Here's what we're going to do. If you agree...of course. You and Clyde here," I motion toward Clyde, he bows, "you're going to arm wrestle."

"Why?"

"Well. To see if Sally farted."

The man scratches his head, straightens up, twists his face oddly.

"If Clyde wins..." I say, "it wasn't her. Actually, no. I have a better idea," I take another long swallow, "you can arm wrestle Sally. You can. Yeah. If she wins it proves it wasn't her. If you win, it proves it was. What do you think? Not at all logical, I know. But hey, arm wrestling an albino, a beautiful, sexy, albino. That could be fun. Really fun. Yes, or no?"

"Yes," he says, no hesitation and he sits down across from Sally, rolls up his sleeves. Sally doesn't have sleeves and her arms are thin and graceful, feminine decoys hiding feral muscle, she's strong. Doesn't look it. Alien muscle.

They get ready, grip each other's hand tightly, no expression, not on Sally's face. The guy is happy. He likes the attention, a chance to prove himself to his wife/girlfriend. She looks puzzled, backs up. I feel like taking bets, no time.

"OK, are you ready?" Sally glances over, winks at me, smiles. The guy nods.

"Go!"

They do, they go at it. At first the man looks overwhelming, he's bigger, more determined, and angry. Sally is small, isn't angry, and she has no interest in arm wrestling. She holds him…sits there, just sits there. He pulls harder. She holds, doesn't move a centimeter off the starting point. The man puts in, presses hard against the floor. No movement. Sally doesn't budge. She inhales slowly, savors the feeling of fresh air filling her lungs, takes a drink, loves beer almost as much as I do. Bartender Sally brings over more beer, a tray full. "On the house," she says. Folks at the bar, other tables, they paid, salute us, shift over, move closer to the action, join the party. The two doorway boys join in, and a priest with two nuns, or was it two nuns with a priest, and roosters, bouncer types, weightlifter types, two, three of them, broad shoulders, muscular legs.

The man pulls, pulls, and pulls. Drops his focus to Sally's breasts, imagines what he can't see. Moisture beads begin to populate the top of his head, and his forehead just above his brows. He's fully invested, no turning back.

Sally takes another drink, leans forward, puckers her mouth, moistens her lips, inhales, reels him in.

The guy swallows several times, grunts, sucks it up, tightens, gives it his all, strains until his face turns red, redder, purple. Damn.

Sally's arm doesn't move, a stone arm, marble, a discus thrower holding back time for centuries. She squeezes the man's hand, not as hard as he squeezes hers, still he whimpers (adolescent remorse of some kind), and tears form, trickle from the corners of his eyes as he grapples with the shock of it all, the reality of his impotence. Sally brings his arm down on the table, hard, a swift thrust. Done. Bam. He loses. She blows him a kiss, takes another drink.

"It was me!" The guy blurts, staring at his woman. "I'm the one who farted."

He did?

"You! It was you!" His woman, she smacks him, whacks him with her purse. Takes a drink, whacks him again. A heavy purse.

The other couple, his friends, they try not to laugh. Can't help themselves. And the Huck Finn kids try not to laugh, and people at other tables, the priest, nuns, roosters, the people standing, they try not to laugh. We don't bother trying. Maybe he's a narcissist, the guy. A man who lies to his advantage frequently and carelessly. A Trump thing to do. A bad guy. Maybe. Maybe he beats women, drowns toy kittens for sport, sucks his thumb in front of empty parking lots, thinks he's an adult.

We clear our table, adjust the chairs, high-five the other patrons, pay the bill, tip Sally, and walk out. High noon. Very hot, little relief, even in the shade. The five of us huddle under Sloppy Joe's corner awning, exchange numbers. Sally puts her arm around Bonnie, "You here for a long time, a short time, visiting friends, own a place, work here, live elsewhere? Tell me everything. Myself, Ben, Des. We just arrived. We're staying at an inn down the street. We make movies, will make movies, high end designer porn. Porn your eyes can feel. Interested in joining us?"

Bonnie hugs Sally, a tipsy, bubbly hug. "We are, sure, of course we are," she says, speaking for both of them. "That's what we do, who we are. We porn for money. Money, money, money."

"Perfect," Sally puts out her hand. Bonnie takes it, shakes it, pulls Sally in for a full body hug. She knows her anatomy, how she looks from different angles, how other people see her. She embraces Sally like something more is going to happen between them, it doesn't. They kiss each other's cheek, hug again, hug me, hug Clyde.

"We'll talk soon," Sally says

"Yeah, soon. See you."

"See you."

They walk away, melt into the gathering crowd. Ubiquitous vanishing points. From our point of view everything is melting into something.

"That's great Sal, we've got our starting actors. We can use both of them. Use their real names. Bonnie and Clyde. It's great stuff, God answering our prayers."

"You think Bonnie and Clyde are their real names?"

"Doesn't matter. We can say they are."

Des wedges herself between us, begins walking us toward the Inn. "Ready for a swim, folks?"

Water.

Sally loves water. "I'm ready," she says, "definitely. Just the thought of swimming makes my hair tingle, every hair."

Excited now, she walks us a little faster.

"Makes your hair tingle. Really. You can feel that?"

"You know I can Ben, I can feel your hair tingle."

"You can, how? There are no nerves in my hair."

"Not that you can feel."

Sally, the albino, the alien, miracle worker, the second coming, of course she can feel hair tingle.

Back in our room. We think about putting on swimsuits. Only think. Turn on the TV, don't watch it. Lay down on the bed, the floor. Fall asleep, leave the planet for a windless world far away, our weariness lost in the mist of breaking waves...afterlife dreaming, cavernous sleep.

Days on the road caught up with us. Drugs and alcohol caught up with us, regeneration running its course. We sleep long and deep, a comforting absence of purpose consuming us. Twenty hours vanish, vanish completely.

Kids drowning in their cell phones, and big people. All the people at subway stops looking down, they fall into their phones, begin thrashing about, crying for life preservers. Life preservers for phone drownings haven't been invented yet.

Twenty hours.

Gone.

# ONE HUNDRED FOUR

The Inn's courtyard, sunlight filtering through the leafy trees, the palm fronds, cutting across the staggered roof line, the uneven walkways, clusters of flowers, tables. People, many people. Seems like all the inn guests decided at once to come out for food, to satisfy curiosity, check out the competition, shop for intimate favors.

Late lunch, early dinner. An in-between time of day. We pick a table near our room. Simple fare on the menu. Hamburgers, chicken sandwiches, fruit bowls, chips. Relaxing, we sit back, scan the field, the aspirations of our fellow patrons. Des begins clicking photos. An everything group; blacks, whites, Asians, Arabs, Chinese. An Abby lookalike. A man on stilts, without the stilts, damn tall. A redneck, coonskin hat, buckskin shirt and leggings, no Bowie knife, bristly beard, big arms, two cowgirls with pigtails on either side, both blond. Dumb blond jokes. Are there any male dumb blond jokers? Must be. Lots of dumb males. Several drag queens, homos, a couple from the Dykes on Bikes gang, a Transsexual, transvestite, transgender whatever. *It. They. Them.* Too many to keep track of. A clutch of leggy models, and us, others like us, others not like us, and those no one is like. Festival participants. Everyone is, even if they aren't.

The manager. She waves. Stops at our table.

"Look at you, folks. Look at you. All Keyed in and you've only been here a couple of days." She sits down. "Listen, I know you're thinking it. I know you are. I can see it in you. You're thinking you want to stay. Build a life here. Take it slow. Take it easy. Everyone does, everyone thinks that, but you folks, you really do need to stay."

We nod.

"You're right Mam," Sally says.

"Abagail, the names Abagail."

Chickadees. Several. They're looking for handouts, scraps, fighting over what they find. Little birds fighting, cute little birds. Something wrong with that. Each table has breadsticks in a glass. I take one, break it, throw the chicks a few pieces. They begin fighting. Humans with feathers, selfish little humans with feathers, and beaks, small brains. Fuck. All the eyes in the world that are open and seeing the world at any given moment, a collective view of reality from many angles, a more objective view. We can have that view. May have long ago. The aboriginals. Until they learned to covet from outsiders theirs was a grand vision of human potential. Sally explained it, said her earliest relatives were Aboriginal.

"Abagail, that's a beautiful name. A musical name."

"And you're Sally. Yes. The whitest black woman from Africa. A National Geographic story. Long time ago. I remember. And Desiree, in front of or behind the lens, 'desire with an E.' We've seen your films. "And you sir, you're Ben. Benjamin Mamott, sniper-knife-thrower. My mate, my jolly John, he's Jock, Jock Daniels. Jock loves knives, he recognized you when you checked in. Celebrities, all of you. Great to have you Want a complimentary bottle of wine? I'll send one over."

She smiles, gets up, hugs a woman standing at the next table. They walk off together, lots of laughter. Big women, both of them. The sharing kind. An Aboriginal past. We all have one.

A waitress comes to take our order, she's small, thirty maybe, the body of a gymnast.

"Have you decided?" she asks.

"Gail, wait." The manager's Jock, he hurries over. A gallant man, someone you're sure can tell unforgettable stories. Grand, unforgettable stories. He's fast on his feet.

"Gail, these folks, they're our guests tonight, no charge," he says, a slight lisp. "And give them a bottle of wine, the Duckhorn Cabernet. The one I've been saving." He turns to us, "Hey, I'm Jock. I own the place. What to say, 'Great to have you,'" he gestures, both arms outstretched. "Let me know if you need anything. Love you guys." He turns to leave.

"Wait! Thank you," I say, and I stand up, shake his hand, nod to the six-inch knife on his belt, the sheath partly hidden in his pocket–some guys do that, makes the knife look smaller.

"Nice knife, very nice. You use it much?" He laughs, "All the time friend, all the time. You want it?" "What?" "Sure, it's yours, if you want it. I'll get another one. I'm due. Had this for years. New would be a nice change. Please, take it." He pulls the sheath from his belt, his pocket, hands it to me. The blade has a black handle, shiny, gouged, a little heavy but sharp, very sharp, sheath is worn. A gift from a stranger. When does that happen, not often? The Keys. What took us so long to get here.

"Have you tried throwing it?" I ask, a little hesitant. Not sure why.

"A few times," he says, "nothing special. Hey, I know. You throw it, Mr. Mamott. For me, throw it for me. Show me the way, friend. Entertain an old sea dog. There," he points at a wooden owl at the top of the stairway. "Can you hit that owl? From here, this spot? Y'all stay for free if you can. And free wine day and night, wear whatever you want, walk naked if you want, the place is yours. I'd love to see you throw. Love it."

"Free everything?"

"Yeah," he says. "Free everything...mostly everything."

"OK," I agree, "great. Let's do this. Have someone steady that owl, make sure it doesn't fall, move people around, have them stand back, out of the way. You never know, I could miss, the blade could bounce, ricochet and stab someone. It could."

"No, not you Ben, never. You're teasing."

Was I? One time, at a knife throwing competition, a guy there, one of those flamboyant types who dress in bright colors and walk mean. When it came time for him to throw, he relaxed his arm, angled it, looked into the stands, saw a girl there he once wanted to marry. Still wanted to marry. At the same time, he made the throw, she dropped her top

375

to show him what he's missing. His throw went off mark, far enough that the blade bounced off a post and hit a lady circus performer with lots of pirate tattoos. Cut her arm. That lady was so angry, she chased the guy down, caught him, tied a rope around his ankles, attached the rope to a truck and dragged him away, his butt skidding along the pavement throwing up sparks. They turned it into a new circus act. Wasn't my knife, but it could have been.

"Free stay and wine. You did say that, right?"

"I did, sir, I did indeed. Everything in the house is on the house."

"Right," he says, and he turns and runs up the stairs, leaps even, very excited. He's wearing a pair of cargo shorts and sandals, black sandals with gold buckles, a gold chain on his neck, gold earrings, a gold nose ring. Loves knives.

Des sets up her tripod, her camera. Sally opens her phone to video. "OK, Ben. Ready."

People begin to take interest, stop what they're doing to watch, all the odd people. We're odd, odd in our own way, most everyone is, maybe everyone. People. Humans. We have no problem getting along when we want to. I roll the knife in my palm, make a show of sorting out its balance, the weight, where to hold the blade for a long throw. Guys behind me take bets. The girls take bets.

A bird lands on the owl's head, a curious pigeon, mostly white, bit of grey. I cock my shoulder, set my arm, my wrist, make the throw. The knife sticks the owl between the eyes, just below the pigeon. It jumps up, the pigeon, frightened, poops and flies off.

Laugher, thunderous applause. Lots of clapping.

People cheer they're thrilled. Impromptu entertainment. Free happiness. Feels good to make them happy. Lots of smiles. A free stay, wine, a pass on wearing clothes if we want.

Applause…a full round of applause…for me.

Cool!

Very cool.

# ONE HUNDRED FIVE

We spend the rest of the day at the beach. South Beach, the end of Duval, crowded. Sand feels used, looks used. Several old nudist couples, flayed out on their blankets. Drying fish, salted pelts, prunes, raisins with heads.

A vacant spot next to the pier, we take it, lay down in the sand. The warm, old sand.

"Hospitals. How many times have you been in a hospital, been sucked into excessive hospital expenses, impossible to escape? And ambulances? And medicines?"

"We're at the beach, Ben. Relaxing."

"I know."

"And..."

"And what? It is just a thought, Sal. These people, most of them, they look healthy, but maybe not. We look healthy but..." Sally stops me.

"We *are* healthy, Ben," she raises her skimpy top. "Do these tits look healthy to you?"

"Yes, yes, they do. Definitely."

Des raises her top.

"And these tits?"

"Yes, those too, very healthy."

We dive off the pier to entertain ourselves, it's fun. People shout, "It's too shallow!"

We dive anyway, many times. Swim until every part of our body wrinkles. Wrinkled people. A world filled with only wrinkled people.

Wrinkled skin bipeds. They're out there somewhere. When we leave the water—when Sally and Des leave the water—everyone at the beach stares, even the beach stares. Little groin and nipple patches are all the girls have on, thin tie-strings keeping the patches in place. A great look, impossible to omit from the view, everyone stares.

Des wore black patches, Sally white. Very healthy.

Still damp and salty, we rent bikes, tour the streets, chase roosters. Come back to the Beach Café. It has a bar, food. An open-air place, about 80 degrees, feels more like 90. We take a table.

"I'm hungry." Sally sticks out her tongue, snaps it back in like a lizard.

"You're always hungry, Sal."

"I'm pregnant."

"Right."

Home in the Keys. At home in the Keys. We are, and we love it.

A waiter comes to our table. Reminds me of Adam.

"I'll have a beer," I say. "Cryonic cold without the body."

"You got it man. Cryonic cold coming up."

A cheery waiter.

The girls order beer, water, and sandwiches. I add nuts, three bags. Sunny Florida. All the sun you can eat, hurricanes for free. Milk and honey days. Joyous days. Beautiful days. Beer days, drug days, Fest days. We have money enough and time enough, life is good.

"Ben, Des, I have an idea, listen," Sally takes our hands. "Let's scuba dive tomorrow, before the festival starts. Find someone with a boat, an underwater camera, and extra tanks. Several extras. We can shoot a trial underwater slow-motion porn clip. Slow-motion underwater erotica, liquid erotica. No one's done that, not that I've seen. Have you?"

"Not me," I say. "Underwater nudity, mermaids without tops, I've seen that. Nothing more, nothing that can pay the bills, buy a roof over our heads, baby food, overpriced medicine."

"People working underwater…" Des holds her breath, holds it for about ten seconds, then spits out, "Bridge foundations, aquaculture work, treasure hunting, we've seen those, nothing erotic there. But it doesn't matter, does it, not really because our sex scenes will boil the water, stiffen seaweed, make sharks of guppies, guppies of sharks, raise the dead just like Jesus. I'm in, Sal. All in."

"Me too," I say. "I'm in."

"You'd better be." Sally pinches me, pokes me. We shake on it, drink on it, eat and drink on it, drink, and drink on it. We drink a lot. Sally goes to the bathroom, comes back without her suit on. "Too restrictive," she says. Does anybody notice? They don't.

Normalizing nudity, erotic skin, legitimizing it, welcoming it, fearing it less. Sally's doing that, and Des is doing it, and Amy (wherever she and Loki are, Amy's doing it), and Key West's Fantasy Festival…an alien invasion plan. That's what it is. A better plan than love of freedom without the spirit of unity.

Time to move about, befriend our new home. Des pays the check, a fair price for what we ordered, takes off her sandals and walks us down South Street to the Southern Most Point in the US. 90 miles to Cuba. That's what the buoy says. Cuba, just beyond view. Another world, another adventure land, new roads, new voices. Not far, not at all far. Closer than the Bahamas.

Lots of beautiful homes on South Street, a museum, trim yards, well-watered plants, tidy trees,

and the occasional senior sitting on a porch, rocking, imagining what was before as being more significant than what will come. All seniors do that, a lesson their grandchildren teach them.

Key West. A comforting warmth of day takes us, almost carries us as we head back to the inn. A slow, relaxed, nowhere we have to go pace.

The Keys. Except for the gun part, Hemingway had it right.

Vacation life.

He had it right.

Sally put her suit back on.

Sill looks naked.

No one notices.

# ONE HUNDRED SIX

**P**avement is warm. The sidewalk. Several guys walking toward us, bulging guts, fat tattooed arms, open shirts, no buttons, stains on their pants, big leather belts, fake rodeo buckles. Three of them. All wearing red "Make America Great Again" hats. When we reach them, they block our way.

"Damn girls, you're beautiful."

That's what they say, what guys always say. Every time. They never think about it. They just say it, follow what was said before, done before, thought before. The need for identity validation from other people, incapable of self-validation.

I half smile, remind myself to control my temper, avoid scaring Sally "Guys," I say, "Listen, a little more imagination, please. Really. What you just said, Christ, everyone says that. Everyone. It's fine. No worries. Say it again if you want."

"Really? Everyone?" The shortest of the three, a gold chain on his neck, lots of body hair, steps to the side slightly, and a little toward me. "Everyone?"

Out of towners. Festival people, maybe. Trump supporters, no doubt. "Sorry," I say. "Sorry. No, you're right." I lose it. "Not everyone, just dumb fucks like you."

Nobody moves. Silence…the thick kind that covers history with lies. It leans into us, envelopes us.

"Move," I say.

Jock's knife. I left it at the inn.

"Now!"

"Move now. Us," says the largest of the three, the fattest. "You got balls old man." They all laugh, almost violently. Looks like their faces will burst into strange shapes with no means of reconnecting.

"And if we don't?"

The eyes. There's a look, something deep in a man, deep in anyone too often aggrieved, that talks through his eyes when he can't take it anymore, when all he thinks of when he thinks about people is how often he's been betrayed, lied to, cheated, dismissed, forced to defend himself against unfair odds. A look that says "I can die here. Can you?"

"Move!" I say again, sharpening the word with my teeth, attaching it to the head of my spear, the tip of my arrow.

They hesitate. Sally gets behind me, Des behind her.

"OK, man. Right. Chill, dude. Chill."

"Right. Chill," I exhale, feel Sally breathing through me, something exhilarating. "Guys, listen, a suggestion, a friendly suggestion. Change the wording on your hat. Russia. Your hats should say "Make Russia Great Again. The A to an R, you should change that."

The shortest, his gold chain wagging, turns to me, "What, mister, you some kind of politician?"

"No," I say, and I pause. Hold back. Not sure why but I feel sorry for the guy, for all of them. Trying to be nice when I want to break something…a change in me? Maybe.

They start to move on. Wait," I say, I'm having a thought. Those hats. And why are you here? Are you joining the Fest?"

"Yeah," they all say, yeah, get excited. "We're here to help put air into the Trump balloon, the centerpiece of the Trump float."

"What!" Sally steps out. "A Trump balloon!"

"Yeah lady," the small guy, he speaks before the others. A big ass balloon, like the ones they use in the New York City Macy's parade, damn big."

"Might be too big," says one of the others.

"Nah, can never be too big."

"Sure, it can," says another.

I intervene. "Guys, gents, what I was going to say, those hats, do you mind," I lift the hats off their heads. "Des, if you would," I reach for her.

"Here's my thought, guys, here's my thought." And I put all three hats on Des with each brim facing in a different direction making the hats look a flower with red brim petals. "This look," I say, this is a cool look. If you're going to be on a float, even around a float, and you have on three hats like this you'll all look the part of Trump helping to plant flowers of greatness in everyone's yard, their kitchen, attic space, and out house."

They look at me. All three. The same look. I can't decide if they're thinking or waiting to be told what to think.

"Try it," I say. "It's a good idea, really, do it and you'll love it, everyone will love it."

They move past us, begin talking between themselves, whack each other, put their hats back on.

"Benjamin Mamott. Damn you!" Sally punches me. "

"What's that for, Sal?"

"In the beginning, you scared me, and Des."

"Sorry Sal, sorry. Sorry Des. I did lose it. I did. You're right. But not for long. You think I'm a bad man?"

"No hubs, I don't. Never have, never will. You're blunt, that's all. Bad is something else."

I get a kiss on each cheek, a quick grab. Love it when Sally does that. When they both do it, even more. Makes me feel wanted.

"People shouldn't be made to do or believe anything," I say. "That's all. Bullies, dictators, tyrants, oppressors, whatever mantle they wear, they eliminate choice, take the one thing from people that makes them most unique. Being told what to do. I'm not good at that."

"I know hubs. Want a raisin?"

"Yeah."

Sally pops a raisin in my mouth. No idea where she keeps them. Alien pockets, do they have pockets, need pockets, have they evolved beyond pockets? Both girls take an arm, we continue walking. Pass two middle-aged gay guys pushing a stroller. A male child in the stroller, wide blue eyes, clear skin, a little jovial face, rounded smile, a victory baby. Free tours of infant genitalia, ridiculing nature.

Innocence feeding the world.

A bad man.

Am I?

# ONE HUNDRED SEVEN

America. A capitalist dictatorship, that's what we are, what we've always been. Whoever has the most capital dictates.

Suddenly feel like gambling, watching Sally win on the tables. Watching Sally anytime is grand, but at the tables, when she picks up her cards and I know she knows what the cards are before looking at them, it does something to me, makes me wonder about the control she has over her mind, over the minds of other people. Over my mind. Even among albinos, Sally is exceptional. Maybe she really can control people's minds, walk into their heads, change the course of history. Maybe she's doing that. Why she's here? A new coming. Maybe she's already set in motion a series of events designed to realign our political process, to erase Trump utterly. Dictator Don and all his Red Hat sycophants – gone. All of them. Why not? No more Trump please-remember-me-I'm-better-than-you highways, state parks, buildings, towers, golf courses, resorts, games, books, doilies at the bottom of trash cans, "The Wall." Everything gone. Every Trump image and word spoken by him removed from magazines, news outlets, government offices, history books, toilet stalls, garbage trucks, sewer treatment plants. No presidential portrait. Gone. Deleted utterly from human memory. If Sally could do that? Damn.

Starts to rain. Then pour. Warm rain, comforting in a way, a bit threatening. We run. Splash each other, frolic like young animals, juveniles enjoying the spring of youth. Three or four blocks to the inn. Des arrives first, fast on her feet, opens the gate, a group of kids are playing on the porch entrance, couple of them are already bar coded, tattooed, branded…trash-age beginners. I can see in them, future parents, using tattoo location trackers on their children to keep tabs on them. "Never Lose, Never Lost" location trackers etched into the souls of the feet at birth. We walk past them, through the courtyard to our room. Our first Key West home.

> *Rooms. Inside rooms we can be anywhere, in any country, any place, any time of day. We can disappear in rooms, be who we want to be. Be who we are. Rooms gives us control, a place to hide when tricker or treaters knock on the door unexpectedly. Rooms within rooms, we're always inside something. Inside and comfortable, the door closed, windows open, curtains drawn, we strip, wrap ourselves with dry towels, thick, dry towels. Wring out our suits in the tub, hang them to dry on hooks, doorknobs, and the shower door. Jock left us a bottle of wine, a 2013 Duckhorn Cabernet, and a corkscrew, several glasses, olives, cheese slices and crackers. I open the bottle, pour half glasses. We clink, toast, swirl, and sniff, check the legs, nice legs, take a sip, several, then we gulp, big swallows. Not sure why, no way to drink rated wine. Finish the bottle, open several cans of beer. More alcohol in the blood…always room for more alcohol. We feel like getting drunk, no reason. No need to have a reason. The three of us on the bed, wrapped in towels, a blank tv screen in front of us. We exhale simultaneously, share a mutual vision of comfort, happiness, and security. A rare moment.*

"Hey, I have an idea." Animated beyond her norm, Des sits up abruptly. "The other Hemingway haunt, maybe the first…Captain Tony's. Let's go there for dinner."

"Captain Tony's, sure, we can do that," I say, and I light a joint, take a hit, blow smoke rings toward the ceiling, roll my gaze over the visible curves of Desiree's body. She's younger than Sally but Sally looks younger, acts younger. Beautiful women. Can't imagine a world without beautiful women. Wherever I go, wherever I've gone in the world, and I've been around and back, if I see a beautiful woman at a train station, a restaurant, walking down a street, wherever, I always feel better about being in that place. All men do, and women. I've heard that.

Amy and Loki, images of them drift into my thoughts, when they first met. A good match. Fun to be there. I wonder how they're getting on. Smile thinking about them, imagine a lizard eating Loki's flowers.

# ONE HUNDRED EIGHT

Rain stops. Sunlight on silent horses' rushes across the sky, lights the inn courtyard, the surrounding trees, crashes through the curtains into our room and licks our faces. We stay inside, open a jar of peanuts, bag of Fritos, a bottle of wine. Sally checks the cabinets and drawers, finds a board card game. Sequence. 108 cards, two decks, two rows of five chips in a row wins the game. We play several games. The first couple finish too quickly so we change the rules, play until the entire board is filled with chips. We call it Sequence plus. Whoever had the most rows after all the cards have been played wins. Sally won every game, even when she had bad cards.

Mind reading. Was she? Maybe. Probably. Trump. Sally has him, is already climbing his legacy, chewing through the lies, the betrayals, the shameless backroom deals, selling our freedom for his, his favoritism, nepotism, his blatant acts of treason, bullying and fraud, his disregard for the law, the oath of office, the constitution, the freedoms that made his corruption possible…she has him, is gnawing through his baren conscience, spitting him out, erasing him, lifting the veil. Dumb fuck. Pit Bulls and albinos, they never let go.

We play sequence for hours, a childhood pajama party without pajamas, talk about butterflies, how it is that they appear to have no clue where they're going yet still end up in places, eat, find mates, make more butterflies. And bruises on fruit, we talk about them, how bruises get there. Bruises on bananas, apples, pears. Were they dropped in the field, on a warehouse floor, on a boat dock? Were they packed too tightly? Did someone throw them, make a sport of it, put stickers on the bruises to hide them? We talk and talk, and we smoke Simbana's weed, drink, snack, fool around, touch, simple touches, affectionate, lots of rubbing and massaging between turns, between games. Nothing like massage. Every day, everyone in the world should have a massage, a legal happy ending massage. No minors, no coercion. No modesty slavery. No guilt slavery. A moral pleasure-focused world. What would that be like?"

Almost dark. Bottles done, hollowed out, every drop consumed. Still have some pills, lots of pills, more weed, Viagra.

Sally stands up. "Well...time to get dressed!" she says, very cheerleader like, and bouncy.

"Do we have to?" Des sounds serious.

"It's a Pre-Fest Day, Des. And it was your idea to go out."

"So."

"So?"

"Girls, ladies. We can go out or not, you can wear whatever you want or don't want. Dressed or not, you're beautiful either way, but naked, if you want to go naked, I'm all for that. Nothing more beautiful than a naked woman. I think so."

"Really. You think so."

"I do, sure."

"And a naked fat woman?"

I halt, take a breath. "Right, yeah, that's something. Yeah, hippos, whales, walruses, they're born fat. Women aren't born fat."

"So fat women are ugly?"

"No, fat on women is ugly, not women."

"Ben...." Piercing eyes.

Four of them.

Holding a pair of twos, not even a pair, something less than twos. I stop talking.

Sally puts on a sleeveless blouse with two buttons, a light grey cotton skirt, white sandals. She looks great, magnificent, shimmers like dust drifting in the moonlight. Can't take my eyes off her. Lots of skin, showing it for free. I slip on a clean pair of cargo shorts, worn, dark brown, my old sandals. Tuck Jock's blade into my right pocket, run the belt through the sheath loop. Sally insists I leave it behind. I do.

Des grabs her camera. She's wearing transparent paint…bartender Sally paint. She got the name of the guy selling the paint, no idea when or how.

On our way out we exchange greetings with several guests, traverse the slanted stairs and out the gate. Onto Duval we go, Sally on one side, Des on the other, me in the middle. The sandwich man. Good title for a movie.

The sidewalks are packed. People spilling into the streets blocking cars. Lots of honking, noise, whistling, shouting, and laughing. A broad-shouldered Black man with big whiskers, rabbit ears and a boom box rolls by, forces everyone to listen to crap rap monotony, always the same monotonous beat. The Temptations. What would they think? The Supremes, James Brown? Smokey Robinson. Beautiful music, what happened to beauty? Trash-agers. Losing interest in beauty, in beauty's ability to elevate the positive. Is that good?

A jazz quartet on the far corner, three girls, one guy. The girls are painted to look like the instruments they're playing. A Double Bass with tits. I like the look. The guy wore a suit. I thought so. Objectifying women, maybe. Had to be sweating underneath that suit. Suit could have been painted. Artists, if they're good, they can do that, trick the eye.

Country western came along further up the street, a couple of guys playing beat-up guitars, empty cowboy hats sitting in front of them. I toss in a buck, two bucks, wonder if they've ever seen a horse, ridden one, been kicked by one. Fantasy Fest. People everywhere, all sizes and shapes, bundles of shifting colors, people colors tied together by permissive merriment; the allure of fantasy seeping into reality, reformatting social norms, evolution. Why not? We keep walking, dodging obstacles both moving and stationary. Lots of lights, painted bodies, partially painted bodies, shops set up to paint bodies, dozens of them, breasts are out, bare legs, backs, stomachs, couple of Johnnies, couple of hairy asses. How to paint a hairy ass…fuck, who knows? Spray paint, that's what I would use, and a blowtorch.

There are kids, too, normal kids with normal parents. Wonder if they're headed to some kiddie festival, if they'd be in town tomorrow. Maybe they aren't normal. Maybe they're painted to look normal. Maybe everyone is painted to look normal. Maybe they aren't kids.

Simbana's pills. Did I take one? Did the girls take one? More than one?

Can't remember.

Probably.

Likely.

# ONE HUNDRED NINE

**H**emmingway haunts. Captain Tony's. More intimate than Sloppys. Custom tacky, disobedient. Music playing, very festive. Dozens of dollar bills tacked to the ceiling. I look for a five, don't see one. Hanging tree doppelgangers meandering through the din. Casual, human. We like it. Feels like an entry parlor for a Nevada whorehouse...an old one.

Sally leads us in and heads straight to the bar. Cards tacked everywhere, bras, in the rafters, old license plates, posters, tourist shirts, personal notes, ribbons, pool tables in the back, racks for the 'ques, obligatory photos of Hemingway, and stools. A large array of stools. Stools with names on them, famous names. Dylan, Clapton, Eastwood, De Niro, Pacino. Did they actually sit on the stool with their name on it? Not likely, but maybe, and if they did, did they sign the back, the underneath of the stool? Has anyone checked? Can nobodies have a stool? I wonder. My old trailer had a stool. Nothing underneath... maybe chewing gum. Paradise. What it was. Places are more like ideas than places. Ideas more like places than ideas. Nothing's certain, not really. We think repetition and familiarity make things certain. They don't they only make the illusion of certainty more certain.

A couple's getting up. The girls take their stools.

"Look! Bras!"

Sally points. Delighted.

"More bras than dollar bills!"

It looks like that. Lots of bras, dozens of dangling, waving, endearing bras. Thick bras, thin ones, old stringy ones and new ones, see-through bras, bra cups filled with memories, fond memories. Lots of bras.

"Des, have you ever been to Markleeville? It's in California, a couple of throws south of Lake Tahoe"

"No."

"Ben, tell her."

"Sure, but can it wait, or you tell her? I'm off to the boy's room."

"I'll tell her."

"Be quick," they say.

I am. I was. When I return, they both have beer, Sally hands me one from the counter. Good and cold in a Captain Tony's iced glass, one with Hemingway's face on it. Sally is still talking about the Bra Bar in Markleeville.

"...so," she says, "the bras here remind us of that. Ben got into it with a couple of guys. You know how he is. There was a scuffle. To distract people I tossed my blouse, no bra, missed the rafters. This sturdy looking girl, she opened her shirt, took off her bright red plus size, tied it to my blouse, and tossed them both. She made the rafters, people cheered, we ran out."

"You ran out?"

"We did, yes," I said, rejoining the conversation. "And we forgot to pay the bill."

"Did you go back?"

"No."

"Can't you be arrested for not paying a bar bill?"

"Maybe, probably. We never asked. And, ladies, here's a thought. Could be good. Bars with bras in the rafters. Bra bars. A chain of bra bars. We could build them, franchise them. Cover the country in bras, the world. Cover the world in gigantic bras. Massive, huge things, use them to cover the poles, slow down global warming, confuse the polar bears."

"Ben...which do you think has more bras, Markleeville or Tony's?"

I look around. "Tony's, Sal. Tony's is older."

"Tony's, right, probably Tony's."

"But maybe not. Maybe Markleeville has a bigger higher ceiling, room for more bras."

"Right, and bra density matters as well."

"It does," I add, "and then there's bra size, how many small-breasted bras can you fit into one big-ass bra? The bar with more bras could have lots of small bras. Maybe no big ones at all. Would that be fair? Would fairness matter in a bra contest? Can bras have bra babies?"

"Bra science, Ben. Must be a bra science behind it all."

"Right, bra science."

Beer is an easy, uncomplicated drink. We drink, talk, get another round, order food, sandwiches, pie, more beer, listen to the band. The Cocky Roach Band. Four guys, lead singer, a guy on organ and drums, bass player, and a lead guitar and rhythm. They're good, a local dance band.

"I should be shooting," Desiree says, feels remiss. "Let's see if I can get permission."

More people entering the bar, bodies painted, bodies without paint, few in-between. Outside, people are tossing coins into the fish mouth, trying, quarters mostly. I look around. The counter's full, the stools fully occupied (roosters are taking bets on how long people will sit on them), pool balls are rolling, beer's flowing. It's getting crowded, louder. Exuberant conversation enchanting the mind, music the heart, people dancing. It's good, the mood. All kinds of people, every kind, all in the same Fantasy Festival mood…peace on earth. Salutary purpose fulfilled. That's how you do it. Put on a big ass Captain Tony's international drink along. Make all political views welcome, all sexes welcome, all beliefs welcome, but drink must be had, smoke and drink, and more smoke, and more drink, and plenty of food, and fucking, have to fuck, enrich the pot, the back rooms, the alleys, streets, the dance floor. No carnal equanimity without carnal exercise.

We dance, dance and dance some more. Ritualistic sensual excitement saturating our senses. Des begins shooting a video of Sally. Rapt, sexy, otherworldly. People stop to watch, they have to. No choice. The white wonder, her undulating hips, sparkling breasts, pouty red lips, she has them in an instant. My wife. Her dance. Her beauty. Her lightness of being. She appears as air through an open window, tossing the curtains. Her liquid arms and legs, tales of erotic mystery, fragrant and seductive, radiate through the crowd. Des joins in. Others do as well, they're hypnotized, taken under her spell utterly, they're living in the present, for the present…for beauty. Politics be damned, social norms be damned, psychological trauma be damned. Several small women with chubby cheeks, a couple of Adams (I dropped fag, replaced it with Adam, an experiment), and an old Andean-looking woman with a cowboy hat, they all move with Sally, mimic her in unison. Sally drifts toward the band, joins them on stage, slows the rhythm, they switch to a sultry number as she cups her hidden breasts, hints at letting them out for a full parade. Sally, she loves taking her clothes off.

Onlookers cheer her on. "Striptease! Striptease!" They shout their desire, empty their glasses, ask for more. More beer, more albino skin, more skin. Sally gives it to them. On her toes, she spins, unbuttons her top, lets it drift, a spirit thing freed from her body…mist, or bird plumage falling from a great height. She catches it with the tips of her fingers, throws it to the rafters. One of the buttons hook a bent license plate, secures it, leaves it there swinging, softly swinging. A shoe, another shoe, her skirt, bra, the one she wasn't wearing. The whiteness of being. Des filming it. She keeps filming with one hand while the other removes her own transparent top, joins Sally on stage. She throws her top to the rafters, misses hooking it, throws it again, it catches. Cheers ring out. I can't see it, there's nothing there. Or maybe there is.

The girls are on, the place is on. A Fan Fest Key West rodeo, arms waving, bulls kicking, the crowd screaming.

Hemmingway, did he experience this? The unvarnished libations of joy. The nudity of it all, the crawl of life through every pore in the human body. All the girls, tits out, royals out and on their way to happy endings? He would have liked it, joined in, striped with the girls, tossed his 12 gauge, written about it in a dozen volumes titled, *Shotguns Can't Dance*.

Drugs and booze taking hold. Rules dissolving, present happiness, how to make it last. We keep drinking, keep at it, the band flips, 'halleluiah,' begins to undress as they play, the bartenders undress, toss shirts, hats, shorts, skirts…outside the bar, almost everyone begins undressing, maybe everyone, everyone dancing, drinking, smoking, all of them laying down tracks for God's greatest hit. No complaints, no fights, no trouble, no need for justice. Bonnie and Clyde come in- join the party. Expand the level of revelry to a higher octave. Des keeps filming, the band plays on. Sally finishes her routine with a slow motion back flip that leaves her standing on her hands, forward facing with all the flesh that makes her Sally visible for all to see…to walk into, dissipate into.

Blunting it at Captain Tony's. We are. All of us. Laying down tracks, laying them down. A hit movie in the can, our first. Living the American dream, making it happen. Being life, we are. No time to imagine or remember it.

Cocky Roach, exhausted, spent of all their charms, they shut down, take their applause, a final bow, pack up, light up and leave the stage. People mingle, try to mingle, little real comprehension of where we are in the universe, how long it takes for water to boil. Too drunk to play pool, we don't bother, can't find our clothes, pick up other people's clothes, nothing fits properly, dosen't matter. Des has her camera, valuable material for our first porn flick: *Key Holes*.

Albino Night, that's what Tony's calls it, how it came to be known and billed every year after that night.

Sally got a stool named for her. A white stool.

She signed it, underneath.

# ONE HUNDRED TEN

We're moving. strolling, not that it could be called strolling.
"The inn," I ask. "How far away is it?"

No answer.

"The inn, how far?"

No answer.

Alice in Fantasyland, a walk on pavement pitted with shifting rabbit holes, deep, cylindrical, whirling toward the depths, rabbit holes. A haze of moving shades textures the air. Ornament people filling the spaces, walking through each other, connected, disconnected, submarine shadows crisscrossing prehistoric seabed's, places in the mind we have yet to visit. Drunk people, happy drunks. Happy stoners, some heavy hitters curled up in corners.

"This way, Ben." Sally pulls me toward her, I pull Des. River's meandering, draining into oceans, becoming oceans, ocean babies. Lots of babies. Fatherhood. Me... Fuck. We make it back to the inn, not sure how, or who we were before the inn. We stagger to our room, lie down...crash.

Rabbit holes, rabbit holes, how deep do they go, whomever we ask, no one seems to know.

Voices. Glasses clinking. Hushed voices. More clinking. Am I still asleep? Can't tell. Can't make out the time. It's dark, strange, the sound of something falling that doesn't hit the ground. I get up. Hard to see. Light coming from outside, just enough. Pool lights, maybe. The girls are sleeping. Beautiful, both of them, but Sally's mine. We're married. I like being married, owning, being owned.

The power to regenerate society, species longevity, it holds you, adds meaning. Meanings. Christ. I don't care much for meanings, everyone has them, I have them. Why? Does meaning change anything? Trying to be someone I already am, improvising reality. Therapists would say that. Wave their mind fuck, new age books in my face, cast me in their image. Try to. Therapy for Therapists, the book. Someone should write it. Probably did. No one read it.

# ONE HUNDRED ELEVEN

"Drugs," I say, gazing up at the ceiling. "I love drugs."

"We love drugs" Sal and Des chime in.

"From the beginning," I continue, "in the beginning, after God created space, black holes, and shopping malls, he created caffeine, diet pills and prescription drugs. Vicodin, Norco, Oxycodone, and he created headache pills, and psilocybin, opium, heroin and smack, and meth, and wine and beer. Beer was last, had to be last."

"Are you sure?"

Sally sticks her tongue in my ear, blew air in it. Tickles all the way to my toes , all ten toes. Very odd.

"Yes," I say. "Beer was definitely last. It was last because beer, even bad beer, is damn good when it's ice cold and God, to keep Satan; his twin brother, from drinking his beer, decided to make ice before making beer. That's why beer was last."

"Really?"

"Yeah, it's God's honest truth, I swear. Satan, you know, he hates the cold. So, God figured he wouldn't drink cold beer."

"Was he right?" Sal and Des, they're both on the bed, elbows down, hands on their cheeks, big smiles. Campfires stories, goblins, witches, and big foot hiding just beyond the campfire glow waiting to snatch you away.

"Yes, he was right. Satan didn't drink the cold beer. He stuck his finger in it, heated it up, and drank it hot, sizzling hot. All the angels say so. They know, they drink with him. They do, but angels are wine buffs, wine mostly, high scoring wine. While Satan drinks beer, they drink wine. Black hole wine, a lot of tannin in black hole wine. And stardust."

"Ben."

"Really, wine mostly."

"Ben!"

Caught…again. Nonsense for the sensible. I return to the ceiling, to staring at it. I like doing that. Altered states augmenting reality, imagining impossible things. Illegal drugs. Legal drugs. Humans love them. It's in our nature. Without drugs man would not be man. Maybe we can make man illegal. Would make the earth happy, and lots of endangered animals, plants, bugs, and fish…would make the fish very happy.

Outside, Key West's Fantasy Festival is full on and kicking up its heels. All the joyous voices, music, horns, whistles, laughter. We hear them waking the romance of congenial revelry. America's most profane irreverent unabashedly absurd anything goes freedom of speech, freedom of mind, freedom of body, clothes optional, sex optional, swearing optional, PC optional, God optional cultural event….

The gates are open.

We sit up, suddenly realize we're too warm, our bodies shimmering with moisture, no air conditioning, no fan.

Sally gets up. "Who wants to shower first? Or with me?"

Most people, when they leave a bed, a chair, a couch, whatever, as they stand up their weight transfers from butt to foot and you can see that happen. Not Sally. She goes from butt to foot without shifting her weight. Every time I notice it – that gravity doesn't like her, can't grasp her, age her like it ages the rest of us – it baffles me and I have to think about it, wonder if our kids are going to levitate, have wings or not, read minds, breathe underwater, fly faster than the speed of light.

I don't feel like showering, too hot, not hot enough, too lazy, too tired, too old, too something…I go to the fridge for a beer. Des joins Sally. A beautiful morning. The three Trump guys, I wonder how they're getting on with their balloon, and what happened last night? Life. It can only be lived in the present, not in the past or future where our ego — the high seat in our head directing our identity — resides.

Misdirects it is more like it. Ego, only man has an ego, thinks more of himself than the world in which he lives. Sally acts like she has an ego, pretends to take things personally, she doesn't though, I can tell. She moves on from moment to moment unattached. How?

Sally, the white Buddha, Christ with breasts, alien ancestry, she loves me. What more do I need to know about her, about anyone?

# ONE HUNDRED TWELVE

Almost noon, very bright, hot. Clothes are clinging to us more than comforting us, comforting anyone. Moisture, a wet world, oceans, rivers. Love rivers. River's hurry along encountering obstacles every moment of their lives. They adjust, go through, around, over, under whatever obstacle greets them. They don't complain, "oh, that branch, it scratched me." They don't cry when they hit rocks, moan when the sun gets too hot. They just carry on. Good to be more like a river. Feels like we're swimming in our perspiration.

On the corner of Duval and Angela, Des found a body painter. Female, a brisk look, young playful lips, enthusiastic eyes, bar coded; following the herd. An empty chair next to her, a beat-up folding chair, a wood table next to the chair, splotches on it, stains, faded colors, dents and gouges, the kind that come from maintenance disinterest. Lots of paint cups on the table and jars with brushes, they look like make-up brushes. Crayons, an old airbrush, body tape, a mix of bright colors, stencils, sponges, ribbons for threading piercing rings, nipple rings...she has them, nipple rings, both breasts. She's body painted top to toe; a kaleidoscope filled with water look.

"I'm Rutty Ann," she says, and she extends her hand.

We shake, all of us.

"Rutty Ann? That's unusual."

"I'm unusual, like you all," she says. "Don't see many like you three. Nowhere I've been anyway."

"Rutty Ann. It's the name your parents gave you? Sorry. I don't mean to pry. Just curious." Des demurred, very cute, made her more attractive.

"Yes, it is. My parents were hippies, are hippies. Monterey Beach hippies, transplanted from Kansas. They thought Rutty Ann was "cool, man." Utterly unique. I can change it. Might do that."

Sally got to the point. "Do you, body paint? It looks like you do."

"Yes, but not full time. Fest time is when I paint. Otherwise, I pole dance, work the tattoo parlor, show off my tattoos, write poems, teach yoga and karate."

"Oh…"

"I can paint you, mister," she looks at me. "Paint you all red, white, and blue. You look like patriot material."

"Do I?" Never thought of myself as not being a patriot, or even being one.

"Do it, Ben, let her." Sally nudges me. "Sit down, we'll watch."

"How can she paint my ass with me sitting on it? And look at this chair, it's wobbly."

"Sit still for your goober, cullions, chest, face, legs," Rutty says, "stand for your ass."

"My goober?"

"Mister, for now, just sit. Stand for your gluteus maximus, once the sitting's done."

"Right."

"Yeah, Ben, that will work. It's a fun idea."

"OK."

Outnumbered, I agree, remove my shirt and shorts, and sit down. Body painted on Duval, definitely not a California thing to do. It could be. Rutty goes to work. Her paints, her 'real' paints, are lined up next to plastic bins filled with fake tattoos for kids, starter tattoos, crawling-to-walking tattoos, trashager training wheels….

Calculated social change…it begins with the most receptive. It begins with kids, kids conscripted for choir boy programming and molestation. Conscripted for God is Great programming and molestation. Conscripted for Satmar modesty slavery programming and molestation, for Boy Scouts programming and molestation, for NRA young shooters programing and molestation, for *Heather Has Two Mommies,* born gay, orientation entrapment programming and molestation. All the eat-your-peas, sit-up-straight, do-as-you're-told familial programming, consumption programming, cultural programming, religious programming, lifestyle programming, gender programming, they all start with kids. The first person, persons, institution, organization to program kids controls future change.

Innocence. It lasts about an hour after a kid's born, not even that, minutes maybe.

Sally, the taste of milk. That's what she looks like. Not at all sure how she does it, how she does many things...who she is, what she is, really...not sure about that either, not that it matters. I stare at her with no hope of self-control as Rutty begins making me into a painted man. A popsicle American. Good to have missed the burning man at the stake bit. The burning woman, burning whoever inquisitors found sinful in the late Middle Ages, bit. At that time, a painted man...cooked, he would have been, cooked.

Embarrassed, suddenly shy, Sally catches me adoring her, looks at me. A warm, "I love you" look. Kisses me with her eyes.

"Hubs, here's a thought."

Rutty begins with a large house paintbrush size stoke of red paint on my forehead, takes it all the way down.

Sally comes in close, tucks her voice into my ear, "Want me to rub some that paint off... Rub-a-Dub dub, as soon as Rutty finishes?"

"Rub paint off what Sal, exactly," I say, feeling all warm and cozy inside. Loving Key West more each moment.

Public love making. Was it permissible, acceptable, plausible in a world so fearful of pleasure? Right there on the street? Plenty of daylight as witness, and people, and trees, not a lot of trees, and roosters, lots of roosters…a dozen waiting in line.

Painted skin. It feels weird. Dressed and undressed at the same time. It feels like that, like even though I'm hiding behind the paint, I can be seen with no effort at all. A not nude, nude man. *The not nude, nude man.* Another possible title.

"Look at me Sal," I point down. "My hammer's off the bench."

"He is, it is, you are, yes."

Rutty brought another stroke down.

"What should I do?"

"Ignore it. Have a raisin."

She hands me one.

"Ignore a phoenix rising, who does that?"

"Exposed phallic symbols are normal, Ben. Religious even, sacred in some places. India,

Bhutan, Bangladesh. Lots of places. Think monk, think Madman of Bhutan and you'll be fine.

All these people here, look at them. As much as we're not offended by anything they're doing, or look like, they're not offended by anything we do, or look like. Ignore it and turn around, let Rutty paint your gluteus maximus.

"Your butt."

"OK."

# ONE HUNDRED THIRTEEN

Renewal. Spring celebrants. Ships gliding into harbor, laden with the weariness of travel and the practical joy of success. We're a long way from Paradise. Far from the carbonized trees, the skeletal fences, the charred cars, burnt bodies, hollow skulls, melted eyes, lips and tongues melted, burned-out homes, the littered remains of dreams coffined in ashen mud, cinder smells, coals smoldering in the mind, hungry for greater destruction. Paradise. Too few angels protecting it.

"Ben."

I look up. Rutty's almost done with Patriot Man. I feel like I'm shrinking as the paint dries...feels like it dries. Maybe not. I try to remember, 'What pills did I take, did we take?' Memory, we live on memory, we do. That it means so much to us to relive memories is surprising, like living in a graveyard is surprising, if you think about. My mind lifts off, my senses, the world, how different it sounds when I listen to it with attention focused on both focal and peripheral hearing. It sounds bigger. Much bigger.

"Ben. What day is it?"

"August first. Why?"

"Why!"

"Ben!"

"Yeah. Sal. I'm here."

"When did I arrive on Earth?"

"What?"

"When was I born? What day?"

"August first," I say. "Maybe. Or...Oh, fuck!!!" I take a deep breath.

"Damn, Sally! Christ!!! Fuck! I forgot. I forgot, Sal, and I did everything I could think of to remember. Phone notes, post-it notes, wrote it down in my calendar. Damn. We must celebrate. Sally, I love you. Happy, Happy Birthday, wife. Happy Birthday!" We embrace. My mind spitting at me, kicking me. Of all the things to forget...a second time. Sally's pissed. I can tell, feel it coming.

"Ben, how could you forget, again? Christ! It's not like you're writing a book, making a movie, building a housing complex, preparing for a flight to mars, launching a new religion.

"I don't know Sal. I tried; I did."

"Tried?! Not hard enough," she says, and she turns away. A beautiful woman, always beautiful. "It's time for lunch. Des and I are going to that restaurant right there, that one," she points. "We're going to sit down and eat. Alone."

She grabs Des, crosses the street, weaves through the people, a break in the fence line, and takes a table under one of the courtyard umbrellas near a hedge, a healthy row hedge, very green, a corner view.

I look at Rutty, she's done. Not sure how I feel, scattered, for sure, looking around for how to fix this. I pull a twenty from my shorts, pay her, put my shorts back on, my shirt. Party mood is gone. Sally's birthday. I need to buy her something immediately, even faster.

Not good at beating myself up, but I try. Inside I keep kicking. Damn. How could I forget.

Fuck.

Fuck, fuck, fuck.

# ONE HUNDRED FOURTEEN

I feel like pushing my way down the street, hitting something, someone, stepping on small dogs, rodents, any size...screaming, 'fuck, fuck, fuck.' I don't. Not one swear word, not one act of violence. Too stoned. The joint's done, connoisseur's blend, I take a final hit. Nepalese hash and weed. Don't feel like being angry, even at myself.

A couple of streets down I find a bar, get a beer, a shot of tequila, two shots, three, another beer, feel better, cooler, calmer. Need to buy a gift for Sally. A piece of 'don't be mad at me jewelry,' something.

"Another beer mister?" Asks the bartender.

"Sure, one more."

"Ice cold, correct?"

"Right. Ice cold, cryonic cold. Yeah," I joke, "imagine bringing a beer back to life in a couple of hundred years. What would it think? Would it be able to relate to other beers, find a girl beer, be invited to parties?"

She raises her brow. No comment.

The bartender's a nice-looking woman, a big woman, tall, graceful, late fifties, good skin, sharp features. She pulls a mug from the fridge, draws a beer, swaps it for my empty, leans over, checks to see if anyone's looking, "I know a fortune teller." she says.

"I don't," I say, abruptly. Could have used one. "Oh, shit! Sorry lady didn't mean to snap. I know *of* fortune tellers, but I don't know one, not as in a real person sitting behind an array of cushions surrounded by all manner of odd relics. One of those. I don't know one of those."

"You talk a lot, don't you?"

Do I? Not sure if I do. Like everyone, when I talk, I talk to be understood, and I talk until I am understood or give up because I don't expect to be understood. My mind goes blank. No words escape the alphabet, pop out my mouth on colored hang gliders.

"Would you like to meet her?"

"Who?"

"The fortune teller. I just mentioned her."

"You did, that's right. I remember." I take a long swallow. Love cold beer on a hot day…more so on a hot day that's Sally's Birthday and I'm stressed over where to find a savior gift.

"Any question you have," says the bartender, "any question at all. Past, present, future. She will know the answer."

"Impossible," I chide. "No one can know that much. Really, lady, come on…."

"My names, Sara lee," she says.

"Oh, OK, Sara lee, that's an amazing suggestion, story idea. It is. Really. Impossible, however. Just impossible." I take another big swallow, several hits off a joint I just rolled. Can't remember rolling it.

"She keeps a room above the bar, The Teller. You can reach her by going up those stairs over there." She points to an open door leading to a series of bright red steps. Steps that appear something like a smile with big teeth.

"But why would I want to talk to a fortune teller?"

"Everyone wants to talk to a fortune teller, Ben."

"How do you know that? The Teller…About everyone. And how is it that you know my name?"

"The Teller. Before you got here, she said you would be coming in."

"But I need to get my wife a birthday present."

"I know. She told me that as well."

"What else did she tell you?"

"She told me you would ask me what else she told me."

"You're kidding, right."

"She's just upstairs, ask her yourself."

"OK, I will, but later. For now, I have to get my Sally a gift. "I'll be back."

"I know," she says.

Of course, she does...I think that, walk out.

The parade is on. More and more people join in. Cigarette smoke, joint and pipe smoke drift between reveler's dancing, holding hands, talking excitedly. The music hits full rock and roll, gets louder as a float goes by, a truck of some kind, made to look like a pirate boat, two guys dressed like pirates running it. They have a cargo of 'good for the eyes' pirate girls. Exquisite pirate girls scantily dressed, without body paint. Just wraps, scarves tied around their waists, their breasts, their legs, and arms. One by one, as the float rolls along, the girls toss a scarf here and there to spectators, the guys do the same, sort of.

I follow the float. Fill myself with the rhythm of strangers becoming friends without meeting each other – a kind of harmony found in high places of the mind, and mountain tops that share the sky without complaint.

Feeling better, more relaxed, hopeful, I look around. There are so many naked painted people mingling in and around the parade floats that distinction of form is beginning to slip. Hard to tell who is man, who is woman, what is not man, or woman, what is anything at certain points. The Key West Fantasy Festival Parade. It's a parade's parade. The parade all parades in the world want to be, would pay to be if they had any money.

I keep walking, checking shop windows, blending in. Nude in public. I was. Pants and shirt were off again. Don't remember doing that. Painted red, white, blue, and nude. Feels good to walk, to just walk along like Adam and Eve in the garden. Running naked in the woods, walking naked on a beach. Walking naked on the street, it's different. Less nude, more nude, I can't tell. Feels good, that's all. No self-image for walking naked on the streets.

I pop another Viagra (a Simbana thing to do), check for my shirt and trousers. Can't remember tucking them under my arm. Just ahead a jewelry and crafts store. I break off from the parade, weave through the crowd, walk in.

The store has two counters, a man behind one, a woman behind the other, both are body painted. The man's wearing a wig, big nose, a Hitler mustache (never understand that), the woman lacks expression, wears thick, yellow tinted glasses, looks blind. Can't hide the anemia, they can't. Maybe they're painted to look anemic. Pallid paint, as opposed to regular paint, paint made to make you look ashen, bloodless. It had to be different from regular paint.

I browse the jewelry displays, pick out a gold chain and locket, bargain a bit, two hundred dollars

even, no tax. I pay, have them wrap it with a bow, find a card at another shop, some flowers,

and hurry back to the corner restaurant. Hope the girls are still there.

They are.

Sally waves me over.

A big smile

Sometime in my thirties I went to Istanbul. The Grand Bazaar, crowded, dense patina smells, grasping odors, ancient dust lurking, finding its way, coating new baubles, shoes, carpets, bowls; life's souvenirs and necessities, everything a human could want. Turkey was magnificent. Amazing colors, beautiful women, belly dancers, ancient ruins. Ephesus, grand and still alive. I stopped at an old mosque a few miles from my hotel, very personal, small compared to Hagia Sophia. A wedding taking place. I followed them outside, found a sheltered place to stand, an alcove, snapped on a 300 mm lens, began shooting photos. The bride was extraordinary, shimmering; an image drawn from medieval history, a butterfly princess saved from dragon fire by her knight in shining armor. Not quite. The groom, the other men, they were just guys, typical guys. Several looked over, looked at me, angry looks. One, maybe 17, 18 years old, broke away from the group, ran over to me shouting, a knife in his hand, thin blade, shinny. He stopped in front of me, just out of reach, just. I was bigger and older. Felt big, what it meant to feel big.

"You take one more photo," he said, "I slit your throat."

Decent English. Easy to understand. The procession continued. I considered waiting until it passed behind the next building, then grabbing the little fuck by the throat and choking the shit out of him. Too risky. I relaxed my camera, dropped it to my side.

"Sure," I said, "no problem."

Satisfied but still angry, still wanting, he hovered.

"No problem," I said again. "No problem at all."

He left. I photographed him walking away, got off a couple more clicks of the bride. She was gorgeous, inviting, no veil, pale brown skin, thin, she walked like a dancer, a runway model, every step rehearsed, planned. I imagined doing her right there, with all her knife-wielding mud slingers looking on.

That's what I imagined.

Muslim guys, women scare the shit out of them, and pigs.

# ONE HUNDRED FIFTEEN

Hot, damn hot, more people, well past noon, scorching.

Sally, always a vision. She stands, pulls out a chair for me. I hand her the card, the flowers, the package. She puts the flowers in a water glass, reads the card, opens the package, the locket. I wait, hold my breath... an odd sensation when you're not under water.

"I love it hubs. A baby picture locket. It's perfect. I love it, love you. Thank you, hubs," she says, and she gives me a kiss, a deep absolving kiss.

I sit down. Sally sits, finishes her sandwich. I'm not hungry. Des is, she always is. She eats everything on her plate, every time, licks empty bowls when she can, uses her finger to scrape crocks and cups, her tongue to dig inside catsup and mayonnaise jars, likes to sleep on the floor. An animal of some kind. She has to be, definitely. And she's wearing transparent paint. A stunning look. I keep thinking she's nude...but she isn't.

We hit the street.

Everyone's happy. Everyone in the restaurants, on the floats, in the stores, the shops, the bars. Defining the streets as open to pleasure and communal harmony, people are doing that. An amazing thing. So many happy people, such variation in human appearance and behavior, so much skin. Every kind of body, body color, and body add-on is on display...the fully painted body, the half-painted body, the somewhat painted body, the lightly painted body, and Des versions...all of them out there, on the street. People being who they are, intermixing without discord. Porn star reality, no fear of the flesh, no fear of insulting, of being insulted. Key West's Fantasy Fest: The united altered states of sticks and stones may break my bones but differences in skin color, race, ethnicity, politics, religion, orientation, and breast and hammer size, will never hurt me.

"No difference between happy people." Sally, she says that. Says her father said it, that her father's father said it before him. I look around. Look at all the people, continue to be amazed, uplifted by how different they can be without being violent or manipulative. I see no Nazi cross-bearers assigning sin. No hyper-PC inquisitors demanding compliance. No need to hide behind the lies clothing tells.

Life as it should be. America as it should be.... It feels good.

We walk and sit, walk and sit, take in the crowd without feeling crowded; like people are there, and not there at the same time. We walk and sit, eat, and drink, smoke, and drink some more, pop pills, pick up some box wine, drink it. We're having fun, being fun, fun for each other. Everyone there, we're there for each other as much as we are for ourselves. Goodwill on a roll, placing our bets, playing the game, we're all in.

I hold Sally around the waist as we slip along, feel myself as weightless as I imagine she feels. Love that feeling. A lucky man, that's what I am. At the end of it all, the luck of having Sally at my side...I feel it as a pounding in my chest, as something vital. Duval. Walking Duval. Living the fantasy: the reality of make-believe alive in a dream others are dreaming. Streets are filled with chatter. An array of sideshows inside sideshows, we immerse ourselves in them, play our part, anything we can imagine appears before us on the street, in the windows, on the roofs. Nothing seems attached, to belong to anyone. Amazing grace, amazing costumes. Few masks, very few, nothing hidden, nothing to defend.

> Some bodies are painted so beautifully, with such depth and precision that thought of throwing out the body and keeping the painting comes to mind. A bazar thought, *Walking Dead* bazar. Something for the Guggenheim. MOMA. Art Basel. Des found a bra store, we press our faces to the windows,

girls working there are hanging loose, sharing their goods, barely painted, just enough to call it paint. Lots of clothing stores selling clothes during a mostly nude festival. Weird, if you think about it.

More and more people arriving, fearless, painted naked revelers. We keep walking. A guy on a bike with a monkey, accordion, and drums rolls by. He's young, the guy, thick dreads, thin goatee, his body's painted to look like a monkey. He painted the monkey to look like he shaved it to look like a weightlifter. A good trick. The monkey waves as they ride by.

Duval is bulging with oddities. Lots of Super Women, not so odd as popular. Two ultra-fat guys, twins, the Fat Marathon winners, too fat for the eyes to see them all at once, riding pink grocery carts with baskets full of fried chicken. I look for the Trump guys. Keep expecting them to pop in, or in and out…convert to reality, something. And there are half people. People half-dressed, trying to fit in, to let go. Too shy to be themselves. Not a lot of them.

It's getting more crowded, more liberating as more bottles open, as more spiked soda gets passed around, and beer, and hookahs. And there are more floats, new acts, they keep coming. Lots of bodies, tall, short, rotund, scrawny, protruding bellies, fat asses, fat arms, fat legs, cellulitis everywhere, even on the fingernails, and crusted old people with wrinkled, sagging body parts, all of them, everything sagging, gravity winning.

In any other setting the fat and sag would appear gross, disgusting. Not today, not in Key West. Today, every guy, every girl, every Tom, Diana, and Harry that wants to sick his finger out and say, "Fuck you, world!" I decide what is right and wrong. They are there on the street, with their fingers up. And we are there, our hands raised, our fingers up.

No difference between happy people.

# ONE HUNDRED SIXTEEN

"Ben, cats. Over there next to the ice-cream stand, by the alley."

"Cats?"

"Yeah, over there. Three male cats. All the same color. They're standing on their hind legs in line. See them?"

"In line. Standing? Yeah, I see them. Looks like they're waiting for something."

"It does, yes."

"A female, maybe."

Then, as it should be, a female steps out. She's graceful, happy to display her beautiful fur coat, to flash her lengthy lashes, to wave her fluffy tail.

We keep watching, staring.

"Listen Ben, you hear that. She's purring. Purring loudly." I can't hear it. Sally can, her ears are more like radar dishes than ears, she can hear ants crying, even when she's asleep. "And look at that. One by one each male presses his ear to her chest, listens to her purring, and hugs her."

"That's interesting. It really is, Sal, more than interesting. Are they paying her, do you think? The males. Are they paying her to comfort them?"

"It looks like they are."

"With what?"

"Cat litter."

"Is that normal?"

"I don't know."

"Is there anything cats do that's normal?"

Up Duval, a couple more blocks, we find a bar, the same bar I was in earlier, the fortune teller bar. Odd, maybe not. We squeeze through the doors, ease ourselves between two couples leaving, and a horse, or mule, hard to tell the difference. Shouldn't be.

"Sara lee," I say, a little too enthusiastic, and I open my arms...old friends after meeting once. "I'm back, Sara. And this is Sally," I introduce her. "And the sprightly lady next to her, she's Desiree the desirable, our camera woman."

All smiles, everyone in the bar, all smiles. Even those who have no idea who we are, that we are even there. They smile. Smiles are easy today, everyone's buying them.

"Desiree," says the bartender, "you're not wearing any clothes."

"I know, ma'am, it looks like that."

Eyes on Des, eyes in the bar. They all look.

"Paint, it's transparent paint," she says. "That's what I'm wearing. You can't see it; can't see me." We all look, harder.

"And what can I do for you Ben, for your Sally, and you Des, what would you like?"

"I'd like a beer." I speak first, not a gentlemen move, too hot. 105 humid degrees outside. I can feel it, the heat, crawling along the floor, onto my feet, up my legs and into my head where all the levers are.

Sal and Des go for a couple of frothy drafts.

Sara lee turns from the counter, begins sorting our order, speaks over her shoulder, "And the Teller," she asks, "do any of you wish to see the Teller? Learn what can't be learned. Hear what can't be heard?"

"I do, absolutely," Sally jumps, almost, pulls me to her. "This is great Ben; I love fortune tellers. If they're connected, enlightened... and the good ones are. They can see from inside the present out, traverse backward or forward in time as 'the awareness of.' It's an ancient perspective; the awareness of; a vision of reality before ego intervened to form attachments. Tellers can walk us through that door, allow us to see through them into a world without ego in it. It's wonderful, like walking barefoot in a warm rain before it touches the ground, a kind of seeing without eyes. Like that, Ben. Something like that."

Curious, confused, captivated, Des has a question. "What happens" she asks, "if a Teller passes on what she observes, tells someone, "Oh, you're going to stub your toe on the corner of the closet door tomorrow, at exactly 8:12 pm. And it happens, like she says, to the minute. Does that make her a participant in the future at the time she made the prediction?"

"It does, yes" returns Sara lee, "and it does not. Seeing cannot be seen, cannot be the subject of its observation. Transparent paint for the soul, reveling what is visible," she adds, "that's what it does, and she smiles at Des, winks. Looks like a wink.

Life is only confusing if you're confused in it.

"Ok," I say. "Sure. We'd love to meet your Teller. And how much does it cost?"

"No charge."

"She'll talk to us for free. Why?"

Sara lee hands us our drinks, lowers her voice, "The fifty thousand you have stashed away, it's enough to satisfy the greater part of your immediate future needs, but you must conserve when you can. The Teller wants you to save your money."

"Ok, thank you. I think."

I look at Sally. She winks. A lot of winking going on. But how? For Sara to know we have fifty thousand tucked away, what would it take, or did it take for her to learn that? She couldn't have, that's all. Mummies with hip replacements. Future electro-sapiens prospering without stomachs or eliminatory canals. Impossible thoughts. Thoughts without beginning or end. What to do with them? I look at Sara lee. She's drying a glass, playing bartender…is she? I wonder what's in the beer, if it is beer.

We follow her up the toothy bright red stairway. Would it make sense to create a toothbrush for stairs that look like teeth? A stair's toothbrush to keep the stairs clean. Not likely, but if there are enough toothy stairs around....

Up we go. One ahead, one behind. Ahead and behind, always a line, someone ahead, someone behind. A long flight of stairs, only a one-story building but up and up we go. Feels like we're working our way through the 463 steps to the top of the Duomo. Wouldn't be surprised if we popped out at the top for a view of Florence. Not at all surprised. After what Sally did to Oscar, or in some way influenced what happened to Oscar, surprised by magic, that magic exists...I'm not surprised, not anymore. In many ways I'm relieved. How Sally can do what she does, be as she is makes sense if what we do not understand is called magic. Sally, Sally is magic, aliens are magic...if they're here. Are they here, aliens? Have they always been here? Are they more of what we are than we are ourselves, or what we will become if we survive ourselves? Or nothing. Are they transparent paint, the soul of our species inviting us in? We keep ascending, up and up, and up, then, at the top, a hatch opens onto a balcony with a view of the street below and the merriment of free people sharing their freedom. To the right of the balcony two carved doors open. Trees on both sides of the doors motion for us to enter. We do. The room before us is not grand, not even well lit. Paintings on the walls are old master works. Each painting (rich with the glow of aged oil and glazes) depicts an animal of some kind changing into man – a female or male human being representing man. The floor is wood with fine carpets elevating the beauty of white pine grain. A rustic cabin feel, the room has that feel, a durable sense of things that contrasts sharply with the thin woman sitting in front of us on a small sofa behind a glass coffee table so clear that items sitting on it, a football, two cups without saucers, and a couple of pin-pong balls, look like they're floating.

"Oh, please," she says, and her voice sounds familiar, familiar like a memory that shapes other memories into a self-image sounds familiar. "No formalities here," she chirps. "We're old friends, but you know that already, that's why you agreed to come. It's been a long time since we last met. And Sally, look at you, you're a woman now, a mother's woman. Mothers of the womb, we know them well."

Old friends? How? I'm starting to lose it, parts of my brain detaching, vacating reality. Could be. And maybe not. Sara lee steps into the room (I thought she was already in the room), sits down next to the Teller, and slowly, as she sits there, just sits, and the Teller sits, as they both sit, they merge into one person. She, they, them, those, had my attention, definitely, and Sally's, and Des, and anything else in the room with eyes.

"So, what do you want to know?" Asks the Teller, tellers. "Anything. Ask me, anything?"

For a moment, cheers from Fantasy Fest revelers beyond the closed doors, the thick stuccoed walls, get through. Sally hears them first, then Des and I at the same time. We all nod. It's a game. All this, this Teller intrigue, it's a game. Some part of the unexpected we should expect from perhaps too frequent consumption of Simbana drugs and smoking her weed. Oddly, the Teller, Tellers, had something of a Simbana feel to her, them, they, those, whatever the fuck, and why does it matter. Are people really like that, more than one, and one, at the same time?

"Excuse me," I say, ask, as the three of us sit down on a sofa opposite the glass table. "Is that one question for the three of us, or one question for each of us? And is it more of a make a wish kind of question or an 'I need to know the truth' kind?"

"The decision is yours," says the Teller, "and it's one question between the three of you. You must first agree on the question before asking it."

The thing life is, most consistently, is hungry. Living is consumption of some kind for everything that lives. Hunger. Maybe God is hunger. I can ask. See what the girls think.

We huddle together on the sofa. Forget we're in a room with a woman who just absorbed another woman. Or was absorbed by her?

"Sally, what do you think?" Des and I speak at once. The first time we do that. And how does the Teller know Sally? We think that at the same time as well.

A question. We can ask one question. The old standards are there. "Where did we come from?" "Why are we here?" "Where do we go when we die?" Great questions, the old standards, after centuries, they're still with us. Why? Are we afraid of the answers, or we can't hear the answers? Are they still questions? Do questions grow old and die without answers? Life. Fuck. We're born, we live, we die, that's it. Nothing anthropomorphic in that, nothing at all. Here and gone. That's it.

"I think," Sal says, "that life's single most essential question, if there is one...the three of us sitting here, talking to Madam Teller, Tellers, are not going to decide on which question the question is, ask the question, and get it answered today."

An Indian. For days he's been hunting alone. Cautious in the deep woods, the sometimes cavernous forest greens. But for patches of light, and the occasional meadow space, all is in shadow around him. He's hungry, middle aged, a wife to feed, kids, he stops on a rock. Rocks silence footsteps, he likes rocks. Rays of sunlight break through the dim, illuminate the rock he's standing on. The trees, their world within which he breathes and lives. He feels them guarding the silence, listening to it, conversing with it. Standing guard, as they always have, as they have been taught to do, each tree preforms its task, never doubting the value of its place in the world. The Indian can feel that in them. Feel them inside himself as he stands on the stone, a nearly dry stream trying to flow around it. The day is warm. Like today. Sally, Des, myself. We all feel ourselves to be that Indian, see him in each other, see ourselves standing on that stone, seeing what he sees, what he saw when he lived... I can't grasp it. Not really. What it means, what it does not mean.

Sally takes my arm, I nod. It's time to leave. Past time. Together we thank the Teller and stand up. As we do, as we stand, the big, engraved doors open, and bears come dancing in. A choir of singing dancing bears, and with them dancing girls holding bouquets of colored flowers in their hands. They're all singing and dancing, the bears, and the girls. They're singing loudly and tapping the floor with bright silver canes. And they have on tap shoes, they're all tap dancing. We have no idea what their singing, if it's a song, or even if it's real singing. Sound is there, we can hear them. Then, for no reason, and we look to the Teller...tellers to see why they run out the door and jump off the balcony. Unbelievable. All of them, they ran and jumped. Did they land on anybody? All kinds of bears and girls pancaking and pancaked on Duval. Did they do that? We hurry to the balcony rail, look over. Nothing there. No bears, no girls, no flowers.

The Teller, Tellers, them, they, join us on the balcony, look over the rail, only revelers on the street, no girls, no bears, no 463 steps to the street, no surprise. She lights a cigarette, inhales, asks, "One question. Do you have one?"

"I do, hubs," Sal says, and she takes my hand, takes Des's hand.

"Ask it, Sal, sure," I say.

Des agrees, "Of course, Sally, ask."

"Am I pregnant?" She asks. That's her question.

"Of course, you are, dear Sally, of course you are," the Teller says, and she embraces Sally. "We're all pregnant."

That's it. With the last letter in the last word she says, the letter T, she vanishes behind an open window. Hadn't noticed the window.

"OK." That was, different. We all agree, sigh, stumble back outside and onto the street, the bar behind us, no longer visible through the jovial ambiance filling the streets. A relief to be walking. Were we in the bar? We're thinking that. Can we prove it? Did it happen if we can't prove it? The human ego. Do animals have an ego? Scorpions, bugs, ferrets, wolves...they have character, a personality of some kind, but not ego. Learn what can't be learned. Hear what can't be heard. Did we?

Warm, very warm. We continue down the street, pass, and are passed by more floats. Beautiful floats, floats that look like gardens with painted people for flowers, windmill floats with people painted to look like windmill blades going round and round, and each time they go round, every loose thing on a body flops about. A comical look.

Another Jolly Roger boat-float wheels by, more alluring. Mermaids calling from the rails, mesmerizing vixens flaunting their curves, enchanting the senses with forbidden wants and desires...pleasure at a discount, free of charge for sinners. Confetti drifting, lots of street acts. Simplifying ego self-indulgence, taking it to the streets, so many elastic variations in the love we have for ourselves. And we should love ourselves. Who else will if not us?

They go by, the acts. The many acts. Between hits, they go by. And it's gotten darker, noticeably darker, but it's just past midday. Or is it? One man shows, group shows, acts enacting acts. They go by, and by. We keep drinking, smoking, blending in. Romance reality, a heartbeat, we were in it, some kind of heartbeat. The heartbeat of man. A species heartbeat. Fantasy fest. Is that what it is, mankind's heartbeat. It could be. What else, if not the Fest? If not all of us on the street, the hundreds of us on the street talking, mingling, milling about, relaxed, and happy.

Then we see it. Everyone sees it. Some half dozen or so blocks up from the southernmost point of the US. A good distance up Duval, we see a Trump balloon coming toward us with two spotlights shining on it, making it so bright, that streets, homes, people, roosters roosting in the trees, they're all illuminated like midday daylight. Very weird. The balloon is at least ten stories high. It's a massive thing tied to a float by multiple lines of rope. The float, a flatbed truck stolen from Mexican immigrants, is driving up Duval. As big as it is, huge as it is, we have no idea how it got that far without knocking down buildings, people, powerlines, guys on bikes with monkeys. Maybe it didn't. Maybe they filled it with helium right there, right where they are?

With a lurch the balloon jerks toward us, the big Trump balloon. It stumbles, if balloons can do that, and knocks out power lines, scares the crap out of birds, lots of birds, and people, and poodles, everything but the roosters. We watch, the Fest pauses, everyone looks, all of us. A damn big balloon, damn big. Or maybe it's just fat. A fat balloon. Balloon fat. Never thought of balloons as having fat, but the Trump balloon does. One can see that, anyone can. It's easy to see. A kid. He looks to be fifteen or sixteen years old. He walks out, stops in the center of Duval, pulls back a fine Mathew's V3 bow, and lets loose. A beautiful arrow spinning all red, white, and blue as it drove through the air and hit the Trump balloon dead center in the belly. Sounds like the balloon yelps, or cries, might have cried. Trump would do that, he would cry. Hot air begins escaping the balloon, must be hot. Sounds like it's hot. Trump's left knee begins to sag, the three Trump guys (wondered where they were), their MAGA hats stitched together to look like flowers, they come running out, try to prop up the knee. At the same time, a couple of hefty roosters, out to impress the girls, begin pecking at the balloon's ankles, at its feet. They're furious peckers, pecking, pecking, pecking. Roosters can't dance but they're very good at pecking. Maybe they can dance.

People began yelling. Mostly at the Trump guys trying to keep the balloon afloat. "What are you doing?" They yell. "It's going to fall. Get away from it."

And the balloon, it does begin to collapse, grows weak in the second knee.

"It's too big to fall," the Trump guys shout back. "Don't worry. It will be fine." They say, and they act confident, very confident until both knees give way, and the Trump head slumps forward over its chin and begins to crumple, to gasp for air, then splat, the balloon hits the ground so fast and so hard that balloon pieces fly everywhere. Everywhere. Trump litter everywhere, on everything, tons of it, incredible, all over the place. Trump litter on the people, on all the revelers, and the bears, and the girls, all over the houses and shops, everywhere. On everything. Lots of Trump litter. A real mess.

And the three Trump guys, damn. What do they tell the boss?

Lie. Good idea for them to lie.

# ONE HUNDRED SEVENTEEN

"Clyde.... Is that Clyde?"
"Where?"
"Looks like Clyde."
"Where, Ben?"
"There, by the corner light."

Almost dark now, the earth rolling in space, playing chess with time, few clouds, humid, a bit cooler, not much.

The parade is back on. Big balloon litter has been collected and hauled away. The Trump guys made a bit of money talking to TV crews, talk show hosts, roosters. Sidewalks and streets are vibrant with animated departure from conservative variations of dress and undress. Between the floats, before, after, and on the floats, people inhale life with rejuvenated cheer, so many people, all of them relying on the currency of good will. Can it last...reliance on good will? Do we want it to last?

> A mankind without conflict wasting resources, without self-disfiguring ego attachments consuming identity. What that mankind could do...what we could do.

Dusk thins the view, people in it, drifting, fading in and out of focus, blending together. A lot of kissing and hugging. Carnal revelry baking the senses, flexing the mind. For a few hours barriers between differences fall away.

"It is Clyde. I'm sure of it."

"And Bonnie, is she there?"

"I think so, can't quite see."

"Yeah, Bonnie. I see her."

"We need to talk to them."

"I know. Business talk, future earnings talk."

Sally takes hold of me, takes hold of Des, walks us, slips us through the crowd (a fine web of category five merrymakers pushing for six). Gets us across the street, the intersection.

Bonnie is filming us as we approach. Des films her.

"Bonnie and Clyde!" My voice is loud, almost a shout. "Look at you guys," I say. "Great paint jobs. You look just like the real Bonnie and Clyde. How'd you do that? Fantastic stuff. Fantastic!"

I'm too zealous, feel like it, no reason to. "Great to see you. Wonderful."

Clyde slaps me on the shoulder. I slap him, press my nose into Bonnie's camera. She zooms in, on what...stops filming, hugs me. Always good to be hugged by a beautiful woman. There's a rare pleasure in it, like knowing you've seen something others have seen but it's too precious to talk about or describe.

Altered states. Higher states. Chocolate chip cookies. Frozen yogurt. A good mood. I was in a good mood. Felt even better knowing I was in a good mood. Love good moods. (How to package them, market them. Christmas, Valentine's Day, Mother's Day, Easter...holiday vendors figured it out). And Sally, Des, they're in a good mood. Everyone, the whole place, nothing but good moods.

Paradise ashes sinking beneath the waves, the beginning meeting its end, our sadness no longer smoldering behind cheerful behavior; mute wounds dissolving into layers of unwashed revelry, decadent honesty.

Bonnie and Clyde. They're old friends now, feels like it. And the three girls with them. The college hookers we thought were college hookers, they *are* college hookers. Their names, have to ask their names, remember to ask, then remember to remember after asking.

Clyde takes out a big ass joint, cigar size, lights it, takes a grandiose hit, passes it to me. "You guys still planning to make porn flicks?" He asks.

"Yeah, we are," I say, savoring the weed, its smell, how it filters through the blood into ideas and perceptions. "We are. Love story porn. Sally's writing it. Romeo and Juliet, Private. Really, classic porn; sense food for the eyes.

"Anyway. We have many, are open to ideas; *Key Holes* will be our first title."

"Key is for Key West, right? And holes...."

"Holes is for holes. Imagine what you will."

"Cool!" Clyde says. "*Key Holes*. A great title, Ben. I can play Romeo, Casanova, any of those guys. And Bonnie," he takes a hit, "she can do Juliet. And Alice, Alexa, and Andrea (the college girls), they can be chambermaids. Look at us Ben, Sally. Look at us. Are we good looking or what, we are, yes, we are. And Bonnie's rack, it's perfect. You can see that, perfect." Bonnie smiles, "her ass, everything, perfect. And my master performer...you'll have no complaints ma'am. Not one. Never had a complaint, not one. And the girls, our three As, they're up for any kind of tumble you can conjure. So, tell me, tell us, do you like what you see? I'm sure you do. We're good. Good product. We like what we do, can't get enough of it. Flesh, the sense of touch, flesh demands to be touched. All people feel that demand. We get to satisfy it." Clyde talking, selling his game, pitching for a home run. "We work hard. We do," he adds. "We're good, that's all. We can make a lot of money. Make you money, a lot of money."

Our life coming together. All it took for us to get to the Keys, to focus on a new course. More than we can remember...it took more than we can remember.

Arm in arm, we begin walking with Clyde and company. The streets are packed, hundreds of people drinking, laughing, talking nonsense, talking sense. Seeing the world from the point of view of other people. I am. I'm doing that. Feel like I'm doing that. Like I'm outside my head looking around without my point of view obstructing the view, without Ben, just the grand Fest from the point of view of people I look at. A familiar strangeness about it, other people's point of view. And all the space between points of view...are there people there as well, eyes we can't see, seeing us and what we can't see? Simbana's house. Are we still in it?

New floats keep coming, a group wearing Rio-like headdresses and feathers, showgirls. Several, three or four, wear minimal feathers, feathers made to look like eyelashes attached above each breast. The rest, along with their headdresses, have lines of yellow feathers running down their spines and legs, yellow, and bits of red. They dance. We watch; others watch. It's beautiful in ways that requires new words to describe it.

We keep walking. Feel rich in the presence of so many friends and general good will. A band, playing in a bar, competing with the street noise. A happy noise, the kind children hear listening to each other laugh.

Then, suddenly we're inside a bar, inside and standing at the bar counter. No idea how we got there, or which bar we're in. Card Sound Bridge. Memory gaps, what do they mean, really? Does it matter? To whom, if it does.

"Ben!"

I listen, collect my hearing, try to focus.

"Ben!"

That voice, I know it.

"Ben, Sally! We found you!"

Unbelievable. Un-fucking believable, again. How? It's Amy, Amy, and Loki. They biked down from Lauderdale on Loki's Hog, got painted, nothing special, a bunch of those swirly looking things that hypnotists used to expose people's inner lives. They spent the day looking for us.

"This is great, Loki, Amy, stunning. An amazing Fest, amazing, and you've just made it more amazing. Damn, great to see you guys. Great. Hey, meet Bonnie and Clyde, they drive old model T's, rob banks, shoot people, get shot at. We're going to use them in our first porn film, *Key Holes*. And this is Alice, Andrea, and Alexa (I remember their names.), we have roles for them as well. Sally's been working on the script. A Romeo and Juliet storyline with lots of hide and seek, sword fights, sex games, and all manner of positions known and unknown in the kingdom of procreation…a Kama Sutra upgrade."

"Great to meet you, Loki," Bonnie says, and she hugs him, hugs Amy.

We order drinks, beer mostly. Cheers all around, and more beer, and more music, and more good will. The currency of good will. Our most valuable currency too little valued. But not today.

"Amy, Sweet," Loki pulls Amy to him, kisses her. "You want those three girls over there all over you? All over me. Here. Now? Alice, Alexa, Andrea…you want them, buttering the bread, watering the willows?"

"Hey," Clyde intervenes, raises his voice, "girls, guys, I have an idea. A game idea."

Everyone boos…not everyone. We did.

"Wait, no wait, this is good," he says, "Here's what we do, and listen," he says, "I'm going to put money on it, big money."

People are listening, now they are. Money does that. Big money does more of that.

Taking the stage, Clyde does, and he can act. He's convincing, even before he speaks, very convincing.

"I've got ten thousand US dollars right here in my pocket." He points to a wade bulging from his right pocket. And it's yours. Ten thousand to anyone who can walk without falling, across a pole placed between two chairs, while chugging at the same time, and without taking a breath, a full 750 ml bottle of double malt scotch.

"Challengers. Are there any challengers.?" The voice of an auctioneer. Clyde has one.

A guy steps forward, a small skinny guy with owl-like eyes and a goatee that twists to the left when he moves his mouth. After him three women step up, then two more guys. All of them seem capable. Like they mean to win. I step in as well. And Sally. (We can use the money.) There we are. Four women, four guys. The night pulling us to her, diming our dependence on daylight. Clyde sorts out the scotch bit with the bartender, some kind of special deal. They find a pole to balance on in a backroom closet. One of those five-foot-long wooden poles you get in hardwood stores. The do is on. A big do. There's money in the hat, a show in the ring. People notice. Clyde, he's got them hooked and he's reeling them in, working the mood. He's working the mood. The porn highway begins with side roads. Clyde knows the side roads, and Bonnie. They have good experience with sideroads. Well removed sideroads. Good experience, to a point.

"Folks, all of you here, and hearing my voice," he looks around, eyes are on him, all the eyes he can see. We feel him absorbing the attention, feeding on it, growing into another Clyde, the character he always wants to be in real life.

"This pole," he says, and he holds it up like a war lance. "If you can walk this pole from one end to the other without falling while chugging this fine bottle of double malt, the ten thousand in my pocket...it's yours. All yours. A small lottery night to end a fine Fan Fest Day.

"Takers, do I have any takers. One out of eight?" he says, and he lays the pole across two sturdy tables with chairs on each end for steps.

We look at each other. Sally doesn't move. I don't move. Sally knows something, made a calculation. Better to wait. A lady, a fat lady, she steps up.

"I'll go first," she says. "I can do it, no worries. I can walk the pole, down a 750, make that ten in your pocket my ten... no problem. One player. That's all you need to lose, and I'm that player," she says, and she folds her arms, stiffens her back, glares at Clyde. At everyone.

"But, lady, shouldn't you wait. You could, well, because, well, you're, you could break the pole once you get to the middle."

She doesn't react, feels no offence. We think that, everyone there... all those closest to the table with the pole, the many on-lookers, we all pause, hold our breath. How can she feel no offense? Offence strengthens ego control over our identity, makes us feel important, meaningful. Meaningful enough to defend our importance. We all want that, but not her?

"Are you judging me?" she asks.

Clyde doesn't stammer, but he does find it difficult to speak. "No, lady, not that. All I'm doing is adding, weighing, and measuring empirical evidence. It looks to me like you're about 5 foot 2 inches, maybe five three, and you've got to top 190, maybe 200 pounds on a bad day. That wight, on the middle of that pole laying across these two tables, that weight, that number," and he tapes on the table for effect, "it could break the pole and bring you crashing to the ground, hard, very hard, and very painful. It could. Then again. With all the fat… well, anyway. It's a high likelihood that' you'll break the pole. That's all I'm saying. Facts, they don't lie, but they are not entirely formed either. Application helps them form, expand into greater accuracy. You'll crack and break the fucking pole, if you walk the pole. That's what I'm saying."

"No. That's not what you're saying. You're judging me. All of you. That's what you're saying, what you're doing. You're judging me, trying to make me feel inferior. It's not nice, judging," she says. "Don't do it. Don't hurt my feelings, sap my confidence. That's not nice. And we must be nice."

Nice, fuck. A dip in my good mood…I want to smack the woman, tell her to grow up, get a life. Walk the pole, or don't' walk it. That's all. Why all the extra drama. Fuck. Liberals. They don't know when to stop whining.

"Ok, fine, lady, fine. You go first." Clyde says, and he reaches out to help her up and onto the table. Once she's on it, he backs away acting like distance between himself and the player is expected routine, normal in every way. And he stands on a chair to give himself a better view. A better view and greater control. He holds up a mic, talks into it. Enlarges his voice. Not sure where he got the mic.

"Ladies and gentlemen, and everyone in-between, our first contestant, is one miss…." He looks to the lady.

"Amanda Jason Wallace," she says.

"One Miss, Amanda Jason Wallace. She's going to walk the pole while chugging this fine 750 Malt." He hands her the malt." She takes it eagerly, happily, greedily. Maybe all she's after is the free booze. Could be.

Off she goes. Not even a glance at the pole before stepping on it. Somehow, she manages to get a good step forward. Her head back, not looking, chugging like a fiend, she takes another step. Lands well, good footing, she keeps chugging, takes another step, and another. She's almost halfway, still not looking, just chugging and chugging. She loves chugging, you can see that, she loves, it, and she takes another step, her last…the pole cracks, it's sound splits the ears like a whip stripping bark off trees. It stings, disorients the mind…she falls. With all her weight, she falls, lands on the table next to me, takes me down with her, grabs me as we fall and rolls with me, pulls me to her, even into her. It feels like that. Very weird, weird but warm.

# ONE HUNDRED EIGHTEEN

Sally pats me down, brushes me off, takes my arm, pulls me aside, whispers, "Let's go to the beach, swim. Just us. Do things. Surprise each other."

I agree. Sure. Sally in the water, she's like water.

We sneak out, make our way down Duval to the beach, the pier, walk out to the end, no one else there. We sit close, rub, touch, hold each other, play adult games, hang our feet over the pier's edge. In the distance, the far distance, we see lights, lights on the far side of the darkening horizon, tiny flickering lights.

"Cuba, must be Cuba."

"Yeah, great pot, great hash. I've heard that, and they love porn."

"Everyone loves porn, Ben."

"Yeah, sex. Where would we be without it?"

Sally pokes me. "Hey, let's swim to Cuba."

"Swim? You're joking."

"No, we can do it, absolutely."

"Now? It's a long way, Sal."

"Not really. Ninety miles isn't far, we've done seventy-five and went hiking right after. What's another fifteen?"

The albino. She knows things. Girls, what don't they know?

"OK," I agree, and I wait, listen to the waves, to old highway sounds playing in my mind, desert murmurings, the wash of fresh breezes across open plains under a starlit night, and I visualize ancient skies swollen with lumbering clouds, the aquatic blue of deep seas, far-off peaks climbing higher, searching, reaching for Everest glory.

Traveling. Exploring the roots of life, her complex nature. I love traveling. The deep inhalation of nameless vistas; an invitation to think like the gods, to be a god unattached to time and place; a conscious speck passing through the dim. Uncommon revisions of reality, who decides them? The beginning of life, the first Nature, is there such a thing? And endings, do endings ever end? Are we ever free of being inside something?

"Are you sure, Sal?" I look at her, tilt my look. "Sure, sure. 90 miles. It's a long way."

"I'm sure, Ben, seriously."

"Seriously."

"Yes, no worries. The mothers. They're coming with us."

"But..." I'm holding a pair of twos, always twos.

"Ben," her eyes, they take me, always take me, swallow me, love me. "The odds, Ben, I can see them. They're on our side."

"You are part fish," I say, "that's true. An easy swim...not exactly, but OK, sure."

We leave our wad of clothes. Drop them on the pier, walk to the beach and wade in. The water's warm, comforting, stars overhead inviting and bright.

"What about my tool, my extended extension," I say, and I point. "Viagra."

"How many?"

"I don't know."

"You're hard as rock."

"I know."

"For how long?"

"Till now, most of the day. I think so."

"OK," Sally says, "then we better make good use of you." And she grabs hold, splashes water for effect, plays 'batter up.' Have no idea what it means but it feels good. We're almost waist deep in warm water, Sally pulling me out to sea, drawing me in, crafting uncharted landscapes in my groin, cranking up the heat, pulling the wagon....

Warm water. Loki's pool. Amy and Loki…when they first met, their beaming faces drift into my mind. I see them. A good match. Fun to be there. I smile thinking about them, imagine a lizard eating Loki's flowers…

He sees the lizard, Loki, damn big, it's 15 to 20 yards out. Just beyond the pool. He grabs his .22, opens the window, slowly, makes no noise whatever. The lizard's moving from flower to flower eating their tops off, Loki raises his rifle, lines up the shot, slides his finger over the trigger, begins to squeeze off a round…the lizard stops eating, stands up on its hind legs and walks over to the window.

"Listen bud," he says to Loki, "I know what you're thinking. I'm a lizard eating your flowers. That's what it looks like but ask yourself this. Can lizards walk? Can they talk? Did I walk over here? Am I talking to you?"

Loki nods. "Yeah, you did, you are."

"OK," says the lizard, "then you understand that I'm not an ordinary lizard."

"I do, I understand," Loki says, and he lowers his rifle.

"Fine," returns the lizard, and he walks back to the flowers, begins eating them again."

Loki squints, rubs his eyes, lines up his shot again, is just about to pull the trigger when the lizard stands up again, walks to the window and begins talking.

"Really Loki? You're going to shoot a walking, talking lizard? If I were you, I'd think about that. Consider how much money you can make recording me, posting the recordings online." Again, the lizard walks back to the flowers, and again he begins eating them.

"I'm just imagining all this," thinks Loki. "Yeah, I'm imagining it." And he shoots the lizard just as it bites off the top of one of his favorite flowers. The lizard shakes and twists, rolls over, belly up, staring at the sky. Loki runs out to finish him off, leans down, stares at him, his mouth slightly agape.

"Call an ambulance, moron. I'm bleeding." The lizard points at his wound.

Loki stares.

The lizard shouts, "Wake up man! This is real. For Christ's sake call an ambulance. It's written in the script. Did you read your copy this morning? It was quite clear. Now is when you call the ambulance."

Loki stares.

433

Learn what can't be learned.
Hear what can't be heard. Have we?

Made in the USA
Middletown, DE
03 December 2022

16902342R00245